Simon Williams

Secret Roads

BOOK II OF THE AONA SERIES

Thanks to all those who read and spread the word about Oblivion's Forge.

APHENHAST

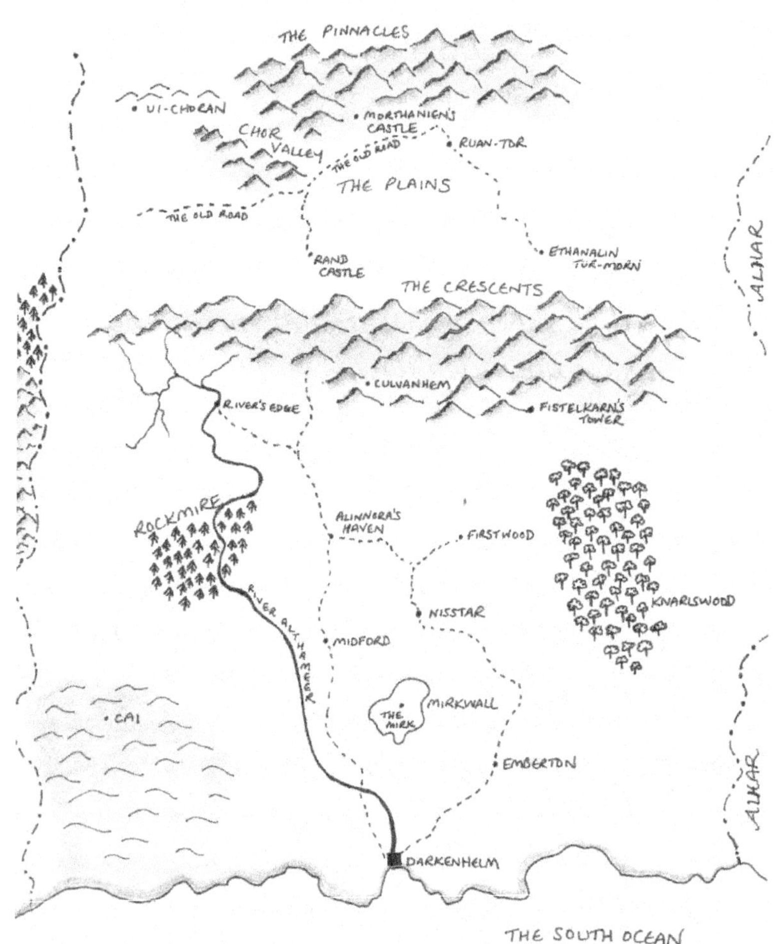

THE PINNACLES
UI-CHORAN
CHOR VALLEY
MORTHANIEN'S CASTLE
RUAN-TOR
THE OLD ROAD
THE PLAINS
THE OLD ROAD
RAND CASTLE
ETHANALIN TUR-MORN
THE CRESCENTS
CULVANHEM
FISTELKARN'S TOWER
RIVER'S EDGE
ROCKMIRE
ALINNORA'S HAVEN
FIRSTWOOD
KNARLSWOOD
RIVER ALTHAMEER
NISSTAR
MIDFORD
THE MIRK
MIRKWALL
CAI
EMBERTON
ALHAR
ALHAR
DARKENHELM
THE SOUTH OCEAN

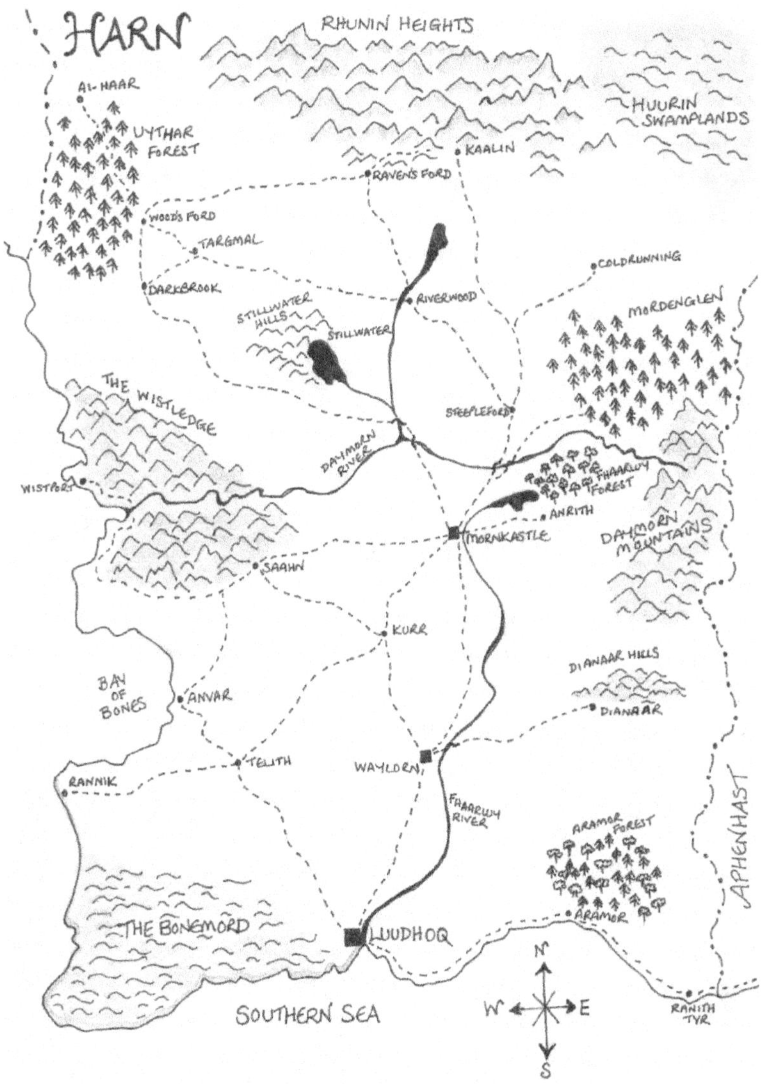

HARN
RHUNIN HEIGHTS
AL-HAAR
UYTHAR FOREST
HUURIN SWAMPLANDS
KAALIN
RAVEN'S FORD
WOOD'S FORD
TARGMAL
COLDRUNNING
DARKBROOK
RIVERWOOD
MORDENGLEN
STILLWATER HILLS
STILLWATER
THE WISTLEDGE
STEEPLEFORD
DAHMORN RIVER
FHAARLUY FOREST
WISTPORT
ANRITH
DAHMORN MOUNTAINS
MORNKASTLE
SAAHN
KURR
DIANAAR HILLS
BAY OF BONES
ANVAR
DIANAAR
TELITH
WAYLORN
RANNIK
FHAARLUY RIVER
APHENHAST
ARAMOR FOREST
THE BONEMORD
ARAMOR
LUUDHOQ
N
SOUTHERN SEA
W E
RANITH TYR
S

I – The River Runs Black

I

Two great sorcerers lay dead, devoured in the twilight of their days by the dark creatures known as the *choragh kin*, whose strength had grown with the promise of their ancient enemies the *marandaal* reaching into the world.

Morthanien, feared and reclusive warlock of the cold wastes near the Pinnacles and a man whose grip upon sanity had loosened, believed he had heard the voices of the long-lost *illeagh*. With his last remaining strength he headed into the mountains, feverishly certain that they called to him. He was never seen again; at least, not by creatures that anyone believed in.

Shimlock of Mirkwall, whose sprawling mid-Hastian castle home had once been an entire citadel, and which now lay forever wreathed in the *mirkfog,* had also grown weaker, but for a different reason altogether. Slowly but with grim resolve the dark creatures of Aona, those creations formed through the madness of the ancient *choragh* dozens of centuries ago, had claimed piece after piece of his vast abode, as he aged at last and there came a dimming of the threshold. Eventually they came for him as he lay awaiting his death, fading in pain. At the moment of his passing, Mirkwall became theirs, and Shimlock, last human denizen of a once proud citadel, was no more.

Fistelkarn of the Round Tower might have been considered a lesser sorcerer by his dead compatriots, but he was at least still alive. However, as he sat and wrote a message to a half-forgotten friend in the small silent hours before dawn, even he could feel his fortitude slip quietly away. Like Shimlock helpless in his remote fastness as the *kin* burrowed towards him, Fistelkarn had known the end was coming for a long while, had felt the sudden onset of frailty and absent-mindedness that should have been his to suffer more than a century ago. He had found it difficult to seize and work the invisible talents that had been second nature to him for so long, and whenever he did, exhaustion and even agony gripped him for a long time afterwards. It could not have happened at a worse time, but there was nothing to be done about that.

Like his deceased compatriots, Fistelkarn knew that the *choragh* were abroad again in Aona, spreading from the dim and unvisited places of the world. When their eternal, implacable enemies the *marandaal* came, to destroy all of Aona, then the world would be a dark place indeed for all the younger Races, caught helplessly between two evils of vast magnitude. Fistelkarn feared not only for the lives of the millions who would be swept up into this storm of opposing powers, but for the existence of life as it had become, for the Age of Enlightenment itself.

If we must see the end of this Age, he had thought again and again, *then let it not herald the return of* choragh *mastery, of enslaved Races, of fear and terror without end, without limit.*

He watched as his writing hand shook and clenched suddenly, and an ice-cold needle of pain shot through his arm. Fistelkarn did not drop the quill, but his knuckles whitened until it seemed they might burst through his leathery old skin. Tears pricked his eyes. He took a deep breath and tried to quieten the sudden frightened thumping of his tired and ancient heart. The pain ebbed and then subsided, leaving him weak and tremulous.

Let it end soon, he thought. *Let this misery and decrepitude end soon, but not until I have done what I can here. If that amounts to nothing, then so be it. I'll bow my head to the final darkness and find solace in the quiet earth. I fear only for those who linger in this world. My struggle is nothing compared to what theirs will be.*

From somewhere Fistelkarn found the strength to continue writing. He bowed his head and hurried about the task, not knowing where or when the next agonising spasm would strike, nor for how long it might cripple him.

"*Serina,*

A long time has passed since we last met, and no doubt we might find much to talk about if circumstances were different. But I must be brief. This will, I am certain, be my last missive to you.

It is the third day after Ildar's fullness. I am three leagues north of Nisstar, and soon to enter that den of depravity. My companions and I seek to convince those who rule there that their continued oppression and enslavement of the other Races- most notably the luyan, *as you will be aware- can lead only to their own annihilation. I suspect, as I am sure you do, that the* choragh, *thought long gone even by those few who remember their name, have infiltrated the Rising. Ever have they fed upon the hatred occasioned by the younger Races upon one another. This, together with the coming once again of* marandaal *to Aona, can only quicken their ascent.*

I am sending two of my companions to you in Rockmire, partly because they are luyan *and so cannot enter Nisstar- but also because I feel they may be able to help you in your resolve to bring sanity to that gathering.*

I suspect you will be more interested in another companion of mine. Her name is Jaana. In Culvanhem, some of my companions were attacked by a choragh- *a minor one, but no less a threat for that. It could not harm Jaana. Indeed, its attempts to do so weakened it somehow, as far as I have been able to tell.*

After we left Culvanhem, Jaana revealed to me that she had sensed the movements and machinations of a diafagh *she had encountered previously, on our way to the* crommar *stronghold. She has powers that may be used against them, there can be no doubt of that. But she will need a teacher, someone who has experience of guiding acolytes in the*

Powers. Are you willing to be that teacher, if circumstances permit? I can only hope so.

Jaana may even be a descendant of the First, those few amongst the enslaved younger Races who stood against their choragh *masters, and, it can be argued, brought about the Age in which we now live. If so then her importance cannot be overstated, and I must personally keep the girl safe until you meet her yourself.*

I will ask Fauli and Lyya- who you will hopefully soon see- to meet myself, Jaana and my other companion, Tyrameer, at dusk on the first day after the next full face of Ildar, twelve days from now, in Alinnora's Haven. Regardless of your progress or otherwise with the Rising, I strongly suggest that you go with them to the meeting place. All those who are able to must stand together for the sake of the Races."

Fistelkarn read through his shaky script. He peered closely in the flickering lamplight, dissatisfied with his words but unable to find others. *Too many,* he thought morosely. *I could never be brief, even in times of urgency. I always want to say more than I have the time for.*

He rolled and sealed the paper before heading slowly downstairs. As he walked he winced at a new flaring of pain, this time in his right knee.

The aged sorcerer made his way through the side exit of the village tavern and into the chill air of the barrelyard. Almost immediately, a small and utterly silent figure moved from behind a stack of barrels and boxes. Behind the hood of the *ko xhoth*'s robe, large red eyes gleamed faintly. Fistelkarn bent down and placed the message into the creature's outstretched claw. "For Serina, in Rockmire," he said quietly in the creature's own language. "No one else must see it. Take the swiftest route you can. Stop for no one."

The creature nodded almost imperceptibly. A moment later it had vanished from sight.

Fistelkarn remained standing in the yard awhile longer, his laboured breaths drifting up into the cold night. He lifted his head after a while and observed the myriad of stars that dotted the night sky. He felt a powerful hatred and fear for the unknowable enemies that lurked amongst them, which would soon come from out of the vastness.

Will I live to see the horror to come? he wondered, and hoped by all the Powers that he wouldn't.

II

As winter tightened its grip on Ruan-Tor once again after a brief and unexpected respite, a collar of fear encircled Ulan Kadur, chief guardsman of the Lord Protector's fortress and the man who had helped organise the murder of the Lord Protector, Vothangrane.

Since the return of Rocan and his men empty-handed some weeks ago- Rocan had put all of his famously religious fervour into the pursuit of Vornen Starbrook, possibly with the intention of hanging him out in the wilderness- Ulan had done his best to avoid the leader of Ruan-Tor's men-at-arms. Rocan's talent for sniffing out suspicious behaviour was legendary.

As his new masters commanded, Ulan had dutifully remained silent on all the matters to which he was privy. Initially he had felt a sense of relief when Vothangrane was finally put to rest six days ago, on a blustery grey Lastday afternoon as sleet angled spitefully across the boneyard. That relief, however, proved to be short-lived. An urge to flee Ruan-Tor as Vornen had done consumed him now, but of course he could do no such thing. Ulan felt a measure of guilt and shame for his actions, but fear for his life overrode such feelings. It replaced them with cold sweat and panic as he lived from moment to moment, doing what he had to do and mumbling a grateful, incoherent prayer at dusk each day. If he fled, the *choragh* would hunt him down and find him swiftly even if by some miracle he made it past the town gates. Their methods might be brutally straightforward or they might be hideously subtle. There could be no way of foretelling the manner of their retribution, but an example would surely be made of him.

Ulan had suffered horrific dreams over the last week, dreams that he knew were warnings from his new masters, from which he awoke screaming and scratching at himself, as if his woes could be so easily dealt with. In most of these nightmares he found himself in faraway places, such as the distant south or even the long-abandoned desert realm of Alhar in the east, a place he had never journeyed to and surely never would. Perhaps these were locations where he might fancifully consider himself beyond the reach even of the earth-lords. Yet they found him, as the tightening ball of terror in his heart knew they would, and they forced him to commit unspeakable deeds in these lands, often against those who had welcomed him. Such nightmares seemed to last for many days.

Ulan was not averse to violence- no doubt this was one of the reasons he had been chosen- but these acts sickened and frightened him even as he carried them out, until at last he was cast out of the portentous nightmares altogether and woke suddenly, clinging forlornly to his soiled bed sheets and whimpering promises of eternal obedience to the shadows.

Most mornings, Ulan woke to find a blizzard swirling down outside. He would watch it for a long while, as miserable thoughts ran skittishly around in his head. The fortress had become an emptied and silent place these days; although the *choragh* and their eyes-and-ears remained invisible to everyone else in Ruan-Tor, still their presence, the shadow that they cast, was palpable. Servants of all ranks had handed in their notice. Even the new interim Lord Protector, Amos Relf, was rarely seen out of his office in the distant eastern wing of the fortress, which was not a place of mourning so much as a place cast in intangible darkness.

We have new Protectors now, he reminded himself one morning, *and the enemies they spoke of, those who would seek to bring ruination to all Aona, will not take Ruan-Tor. What I have done, I did for the greater good.*

He repeated those words over and over, in his mind and then aloud, like a prayer or a mantra that he would eventually believe if only he repeated it enough times. At the same time, other thoughts darted through his head, visions of a future Ruan-Tor, a last stony outpost in a world where either the *choragh* or their foes held sway, where humans were bred for amusement, or meat, or sacrifice, or all three.

It had been set in motion; there could be no way back, and only one way forward lay open. Ulan wept as he stared out at the snowstorm and cursed the day he was born.

III

In distant Luudhoq, Garret of the Seven arrived in a room long-forgotten even by his compatriots, to indulge in a ritual; one that might to an observer appear to be a curiously *human* trait. He was human, although Harn had somehow made the Seven more than that. They had lost all capacity for love and compassion, but they had gained so much more.

His was a daily routine. Just before the sun rose he would unlock the door at the back of his study chamber, and step forward not only into the dusty confines of an east-facing room but also into a world he barely remembered. The world into which he had been born.

A world now long gone.

The room held no furniture aside from a table, upon which a small, square shape lay, composed mostly of metal. It was a type of metal that could not be mined here in Harn; Garret could not remember its name. This small box, less than a

13

fingernail high, had only one purpose, which was to play the music of the old world. It could, in time, have easily held *all* the music ever composed in that unreachable place, but Garret, like all the Seven, had fled his home with only essentials and what little else he could grab. The box, he had found out much later, contained one piece of music only.

He had placed it on the table in front of the wide east-facing window for a good reason. The box worked by using the power and the heat of the sun, storing some of it so that it could- if he ever wanted it to- play its music even at night or when dark clouds covered the sky.

Garret waved his hand over the box and stood by the window, eyes closed. He felt the faint heat of the sun begin to wash over him as it rose over the towers and rooftops of eastern Luudhoq. A moment later, the music began to play.

A melody that now seemed indescribably alien rose into the air. Slowly it rose to a crescendo before the multitude of string instruments faded, replaced by a hundred human voices, male and female, singing in unison. The words themselves were meaningless to him; they were sung in a language of the old world. He had no idea which one. Yet this passage of the song affected him more than any other. After more than a thousand years, he was at a loss to work out why.

As the music eventually faded into the backcloth of silence, Garret uttered a long drawn-out sigh. His head slumped forward; his shoulders sagged. His response to the ending of the music was the same each day, involuntary and resigned, as if he lost something of himself each time the song drew to a close.

But I have nothing more to lose, he thought, turning his head slightly in order to see his reflection in the full-length mirror fastened to the side wall. *Nothing more,* he decided as his gaze took in the sight of his own face, stranded forever in middle age, unremarkable in all ways but one- the look of utter desolation in his eyes.

14

"I want to die," he whispered. It was the same plea he had uttered each morning for perhaps five hundred years as he stared helplessly at the sight of his own misery.

He had of course tried to kill himself many times, and watched as he healed inside and out, his body relentlessly determined to last until the end of time itself. For a moment he recalled how hundreds of years ago he and Issele had tried to produce children, thinking that perhaps then the two of them might finally die- they had all tried, at one time- but their efforts had always ended in abject failure. The powers bestowed upon them had come with another price; not only were they apparently destined to live forever, but they would never produce others who might take on that mantle in their place.

The Seven are Eternal was a common saying down in the city where mortals scurried like ants about their trivial lives, blissful in that mortality for which he and his six compatriots yearned.

A sudden, familiar urge overtook him. He went to stand even closer to the window and stared down towards the city streets far below, helpless in the face of the sheer hatred that poured through his mind. *I knew it would happen soon,* he thought. *It's been what- an Ildarian month or so?*

As he concentrated on one area of one particular street, where the usual hustle and bustle of the morning was already building, his sight swept down to that place, so he could see all the people gathered there or walking by as if he hovered no more than a dozen hands or so above them.

A middle-aged woman carrying a large basket of goods caught his attention. She perused the stalls nearby, pondering what further food to buy. Every now and then she would exchange pleasantries with one or other of the stallholders. She seemed amused, or perhaps she was simply in a good mood; after all, the weather today was unusually pleasant for this time of year, and Luudhoq looked resplendent in the morning sunshine.

He closed his eyes, and made a sudden fist with his left hand, imagining her heart caught within it.

Her expression changed; Garret opened his eyes and watched closely, fascinated. Sudden bewilderment, then terror. She opened her mouth, to say something or perhaps cry for help, but the agony was too great. Finally, as she staggered to her knees, the basket and its contents tumbling across the flagstones, he saw a third, more interesting look in her eyes; one of dull realisation, acceptance.

Then she fell forwards into the street, dead.

And there it is, gone just like that, he thought. *From a smile to a silent scream in little more than a fleeting moment. Did she know how lucky she was? Of course not.*

But Garret's attention was pulled back from his grim celebration in an instant. The hair on the back of his neck stood up. A chill settled in his stomach, a sense that he shared his secret chamber with something inexplicable.

For the first time ever in this world, the music box had started to work without his command, and the music it began to play, a song he had never heard before, filled his heart with terror.

IV

Full darkness had fallen on the forest of Rockmire. Around the tent in which she sat, Serina could hear the sounds of muted conversations amongst soldiers of the Rising, some of them gathered about their camp fires, some of them walking to or from the camp- either on their way towards the city of Nisstar to scout for information, or coming back with whatever knowledge they had harvested. From what she could tell, the Rising had got better at that particular activity, although much of their preparation remained a shambles.

The most interesting piece of the Nisstar puzzle, as far as she was concerned, was the way in which the human society had changed since the One Church had assumed power within the city walls. Given a freedom to commit all manner of depraved and foul acts provided that they paid homage and silver to the Church, more and more people had chosen to do exactly those things, particularly against those unfortunate people of the other Races who had been trapped within the city and forced into slavery, or worse still, a gladiatorial arena from which the only escape was failure to rise from the dust.

Serina's lip curled in a cold smile. *I have moved on again, it seems. I think of them not as creatures now, but less than creatures. Here I am, a human amongst the Rising, where we number only a few, despising many of my own Race. We condemn them as a faceless enemy, or one with a single face. But what do those gathered here truly think of me, of my presence here?*

That was a difficult question to answer and an uneasy one to ponder. There had been little outward hostility towards her, once the commanders of the Rising had begun to realise that she would to be an asset to their cause, and once Ilumor had said as much. They were not entirely stupid, and in any case they quite rightly feared Ilumor. They commanded the folk of their race and region who had followed them here, but they answered to Ilumor whenever he chose to give orders.

But she was still human, and their relief at her decision to remain alone in her tent most of the time when not required- alone, that was, except for Gaan the great silver wolf, who came and went as he pleased- was obvious.

Yet although they had grown more organised and better-trained and their resolve- quite simply to raze Nisstar to the ground- burned as brightly as ever, still she could not decide whether or not the Rising was destined to triumph or fail. Foretelling had never been something she had any talent for- although she had pretended to from time to time, as necessary- who would openly disbelieve a witch?

The Rising had not looked beyond what boiled down to a simple act of revenge, and therefore no consideration had been given to the consequences after the dust settled. This was little more than a loose alliance forged from the hatred felt across the land towards the settled human societies in their stone towns and cities. Underneath the passion that could easily be stirred up by the rhetoric of hate, little existed to unite the Races- and so, what might happen if they did eventually triumph and returned to their homelands, depleted and untrusting of their comrades, perhaps blaming one another for losses incurred? The *crommari,* close-knit and suspicious, would remain within their vast rocky cities in the Crescents and plot endlessly. The *luyan* and *du-luyan,* always naturally wary of each other, would become openly hostile. And as for the *ko xhoth,* with their webs of intrigue and lore pilfered from who knew where...

A shadow fell over Serina's thoughts.

She knew of Ilumor's approach long before his soft footfall could be heard outside the tent. To Serina's mind he moved like a concentration of darkness through the encampment, causing a ripple of fear wherever he went. Soldiers and commanders alike shrank back from him, moved a little nearer to their fires, averted their eyes and wished themselves elsewhere, praying that he would pass by with nothing to say to them. She could not help but flinch when he pushed aside the cloth flap that let in the night air, and wandered in unannounced.

His eyes darted about the place, seeing Powers knew what, or perhaps nothing at all. Finally they rested on her. At Serina's side, Gaan growled softly, ready to leap and rip the man's throat out. No man would be swift enough to stop him. But she also knew that Gaan would be dead and ruined before he even reached his target. Ilumor was something far more than a human man. *And yet something less,* she thought. *Whatever human part remains, it shrinks and fades with each passing day. Powers, if I could only undo the summoning that brought him back!*

"Serina," he said softly, and sat cross-legged on the ground in one easy, fluid movement. Serina found herself drawn to that motion, and willed herself to look away. *Something dark lurks in everything he does,* she reminded herself.

"You still have so much to tell me about your cause," Ilumor remarked with a smile. "But then again, I have found one here that meets my own ambitions." His dark eyes glittered with merriment. A gust of breeze blew in through the tent opening and caused his hair to move across his face a little. As he smoothed it back, he looked almost like the man she had known so long ago. Almost. But the laughter in his eyes held a madness that sent a shiver through her.

"All of Aona faces the abyss," Serina found herself saying. "Tales come from the north of Gates and Gods and slaughter. The Races prepare for war. *That* is why I summoned you, why I took you from the Road. There are few of us to stand and defend the Races when war tears the world apart. The humans..."

"...slaughter each other, as always." Ilumor laughed. "Is it not the Race that finds it easiest to turn its back to itself? You and I, Serina, we are alike in one way. We have moved far from what we were born into the world as, so long ago. You talk of protecting the Races, but you detest humanity. You wanted my help, but you fear me. You're a woman of contradictions."

"It seems our paths have grown further and further apart." Serina found herself scratching at one of the amulets around her neck, and with an effort she managed to stop.

"Hardly, as we sit together here in a common cause." Ilumor blinked and offered a gentle smile as if bemused at her words.

Serina changed the subject. "Tell me, Ilumor, about what you've done for all these years, and with whom."

"I have slept while awake, you might say." He uttered the words casually. "Somewhere within the Silver Road where you sent me- or should that be *along* the Road? Location means nothing there, and a name is everything. I wandered, until the old ways... caught me. They are coming to life, you know, for want of a better expression. But then, they never completely went away. They just slept, and waited. It's like the tide going in and out on an endless beach, Serina."

She took a deep breath. He talked of the *choragh* and their minions- of whom he was surely one- as he might talk of acquaintances. "There is no place for you amongst the Rising," she said abruptly. "The Races last endured your masters in an all but forgotten Age. They shall not bear enslavement again."

"Oh." A smile creased his lips for a moment. "Are you certain?"

"I ask you to leave this place. The Rising will do as they will without your goading them on. If you serve the Old Dark then serve it somewhere else."

Ilumor seemed to be listening to someone or something else, head cocked to one side. Finally he returned his attention to her, languid, almost contemptuous. "Why do you think we were awakened?" he asked. Serina's stomach crawled at the sound of the *we*. She did not answer, although she had a fair idea.

"Enemies come from the stars." Ilumor grinned. "But with every drop of blood spilled as the Races vie for power, our own strength grows. Only *we* have the strength to face the starspawn, the destroying light. Only *we* can safeguard Aona. As for the Races and their fate..." His lips twitched, and presently he laughed out loud, a coarse baying that rose like madness into the night sky. All around them, people fled to other clearings. Some of them shrieked prayers to their various Gods as they tripped through the darkness and spilled their belongings.

Serina sat and watched Ilumor until his eyes ran with blood and his hands shook so fast they became a blur. She had no belief in any Gods that might save her. Only the natural forces, the Powers, held her world together, and the light and dark ways in which they were reflected.

But in this moment, it seemed that Ilumor's shadow was all that remained in the world, and the last thing she heard in this life would be his endless, inhuman laughter.

II – Winter's Eyes

I

The pain has gone!

The sight of the girl as she turned and fled up the stairs, scrambling and slipping in her frantic attempt, roused Amethyst from her stupor. She blinked, pulled sharply back into awareness by the motion and the sound. A moment later, somewhere in the gloom upstairs, a door slammed shut.

Amethyst took a long, slow breath. Outside, the silence was punctuated only by the slow drip of the melting snow as it slipped from the roof and through the broken guttering.

The absence of any kind of pain in her head, or even any residual *threat* of pain, confused her. The heaviness, the *lurking* inside, like a baleful eye that roamed within her mind, had gone, as if something inside her had suddenly crushed it.

Despite her overwhelming relief and shock at the lifting of her curse- however temporary that might be- a thirst for vengeance filled Amethyst's thoughts like never before now that she had the strength for it. *If I leave this place without her,* she thought suddenly, *the affliction will return. I have no doubt of it. That girl is my path to sanity, my path to vengeance.*

She raised her hands briefly to each side of her head, suddenly fearful that the agony would flare up once again, worse than ever, as if to give her fair warning.

It did not.

The answer was simple. She had only to keep this girl with her- bind her arms and legs and strap her over a packhorse if it came to that, and if they could find such an animal still alive- and then she could hunt down the witch

22

who had forced her onwards, league after weary league, through the bitter winter of the Crescents and the barren lands beyond to this forsaken, ruined town whose people mostly lay dead under the snow.

If I can make it through the mountains, she reminded herself. *I managed it before, but the snows hadn't arrived.*

A man watched her from across the room. Amethyst had been vaguely aware of his presence, but only now did she turn to look at him properly. "Do you know her?" he asked.

In a manner of speaking, Amethyst thought, but she still felt too muddled to reply coherently. She turned and slowly began to make her way to the stairs.

"Where are you going?" her companion added just as she reached the first step.

"She is coming with me," Amethyst told him without looking back. "If she dies along the way, so be it."

Pausing as she reached the top stair, Amethyst considered suddenly what might happen should the girl perish. Would her agonies return as she feared? Might she be pulled apart inside by some final excruciating pain? *I must keep her with me,* she told herself, *and I suppose I must also keep her safe until I find the witch-woman again.*

Behind one of the doors on the landing came the sound of quiet sobbing. Amethyst pushed against the door, found that it had been blocked by something, and shouldered it hard. The door burst open, and the flimsy chest of drawers that had been placed against it splintered and fell back. Amethyst kicked aside the attempted barricade and walked over to the corner where the girl sat curled up, hands covering her face as if by failing to see this intrusion on her world she might somehow make it go away. Amethyst felt a twinge of sympathy for her, but steeled herself against it. *That will not do,* she told herself. *She will be my prisoner. That's the way it must be.*

"You are coming with me," she told her.

The girl opened one hand a little, and a pale blue eye stared in disbelief, then watched as Amethyst rummaged quickly amongst the ruins of the drawers to find clothes that might be better suited for travel. Even with the sudden warming of the air, the girl would quickly perish wearing only a thin dress and sandals.

Trying to ignore the rank odour of the bedchamber, she eventually found a pair of breeches and wool jacket- neither of which looked as if they had ever been worn- and tossed them over to her new charge. "Put these on and be downstairs immediately afterwards. Bring anything else of value- provided it's small. If it cannot fit in a belt pouch, leave it behind." Amethyst gave the dank, miserable bedchamber a final cursory look. She doubted whether the girl had anything of value to her name, small or otherwise. "If you know where coins are hidden here, show me. And if you're thinking of hiding a knife or dagger about your person- *don't*." She smiled tightly at her. "Very few people know their small-blades better than I do."

Amethyst left the girl to change her clothing and made her way back downstairs. Ignoring the man's quizzical look she sat back in her chair and waited in silence. She listened intently and kept half an eye on the snowbound track outside in case the fool girl decided to try and force open the window and jump out in an attempted escape. She would not get far even if she failed to break either or both legs.

"My name is Vornen," her companion said after a while. "And that's Suli over there." He gestured to the woman who slumbered by the hearth.

"I'm Amethyst," she said, frowning at the interruption. A creak and a thud sounded from upstairs. She wondered what the girl was up to, and for a moment feared that she might even try to kill herself. *They seem to like doing that around here,* she thought with a shudder, and wondered if she ought to head back upstairs and supervise her young charge.

Vornen had not finished. "I heard what you said to the girl. If you bring her along, she will be your responsibility alone. If you're coming with us, that is." Amethyst glanced across at him, but his gaze was now fixed upon the woman, who was now awake but continued to stare into the fire like a mad diviner, oblivious to everything around her. "I have Suli to look after."

"I'm headed south," Amethyst said. "Until we reach the middle lands, and then east. You?"

"South," he said, and turned his head that way. "I think I have to."

Amethyst suddenly remembered that she had fallen as she stumbled towards the tavern. *I saw him just before I fell,* she recalled. "You saw me fall in the snow. You saved me."

He nodded. "More than likely. You... didn't look like a Tur-mornian woman."

"Would you have saved me if I had been?"

Vornen gazed out at the snow for a while. The breeze sighed around the building as if in mourning. "I don't think so," he said eventually. "It would have been a mercy to let you die." He glanced at Amethyst again, his gaze suddenly sharp. "Which do *you* dream of?"

Amethyst was taken aback, but she understood the question. "Neither," she said, looking straight back at him. He nodded, his relief obvious. *If I'd said that to almost anyone else I've met in recent times, they might have killed me,* Amethyst thought. Aloud she said, "I will be watching her every move. I will even keep her tied to me when I sleep. I'll kneecap her if I have to."

Vornen raised an eyebrow at that. "Certainly, taking her out of this place is a kindness, and she will need to do as she's told should it come to that- but kneecapping?"

"As you said, she's my responsibility," Amethyst told him, "and believe me, Vornen- this is no kindness."

Vornen looked as if he wanted to ask more about this sudden and strange arrangement, but he said nothing more. As he had explained, he had his own responsibilities. Amethyst stole a glance at Suli, who remained as lost in her world as they were all lost in the real one, as far from awareness as they were far from civilisation.

"The Gate did it," Vornen said softly. "The Gate pulled her here and then it ruined her. She was drawn to it. We both were. Maybe she would have been cast into the abyss if the Gate had not been shut away from this world." He looked down at his boots. "Maybe that would have been better."

The snow continued to melt outside as they began to pack what they could reasonably carry and ransacked anything of value they could find from nearby abandoned outhouses and stores. Amethyst kept one eye on the nearby tavern, watching to see if the girl had emerged yet. They found a few knives, cooking bowls and water flagons, along with a couple of woollen robes, and in one house a small pile of silver crowns left half-counted on a table. *No matter what they were doing, sooner or later everyone abandoned their lives and headed towards the Gate on the hill,* Amethyst thought with a shudder as they shared the money.

They returned to the tavern to pack their finds properly, and Amethyst's new companion finally made her way downstairs. She crossed over to the window and watched as swiftly melting snow ran in rivulets from the gutters. "You may as well tell me your name," Amethyst remarked, "as we'll be spending the next few tennights together, I imagine. I am Amethyst."

The girl half-turned. She appeared to be caught in a daydream. "I'm Ileana," she murmured. "Look! The snow is melting."

"Which is why we intend to head south whilst we can," Vornen said over his shoulder. He had been making odd marks- mostly crosses and lines- on a map of the Crescents. Amethyst guessed he was planning a route through the mountain valleys. *The quicker the better,* she thought. *I've had more than enough of this grim place.*

"Winter is drawing breath, as some people like to say," Vornen continued, and glanced at the girl's continued calm observation of the scene outside. "Ileana, you realise everyone here is dead or as good as, don't you? You know they abandoned whatever they were doing and headed to Tur-morn Hill? They were compelled by the opening of the Gate, by the reach of the *marandaal.* Do you understand me?"

Amethyst gave Vornen a sharp look. She had heard that name only once before, and had not expected to hear it again so soon- certainly not from him. How much did he know of such things?

Ileana reacted only with a shrug. Clearly the name and even the event meant nothing to her. "I don't know what you're talking about."

Vornen gave her a second look, suddenly intent. "Did you not feel the call of the Gate, Ileana?"

She stared back at him. "No. That's why I stayed here. I pretended to have the same stupid dreams as everyone else, or else they would have probably killed me. But I didn't really have such dreams. And I don't care that everyone is dead. I hate them all." Her words had a venomous edge to them.

Vornen stared at Ileana for a little longer, then returned to his odd map-marking. One hand, Amethyst noticed, strayed towards the hilt of the black-hilted sword he carried in his belt, and lingered there awhile as if drawn helplessly. Vornen appeared not to even notice, lost instead in his scribbles and thoughts.

The Gate, Amethyst thought numbly. *Even I felt the pull of the Gate.*

She could recall that horrifying moment in perfect detail, and feared that she always would, even though at first her memories had been so confused. Stars within the Gate, a being fashioned from pure burning light, the screams of maddened worshippers- worshippers of oblivion!- and then the enemies of that light- black, swirling shapes that turned and dove and *consumed* the light as it poured and reached from out of the Gate to touch this world. Amethyst had thought at first that the black shapes might be birds tainted with some powerful sorcery, but they were too fast. They changed appearance at will. They were silent- and their arrival had set off roars of fury and frothing madness amongst Ethanalin Tur-morn's people as they huddled on the slopes of Ailach Tor, a heaving mob drawn helplessly to the abyss that opened at the summit.

Light and dark, Amethyst thought, her gaze drawn directly to Vornen's sword although she had no idea why. She closed her eyes to try and banish the awful vision, but still she saw only the apocalyptic chaos that had torn the day apart. *Light and dark, but all of it evil.*

And those people who had gathered on the hill died once the light had been drowned out, as the Gate faltered and changed from doorway to stone and back again a dozen times. The dark shapes had cut through them, or the hard, snow-covered earth had opened up to snatch them into its cavernous depths.

Even in her horror, Amethyst had eventually managed to turn and stumbled away. She had not been the only one, but aside from Vornen and Suli, as far as she knew no one else had found their way back to the town. They had frozen, or been cut to ribbons.

And I would have frozen as well, had Vornen not found me, she thought. *But why did the dark things leave me unscathed? Because I was not a worshipper of the light?*

Because I hadn't been taken by whatever madness had afflicted almost everyone else in this town?

She would never know. Other than Ileana, no citizen of this place remained alive to be questioned, and even if someone here still clung to life, how lucid and sane would they be?

Amethyst glanced across at Ileana. *She felt nothing of the Gate! Certainly she must be different to everyone else who lived here. And that may even be why the witch-woman wants her so badly.*

When they had made ready and ventured outside once again, Vornen breathed in the air and nodded. "This is fortuitous weather. We need to make the most of it and head as far south as we can through the Crescents. If we cannot reach their southern limits, perhaps we can beg hospitality from the *crommari* that dwell in the mountains, though it's never easy to gauge their likeliest response. Few have ever understood their customs, and they make little effort to understand ours." He gestured around them. "This will undoubtedly happen again, in other places. I wasn't sure, but now.."

His gaze turned to the south, and for a while he seemed lost in something more than thought. To Amethyst, he looked almost as if he listened to something that only he could hear. His lips moved silently, and once again his hand stole to the hilt of the black-bladed sword in his belt. This time though, it sprang suddenly away as soon as he had grasped the weapon, as if his hand had been thrown back by some invisible force- yet despite the violence of that movement Vornen appeared not to even notice it.

Amethyst found his detachment oddly disturbing in its suddenness. She looked away, uneasy.

Suli's attention, meanwhile, was fixed in the direction of the hill to the east, littered with the recently deceased. She looked as if she might be searching for something, her head turning slightly one way and then the other as if some scent or sight might arrive that would tell her what to do. *Gods, I am walking with the insane,* Amethyst thought, shaking her head. *Once this sorry business is all done with, I'll head back to Darkenhelm on the fastest horse I can buy. And then I'll be done with travel, done with the lure of adventure.*

"The rivers in the valleys may burst their banks if the snow continues to melt like this," she pointed out eventually. It was an obvious thing to say, but something had to be done to break the unsettling silence.

Vornen nodded slowly. "They may indeed. But we'll have to take our chances." He returned his attention to the Crescents that lay directly to the south, the forbidding shapes of which rose like an impenetrable barrier east to west as far as the eye could see. "Floods can happen suddenly in the valleys," he added. "Tell me, Amethyst- have you ever made your way through mountains such as those?" He raised a hand, smiling suddenly. "No, of course you have- you must have done to be here at all."

"I did travel through the Crescents by myself," Amethyst said with a shrug, "although the paths were well worn trails far to the west of here- and it was before winter's full force. I took the mapmakers' routes." She smiled faintly. "I thought they might make for the safest journey."

"Still, most people would never manage or even contemplate it." Vornen looked as if he had more to say, but once again his attention was wrested away by something distant. Amethyst looked at him and a strange thought occurred to her. *He's looking over the horizon.*

She almost laughed out loud at that, but when she thought about it again, the idea did not seem in the least bit amusing. She watched, drawing a little closer out of curiosity, as Vornen drew some more marks on his makeshift map with some charcoal he had found, holding the map down as it rustled in the breeze. Then he stared at the scribbles he had made as if unable to comprehend why he had just drawn them. His right hand trembled suddenly, and then once again found its way to the pommel of his sword. Amethyst looked from Vornen to Suli, and then to Ileana. *Gods, what wrongs did I carry out in some former life,* she thought mirthlessly, *to have ended up here, stranded and lost in a town of the dead, with these people as my companions!?* She knew the sentiment was not entirely fair, but it could not be helped.

Vornen cleared some snow out of the way with his boots and squatted on the ground, still intent upon his drawings. Suli went to sit near him, but she neither spoke nor looked at what he was doing. Watching them for a while, Amethyst's frustration gave way to pity mingled with guilt. Vornen had told her a little of their story whilst they ransacked a few of the nearby buildings, with Suli in the tavern. The two of them had been lovers once, a long time ago. Then she had left their home town- some place even further north that she had never heard of before- and Vornen had been exiled from it sometime afterwards. Until a chance meeting here in the desolate settlement of Ethanalin Tur-morn, they had never seen each other again.

"And she saw me first," Vornen had told Amethyst with a rueful smile, as they picked through provisions in a storehouse while Suli remained sitting huddled by the fire in the tavern, wrapped up and sleeping again. "She tried to kill me. The madness had taken a hold of her. Her mind comes and goes now. But the tide is going out, and I can do nothing about it. The waters of sanity are draining out of her. I'm losing the little that's left."

Vornen, she decided, was a man of some complexity: knowledgeable and intuitive, yet at the same time a slave to something invisible and intangible.

"If Gates open," Vornen said suddenly, turning to face her, "then I'm compelled to go to them. Sometimes I even catch a glimpse of a place on the other side. But most of the time, even if I see anything at all, I forget about it. That, at least, is a blessing of sorts."

Amethyst thought for a moment. *So I was right,* she thought, *but I didn't expect to be. Not like that.* "Then you were forced here?"

"Oh yes." He laughed unhappily. "And now I must head south. Luckily, the direction makes sense at the moment."

Amethyst nodded. She thought for a moment that she understood- *I know about the pain of compulsion,* she reflected- but she had never met anyone quite so confusing or confused.

As she waited patiently for Vornen to finish his scribbles, Amethyst wondered briefly what had happened to Elluron, the traveller she had met briefly on the way here, and another man to whom she owed her life, though she could remember almost nothing of his rescuing her from the makeshift prison in which she had been held. Elluron had known a great deal about the madness that was blighting people everywhere, or at least that had been her impression of him. *His eyes,* she thought suddenly. *When they caught the sun in a certain way, they seemed... what were they like? Gold and lilac at the same time? I've never seen eyes quite that colour before. I've met unusual people, but he was something else entirely.*

"I had a dream that someone would come for me," Ileana spoke up. "That's the only dream I've had for tennights now."

Amethyst blinked and glanced across at the girl. For a moment she considered telling Ileana of the dreams *she* had occasionally had of *her,* but decided against it for the moment. The girl did not need to know. "Did you know it would be me?" she asked casually.

Ileana shook her head. "I just knew someone would come. Someone from far away." Then she added quietly, "What will you do with me?"

"For now, you'll stay with me. There's someone I need to take you to." Amethyst wondered if she might ask who, but Ileana seemed barely to hear the answer, for like Vornen her attention had suddenly become fixed upon some distant, unfathomable point.

In that instant, Amethyst felt truly alone- far from home and with companions whose time was spent playing out their lives only in their own minds.

II

By late afternoon they had covered the mostly flat distance between the town and the mountains under clear skies, and headed through a wide valley between two of the smaller northern Crescents. Although the air was nowhere near as chilly as it had been, a stiff breeze blew down the valley, occasionally changing direction. It made the journey that much colder, although at least the wind blew mainly at their backs.

Numerous caves and tunnels, ancient attempts at mining for precious metals, littered the mountain slopes. Those who had sought such wealth were long gone, no trace of them remaining except the intrusions themselves. Amethyst, who knew her history well enough, recalled that the Tur-morn silver mines had once been the busiest in the land- but they had been poorly-run, mysterious accidents and incidents had plagued the mining operations, and eventually, despite the considerable wealth they had at first generated, most of the mines this far south of the town had been shut down.

Once the light had deteriorated too far for them to continue, the companions rested in one of the lower hillside caves for the night, protected from the increasingly chilly wind. At one point, Vornen voiced his fear that the snow would soon return. "Then it will cover rotting bodies this time, in Tur-morn- unless the carrion have plucked them bare already," Ileana said with venom.

"You harbour a lot of hate for your people," Amethyst commented.

"They're not my people any more than *you* are," was Ileana's spirited retort, which itself gave Amethyst a sudden thought. "Have you spent your entire life in Ethanalin Tur-morn, Ileana?"

The girl stared at her, pale blue eyes suddenly suspicious. She then looked sullenly at the ground. "Why do you want to know?"

"Because it may tell me why I was forced to find you," Amethyst said. "I suggest you answer me, Ileana- or perhaps I'll show you the pain I've had to suffer because of you."

Ileana blinked in bemusement, then shrugged. "I was left there when I was three years old. At least that's what I have always been told. My parents sold me to Tuin and Arla, the tavernkeepers. I know nothing else about them, and I was told never to ask. And I'm not scared of you, Amethyst."

"You should be," Amethyst said grimly, but Ileana shook her head, dismissing the possibility. "You're not that sort of person. You wouldn't inflict pain just like that. What's it called? In *cold blood*. And you're taking me with you for a reason, yes? Why do that if only to hurt me? You could have just hurt me back in the town."

Amethyst stared at her for a while, trying to ignore Vornen who had made the situation still more humiliating by laughing out loud. Finally she nodded brusquely. "Very well, Ileana. It's not your fault that some witch cursed me, forced me to find you or endure agony for every step I took further away from you. The fault lies with her- and I swear I will seek out that hag and cut her to pieces."

"Amethyst," Vornen spoke up, as Ileana stared open-mouthed in the wake of Amethyst's outburst, "have you ever wondered *why* you were commanded to find Ileana?"

"That's hardly my concern. I was simply in the wrong place at the wrong time. If not me, then it would have been someone else passing through."

"But it may serve to explain a few things," Vornen reasoned as he scattered firepowder over the twigs they had gathered before the onset of dusk. The women- even Suli, who sat further back in the shadows- watched as he struck the flint in his hand; moments later, smokeless flames leapt up from the kindling. As they moved a little nearer to enjoy some of the heat, Vornen continued, "As you said, I expect you were chosen simply because you happened to be in the wrong place at the wrong time. But perhaps this witch felt compelled to force you on that quest simply because she had to be certain, or as certain as she could be, that you would eventually find Ileana. Her method was harsh, certainly, but it shows one thing clearly. Ileana is very important to this woman."

"I don't want to be handed over to her," Ileana said immediately, shaking her head. "I would rather take my chances with the two of you."

Vornen laughed at that. "Be careful, Ileana- that might be considered a compliment."

Amethyst sat in silence for a long while, pondering the matter. "We'll see what happens," she said finally. "Certainly, I owe her nothing but vengeance. Why could she not have sought Ileana out for herself? Still..." Doubt and fear rose as she considered what the witch-woman might be able to do if she refused to hand over the girl. Amethyst's right hand rose to the side of her head, as if by doing so it might ward off a return of the agony that had consumed her life. She remained unaware of the motion.

Vornen said nothing.

During the night, the wind rose to a howling gale. At its worst, the storm sounded like a gathering of banshees screeching their way down the valley, pulling at withered shrubs as if to tear them from the earth. Even when it abated a little, still it sighed like a desolate and restless soul. Sleep was all but impossible.

Vornen lay on his side, listening to the mournful sounds out in the valley. He stared across at Suli, who had turned to face him. Dim light from dying embers flickered across her face. Her dark eyes looked like holes. *Gods, you were so beautiful once,* he thought. *Now I see nothing but misery and madness in you. You can no longer even talk to me. I can't remember the last words you uttered. When did you last speak?*

He remembered after a moment. *If someone wishes to gnaw the poisoned flesh from my bones, they are welcome to it.* She had said those words, and then quietly laughed as if they constituted some sort of dreadful joke.

"Suli," he said quietly, wondering if he could elicit some response. But she said nothing. Perhaps she had not heard him, or perhaps her mind was simply elsewhere. He felt a sudden, powerful desire to reach across to her, touch her- not lustfully, but to offer a crumb of comfort to this broken shell of a woman. Yet he stayed his hand, fearful of how she might react- and even more afraid that she would not react at all, that it would be like trying to wake a corpse.

Eventually Vornen forced himself to turn away, unable to bear the sight of her. *It's the most miserable thing,* he reflected darkly, *when love has gone, replaced by nothing more than pity.* He could still feel her gaze upon him, more a fixation than a stare, and although he did not turn round again to face her- for some reason he feared what he might see this time, even though he knew that was a ridiculous notion- his hand strayed to the hilt of his sword, and remained there for the rest of the night.

Several paces away, Amethyst listened to the wind and wondered how it could possibly make such hellish noises. When it eventually calmed a little, Ileana spoke up quietly. "I'm scared."

Amethyst glanced across at her. "Of the wind? The sounds it makes?" That was the first thing that came to her mind.

"The woman you said wanted me for something." Ileana paused, no doubt thinking something over, and then asked, "Did she really torture you to make you find me?"

Amethyst sighed and wished she hadn't mentioned the matter earlier. "She used some powerful weave of witchery. The agonies I suffered if I so much as walked too far in the wrong direction were..." She shook her head, unable to describe them. "You don't need to know."

Ileana said nothing but shuddered and drew her blanket closer about her. Amethyst was suddenly reminded of the girl's tender age. How old was she- thirteen, maybe fourteen? Certainly she was too young to have to endure this miserable journey, although she would hardly have fared better in the frozen graveyard of Ethanalin Tur-morn. What would a survivor do in a place like that? Eat until nothing remained to be eaten, and then slowly starve? Which would come first: death or madness? Or might there be a few other survivors, who would butcher her and feast upon what little meat they could pull from her bones? Amethyst shut her eyes and willed away that dreadful image.

"I had to bring you with me," she said eventually. "I want you to realise that. If I had not, the agonies would have returned. I'm sure of it."

"It's done now," Ileana said, and turned away.

III

The morning dawned brightly, and mercifully the wind had died down to a light breeze by the time they set off again. As they walked down through the valley, Amethyst reflected deliberately on past times with her family in Darkenhelm, hopeful that it would distract her from the numbing fatigue and ever-gnawing hunger in her belly.

But soon enough she found herself dwelling instead on the tribal lunacy that had set people against each other throughout the northern territories, the rampant talk of *blood lords, earth lords,* the *Great Light of the East* and other names that until the last few months had meant nothing to her. *And in an awful way, it was true,* she thought, shuddering and drawing her cloak more tightly about her. *I saw the light and the dark, the great battle fought in the sky. For a moment, perhaps I even saw the same things that Vornen says he has seen, glimpses of some other place beyond Aona.*

This struggle is affecting the world, she thought. *People flock to the light or the dark, deluded in the belief that Gods have come to the world, to bring an end to the Age. They're being pulled one way or the other, to certain ruin. It's part of some vast, evil plan.*

Amethyst knew in her heart that whichever side eventually won it mattered little, for the peoples of the world would be in thrall to one grim master or the other when all of this was done.

They stopped to rest for the third time late in the afternoon. Amethyst sank down to the ground and leaned against a boulder which had fallen from the slope and come to rest by the side of their trail. Ileana sat down nearby and uttered a sigh of exhaustion that sounded exactly how Amethyst felt. "The further south we head, the less cold it will be, after we make it through the mountains," she said, not sure how true that might turn out to be.

"*If* we make it through the mountains," Ileana darkly pointed out.

Amethyst was about to reply- though later she would never remember what it was she would have said- when a sudden motion on her left wrested away her attention completely.

She had never seen anyone move as fast as Suli did in that instant.

The woman was a blur. One moment she sat on the ground with her head slumped slightly as if she might topple forward, but the next she had already reached Vornen and ripped the sword from his belt.

How? Amethyst thought in shock as Suli fell backwards with the effort, legs buckling under her, yet still managed to spring to her feet a moment later, before Vornen had even realised what had happened. *How can a woman so physically sick do that?*

The answer came to her immediately, and her heart hammered madly at the realisation. *The sword,* she thought, horrified. *The damned sword. It* wanted *her to claim it.* She suddenly recalled Vornen's hand being drawn towards the hilt so many times, seemingly without him knowing.

Vornen looked caught in a stupor, as if part of his very being had been torn away with the sword. Slowly he turned and watched as Suli took several steps backwards and brandished the black blade. To Amethyst the weapon seemed to turn the afternoon darker, as Suli lifted it higher into the air. *Black shapes,* she thought numbly, recalling the horror of Ailach Tor. *Gods, it's the same. The same darkness seeps from it.*

"No," Vornen said weakly. He reached forth a hand and implored her, "Suli, if any sense remains within you..."

"It's no longer yours, Vornen." Amethyst realised suddenly that this was the first time she had heard the woman speak. She had a beautiful, strong voice, at odds completely with the confused and lunatic face that stared back at her former lover. "It's not mine, but I must take it from you. Its purpose lies elsewhere."

Vornen extended his hand again, not in expectation but in desperate hope. Every finger shook. "Suli, *listen to me!* Do you not recall what happened on Tur-morn Hill? Do you remember what this blade *does?* It can *close Gates.* It sets free things that can destroy the *marandaal...*"

I was right, Amethyst thought numbly. *But this evil will destroy its bearer too, given any chance.*

"That's why I must carry it to Nisstar," Vornen whispered. He took a slow step forward, and Suli matched it with an equal backward step. A boulder might have tripped her, but somehow she sidestepped it without looking, as if she knew exactly where it was. "There will be Gates there, Suli, and they must be closed, destroyed, rendered unusable, I know that to be true now..."

"But not by such as you," Suli said, and shook her head. "*No.*"

She turned then, and fled towards the slope of the nearest hill, leaping over a frozen stream and over boulders and tufts of grass. Vornen followed at first, but she turned, more swiftly than should have been possible, and swung the black blade so that it was raised above her with both hands. To Amethyst, that sword now looked exactly like one of the indistinct, shadowy entities that had circled the Gate on Turmorn Hill, cutting through the light that came from a different world to deny the yawning abyss and its unknown contents.

"Leave me or be slain, Vornen!" cried Suli. These were, Amethyst reflected later, the most tormented words she had ever heard. For a moment she felt nothing but pity for this maddened husk of a woman. *Don't take another step towards her, Vornen,* she silently pleaded, as a frightened Ileana grabbed her arm. *She will kill you if that's what it takes. The sword no longer needs you.*

Vornen remained where he was, transfixed in helpless silence. Then Suli turned and ran away into the gathering dusk, and Vornen sank to his knees with a groan of despair.

Amethyst made her way over to him, but she could barely look at the misery etched upon his face. Neither of them spoke. As if in lamentation, the chilly breeze sighed through the broken, bare trees that lined the valley.

We should find somewhere out of the wind to sleep tonight, Amethyst thought absently after a while. As if he had heard that sentiment, Vornen finally staggered to his feet, and they headed onwards.

He did not speak at all until much later, as they gazed out of another cave entrance into the night and watched the great red moon Archaon rise over the jagged mountain horizon. "Now she has the sword," he said. "Or the sword has *her*. It weaves some dark purpose of its own, and she has been made a part of it."

IV

Heavy with snow clouds, the sky darkened swiftly as afternoon became evening, but Suli walked on, careless as to the pitfalls that lurked along the path. Twice she fell, and on one occasion a sharp spur of rock pierced her leg, but she barely noticed. Small rocks that she dislodged or kicked aside tumbled away down the icy slope that loomed to her left.

Suli felt the pull of emerging Gates far to the south, but the pull of the sword was far stronger. Often her hand strayed to its plain hilt, and remained there, gripping it so tightly that it shook and her hand became a blur. When she closed her eyes, she could still see the path before her. Somehow, even in the darkness behind her eyelids, it appeared painted red, earth and stone and blood comingled and then laid out for her to follow.

Her thoughts were muddled and irrational, and they came and went unordered. Her sanity had long since crumbled away, but some awareness remained. *Now Vornen will not have to suffer my fate,* she told herself, and in a rare moment of clarity: *If he does not thank me, still at least his woman-friend will.* She barely remembered the clash of forces, between the sword and the Gate that opened on Turmorn Hill. It was a vague recollection that could have happened years ago.

When it became too dark to see where she was going, she collapsed by the edge of the slope, disturbing stones and hardened turf that tumbled away down the side of the mountain and gathered other debris as they went. Barely conscious, she pulled the sword out into the chill air. The blade was hot to the touch. *It will keep me warm,* she thought before drifting off into a feverish slumber, and it did just that. If anyone had passed by early the following morning, they would have seen her curled up around the blade, which had melted the snow for yards around and even scorched the sparse vegetation that clung grimly to the path, and yet had left her body unmarked.

Her dreams were ecstatic, feverish interludes of lust, which disintegrated into the worst of nightmares. In one of these, she and Vornen made violent love on the shore of a lake. They bit and tore at each other and writhed at the water's edge, until from the corner of her eye Suli saw that the lake's waters were in fact blood that congealed at the shoreline, and that her skeleton and Vornen's lay deep within that thick crimson mass, many times over. *As if we have done this before, and are condemned to do so again, forever,* she thought in dismay, before she was sent tumbling from that horror into another.

Here, she ran around a room whose four walls each moved slowly inwards. They could not be stopped. The room had no ceiling, or if it did then it was so far above that she could not hope to glimpse it. *If I had lived wisely, I could have found a way out,* she thought brokenly, and watched as specks of blood and another, indeterminate substance appeared on the walls and trickled down. With a sudden spasm of unquenchable thirst she pressed herself against the wall and lapped up the sour flow. From somewhere far above, or beyond, she heard faint cries, but they faded the more she drank the blood that now poured into her mouth.

Suli woke violently, choking, and as a first impulse she reached for the sword and cradled it in her arms. Immediately she felt calm, warm and safe. Leaning forward, she spat her own fresh blood onto the ground, but the sight of it meant nothing to her. She rose unsteadily to her feet and staggered on along the path. After a short while she felt *too* warm, as if her insides had started to smoulder, and so she removed her leather armour, shirt and trousers and threw them away down the slope towards the black depths of the ravine, followed by her undergarments. *I am higher now,* she realised suddenly, *as high as some of the other mountains. I can see almost the entire Crescents.* She stopped to observe the harsh beauty of the landscape, the contrast between black rock and dazzling white snow and ice. She held the sword against her breasts, and this time the blade burned against her skin; Suli did not even notice, but she did imagine that it spoke to her, in a voice that was neither male nor female, only an insistent, urgent whisper.

Hurry!

I always want to be this warm, Suli told the sword as her skin grew ever colder. *I want to be warm and be safe and I want to be rid of Gates.*

It's not long now, the sword said comfortingly. *Just a little further and then you will have your rest.*

I am so tired! I have always been tired. Something has been wrong with me for my entire life, something to do with Gates...

The sword said nothing to that, but Suli found that her legs moved jerkily forward again.

At dusk that same day, Suli reached a point on the mountain ridge where it changed direction, turning a corner of jagged rock to lead her abruptly south. She staggered around the corner, and then two things happened. The wind dropped entirely, and in the oddly warm calm that ensued, a creature that at first she mistook for nothing more than a shadow loomed before her. It gained in substance and height until it became seven feet tall, a thin, black-clad being of sticks and bones over which a cloak was draped. Nothing of its face could be seen, if indeed it had such a thing.

Suli fell to the ground, vaguely aware of a shard of rock that broke through her kneecap. She felt no pain, only foul warmth covering her.

Somehow, her face was lifted up and she gazed at the being. Her mouth felt full to the brim with hot blood. A grim redness loomed at the corners of her vision. With hands that shook violently and veins hard and full like the roots of a tree, she raised her arms and presented the sword to the shadowy creature that stood in her path. But even in her baking hysteria, she saw now that the sword was no longer a sword, but a small black glass cube.

The being knelt before her, or perhaps it had made itself smaller in order to look into her eyes more easily. Suli felt that it grinned, although of course it could not, for it had no discernible face. Something that vaguely resembled an arm extended forth, long and painfully thin, more needle than bone. A tendril of insubstantial darkness reached out to her like curling mist to caress her cheek. Suli let out a ragged, defeated sob as it burned into her.

A great gift indeed, the *choragh* said into her.

"Not... not a sword..." The words forced their way out, choked into the thick, warm air. She felt the creature laugh inside her head. *No. It was never a sword. It is only ever what we need it to be.*

The cube was lifted from her hands. Suli felt as if an entire limb had been ripped from her body. *Let me die,* she sobbed inwardly, and of course the *choragh* to whom she had surrendered the artefact heard those thoughts. *You can never die when you are as one with us,* it said softly. *You become a part of the world itself. A world cast once again in our image.*

It ran smoky traces down her arms, and each one gouged fleshy cuts and subcutaneous tissue from inside her. Suli felt no pain. She felt nothing but faint curiosity and a sensation akin to a door closing forever behind her ruined remains.

Now the secrets of the world are yours, for you cannot die, the *choragh* whispered to her, as Suli's remaining memories and emotions tumbled out of her like the tired flesh her new lord picked at dispassionately.

V

By first light the following day the wind had lessened further, and Amethyst, Vornen and Ileana made their way on through the desolate valley, following the path of the part-frozen river. Vornen remained silent and disconsolate, but as they stopped to refill their canteens at one point, he suddenly said, "I shouldn't grieve for her."

"Because she's no longer who she once was?" Amethyst asked guardedly.

He shrugged. "Suli left a long time ago and never truly came back. It was through pure chance that I found her again- if I'd found myself another guest-house to stay in, or if I'd walked to another part of the hill, I'd never have known she was in the same town. The sword will make an end of her." He smiled bleakly. "Perhaps she will cast herself off the edge of a mountain path. Then it will have to find itself a new owner."

Ileana shuddered. Amethyst said nothing, but Vornen added for good measure, "What would *you* prefer- the emptiness of madness, or the peace that death brings?"

"Death," Amethyst told him curtly. "Wouldn't we all? But I don't wish to think about it."

On several occasions during the morning, Vornen stopped and looked around in every direction. Amethyst followed his gaze but she saw only the snowbound peaks and

45

ridges, the loose rocky mountainsides and the bare, windswept trees that jutted out like malformed hands from the barren landscape. "What is it?" she asked finally.

"I feel we are being watched." Vornen stared around again. "Don't you?"

"This is where they'll attack," Ileana said. Vornen whirled round. "Where *what* will attack?" he demanded, but Ileana just shook her head miserably. The breeze blew her mousey brown hair across her face as her shoulders visibly sagged. Vornen cursed and was about to repeat his question when the girl uttered a low, despairing moan and sank to a kneeling position on the ground. Amethyst rushed to her, grasping her hand. "Ileana!" she exclaimed, and watched in increasing horror as the girl's eyes rolled back in their sockets until only white sclera remained visible. Ileana shook violently; it looked almost as if she was being shaken from within, something coursing throughout her body, a mad force that had suddenly been unleashed.

Amethyst stared in mute shock, grasping both her hands, not that that served to do any good. If anything, Ileana became yet more agitated, her mouth opening as if in a soundless scream.

Then came the attack, as Ileana had warned.

Six *crommari* and two larger figures, almost certainly humans- appeared at the top of the slope on the right, a hundred feet or more above them. Inexplicably, the two larger ones proceeded to fling themselves down the hillside. Amethyst watched in bewilderment and horror as they crashed down the slope, dislodging rocks and snapping bushes and shrubs that clung feebly to the eroded surface. Each collision elicited a sickening crunch as bones broke and innards ruptured.

The two figures tumbled to the valley floor no more than thirty yards away, and there they rose, mangled and broken but careless as to their predicament. A dull yellowish glow, liquid and waxlike, glimmered in their eyes, which fixed upon the companions as they dragged their way nearer, arms flailing at their sides.

Amethyst flung six of her blades at the creatures in swift succession. Her aim was unerring; four of the knives embedded themselves deep in the creatures' heads, a fifth punctured the windpipe of one, and the sixth almost severed the right hand of the other.

They lurched on regardless.

Amethyst heard Vornen curse and draw his longknife as she did the same. The abominations had dragged themselves to within ten yards away- and the *crommari,* Amethyst dimly realised, had reached the bottom of the slope- when they stopped suddenly. In the same instant, Amethyst heard Ileana mutter a quiet mantra to herself over and over, in a language she had never heard before. She turned, and saw that the girl now stood by herself, swaying slightly. Blood dripped slowly from her eyes, which had become pure white like the orbs of an alabaster statue.

Amethyst dragged her gaze back from this confounding scene to the creatures that sought to assail them, yet she need not have bothered. They had still not moved. It seemed they could not.

Some distance behind them, the *crommari* waited, suddenly uncertain. They, at least, could move, but they dared take no more than a few more steps forward, perhaps unable to comprehend what had happened to the creatures they had sent forth.

Inexplicably, parts of the two immobile creatures began to snap off and blow away in the wind. They became nothing more than clumps of dirt and dust which were carried further, swept along the ground. What remained of their legs snapped and crumbled. The heads were the last parts to remain identifiable on the ground; Amethyst found herself dimly wondering if at least their skulls would be left once the disintegration of their bodies was complete. Yet these too became dust. Within a short space of time, nothing could be seen that showed these abominations had ever existed, for the dust itself had blown away and was gone forever to mingle with the earth and the air.

The companions stood in mute shock. The six *crommari,* meanwhile, looked on in visible dismay. Then they turned and scrabbled their way back up the hillside, dislodging boulders and snapping shrubs in their fevered haste. Even the dust and disturbance from their exit had settled by the time Vornen spoke. His words, Amethyst would recall later, sounded oddly calm. The horror of what she had seen seemed to shrink back, if only a little.

"I think maybe they came for the sword. Or for *her.*" He glanced at Ileana, a curious expression upon his face.

Mercifully, Ileana had recovered a little, though she was still shaking and exhausted. At least her eyes were as they should be, Amethyst noticed, and blood no longer seeped from them. She gave the girl a little water and wrapped her in a blanket, then held her until she had stopped shivering. When Ileana finally felt able to walk they made their way as quickly as possible- which in truth was with painful slowness- on through the valley.

When night fell, they stopped near a small group of trees, the remains of which might have been extensive woodland once. They at least provided a little shelter from the wind. Vornen built a fire and put a kettle of water and nettles over it. Amethyst had noticed that he had something of a preference for nettle tea, a concoction she had never tried before meeting him. "I even found it kept me off the *kyush,*" he had said at one point, a statement that she doubted very much though she didn't say so.

She was about to ask Ileana if she could eat and drink a little when the girl turned to look at her, and without any warning flung herself into Amethyst's arms, sobbing loudly. She cried like someone who had never wept in her life before.

Amethyst held her uncertainly, completely taken aback at first. *She must still be shocked after what happened,* she thought. *I know I'm shaken up enough by it. The Gods alone know what she must be making of it all.*

She was reminded suddenly of the times when she had comforted her little sister Lona, and a feeling of deep homesickness washed over her as she caressed Ileana's tear-stained cheek, lost in reminiscence. For the first time she reflected on the terror that Ileana must have been feeling all this time- from the moment she had been forced from her home, even if she had hated it, to their encounter with... whatever those creatures had been. *What a life,* Amethyst thought. *A miserable existence in Ethanalin Tur-morn after being sold by her own parents, then this journey through the heart of winter, and now, just when she probably thought things could not possibly get any worse...*

Ileana said nothing of her ordeal or anything else. After a while her sobbing ceased and she fell asleep, leaning against Amethyst, who gently laid her down in her blankets. She and Vornen then talked quietly of their horrific encounter and sat as close as they could to the fire without burning themselves.

"Suli may have been captured," Vornen suggested, "and forced to tell her captors about us, our whereabouts and more importantly about Ileana. I think one thing is now certain, Amethyst." He dropped his voice and glanced at their companion to make sure she was asleep. "I thought at first it might be the sword, but now... it could be that this has something to do with Ileana. Perhaps it even has something to do with why that witch-woman needed her found." He paused, scratching at his patchy growth of beard, thinking for a moment. "She didn't feel the pull of the Gate, nor did she dream of the *marandaal,* the destroying light. You know, I had forgotten the name myself, until Suli reminded me. And it seems Ileana has... other talents. Other powers. Her enemies will come again, and again, until she can no longer withstand them.”

“What were they?” Amethyst asked him quietly.

He looked grimly at her. “I can’t be sure, but if I had to guess, I would say they were *diafagh*. Creations of the Old Dark. The dead, made to rise again to do their masters’ bidding, for want of a better description. Weapons are of little use against them.”

Amethyst shuddered. “Do they have anything to do with the earth-lords?”

Vornen nodded and smiled mirthlessly. “And I’ll wager you had never heard that name either, before you travelled here.”

Amethyst thought of the men she had met who had spoken that name, and shuddered. The time from when she fell down the stairs at the castle, to her arrival in Ethanalin Tur-morn, seemed now like a mad dream. Her encounter with Elluron appeared in her mind like a bright splash of colour and sanity against a backdrop of gloom and madness. “I think the world and its people are going entirely insane,” she sighed. “I have no wish to live in a world like that.”

“Would you kill yourself?” Vornen asked her, and before she could answer, he added, “I’ve contemplated it many times. But I’m a coward, a weak man.”

“Why would you have thought about it?”

“When you’re drawn towards Gates, your life is never your own,” Vornen said, and stared into the flames as if he could see his own past being played back in their light. “Life itself becomes fragmented. You forget things. Perhaps you lose a little piece of your mind every time you see those distant, impossible, indescribable *things* elsewhere in the Existence. A punishment for knowledge which itself never lasts. It’s a kind of... *unravelling*.”

Amethyst shuddered. “I’m glad I can barely begin to imagine it.”

"In Darkenhelm, or anywhere in the South, I expect there are no stories of the Old Dark, and certainly not of the *marandaal*," Vornen mused, suddenly eager to change the subject. "You *are* from Darkenhelm, aren't you?"

Amethyst nodded. *And I'd send myself back there in an instant if I could,* she thought.

"Even amongst the witches and warlocks in remote places, the names of the Old Dark are a myth, no more than tales with which to frighten errant children. When thousands of years pass, even the most ancient history is eventually forgotten."

Amethyst glanced across at Ileana, who continued to slumber peacefully, snoring faintly in the shadows. "The poor girl. To be cursed like this, with whatever power she has..."

Vornen nodded. "There you have it, in your own words. A great power and a great curse are sometimes the same thing. I can't say how she fits into this, Amethyst, but I would put any amount of money on a wager that she *does* fit into it. You need to find this witch-woman for her sake."

Neither of them said anything for a long while. They listened to the night, ready for any sounds or sights that might alert them to another attack, though it was difficult to see anything out there except the grim outlines of the mountain slopes, black silhouettes under the sky. With the wind having dropped, Amethyst could hear the blood pounding in her ears louder than anything else.

"The place where you met the witch-woman," Vornen said eventually. "Could you find your way back there?"

"Yes. I think so. The village was called Alinnora's Haven." Amethyst was confident enough of that; she remembered seeing the name on a sign as she approached the place. Although a fairly small village, it had a widely-used road travelling through it north to south and a smaller one running roughly east-west. The layout of the village itself was not that unusual, perhaps, but she remembered it well enough if only because it was the place where her life had been changed forever. There would be signs that led travellers towards it, she supposed.

"If you take Ileana to that place, then I expect you'll find her again."

"What about you?" she asked, shivering and drawing her blanket more closely about her shoulders. "Will you come with us?"

"Part of the way. Certainly until we are well out of the Crescents, if we get to such a place. But then..." His expression darkened. "I must go to Nisstar, south of here."

Amethyst nodded. She had expected him to say something like that, and was already resigned to the fact. "The Gates," she said. "Were they what you kept looking at, even before we set off from Ethanalin Tur-morn? Were they what you drew on your map?"

"Did I?" He looked confused for a moment, and then shrugged. "I cannot turn my back on them. Oh, I've tried from time to time, but I can't escape their pull, vnot by myself at any rate. But perhaps when I..." His words drifted away; she watched as his eyes glazed over. Vornen stared at the remnants of the fire, lost in whatever thoughts had ensnared his attention.

"I always end up heading towards them," he said softly, after what seemed an age of contemplation. "If I turn to head in another direction, sooner or later I find myself on the road I turned away from. As if the road itself turned around, impossible though that is. So I may as well save myself the bother."

"Nothing seems impossible now," Amethyst remarked with a shiver. She thought back to her own attempts to turn from the path she had been forced upon. "I can understand, Vornen. I tried to resist the direction in which I was being guided, and suffered more each time."

"There, you see. It's different, yet it's the same." He looked up from the fire and into her eyes. "I hope that curse has been lifted from you forever, Amethyst. Whatever else happens."

"Thank you," she said, and somehow managed a smile.

But her expression faded a short while later as Vornen turned his head south once again, a look of lean hunger in his eyes that was not entirely his own.

The following morning was slow in arriving. Low cloud hung ominously, heavy with the promise of snow. The companions wasted little time in setting off across the wide plain, and walked as fast as Ileana's state allowed. Physically she had improved somewhat, but she maintained a sullen, withdrawn silence as they walked. Amethyst thought about broaching the subject of yesterday's horrific encounter, but could find no way of doing so. In any case, she reasoned, there was no sense in causing the girl further distress. Perhaps she would speak of it in time, perhaps not. Amethyst cast many an anxious glance around as they traversed the plain. She had no idea what she would do if the terrible events of yesterday repeated themselves.

Ileana for her part merely stumbled along, slack-eyed and wrapped in her own nightmare.

Morning had long been and gone by the time they reached the other side of the plain, where once again jagged mountains or the shadowy passes between them formed their stark choices. The sun struggled through the milky sky, and the cloud had become a little higher and thinner, for which Amethyst was grateful. If snow had started to spiral down during the morning, she would have sunk to her knees and wept openly. Every part of her ached with a deep, leaden weight.

"Two days, perhaps three, separate us from the southern foothills," Vornen said as they rested on a group of boulders at the head of a wide valley. The valley led roughly southward between clusters of snowbound peaks, and a partly frozen river wound along its lowest point, cutting through cold, boggy grassland dotted with stark bushes and trees whose windswept deformities bowed to the mountains in their midst. *Much more of this,* Amethyst thought, *and I might even forget how I came to be here, and start wandering in my mind even while my body wanders.* She opened her water canteen and took a few sips, wincing at the cold. *Mulled wine,* she thought absently, her teeth chattering. *If only I could turn this water into mulled wine, and build some warmth in my belly.*

She saw Vornen look appraisingly at Ileana, and did not have to ask what he was thinking. The girl's progress, and hence theirs, had slowed during the day. Despite frequent rests and administrations of the few herbal concoctions either of them had in their possession, she had grown weaker. Amethyst knew in her heart that whatever ailed Ileana, it was beyond the reach of such simple remedies.

During her waking moments the previous night- which had been many- and throughout the morning, Amethyst had dwelt on nothing but the matter of Ileana and her enemies. She felt certain that those they had encountered were the least of them. A vague sense of familiarity, as if she ought somehow to know the purpose of these horrific creatures, nagged constantly. *It's something far wider than we know,* she had thought. *Something that will reach out and touch every man, woman and child of each Race in all lands. The Old Dark, Vornen called it.*

"Then we go as far as we can," she said.

Ileana sat wearily on a nearby boulder, almost collapsing. "They will come again," she murmured.

"When? How far away are they?" Vornen asked.

The girl gave a long drawn-out sigh. "Tonight," she said eventually. "In the dark. There are more of them this time. Too many."

Amethyst felt the quiet chill of certain defeat settle into her. Mingled with the fear and panic of knowing their enemies would bear down upon them in greater numbers and imminently, she felt a strange relief, about which she was oddly ashamed. She had been taught from a young age about the value of life for its own sake. Words her father had uttered years ago came sharply back to her. *If you don't value your own life, how can you truly value the lives of others, or life itself?*

But I have always valued it, she thought, *which is why I wanted to explore the world. I wish I could have had the chance to do that, to go to all the places I'll now never have a chance to see. And yet I'd do anything now just to be back home in Darkenhelm.*

"I think we're being watched," Vornen said grimly. His words shook Amethyst out of her black thoughts. As if in response to his words, a small figure appeared from behind a group of boulders no more than forty paces away. It wore a small hooded robe, tied with rope at the front. Instantly Amethyst had her knives ready, and Vornen had drawn his longknife, but the creature hastily dropped the spear it held and took a step back as if to show it meant no harm.

Vornen beckoned the creature nearer, and it made its way cautiously towards them. As it stopped, just five paces from the companions, Amethyst saw the red, wary eyes beneath the hood, and the scaly, almost reptilian face to which they belonged in a little detail. "A *ko xhoth*," she said, taken aback. She had seen such a being only once before, near the borders of Rockmire a week or so before she had arrived in Alinnora's Haven. It had been bartering goods with a small group of *luyan* travellers in a temporary market encampment.

"Why do you spy on us?" Vornen demanded. The creature spread its claws expansively as if to imply that it had done no such thing. Then it pointed further down the valley, and jabbered something unintelligible in its own language. It walked in the same direction, picked up its spear and turned back to beckon them impatiently.

"Even if it means us harm," Amethyst observed, "can it be any worse than what else awaits us here?"

Vornen smiled thinly and strode after the *ko xhoth*, which quickly resumed its swift progress. Amethyst and Ileana followed behind. Further north, snow clouds massed and began to deposit their load upon the land, rolling ominously southwards. Amethyst shivered in the icy breeze and tugged her cloak more tightly about herself.

The *ko xhoth* led them through a narrow ravine ringed with broken remnants of fallen boulders and dead, stunted trees and shrubs. As they stumbled along this rough trail, the light began to fail swiftly, and snow began to fall, thickening the whole while. It had begun to settle by the time the creature led them to a crude cave entrance and pointed at it. Vornen uttered a groan and shook his head, but at the same moment Ileana clutched suddenly at Amethyst, her nails almost digging into her arm. "They are almost here," she whispered, eyes wide with terror, at which point the *ko xhoth* began to jabber away and pointed animatedly at the cave entrance again and again. "It knows about them," Amethyst murmured.

Vornen said nothing, but strode into the cave alongside the *ko xhoth*. Amethyst and Ileana hurried after him. *What other choice*, Amethyst silently remarked, *if Ileana speaks the truth?*

A strange, chilly sensation that had nothing to do with the temperature assailed them as they stepped forward. Then it was gone, and the air suddenly became warmer. Amethyst felt sure, as she glanced back, that the air near the cave entrance shimmered for a moment.

They stopped to light lanterns, and by the glow of the sputtering flames they headed onwards, led by their strange guide into the dark heart of the mountains.

Amethyst woke so suddenly that for a moment she could not remember where she was or who she was with.

Slowly the events of recent days drifted back. She held her head in her hands and cursed quietly to herself. *I could weep,* she thought, *but what good would that do even if I had the strength?*

She heard Ileana stir next to her and then utter a gasp of fear. A small, cold hand found Amethyst's arm and swiftly moved down to her hand, where it remained. Amethyst clasped Ileana's hand and the girl grew quiet.

Vornen was already awake. He suddenly appeared out of the darkness as he lit one of their lanterns. "Both awake?" he enquired pointlessly. Amethyst managed a faint smile.

"How long did we sleep for?" Ileana asked. "It feels like days."

"Half a day, perhaps a little more." Vornen passed her his water flask and she drank thirstily from it before passing it to Amethyst.

"Where is the *ko xhoth?*" Amethyst asked suddenly, noticing that their guide was nowhere to be seen.

Vornen shrugged. "I fell asleep for a little while. It must have left then."

Amethyst handed back the water flask. "Do you think it deliberately saved our lives?"

"Perhaps. Clearly it sensed something and decided we might be safer here."

A dreadful realisation came to Amethyst. "But now we're lost. How do we know which way is south?"

"I know which way the Gates are, no matter the leagues of stone between us," Vornen said softly, "and I know the Gates lie in the south."

They continued along the rough-hewn passageway. It remained uncomfortably narrow for a long time before eventually it widened out a little. Amethyst walked a little behind Ileana and watched her carefully in case she stumbled and fell. The girl looked about to do just that on a number of occasions, but somehow managed to keep herself upright, hands clenched tightly into fists as if she was willing herself to keep upright and moving forward. *Better to keep open palms and ready fingers in a place such as this,* Amethyst, who had already tripped a couple of times, remarked to herself. But she said nothing, too busy watching her own footing and silently pondering the matter of Ileana and everything about her.

That she had some rare, terrible power was beyond question now. But Ileana was also a liability. Trouble would surely follow for as long as she remained with them.

In the midst of such worries, however, Amethyst felt oddly proud of Ileana's stubborn resistance and fortitude, for she herself felt ready to collapse at times as they made their way along the winding tunnel. The strange variations in temperature did nothing to help them- they walked from pockets of warm, dry air into cold, dank vapours that made the walls gleam faintly with moisture, and then on into stuffy, dusty air once again, many times.

Not for the first time, she wondered if Ileana might have had seizures before. Amethyst thought perhaps not, if this stirring of the *old dark* had only now started to happen. And Ileana had apparently felt nothing of the Gate's pull in Ethanalin Tur-morn as the place erupted into madness. Even Amethyst had felt that influence, though faintly.

Why did Ileana not even notice it? she wondered. *Could it be that she is simply attuned to... other things?*

The tunnel started to slope gradually downwards and the air became warmer still, though damper than before. Amethyst's shirt stuck to her skin even more and she pulled irritably at it, cursing under her breath. To make matters even worse, her monthly blood had started and she had no spongeweed or anything else to deal with it. *This could not have happened at a worse time,* she thought angrily.

Here and there, rivulets of water ran from the ceiling to the floor to collect in larger streams which had made natural gutters on each side of the tunnel. Patches of slime and other slippery growth marked the floor in places and required careful negotiation.

After a long time the tunnel widened out into a fair-sized cavernous area, dimly lit by green-hued phosphorescence on the walls as bright as the flickering light of their lanterns. Several large rises in the ground formed natural if uncomfortable seats. "At *last*," Ileana groaned, sinking down onto one. She then made an exclamation of disgust as Vornen tore some of the mossy substance from the nearest wall and held it out to her in one outstretched hand. "Please tell me we have something other than moss to eat," Ileana moaned.

"We do," Vornen confirmed, nibbling a little of it himself, "but this particular moss is the one also known as greenbread. It has restorative qualities, Ileana. I think you should eat some. Certainly it will keep you going for longer."

Ileana peered suspiciously at Vornen as if he might be trying to trick her, then made a face and took a little of the proffered gift. After picking at it for a while, she eventually put some in her mouth and chewed it. "It tastes of nothing," she declared eventually.

"Better than you expected, then," Amethyst said with a smile.

The three of them rested mostly in silence for a while. When they finally set off again Amethyst asked Ileana if she could tell how far away their enemies were. "Or in which direction," she added as an afterthought.

"They're trying to track us on the surface," the girl said, slowing to a halt briefly. She stared up at the ceiling, and then behind them as far as the lantern light extended. "I think they must be falling behind, or maybe going the wrong way. Maybe the snow has become too deep for them to walk through." She sounded hopeful rather than confident.

"Have you ever seen them before?" Amethyst asked. "Before we met, I mean?"

Ileana shook her head. "No. But I know what they are. I dreamed about them. I knew one day they would come." She glanced at Amethyst and smiled. "Perhaps I was as mad as everyone else in the town. Everyone else dreamed about new Gods and a shining light. All I dreamed about was black shapes and men made from inside the earth, until I had the dreams about someone coming to take me away."

Men made from inside the earth? Amethyst did not even want to contemplate what that might mean. For a moment she thought back to Craddan's plainsfolk, who had butchered so many of the castle people as they journeyed east with her as their leader's prisoner. *They dreamed of black things,* she thought. *Were those same creatures present in Ileana's dreams?*

The tunnel through which Vornen now led them twisted and turned through the dark mountain rock. Sometimes it almost doubled back on itself, and on occasion it headed upwards before winding and turning in a downward direction. "Still south?" Amethyst asked tiredly at one point, to which Vornen replied without looking back, "More or less."

Again the temperature changed with disconcerting suddenness. In a few places, the luminescent moss grew so thickly and brightly that the light it gave out outshone the glow of their lanterns.

During a later stop in a small cavern whose walls grew thick with this curious growth, Vornen suddenly said to Amethyst, "I sometimes wonder what it would have been like, if I could have followed a different path."

"A different path from which point?" she asked. "There are so many."

"Ah, well there's the question," he said with a faint smile. "What if I'd chosen not to return to Ruan-Tor? What if I'd never seen you out in the snow in Ethanalin Tur-morn?"

"Then I'd still be lying there now, frozen along with all the others." Amethyst shrugged. "Life is full of *what if,* and *if only.* I was always taught that the turnings we never choose to take don't matter. The only road we need to worry about is the one we're on. I know that from bitter experience."

"That's certainly true for us." Vornen's smile faded. "As I said, if we reach the lower Crescents, I will need to head directly south still, as far as Nisstar. That's where the Gates will appear. And the two of you should make all haste to Alinnora's Haven." He glanced at Amethyst. "That's if you are still intent on it."

"Intent? I *intend* to look the witch in the eye, and look inside myself to see how I feel at that moment," Amethyst said quietly. "I've long been wondering what might happen when I complete this task. Will I still feel the same need for revenge? Will she know that?" A dark thought occurred to her. "Will some new entrapment await me?"

"She only wants me, you said- so you'll be free once you hand me over," Ileana pointed out, and then added without sounding at all convinced, "I hope."

"And you will be anything but free," Amethyst said, but Ileana shook her head dismissively. "Can it be any worse?"

Neither Amethyst nor Vornen commented on that.

"You said yourself that without the sword, the Gates cannot be closed," Amethyst said to Vornen after a moment. "Can you truly not escape them, even if you try?"

"I'm drawn towards them. That's the way it has been for many years." Vornen smiled grimly, the expression accentuating the scars and wrinkles on his face. *He looks like a battlefield,* she thought, *and in some ways that's what he is.*

I thought my luck could not be worse, when the witch forced me on towards her prey- but to be Vornen...

"I can't choose my path," he said quietly. "You already know what that's like."

Amethyst said nothing, but wondered how she might convince him otherwise, without knowing exactly why she was doing so. Perhaps, she considered later, it was just because she detested the idea of a life being wasted in a hopeless cause. But she knew the true reason was more complex and selfish than that. The fact was, she liked the man more than she had originally thought she would, and even enjoy his company. In an existence which had become almost entirely bereft of enjoyment, she did not want to let him go.

And, she thought with a wintry smile, *if I can persuade him from his path, Suli may have done me a favour in a strange way. Ever since he lost that black sword, it's as if the weight of a curse has been lifted from his shoulders. Yes, he's still drawn to the Gates, but if he had the sword still then I'm sure it would have killed him by now. Perhaps it would have made him turn on Ileana and myself before destroying him.*

Silently she gave thanks to Vornen's mad lover from a former life, though not without a pang of guilt.

VII

Ileana stopped so suddenly that Amethyst, who walked behind, collided with her. Amethyst apologised, but in response Ileana merely pointed ahead and behind, and then, inexplicably, at the rough-hewn ceiling above their heads.

"I can sense their movement," Ileana said.

"Those... dead things?" Amethyst asked her.

"Not just them. Others. I can feel them too." Ileana shuddered. "Not all of them seek to harm us. Maybe they're not strong enough. But some..."

"What are they, Ileana?" Vornen demanded. "What form do they take?"

"I don't know," the girl said wearily. "But they're close."

Amethyst glanced at Ileana's wan, drawn features. By the lantern light she appeared thinner, more haggard than ever. She would not be strong enough to destroy these creatures a second time if they attacked, Amethyst feared. In truth, the girl looked barely able to walk.

"These other ones," Amethyst said finally. "Perhaps they will leave us be?"

Vornen laughed bitterly at that. Amethyst threw him a furious glare and repeated the question. Ileana shrugged miserably.

"Those creatures, and everything else Ileana can sense that we cannot, is the work of the Old Dark, the *choragh*, and the *kin* creatures that worship and obey them," Vornen said. "Only they could do this."

"The *choragh*?" For a moment Amethyst did not know what he meant, so tired was she. "Oh. Yes, I've heard the name. Some call them the blood lords, amongst other things."

Vornen nodded. "A myth, or thought of as such. In the south that name ceased to linger many centuries ago, as did all the others like it. I doubt you would find them mentioned outside fantastical stories handed down over generations. They've been given many titles. Earth Lords, Blood Lords, or the Old Dark. Some even once called them the Heart and Pulse."

Amethyst stared at him.

"The heart and the pulse of the world," Vornen said quietly, "as if they are a part of it."

Amethyst had no idea what to say to that, but Ileana did. "Those names have been in my dreams. Many times."

Three sharp turns of the tunnel later, they reached a vast pit, around which the pathway was hewn into the rocky cliff in both directions, the tunnel passage continuing on the other side of the pit directly ahead of them. At this point, the ceiling could no longer be seen at all, and neither, as the companions discovered, could the floor of the pit.

Yet they could *hear* the contents of this chasm. They could hear enough to neither need nor wish to see. The noises that came forth sounded unlike anything they had ever heard. There came a deep, sinuous slithering as if something worked its forceful way through flesh and bone- a cracking of stone and metal, some force rendering apart those materials by sheer force- but most sickening of all, the sound of damp, mouldering bones being rendered to dust, crushed under the weight of something vast and relentless.

"The *kin,* you called them," Ileana said after a while. "They have other names, the things down there. Some are named *thlaan,* others are the *peremar.*"

"From your dreams?" Amethyst whispered.

Ileana backed away from the edge of the pit, her eyes now drawn to the deepest shadows around them. "I've woken up screaming," she said, "because I thought they were upon me, burrowing inside, making their way to my heart. But now I'm so close to them, I know that it wasn't just a dream. Somehow I *know* about them. I *know* that the *peremar* are the heart-watchers, the ones that work their way into people... they..." She shook her head as if trying to clear some interference with her thoughts. "They... search for the secrets, unlock your worst fears. That's what they were made for." She looked down for a moment and and then turned her pale face to Amethyst again. "We should go."

The companions walked on more swiftly, Amethyst taking Ileana's hand. The girl whispered things over and over. None of them made any sense and much of what she said was almost inaudible.

They swiftly made their way along the tunnel beyond the seemingly bottomless pit. Here the ground became slippery underfoot again and the slope precarious in places.

Ileana glanced one way and the other many times, as if *choragh kin* might suddenly melt through the rock face.

Then Amethyst stopped suddenly. "I can hear whispers," she said, and Ileana turned to look at her. "It's *them*," she said quietly. "What do they say?"

Amethyst shook her head. "I would have asked you the same thing. They say nothing I can understand. Sounds without words." An unpleasant thought occurred to her. "Is it some kind of sorcery? What if..." Her voice trailed away; she swallowed hard, trying to contain her fear. Ileana said nothing; her hand stole into Amethyst's and squeezed it tentatively.

"It's their speech," Ileana said after a while. "They're *talking*. They tell me to join with them. They say that we're the same." She shook her head, puzzled by something. "We stole a flame, a handful of earth, a cup of water, a breath of air. If we give back none of those things..."

Abruptly she stopped. Vornen glanced back and exchanged glances with Amethyst before walking on. She could not exactly read his expression, but fancied that it could easily have said: *Which one of us will succumb first?*

They walked for a long time before Vornen wearily called a halt again. Their path had led them downward a little, but whether or not they were headed south, Amethyst had no idea. *We can only trust to his sense,* she thought, too exhausted to speak as she sat down in the rocky cave and winced at the pain in her knees.

Vornen sat in silence, head in hands. She wondered if he was simply exhausted, or if he felt the pull of the Gates more acutely once again. After a while, she moved to sit next to him.

"They draw me closer," he whispered, just as she was about to speak. "There will be three. Even here, deep under the surface, I can feel them." He paused, and raised his head, glancing at her. "*Especially* under the surface. How could that be?"

Amethyst stared helplessly at him. "I don't know, Vornen. I know nothing of these things."

"One way or another, I will go to them," he said, "unless I can be stronger now than I've ever been." He laughed unpleasantly. "That I should hope for such strength now, when I've never been able to summon it before!"

"I don't know about Gates," Amethyst admitted, "but remember, I know what it's like to be forced along a path, to suffer if I even thought of straying from it. I wish we could find a way to remove this burden, Vornen."

He gazed sadly at her. "So do I. I've wished for it my entire adult life. But it can't happen. It's not a curse placed upon me because I happened to be in the wrong place at the wrong time. It's a part of me, and will always be."

They lapsed into silence; there was nothing more to be said.

VIII

For days afterwards, life became a continuous blur of walk and sleep and occasionally stopping briefly to eat and drink a little. Now and again they came across underground streams, the water of which proved bitingly cold but refreshing. The companions filled their water canteens wherever and whenever they had the chance. *After all,* Amethyst thought more than once, *we still don't know when or even if we'll emerge from the mountains.*

Of their enemies, Ileana could sense no trace. Perhaps they had taken another direction, or had decided to hunt other prey. Amethyst wondered on more than one occasion if Suli's theft of the sword had anything to do with it.

The only sounds in this lonely underworld were the ones made by the companions, or the trickle of streams through the rock now and again. They encountered no creatures other than insects that fled the sudden invasion of light and sound into their environment. Conversation lapsed entirely, for the three of them had nothing more to say and they all hoped fervently for the same thing- that they would soon emerge from out of the dark.

It had been so long since anyone had spoken that both Amethyst and Ileana were startled when Vornen suddenly said: "Do you see it?" He placed his lantern in a crevice in the wall and pointed ahead.

Amethyst saw it, but hardly dared to believe her eyes. "Daylight," she murmured. "Can it be?"

As they walked on, the faint pinprick of light grew steadily nearer and brighter. Soon they could see that they headed towards an exit from the underground tunnels.

Shielding their eyes, the companions reached the cave mouth and stumbled out onto the hillside.

Open moorland lay ahead and gradually descended into the Hastian midlands. The bright sunlight and clear sky allowed them to see far into the distance. A thin layer of snow covered the land for about a league ahead of them but thereafter it thinned out to reveal the wintry and brown foliage of cold late autumn.

Despite the chill breeze, Amethyst decided she had never seen such a welcome sight in her life, nor enjoyed blasts of cold fresh air so much. Sighing, she sank to her knees. It was all she could do not to start sobbing, but instead she laughed out loud. Ileana smiled, her eyes wet with tears, and sat down on a nearby boulder.

For a moment, caught up in the sheer joy of having made her way through the mountain tunnels relatively unscathed, Amethyst forgot about everything else and simply revelled in the instant. Only when she glanced at Vornen did her buoyant mood fade. He stood, staring directly south, an expression upon his face that truly chilled her.

It was the look of a man who was utterly lost, had no path to call his own, only that which he had been forced along for so many years.

Amethyst wondered what that would have been like for her, to never be free of the witch-woman's curse, to be compelled one way or the other throughout her useful years until eventually either her mind or body gave up and she fell for a final time, still upon the path but destined never to reach its end.

She shuddered and looked away, but the sight of the open land before them no longer gladdened her heart.

"He'll leave us soon," Ileana said softly at her side. Amethyst almost jumped. She had not even heard the girl approach and sit down next to her.

"He's compelled," Ileana added, as if Amethyst didn't already know. "The Gates will take him."

Amethyst said nothing. They waited until eventually Vornen stirred, as if from out of a dream, and walked over to them. He said nothing, but began walking along a rough, rock-strewn path that wound down the hillside, and after a moment Amethyst and Ileana followed.

Mid-morning became noon, which drifted into afternoon. The companions reached the moorland, and followed a path that widened out into a grassy track as the late sun hung ever lower in the sky. Amethyst noticed that Vornen had gradually quickened his pace, and called to him to stop. He staggered, half-turned and fell to his knees. Then he opened his mouth as if about to say something, but instead of doing that he turned his head to the southern sky again.

"You'll need to head west soon enough," he said after a while. "Alinnora's Haven lies in that direction."

So the time draws near, Amethyst thought, and a curious panic rose within her. *The moment I've dreaded for days.*

But that time had not yet arrived. Inexplicably, when they next reached a fork in the trail, Vornen took the path that headed west. Amethyst and Ileana exchanged glances but said nothing as they followed behind.

He fell a while later, sinking to his knees at the edge of the path, head and arms almost buried in the long grass and heather. The breeze moved his clothing and his hair, but otherwise he might have been made of stone.

Vornen lurched to his feet suddenly, and managed perhaps another dozen steps before he doubled over in agony and suddenly turned, kneeling in the dirt, as if some powerful assailant had pulled his arm from behind and then thrown him to the ground.

His head turned south. With an effort he turned to glance at Amethyst, who sat down next to him. A low moan escaped his lips.

"We talked about this," she said softly. "I know what it's like to try and deny the curse. Don't torture yourself, Vornen. Go where you need to go."

Amethyst moved to sit so he could look her in the eyes and still face towards the invisible, irresistible force that enslaved him. In that moment she felt an almost overwhelming feeling of sadness through which anger and frustration rose. *It's unbreakable,* she thought. *It's an unbreakable force that will lure him again and again until finally his mind and body snap apart, and all for what? Why do such things exist in the world? What cruelty could have created them?*

If only I could break this curse with a snap of the fingers, pull him to his feet and keep him with me.

Oh Gods, listen to you, she thought angrily, averting her eyes. *You wish you were some sorcerer with power over the ways of the world. But there can be no sorcerer who ever lived, who could do such a thing. And still you allow yourself these fancy thoughts.*

Let him go, you stupid woman. Don't mourn him when you turn the other way and then look back to see the speck in the distance disappear forever.

"I won't be responsible for your ruin," Amethyst said, and got to her feet. She looked pointedly in the opposite direction. "Go."

He looked to her and then to Ileana as he stood. "Good luck to you both," he said quietly.

"And to you," Amethyst said, before she realised the idiocy of her words. He smiled, and she watched as the expression faded to become something close to desperation. On an impulse she hugged him fiercely, until he gently freed himself, and stood with his hand clasped in hers.

"*Go,*" she said again, swallowing and turning away. Ushering Ileana, Amethyst strode on along the trail, half hoping that he would heed her words and half hoping he would stay.

They had rounded a corner and headed past a perimeter of woodland before she dared to stop and look behind them. Vornen was nowhere to be seen.

For a moment, Amethyst stood where she was and wondered what would become of their companion. Would the Gate or Gates consume him this time? Or would they simply steal another part of him?

A mad notion came to her; she could run after him, and convince him to stay with them instead. Was that possible? Would the bond that held him fast eventually snap? Or might her selfish actions simply kill him or worse still render him a babbling lunatic beforehand?

Ileana gazed solemnly at her and said nothing. The breeze sighed regretfully in the trees nearby. *Well, it's done with,* Amethyst thought eventually. *It's done with, and he's gone. He's taken the only path he could. But you're still alive, Amethyst- and compared with Vornen you have had a bounty of luck.*

It's done, she reminded herself, and turned away.

III - Dreams and Ambitions

I

Yui woke suddenly, sat bolt upright, and screamed as if she was being burned alive.

From the corner of the bedchamber her father stumbled across in the dark and rushed to comfort the child. As he gathered her up in his arms, she grabbed frantically at him, eyes wide open and fixed on the gloom, hands shaking, nails digging into his hands as if to let go now would be to fall back into the nightmare and never again wake up.

Phyqor did not even feel the pain. He occupied a wretched place where pain itself was constant, an insurmountable wall that enclosed the two of them from the rest of the world. In the twelve grim days since they had fled the prison, never staying anywhere for longer than a night at a time for fear of discovery, Yui's fitful, restless dreams had become drastically worse. A few times, other guests at taverns or guest houses where they had stayed had made complaints about the noise. Not wishing to draw further attention, Phyqor had humbly apologised whenever necessary, even to the point of pressing coins into palms if he had to, and the two of them would leave as soon as possible afterwards, sometimes even in the middle of the night.

He remained fearful that the Council troops who had liberated Darkenhelm still hunted them, although he could think of no reason why they might, except for the petty thefts they had committed whenever necessary. During the daytime, when she was awake and behaved more or less like any normal child, Yui exhibited skills in this area far beyond her nine years, and so far their theft of food had gone entirely unnoticed- by its vendors at least.

71

Still, as they hurried from place to place under the cover of darkness, Phyqor would often cast anxious glances around and behind them, watching for movement amongst the shadows, listening for footfall, trusting only his instincts. Without knowing why or how, he felt certain that no one associated with the former ruling Family would wish to be found by any agents of the Council, and that certainly included the former chief architect of the palace.

This time, instead of screaming endlessly into the dark, Yui turned suddenly to face him. In the gloom of the bedchamber, her eyes looked like hollow pits, her cheeks sunken as if she had sucked them in. *Gods, this is my daughter, and I feel as if I'm staring at a skull,* he thought. He could barely look into her eyes, and the fact shamed him more than anything else. He listened briefly to find out if the disturbance had stirred irate fellow guests from their sleep. Thankfully no shouts of indignation or pounding of the walls could be heard. Perhaps the adjoining rooms were empty. Phyqor was not a religious man, but still he whispered a short, half-forgotten prayer to the old Gods of his childhood. Neither he nor Yui had slept properly for many days, and to be cast out now might make an end of them.

"There's a valley surrounded on all sides by high mountains," Yui said calmly, and Phyqor felt as if his insides had suddenly fallen in on themselves, for her voice had changed, had become deeper, as if a grown woman was speaking through his daughter's mouth.

Oblivious to his shock, Yui continued monotonously, "In the centre of the valley is a small stone bridge that a river once flowed under. The river has gone now. Even the water has fled this place. The riverbed lies dry and dusty. The bridge is darker than it should be, black like a deep hole. When light touches it, it becomes darker still. On top of the bridge..." She stopped suddenly, and then gasped. Her eyes widened as if in shock or pain.

"What is it?" Phyqor whispered, holding her hand gently. "What do you see, Yui?"

"*Black.*" The child's voice trembled. Her head turned swiftly one way then the other, as if she searched for something in the gloom. "Blackness comes out of the stones... it's a river again, and it's a doorway, but it *moves...*" Abruptly she stopped and fell back limply onto the bed. Her eyes closed, but Phyqor had no idea if she was asleep or not. In all likelihood she occupied some grim place in between dreaming and waking.

He could not sleep now. The vision that Yui had conjured simply by speaking into the darkness had seen to that, and every time he closed his eyes he could see it. *A real place, real beyond doubt,* he thought numbly. *A place that she could never have been to, and yet she sees whatever happens there.*

He stared as she slept fitfully, lips occasionally moving as if in silent recital of something. *I wish I could help you. I would do anything to give you peace. I'd take your visions and suffer them all forever, if only you could be rid of them.*

With helpless tears in his eyes, he sat and watched his daughter's every twist and turn, every faint gasp of pain as the night wore on, until eventually the first light of morning fell upon her tortured body.

II

Nia had always suspected that the *liberators* of Darkenhelm- how that word made her smirk- would feel somewhat less well-disposed to her after the overthrow of the militia that had held the citadel with an iron grip. Xeth Korriston, leader of Aphenhast's Council of Priests and presumably supreme leader of the entire land now, would have set in motion a way to have her quietly removed. After all, she was one of the few people in the land who knew that the coup of

73

Darkenhelm had been nothing but a manoeuvre to dispose of the ruling Family. She and Xeth were the *only* people who knew that inside that trickery, more trickery dwelt. She had assassinated Darkenhelm's temporary ruler Kown Malakray by carrying an object of sorcery into his office and handing it to the man himself, although even she had been taken aback by the further effects it had had. Every guardsman, soldier and man-at-arms within the palace had also fallen dead to the ground.

Nia had been surprised and more than a little perturbed at the ease with which she was able to carry out the task, but the power of the spellcraft that had been unleashed unnerved her even more.

Amidst the inevitable panic a small contingent of Council troops from Emberton, the stronghold of the priesthood, had appeared- how convenient! They had encountered little resistance at the city gates, and had made the victory look entirely their own within hours. Oh, there had been a little fighting here and there, but Nia suspected that those skirmishes had been staged. She might well be the only one who knew every layer of the story, but no doubt there were others who knew just enough to play their part in this grand charade.

That evening, a note had been handed to the bartender at the inn where she had been staying, just as the confusion and chaos around the city was beginning to turn to jubilation and the Darkenhelm folk realised that their oppressors were gone. One set of oppressors at least.

The note had politely requested her presence at a meeting with a man whose name she recognised as being that of Xeth Korriston's envoy, the following morning. The purpose of the meeting was apparently to receive the remaining payment owed to her. Nia failed to attend that meeting, and it was then that things became interesting.

Three men, or creatures that bore the shapes of men, came for her that evening at dusk. They arrived from three different directions and met outside the tavern. Those folk who were still about their business nearby melted away in a hurry. The people of Darkenhelm were well used to sensing trouble when it appeared, and they had had more than enough of it during the turbulent months of upheaval and military rule. Nia had felt a peculiar taint- like bitterness and metal- as she watched from a distance, even felt the peculiar speed at which these *things* were moving. It was not a kind of sorcery she remotely recognised, but she had no time to ponder its origins, concerned only with survival. Jumping over rooftops and across alleyways, she had somehow evaded them for the time being, but knew that she had only delayed the inevitable. If she remained here, they would find her eventually. She could not keep moving around the city.

Nia decided to leave Darkenhelm immediately, and head west into her homeland of Harn, where even Korriston's sorcerous minions would fear to tread.

Would they?

Sitting on a sack of grain in the storehouse where she had spent that night, Nia frowned, unsettled by her memory of the three creatures that had come for her. It occurred to her that they had not been Korriston's men- or *beings-* at all, but that notion, although it was what her heart somehow told her, made no sense. *Even I don't have that many enemies, do I?* she asked herself, but chose not to dwell on the possible answers. She forced the thought aside, to chew over when or if she had more time. Of course, if *another* merry band of assassins should seek her out, then that would be another worry entirely.

Nia shook her head. Soon none of this would matter. She would be on her way back to Harn later today, if she could *shift*. That would depend on how much rest she had had, but last night had been peaceful enough aside from the scurrying of a few rats amongst the sacks and lone drunkards passing by outside in the dim and misty late hours, stumbling against the walls and occasionally even apologising to them.

She rose from her makeshift bed of sack cloths and walked cautiously to the wooden door, which she had blocked with several heavy sacks of grain before she settled down to sleep. Nia heaved them aside and opened the doorway just a crack. Bright sunlight poured in, and she shielded her eyes for a moment in order to look around. The hour was still early and the sun lingered low over the rooftops. No one walked or loitered nearby.

Nia judged herself to be strong enough for the *shifting*. Besides, she reasoned, as she closed the door quietly, turned away and removed her clothing, she could not leave Darkenhelm until she could make it happen. She could not risk going anywhere near the city gates.

She stood still, closed her eyes and bowed her head slightly. After a moment, the first ripples began to course through her, a prelude to a physical change that would have utterly confounded anyone watching.

Facially, the change was subtle; she might have been slowly turning into her own twin brother. At the same time, her musculature altered, though not drastically. The young man into whom she appeared to turn had a slight build and was around the same height. As ever, the most disconcerting aspect of the transformation was the gradual disappearance of those parts of her that made her female. The flattening out of her chest and the appearance of male parts between her legs were two things that Nia could never become used to and comfortable with. These changes caused a flutter of panic in her even after all these years.

"It's only for a short while," she murmured as she finally raised her head and let out a long-drawn sigh, the transformation complete.

A short while later, the doors to the storehouse opened, and someone who appeared to be a dark-haired young man stepped out onto the side-street. Nia looked around, liked what she saw- which was nothing happening- and with a secretive smile she made her way up to the northern end of the street.

Nia had made her way as far as the Great West Road, which led directly to the western gates of Darkenhelm, when she saw something that made her stop, made her almost forget her hurry to leave the citadel.

What was odder still was that the girl stopped and turned to look at her at exactly the same time. Nia saw recognition leap immediately in her eyes. *Of course,* Nia reminded herself. *She saw through me, even though I was not shifting. She saw the female, then the male, then the female again, just like that. I could tell by the way she looked at me. How?*

In that moment she suddenly reflected on what it was that had made her stop back in the prison. *Not only did I stop but I even gave them the keys to help them out,* came a whisper from the back of her mind. *Why did I do that? What sense was there in it? Why would I even want to let them go? Pity? Perhaps- if I was feeling charitable. But still it makes no sense.*

No sense at all on the face of it, but Nia was essentially a creature of instinct and intuition and knew better than to dismiss that curious meeting from her mind. This was the same girl. There could be no doubt about it. And the look the child had given her- almost of understanding, but without knowing- fascinated Nia so much so that she almost forgot her surroundings for a moment.

Nia raised an eyebrow in surprise as the child began to make her way over, picking her way carefully around passers-by and the odd cart and wagon that rolled along the Great West Road. Her companion followed close behind. Nia remembered him from the prison cell. He seemed to have recovered from his beatings fairly well, all things considered. Who was he? Nia thought quickly. Her father. Of course. She could tell by the way he watched her every movement; concerned, pained. And why else would he have stayed with her once free, if he was simply some common criminal? Was he aware of the child's... *vision?* Nia reckoned that he knew perhaps half of it. Well, that wasn't important at the moment. What *was* interesting was that the girl had not only recognised her, but looked intent on speaking to her. *Why?* Nia had no idea.

The girl stopped a few yards away and looked up at her, wide-eyed. "I saw you in the prison," she said. "Do you remember?"

Nia paused only long enough to ensure no one else was within earshot, except of course the girl's father, who was clearly perplexed. "That's right," she said quietly. Changing the subject, she added with a smile, "And what's your name?"

"Yui," she whispered. "This is my father, Phyqor."

Nia glanced briefly at Phyqor, who stared warily back at her. "All the guards were dead," he said quietly. "Did you..." He said no more, perhaps remembering just in time that they were in a bustling main road.

Nia gave him a vague smile, and then decided to allow her intuition free rein. The words that spilled from her mouth surprised even her. "Your daughter needs guidance, Phyqor. She has a remarkable gift. I can see you're already aware of that. She sees things that other people cannot, yes?"

I should not have said that, Nia thought wildly as Phyqor took a step closer, astonishment on his face. *I should have turned and ran as soon as I saw them, all the way to the western gates of the city.*

A feverish, intensely hopeful look had entered the man's eyes, and Nia was taken aback. What had he read into her words? Clearly she had stumbled upon something greater than she had at first thought, judging by the man's response. She willed herself to play this carefully. He posed no immediate threat, but desperate people were quite liable to *become* threats. Finding a way to help his daughter, she suddenly realised, consumed his life at the moment. But why?

Sweat sparkled on his forehead as he stood before her, despite the cool breeze that angled across the street. "Can you help?" he whispered. "*Please*, can you help her?"

"Yes." As soon as she had uttered that word, Nia knew that something important had just happened. Her life had changed and there could be no going back. She had taken a step forward only to find that the step had been through a doorway, and the door had slammed shut behind her to disappear forever. "I can," she added, keeping her face carefully neutral, although her heart hammered. *Powers, what are you doing?!* a voice shrieked within her mind. *Turn away now, tell them you made a mistake, say anything. Leave!*

Nia looked around and tried to ignore her panicked thoughts. She thanked the Powers that no one had heard their conversation. "We need to talk, but not here. We'll go to that tavern over the square. It'll be quiet enough at this time." She pointed to a large alehouse which had just opened. A large sign high up on the wall creaked in the breeze, proclaiming that this establishment was called the *Hope for the Weary. How appropriate,* Nia thought, but the notion failed to amuse her.

Phyqor looked torn between feverish hope and natural suspicion. Yui's mind was on something else entirely, as she confirmed with her next words to Nia: "Are you running from someone?"

Nia was only mildly surprised at the girl's insight. She shrugged and gave her a quick smile. "Perhaps. And you?"

Yui remained fixated on her own train of thought. "I thought so. But they won't find you."

"I certainly hope not!" Nia's words had a lightness to them that she did not feel.

Yui stared up at her for a moment longer, squinting in the sunlight. "What's your name?"

"Narin," she said. It was the first male name that came to mind, and it was also the name she had occasionally assigned to her male form. "What do you remember from the prison?" she asked her quietly, seeing that Phyqor had been momentarily distracted by some altercation across the street. "What do you remember about me?"

Yui frowned. "Nothing. Only that I saw you before. You were the man I saw in the prison."

Interesting, Nia thought. *She doesn't seem to remember her own insight about me, though I'm still certain she could see through me at the time. And she seems to remember only my male form, not my true form. But I'd better make sure.*

The three of them made their way into the tavern, where a few traders and merchants had begun to file in for early luncheon. Darkenhelm had already become a hub of commerce once again. Nia saw a large number of South Ocean Islanders amongst the crowds out in the market area. Evidently the change of government within the city had enticed them from their ships out in the bay, to engage in trade once again.

The *Hope for the Weary* remained deserted towards the rear. The remnants of a fire gleamed sullenly in the hearth and failed to alleviate the cold. Nia bought a flagon of watered wine for them all- she had plenty of crowns left after relieving some of Malakray's men from what had turned out to be their final wages. As ever, she avoided the pump water, knowing that the water used for mixing to create the *daywine* as Hastians called it had at least been boiled and cooled before use.

They sat down in the dim rear of the tavern, and Nia glanced again at Yui, curious as to how and where such a gift could have come from. Her father's reaction to her first words on the matter intrigued her even more. *There's much to this that I don't yet know about,* she decided. *Now, perhaps, I'll find out how much.*

"Yui, tell this man about your dreams that you have," Phyqor whispered, and the child turned wide-eyed to look at him, evidently startled. "I don't want to!" she whimpered, and Phyqor hugged her gently. "Narin can help us," he said quietly, and glanced again at Nia for confirmation. "You *can,* can't you?"

"Of course." Nia gave Yui a smile of encouragement as the child's gaze turned to her, and poured some of the daywine into one of the cups. "Have a little of this, Yui. You'll feel better. You'll feel brave enough to talk."

Yui drank the beverage, grimacing at the taste, and finished it off before she set the cup down and coughed. *There,* Nia thought. *That may loosen your tongue a little.*

Pure intuition had led Nia this far. But the words she was about to hear would change her life utterly. In times to come, she would occasionally dwell on what might have happened had she ignored her inner self, had she turned resolutely away from this tangle of a nightmare and made tracks swiftly out of Darkenhelm. Days would pass when she wished bitterly that she had done exactly that.

But instead she sat in silence and let Yui's whispered, almost feverish words- a breathless and semi-coherent jumble- wash over and into her. They did not explain her ability to see both her female and male forms. In fact they had nothing whatsoever to do with Nia.

I see the black things forming. Sometimes they come out of the ground and sometimes they come from nowhere at all, suddenly in the air, not black like night but much worse. There are stars everywhere and I can hear a language made out of numbers. The blackness is like a hole, as if the world has a rip in it. It pulls things in. Even people.

Yui's shaky, uncertain monologue did nothing to prevent images of what she saw seep into Nia's mind. The longer she spoke, the sharper those images became. *She* could see the black shapes now, but also others made entirely of light. The sounds of some long-forgotten language from the other side of the Existence assailed her- cold, harsh whispers. *Numbers,* she thought. *Numbers and directions. Paths.*

Great yawning spaces opened up from out of the air or the ground, or both at the same time. Some contained vast, impossible sights, stars near and far that moved or even *changed,* and other, darker worlds that lurked in the void. She gazed down into deep, pungent chasms where thick, languid lakes of some indeterminate substance lapped against frozen shores. *Things* that she could not even hope to describe lurked in that darkness, tangible only by their faint, blood-tinged luminescence and the multitude of forms they took, as they moved in and out of the slow lakes, the icy ground, the great monolithic slabs of rock.

Down and up. She heard Yui's words as if from a great distance, yet still inside her head. *Everything is feeding on everything else. They get stronger.*

"Stop," Nia murmured finally, just as it seemed her *sight* of what Yui spoke of might become sharp enough, substantive enough to pull her in, real or not.

Yui needed no further encouragement. She stopped immediately and uttered the sort of sigh a bowed and defeated woman might utter at the end of her days. It was not the sound any normal child could make. Nia felt a shudder run up her spine as the visions began to fade.

The collisions of unbearable light and monstrous darkness finally fled. The stars winked out. The chasm where the creatures gathered and writhed, abruptly vanished. The rippling of unknown forces over Nia's body ceased. The horror faded, but for just a moment she thought that some semblance remained within the embers in the hearth, and her heart skipped a beat as she turned sharply to stare at the fire.

"Now you see," Phyqor said.

Powers, I do see, Nia thought, her head spinning. *I only wanted to know how this child could see my true form and shifted form together, without her father knowing, but now... now I know something I would do anything to forget.*

No one spoke for a long while. Phyqor seized his tankard and drank its entire contents in one trembling effort, white-knuckled and eyes shut. Yui sat with head bowed. Her hands shook so much that her fingernails rattled on the table. Nia remained lost for words despite her desperation to break the numb silence. The things that Yui had uttered, the memory of the images she had evoked, whirled endlessly in her head. Some desperate importance attached itself to them. She spoke of... what? *Gates?* Nia had read about such things, years ago. But there was more. Black things coming out of the ground? That was something else entirely. Nia did not want to dwell on any of it.

One thing was for certain however, and Nia's senses almost screamed the truth of it. Whatever this girl had seen and sensed was of the utmost importance.

Nia sat back in her chair, her entire world turned upside-down, and regarded the child in shocked silence. *One way or another, you are coming back with me to Luudhoq,* she thought grimly. *And then we shall see what my masters make of you and your visions.*

III

"Luudhoq." Phyqor shook his head, frowning. "We have never set foot in Harn, Narin. Why would we need to travel all the way there for Yui to be helped?"

"I know the city well, and I know a physician and apothecary there who I'm certain can help her," Nia said patiently, leaning forward. She smiled as their eyes met and marvelled at how much composure she had regained during the afternoon. Perhaps the daywine had helped, weak though it was. Powers knew they had consumed enough of it

83

between them. "I do have other reasons, I'll admit. In all honesty"- she reduced her voice to a faint whisper- "...I'm Harnian, as I'm sure you guessed from my accent. I miss my home. I need to leave Darkenhelm, and so do you if you want me to help your daughter. You can't remain a fugitive forever- not in this city. Nothing is certain anymore. Ask yourself, is there anything left for you here?"

Phyqor shrugged tiredly and threw a quick and furtive glance towards the tavern entrance as if he expected a half-dozen soldiers to pour in waving his arrest warrant. "No- you're right, of course. Maybe they aren't even looking for us anymore. I expect all the people imprisoned by the militia mean nothing to them." He sounded like a man trying to convince himself. "When do we leave?"

"This evening." Nia rose and took a silver crown from her pocket. "Buy yourselves something to eat. I'll arrange passage for us on the next coach heading west, and be back as soon as that's done."

Nia was as good as her word. She returned late in the afternoon having bought three seats on a coach heading along the coastal route to the outlying border villages in Aphenhast's extreme south-west. *From there,* she thought, *we will be near Ranith Tyr, and I will rest easier. A little easier, anyway.*

She knew Ranith Tyr, Harn's coastal eastern border town, about as well as anyone who did not live there could. In recent months, she had spent considerable time in the settlement gathering information about the situation in Aphenhast at the behest of her employer, a Watcher who was keen to know as much as possible even about events outside of and unrelated to Harn. That, in fact, was how she had been lured into this country's muddy affairs, although if luck was on her side she would never again consider such a proposition. Ranith Tyr would be a good place to stay for a short while- sleepy and somewhat off the beaten track, it was nevertheless used to a certain number of travellers passing through, so hardly a forbidding place.

Later that afternoon, they boarded their carriage at one of the open squares near to the Great West Road. Nia showed the coachman their documents of purchase, but he barely looked at them, which suited her just fine. Such a man would make an ideal chaperone as they departed the city: one who had no interest in his environment and who was clearly wrapped up in the drudgery of his task, counting the hours until he could stop and drink.

As the coach rolled laboriously up the road, Yui leaned against Phyqor and presently fell asleep, her hand clutching his arm. Nia worried a little about this; what if the child suddenly woke up screaming and babbling, as Phyqor had described her often doing? Certainly it would cause consternation amongst the other three travellers they shared the carriage with- an elderly couple, and a man of middle age who had seen better days judging by the scars he wore. Worse, it might even mean their expulsion from the carriage. And if she started shouting out about what she *saw* in her dreams...

Nia shuddered. Some darkness resided in everything this girl said and did. A taint, a shadow existed inside her, and it had the potential to reach out and touch the waking world. And when *that* happened...

Well, she thought, *as long as we get through the western gates and put some distance between us and Darkenhelm, perhaps we'll be all right.*

Nia almost laughed out loud at that hopeful notion.

Yui stirred and mouthed some soundless words more than once even before they reached the inner gates, which itself was almost enough for Nia to shake the girl awake. Only the thought that she might then start screaming stayed her hand; that, and the considering look that Phyqor gave her from time to time as the coach laboured its way up the street. *Despite my promise he still doesn't trust me,* Nia reflected. *But then, why should he? I too would suspect my own charity.*

Luck remained with them for the moment. As they neared the final bend in the road and rolled to a gentle halt at the inner gates, Yui stopped her restlessness entirely. By the time the sentry- a young man resplendent in the dark grey and blue of the Council- had opened the door of their carriage and checked everyone's documents of purchase before impatiently waving the coach onwards, the child was fast asleep and snoring gently, one arm linked around Phyqor's. *May that continue,* Nia thought fervently. *May that continue all the way to Harn!*

At the outer gates, another sentry opened the door of their carriage and gave each of them a cursory look, before consulting some papers with another, older man. Nia felt her heart skip a beat. She felt certain that her name was on the list of people they searched for, and equally certain that the older man was anything but a normal official of Darkenhelm, no matter how drab his clothing might be. Before the man's gaze rested upon her, she looked down at the ground, choosing her bored-and-tired expression and moving her foot idly on the dirty floor. He did not spend long looking at her. After all, Nia reminded herself, he was looking for a female. Presumably Yui and Phyqor were absent from the list of wanted people- this particular list anyway- for soon enough the door was slammed shut and the coach ushered onwards. Before long they were well outside the city and headed slowly west through open land along the Great West Road.

That night was as bright as Nia had seen for tennights. Ildar's full face hung over the ocean like a gleaming silver coin, and its reflected light shimmered on the waters. *I've seen a similar view from the south-facing windows of my own house many times,* Nia thought, and sentiments of home turned her thoughts once again towards the task in hand, and the possibility of reward for her efforts. Her employer Kelandra made a hard taskmistress, and as cold as any Watcher, but she was at least consistent and fair. Nia remained as certain as she could be that Yui's tormented visions were of Gates, but also other things- creatures from ancient myths that few people knew anything about. Even in Darkenhelm and in Ranith Tyr she had heard rumours of strange, horrific events in the far north of the land, and they sounded as if they had much to do with Yui's troubling visions. *They are related,* she asserted silently. *And Kelandra can find out more about them. Or Kelandra's masters can. Whoever acts on this revelation, it's a demonstration of my unswerving loyalty to Kelandra, to the Watchers, and to Luudhoq. Most importantly, it ultimately shows my continued allegiance to the Seven.*

And that, Nia considered, *should help ensure I continue my quiet life between tasks, unmolested by interrogation, devoid of suspicion.*

IV

They stopped for the night at a small village called Cliff Reach, a tiny place with just two dozen cottages and a small tavern where they managed to find a room- though it did mean the three of them had to share. As she prepared to sleep on the spare mattress that had been dragged into the room for her use, Nia glanced warily at Yui, who had fallen asleep within moments of lying down on the bed. Would she be quiet tonight, or would the entire tavern wake to the sound of her screams?

"So, are you from Luudhoq originally?" Phyqor asked her as he unlaced his boots.

"I am." Nia frowned, distracted as she saw Yui twitching in her sleep. "Do you think she might have one of her visions tonight?"

"She might." But Phyqor was more interested in Nia for some reason. "And do you have any family there?"

Nia gave him a cool look. "I have no family anywhere to my knowledge. I was raised in an orphanage in Luudhoq, if you can call that being raised at all. All I know is that I was found abandoned somewhere in the city as an infant." She sighed. "I'm a little tired for questions, Phyqor. Especially questions about family."

"Of course. Good night." He put out the lamp near the bedside, and presently he too had fallen asleep.

Nia found rest considerably more elusive that night. She hated her past, her childhood, and she hated being reminded of it, particularly when she wasn't expecting to be. *Yes, I've no family, I barely exist at all,* she thought sourly, glaring up at the wooden beams in the ceiling. *I'm nothing except a spy, an assassin, an assistant to a Watcher, something my own people fear. And I'm even proud of my work, so what does that make me in their eyes? Not that they are really my people. No, they have each other- and what have I ever had except myself? No one has ever wanted me- not even my own parents!*

As often happened when she was trapped in her male form, her anger suddenly flared almost out of control. A sudden desire to strike and kick something- Phyqor, perhaps, or the furniture- threatened to take over her reason entirely. With an effort she controlled herself, although her fists shook and tears of rage flooded her eyes.

The following morning, after breakfast, Nia thought about making her excuses and finding somewhere secluded where she might *shift,* if only for a short while. But the tavern privy was open in the back yard, and there was nowhere else available. And, she reminded herself, they were still in Aphenhast. Even though her chances of being apprehended if she returned to her natural self diminished with each league that they trundled westwards, still it remained quite possible that she could be recognised and reported if the wrong person happened to glimpse her. By now, Korriston would be well aware that she had slipped through his net, and those who answered to him would be scouring the land intent on capturing her; at least, those who had not already been punished for their inability to find her.

Leaning back in her chair, Nia watched the wheeling of seabirds outside in the morning air, and idly rubbed at her chin where stubble had begun to grow. She had never maintained her male form for this long before, and unless she *shifted* before they reached Harn, she would need to maintain it for another five days or more- in public at least.

I suppose I can relinquish this façade at nights, with doors bolted, she considered, then added as an afterthought, *As long as I have a room to myself.*

Nia warmed to the idea in quick time, partly because she feared that she might not be able to maintain her male form for much longer. *Not without killing someone anyway,* she thought darkly. And so, for the next five nights, she *shifted* back to her true self as soon as the three of them had retired to their chambers in whichever hamlet or coach-stop they had reached during the day. On the first of those nights, the relief she felt was overwhelming, and she wept quietly to herself in the darkness.

Phyqor was not done with questioning her. "Do you have a woman, in Luudhoq? Anyone special, I mean?" he asked casually one morning.

Nia gave him her most hostile stare. It would have been far worse for him than that, but the relief, the *calm* of fitting back into herself the previous night had improved her mood just enough even if she still had to hold the pretence of her male form during the day. "No," she said flatly. "I do not." *The sanity of womanhood,* she thought, turning away and trying to forget that he had even asked the question. *It's saved him a good beating, or worse.*

Before she drifted off to sleep each night Nia did her best to dwell on more positive thoughts- returning home, reporting her findings to Kelandra, and showing once again how adept she was at her job.

Adept? she wondered, on the fifth night, as they rested in a comfortable inn on the outskirts of the village of Westferry. *Perhaps, but lucky most of all. Unlucky in life but lucky in work. That's the way my coin fell.*

She lay naked on her bed and gazed up at the ceiling. On an impulse she reached over to where she had thrown her trousers, picked out her special coin, her *decision* coin, and tossed it up in the air dozens of times, catching it perfectly in between the fingers of her loosely closed fist each time until she grew bored of the game. *Ah, but I'm a smart girl,* she thought, leaning over to snuff out the lantern before settling down to sleep. *Alone, and plain, but so very smart.*

Her vague smile faded suddenly. *Perhaps I should have used my coin when I saw Yui and Phyqor in Darkenhelm. Star side- I go and talk to them. Earth side- I turn away and never see them again.*

The notion disquieted her considerably, no matter that the deed was done. Surely matters could not have turned out any better- for her, at least. She had been gifted an opportunity to impress, and hopefully make some good money for herself into the bargain.

So why, despite everything, do I feel this occasional dread? Nia wondered, but could find no answer.

Hours passed before eventually she slept.

Westferry was the final stop for the coach, and by this time the three of them were the only passengers remaining, the others having alighted at various stops along the way, so Nia had relaxed a little concerning the possibility of Yui's dreams and visions interrupting the journeys of others, and worse, being reported. In fact the girl had been relatively subdued- only on one of the last three nights had she had one of her nightmares. Nia, having experienced what even the simple retelling of such an episode could do, was thankful that she slept in a separate bedroom, although the desperate wails of the child still woke her up and sent a chill through her heart.

But the next morning, a worse problem than Yui presented itself.

V

Alexia would probably have remained upstairs- she had no appetite for breakfast- had she not recognised the voice of the man in the room next to hers. She then caught his name when it was spoken by the other, younger man who had been sleeping in the room across from his. Suddenly she remembered who it was.

Gods, it's him, she thought faintly. *It's Phyqor. I thought he had been assassinated along with almost everyone else who lived or worked in the Palace. But he's found his way out of Darkenhelm somehow. Maybe he was released from prison, and the Council authorities had no need to recapture or interrogate him.*

Alexia exhaled slowly and allowed herself a brief smile. *Some good news at last,* she thought. Phyqor, the unkempt architectural genius who her family had begrudgingly only kept in employment because of his astonishing building and design work, had been one of her few true friends. They had talked for hours at a time in the palace libraries; they had met on many occasions at the Guild and drank Kyransan *kafa* together.

If he's here, she thought, *then he must be trying to escape to Harn as well.*

She had managed to escape Darkenhelm shortly after fleeing Phain's shop, taking the view that it was either then or never. She had hoped fervently that with most of the Council troops working to restore order and ensure that the palace buildings were secure, they would not yet have secured the city gates. As it turned out, guardsmen were in position checking everyone heading out of Darkenhelm, but as she no longer looked remotely like her description which she supposed had been given out, they failed to give the

91

bedraggled, dirty and odorous girl before them more than a quick glance.

I wonder how many of them would have actually known what I look like in any case, she had thought afterwards, having begged a ride on a farmer's cart for a while. *How had they known to come to Phain's shop? Who could have informed them about me?*

Alexia turned to look at herself in the mirror. She had eaten last night and washed this morning, but her clothing was still the worse for wear and she looked thin and drawn. *I was never a dashing beauty,* she thought, *but still I idly imagined that Phyqor and I might one day be lovers. Given my position I could have had him if I wanted. But I never dared. And I think that hope would be dashed forever if I presented myself to him like this.*

Yet there was nothing to be done about her appearance, and curiosity held a powerful grip over her.

Alexia left her room and started to make her way down the stairs, treading carefully, then stopped, suddenly unsure, as she heard him talking down in the tap room. A few more steps further and she saw him through the open doorway, sitting near the back. With him were Yui and, presumably, the man with whom Phyqor had spoken earlier.

She stopped, uncertain. *Should I just leave them all in peace?*

Alexia reached the bottom of the stairs and lingered near the door. She peered into the tap room again. The air was heavy with the scents of breakfast, and her stomach growled impatiently. Through a side door she saw the innkeeper in the rear kitchen, making mugs of herbal tea with Kyransan honey, while a serving-girl cut chunks of ham hock onto a large wooden serving platter.

Alexia turned her attention back to Phyqor, Yui and their companion, who were looking at a map. The man seemed to be explaining a route to them, and Alexia heard Luudhoq mentioned more than once. *That's probably where they're headed,* she thought. *The capital city of Harn. A good place for them to lose themselves.*

The last time she had seen Phyqor had been in the main Palace Library a week or so before the bloodbath of the military rising. He had been planning the construction of a new antechamber for rare historical documents in the east wing, something that Alexia herself had asked him to do.

But he seemed wary, subdued, exhausted. The man regarded as the finest architect in Darkenhelm had changed. No doubt the events of the last few months had taken their toll on him as they had everyone else. He also had some cuts and bruises on his face. He had healed relatively well, but he had clearly taken a savage beating not so long ago.

Before she knew it, Alexia had wandered over, and as she did, Phyqor saw her from the corner of his eye and turned half around. She felt oddly pleased that despite her terrible appearance he still recognised her. "Alexia!" Even in his shock he had the good sense to keep his voice to little more than a whisper.

"I thought I heard your voice, Phyqor," Alexia said softly. "Last night, and again this morning. Then I heard your name. I knew then that it must have been you."

Phyqor recovered his composure quickly and offered her a seat at their table. "How did you..." His expression darkened. "I'm truly sorry about everything that's happened. I still can't quite believe it all."

Alexia sighed. "No, but I try not to think about it. I will build a life elsewhere somehow." She glanced at the young man sitting with them. "Are you going to introduce me?"

"Of course. You already know my daughter Yui, and Narin is... well, Narin is going to travel with us to Luudhoq and help us find a cure... for Yui's dreams." He smiled almost apologetically. "There's much to tell you, but I'll explain later- if you want to travel with us?"

"I will if you're all happy for me to," Alexia said. Yui merely gave a tired, shy smile; Narin looked flustered and perhaps even a little angry, and Alexia wondered why.

Then his expression changed, and Alexia's heart sank. She saw recognition in his eyes even before he spoke. "Are you who I think you are?" he asked quietly, but the triumphant half-smile on his lips showed that he already knew.

Before she could even think of an answer, Phyqor interrupted. "I suggest we *all* say nothing more than we need to until we're safely across the border. None of us wish to be arrested and find ourselves heading back to Darkenhelm in chains."

No one could disagree with that.

VI

No coaches or traders' carts were available to take them further that morning, so once everyone was ready, they set off on foot following the western track out of Westferry, with the sun still on their backs and a chill breeze blowing from the coast half a league away. Nia's mind raced as they walked, so much that she barely listened to Phyqor's and Alexia's exchange of stories, which began once they were a few hundred paces away from the village.

I don't need to hear their histories, Nia told herself. *I know who they are. I certainly know who* she *is, even if she has made herself look like the drunken apprentice of a hedgewitch.*

It occurred to her that she ought to work some advantage from the fact of Alexia's identity, but in Harn, Hastian folk of all creeds and classes were thought of as one of a kind unless they had any peculiar or useful talent. The Watchers and the Seven had never paid much attention to the political and familial wrangling in Aphenhast- not that much, anyway. *They might get some sort of ransom for her,*

94

Nia mused, *but more than likely they would have no interest whatsoever in the matter. Powers, the two countries don't even have envoys to each other!*

But she had to do something about Alexia. Her presence complicated matters. Clearly, she and Phyqor were friends, and worse still, judging by what Nia had seen and heard, Alexia knew Yui as well, which she should have expected. The child joined in readily with their chat as they walked along. *Yes, you're all so high-spirited this morning,* Nia thought sourly as she glared at their backs. *Perhaps we need Yui to recount her visions again.*

She thought over and over, and willed herself to be logical, not emotional. *How do I work this out? How do I rid myself of this hindrance?*

But the morning wore on and became afternoon, and still Nia had no answer.

They reached the vast, five-hundred-hand high Border Wall before sunset. This great structure stretched from the southern coast as far as the beginnings of the Huurin swamplands in the distant north of the world, a place that Nia had never been anywhere near and had not the slightest desire to visit. The wall was ancient, built back in the distant age when Harn was still one united land, just after the great war that had ended the Age of Blood and heralded the Enlightenment.

She had read that in places along its vast length of five hundred leagues or more, the wall had crumbled, but as far as she knew, those places were guarded even more heavily than the intact parts, at least in the south of the land where the Border Guards were employed. *And who better than the Border Guards,* she mused, *aside from Watchers themselves of course?* The Border Guards were one of the best trained and most respected military forces in Harn, well-motivated, well-paid and masters of more weapons than even Nia could name.

Besides, she thought as she gazed up at the imposing structure as grey-clad Border Guards gathered to stare down at them, *What need have I to enter the country without being observed and checked? I am a citizen of Harn and a servant of the Watchers. I can enter my own land and be welcome.*

Every time she came within a short distance of the Border Wall, she was reminded of the reasons why Harn had enjoyed peace- peace from its neighbouring land at least- for so long. The Wall was not only vast in height but a hundred hands thick, composed of huge blocks of grey and black yieldstone mined from the Wistledge. Yieldstone was so named because it could be cut and shaped with the right tools but was almost impossible to break by force; it absorbed shock as dried sea-sponges absorbed water. Certainly, any attempt to break through the Border Wall using siege machines would end in bitter disappointment and failure.

I always wondered who guards the Wall in the far North, Nia mused. *They have their own ways, little though we know of them. Presumably they also guard their territories in the east in some way.*

She walked ahead as far as the triple portcullis built into the base of the great wall. Between the first and second of these great iron gateways, chambers had been cut into the rock, and from them six Border Guards emerged. "I am a citizen of Luudhoq," she said, "and these three are my companions." She beckoned her companions forward.

"Show your hands, if you please," one of the men instructed her. She recognised him; he had passed her through from both Hastian and Harnian sides on several previous occasions. Nia willed herself to be patient. She was almost back home, and the thought filled her with a quiet relief.

She showed the palms of her hands, and the Border Guard handed her what appeared to be a small, star-shaped piece of metal. Nia knew the procedure perfectly well, and placed the star in the palm of her left hand. The Border Guards watched intently. None of them spoke.

As before, Nia felt the heat of the metal star, felt it *investigate* her- there was no closer word for it. When prompted, she moved it to her right palm. *Even if I am not who I appear to be, the star cannot lie,* she reminded herself. *It will tell them what they need to know in order to let me pass- that I am a servant of the Watchers. It will tell them nothing else, because I'm allowed to carry secrets on behalf of my masters.*

Finally, the Border Guard asked for the star to be returned, and they watched as faint patterns showed themselves in Nia's palms, moving faintly as if affected by her blood and her pulse. Yui, who was nearest to her, gasped and exclaimed, "What's that?! Is it magic?"

"Quiet, child," one of the other guardsmen growled, and they continued watching until eventually the patterns became still, and eventually faded.

The Border Guard who had handed her the star nodded, satisfied, and gestured for the first portcullis to be lifted. The companions were ushered through, and the second and third portcullises were lifted in turn. Nia knew little about the sorcery that had fashioned the star, but she knew that the Border Guards studied the usage of such objects as part of their training, and that they would have recognised the patterns on the palms of her hands. *And in so doing, they would recognise me for what I am, in one sense at least,* she reminded herself, noting with sardonic amusement how they now averted their faces and ushered them all through as quickly as possible. The Border Guards quite rightly feared their masters the Watchers.

If you weren't with me, you would have been turned away, Nia thought as she glanced at her companions and saw the raw, naked relief in their eyes. *Sooner or later, you would have been caught.*

The trees to the south of the road stopped the cold sea breeze for the most part, and the day felt a little warmer as they pressed on. This, coupled with the knowledge that she was back in her own land, if only just, improved Nia's mood immensely. She almost felt like singing, although she had never sung in her life- she had never had the voice for it. With each westward step her optimism grew, even when her thoughts turned briefly to the less-than-welcome addition to their number. She would find a way to deal with Alexia- Powers, there were any number of ways of dealing with her! The woman was a distraction, and a minor one at that. Once they reached Luudhoq, Nia decided, she would find a way to be rid of her.

They reached Ranith Tyr shortly after sundown, with both moons already risen along with the brightest of the stars. Nia smiled to herself as they made their way towards the gated eastern wall of the town. She touched the belt pouch where she had placed her Harnian coins. *Comfort at last,* she thought, watching the glow cast by the town lanterns and torches as they approached. *What's the name of the large guest house where they do those fine and enormous meals? The Bell and Whistle, that's it. I'll dine properly tonight. I deserve it. I'll even buy Alexia a fine dinner. Perhaps a full belly will help her see me as a friend.*

Nia still did not sing, but she whistled a merry tune as the tired companions reached the gates of Ranith Tyr.

IV - Dark Movements

I

Iyoth woke with a violent start. Both of his longknives reached out into the cool dawn air in an instant, as if he expected to see an adversary looming over him. Kian cringed and drew breath sharply. She dared not speak in case he had heard or sensed something that she hadn't.

Finally, apparently satisfied that nothing malevolent lurked nearby, Iyoth sheathed the weapons and stared moodily out across the field, the eastern edge of which they had rested by for the night. The outlines of distant hills, copses and outbuildings- for they were in farming land now- gradually came into view and the crisp, chill air quickly wiped away the lingering remnants of the violent dream from which he had woken. Despite having been dragged unpleasantly into the waking world, Iyoth's mood improved somewhat as he surveyed the scene. Although loath to admit it, he had grown fond of many natural treasures in the human-occupied areas, despite his continued disdain for the humans themselves, who crawled like ants almost everywhere, quarrelling and copulating in equal measure as they spread disease and ruined the natural order of things.

Soon the dawn chorus grew to its height all around them. Kian enjoyed the sound of birdsong. It was not something she ever heard within the misty confines of Mirkwall, and she had only ever been able to enjoy it on her occasional journeys out into the wider land.

Here, she silently reflected, everything seemed peaceful or *normal*. In the forest of Knarlswood, which they had fled days ago, her instincts had screamed to her that everything was wrong. Iyoth had had a suspicion as to why this might be, but it was Kian who had told him and in so

99

doing had revealed that she must have developed some sort of precognitive gift during her years in Mirkwall.

"That woman with the wolf summoned a creature to her," Kian had said during their hurried journey west, as they left the troubled forest behind. "No, a *man*, or something that's part-man. He's bound to others somehow. Other beings."

"What other beings?" Iyoth had demanded to know.

"Like those in Mirkwall," Kian had told him, "but even worse."

Iyoth had taken that to mean that somehow, *choragh* were truly loose in the world once again, a possibility he had feared already. It gave weight to his unspoken fear that an end to this Age might be imminent. Was that not what had happened two thousand years ago? Time then to abandon his life of constant wandering and seek shelter from whatever Aona willed as the fate of the Races.

When he asked her how she could know about the summoning, Kian replied calmly that she had always been able to sense the movements and machinations of such beings, for as long as she could recall. "They were in Mirkwall and had been there for at least as long as me. But this- the summoning in Knarlswood- felt different," she had added. "I had no idea that I could *know* such things. I just did. It was like..." She had shrugged wearily, unable to describe her talent, let alone make sense of it.

Kian was Iyoth's daughter, although she had no inkling of the fact. In the twenty-two years since her birth, they had followed entirely different paths. Pursued by enemies into the misty lands surrounding the ancient fortress of Mirkwall, Iyoth had given his baby daughter over to Shimlock, lord and sole denizen of that forgotten place, more to help quicken his own flight than to protect her. In return, Shimlock had granted him safe passage onwards through the vast swamplands. "You can never return for her," the warlock had warned him, watching as Iyoth made ready his borrowed boat for passing on through Mirkwall's northern expanse. "She is mine now and will be brought up as my daughter."

"As you will," Iyoth had said, barely giving the infant a glance as she lay cradled in Shimlock's arms.

Since that day, Iyoth had thought occasionally about Kian, but until their chance meeting he had made every effort not to dwell on the past. The abandonment of his daughter was hardly something he wanted to recall, and so he had tried to push the matter aside.

Would I do the same now, he asked himself, *if I had to?* Everything had changed. The unknowing infant had become a full-grown young woman, even if she remained naïve to many of the world's ways.

Iyoth decided it was a pointless question to ask. If she had been the age she was now, back then, surely she could have ran with him. He shook his head and silently cursed himself for dwelling on matters of little importance. *The past cannot be unmade,* he told himself grimly, *so stop going back to it. Memories and regrets won't help you survive.*

He had already mentioned his trades of choice- assassination and bounty-hunting- to Kian, for the simple reason that the irreconcilable chasm between them might be easier to bear if she became even warier of him, perhaps revolted by the way he conducted his own life and ruined others. Initially she had indeed been horrified, as might anyone hidden away from the world and its harsh truths her entire life. As they fled Knarlswood, however, she seemed to put it to the back of her mind, perhaps having realised there were far more urgent matters to deal with. Putting as much distance as possible between themselves and that forest, for one.

If the past had been different, Iyoth might even have told her of the pride he felt at that.

They breakfasted on late, softening berries from a winterfruit tree and some small fish from a river that ran nearby- a tributary to the great Althameer, Iyoth reckoned, upstream of all the main towns and cities and therefore likely safe to drink and eat from. Kian looked aghast at Iyoth as he ate the fish raw after deftly pulling the spine free, and he stared back at her. "Not hungry, Kian?"

"Not for raw fish," she said.

"They taste delicious," he remarked, "and they are good for your health."

"Can we not cook them?" she asked, but he shook his head. "There's no time to make a fire. Eat them raw or leave them for me."

Clearly she was hungry, for she took a deep breath and set about deboning and eating one of the fish, although she looked as if she might vomit it back up. Iyoth shook his head at the mess she made and turned his thoughts to the way ahead.

Kian had suggested a few days earlier that they head slightly off their original path for a while, in order that she might look upon Mirkwall again. Iyoth had initially been vehemently against the idea- Mirkwall was the last place he wanted to see- but Kian had told him, "The creatures that dwell there can't harm me. They can't even bear to be close to me. If they could hurt me, they would have done so many years ago. But they always maintained their distance."

"All the same," he scowled, "why go there at all?"

"Something is happening in that place," Kian said. "I can feel it."

Their detour had taken them mostly through open land- small wooded areas and meadows that had long lain fallow, rich with thick green grass that shimmered as the chill wind chased itself across their abandoned expanse. Rain fell frequently, and when the rain had stopped falling, still the stiff breeze pushed the low grey clouds onwards, which meant a downpour was never far away.

As they headed on again after breakfast, Iyoth reflected briefly on what he supposed ought to be their destination- the *du-luyan* settlement of Cai, in the far middle-west of Aphenhast, high in the moorland with the higher mountains of Harn visible further to the west. From the highest ramparts of the castle walls in Cai, the Border Wall of Harn could be seen.

They could stay there, certainly, but for how long? Iyoth feared that whatever evil stirred in the world, it would not be contained. If his people knew that the *choragh* had risen, they would already have plans to combat them. Avid students of history and mythology that they were, the *du-luyan* people knew the old names such as *choragh* and *marandaal,* even if some of the meaning had been lost over the centuries. Most humans, meanwhile, had long forgotten such names and even the history attached to them.

Glancing at Kian, who had taken the lead as they made their way along a little-used grassy track, he made a mental note to teach her the *du-luyan* tongue, and perhaps in time even write it. That she did not know anything of her own people's language shamed him, although the fault lay neither with her nor even with Shimlock. Perhaps the old sorcerer had not envisaged her ever needing to use the language of her people. Perhaps he had even thought he might outlive her, as he had outlived so many others.

During their journey, they avoided the few human settlements they passed near to. To walk through such places would undoubtedly complicate their journey. These days, even *luyan* were viewed with deep suspicion in far-flung rural parts as much as cities, which as Iyoth pointed out meant that *du-luyan* with their dark skin and violent reputation were viewed with open hostility.

"Where do all *our* people live?" Kian asked at one point, as they took a wide detour along the side of a wooded hill, at the base of which nestled one such quiet village. "I learned a little about the settlements and cities, but much of what I read contradicted itself."

"As far from humanity as possible," Iyoth retorted. "There are settlements in the far west, on the slopes of the Daymorn peaks that reach back down into Aphenhast, and in the distant east, near the border with Alhar. Some may have even ventured into Alhar itself. Then there are smaller communities in other places." He gave her a lupine grin. "We're always where you least expect."

"I've often wondered what it might be like to live amongst my people," Kian mused.

"Difficult, I expect."

Kian nodded soberly. "The idea fills me with dread. How could I possibly fit in? But I have nowhere else to go. I can't simply wander the land hoping for kindness or charity."

"Do not think to settle anywhere, Kian," Iyoth warned. "Not anytime soon. I aim to reach Cai in the western moors as soon as possible, but we may need to travel again. We will not be the only ones. The world is changing, and not for the better. Ancient enemies walk the lands again. You know this to be true."

Kian shivered in the chill breeze and ducked neatly under a low-hanging oak tree branch as they emerged into open land once again and the bracken-infested hill flattened out. Rolling hills and meadows stretched away into the serene distance. Even given the inclement weather they had suffered for days, Kian admired the beauty of the constantly-changing view. She smiled absently and drew to a brief halt to observe the scene, before she recalled Iyoth's words and her smile quickly faded. "What will happen to everything?" she murmured.

"We'll find out soon enough," Iyoth said as he strode past her. "Everyone will find out soon enough."

That night they were lucky enough to chance upon an old farmhouse that still retained its roof and furnishings, but which, judging by the dust it had gathered, had lain silent and unoccupied for at least a few years. Kian, who already felt tired and emotional after a gruelling day spent walking and pondering the future, found herself deeply saddened by this mournful, musty place. Whoever had lived here had, it seemed, been forced to leave in a hurry, although she could find no clue as to why. Aside from basic furniture and a few ornaments in the family room and utensils in the kitchen, she found toys and an intricately-carved wooden box with various coloured pieces- a game of some sort, Kian surmised- in a small room that had probably been set aside for a child or children.

She sat here in the gloom for a while, oddly desolate. What had become of these people? Soon enough, a second question came to her: *What will become of me?*

Kian listened to the sounds Iyoth made as he rummaged through each of the cupboards in the other rooms, no doubt looking for anything that might be useful or valuable. *Perhaps I should do the same, Kian considered. After all, haven't I been a thief all my life? Often it was one of my tasks when Shimlock was alive. I was good at it- most of the time. But now... now it feels wrong, even though this house has been abandoned.*

Presently Iyoth looked in on her, and laughed as he saw her inspecting the carved wooden box-game with a view to working out how it was played. "We have no time for games, Kian."

"What games do *du-luyan* children play?" she asked.

"Childhood is a preparation for adulthood," he said with a shrug, "so they learn to survive. To fight. Or learn the arcane arts, if they have the talent for them. All play has a purpose."

Kian turned to stare at him. "If all the Races thought to find ways to end the bitterness between one another, the world would be a happier place."

"You have lived the wrong life for too long," Iyoth told her, "hidden away in the mist and sheltered from reality."

"So *du-luyan* children never play, for play's own sake?" she asked, ignoring the jibe. Iyoth gave her a scornful look and went back to his ransacking.

Kian was exhausted, and after their evening meal she fell asleep on one of the straw mattresses almost immediately, curled up with a blanket pulled tightly about her.

The dark walls and endless corridors of Mirkwall wrapped themselves about her. They knew who she was, and somehow they reacted to her presence. Kian walked along a passageway whose surfaces, above and below and to each side, were stained with mould and cracked in a myriad of places. Water dripped incessantly from somewhere, although she could not see it. Her own footsteps sounded soft and muffled, without any semblance of echo.

She stopped suddenly and listened. The sound of other footsteps nearby continued for a moment and then stopped. Kian turned, unafraid, knowing what to expect. Odd shapes and likenesses retreated into the shadows, into holes in the ceiling or the walls, into the between-places where they liked to lurk. Kian observed their hurried retreat, then turned and continued on her way.

A uniform greyish glow suffused everything, yet it became marginally lighter as she ascended a flight of steps to another passageway, which ran around the perimeter of a tower and so afforded her the luxury of window spaces from which to look out. Tendrils of the ever-present mist that enshrouded Mirkwall and its territories drifted in. Kian looked through one of the arched windows and caught a glimpse of the surrounding marsh before the mist, borne on currents that no one understood, swirled and hid it from her view.

A sudden, urgent thought came to her. Might Shimlock still be alive? Could she perhaps find him and question him? She would know what to ask when she saw him.

She ran in what she reckoned to be the direction of his private quarters. But time passed, corridors, archways and rooms came and went, and still she could not locate the sorcerer's chambers. Somehow, Mirkwall had changed physically, and continued to change. Where once passageways had led through the mournful darkness, now blank and impenetrable walls blocked her way. Behind some of them she heard faint scratching and slithering, the sounds, perhaps, of the castle's unwanted denizens making further amendments to its infrastructure. Where once a staircase had led up to the higher ramparts, a set of crooked stone steps led down, precarious and worn-looking. Some rooms had become mirror-images of themselves. And some entire areas that ought to have existed were, inexplicably, missing in their entirety.

Kian ran as her despair deepened. She tried to ignore the scuttling of the creatures that dwelt here as they kept up with her progress whilst maintaining a respectful distance. Then, as she reached a sturdy, iron-studded door, their sounds and indeed their very presence disappeared completely, to leave nothing but a deep, unfamiliar silence, an emptiness that belonged only to Mirkwall itself.

Kian, vaguely aware that this had never happened before, marvelled at it for a moment and guessed that the door or whatever lay beyond it held some repellent properties. Then she opened the door and strode through.

The scene she now beheld made her entirely forget the creatures of Mirkwall.

The room into which she had walked was some sort of ceremonial hall, crowded with people of various races, all dressed in occasionally great and at least moderate finery, except for the cheerful and attentive servants who darted from place to place, keeping everyone well-stocked with mouth-watering food and exquisite drinks.

Stupefied, Kian wandered further into the room, and then froze in shock as she caught sight of herself in a full-length mirror. At least she was still du-luyan, *but the reflection that stared back at her was taller, a little older, and judging by the full roundness of her belly, heavily pregnant.*

"Pardon me, my lady. Might you care for one of our Kyransan rootcakes?"

She almost jumped at the sound of the servant's voice. Half-turning, she smiled wanly and took one of the proffered cakes and a glass of what looked like watered wine. The servant bowed quickly, flashed a polite smile and hurried away to his next guest. Kian's attention returned to her reflection in the mirror. She reached up a hand to stroke her cheek, and the reflection did the same. Clearly this was no illusion.

Who am I? *she wondered.* Where is this place? Is this still Mirkwall? *Part of her remained certain that it was, for the architecture of the hall seemed familiar- and yet, if this was indeed her fortress home, somehow it had been transformed into a place of light and merriment.*

Suddenly conscious of the Mirkwall from where she had emerged, she tried desperately to remember how she had come to be here. There was an entrance, *she thought briefly.* A door. I was being followed, but now...

Her thoughts became confused. What door? And who am I supposed to be?

The sight of people from so many different Races as they mingled together perplexed her, yet she had no idea why. After all, such gatherings took place every Lightday, and folk came from far and wide to discuss all the goings-on throughout the land. How do I know that? *she asked herself, but even as she did, recollections came of the names and professions of those people nearest to her. It was a little like waking up. She remembered her own name. Blinking in bewilderment, she wondered what it was that had caused her confusion.*

"Anara," a voice murmured in her ear. "Are you well?"

She turned to see a tall, silver-haired luyan man standing next to her. His green-tinged eyes held a mischievous gleam. "Please don't tell me you're planning to give birth here and now!"

She smiled faintly, and at the same time his name came to her. "Cianmor," she said. "I think perhaps I still have a week left." Her smile widened at the thought. "I'm looking forward to holding my daughter in my arms."

"A week of freedom!" He laughed, patted her stomach gently, and strolled off to talk with a pretty young human girl who had caught his eye. Anara placed her hand where his had briefly been. For an instant she could not even recall the name of her unborn child's father, but quickly it came to her.

"Daram," she murmured, and the strangest sensation she could ever remember experiencing came to her. For a moment it made her entirely forget her surroundings. It felt almost like staring into an infinite array of mirrors that stretched into an indeterminate distance. In that moment, Anara knew not only the name of her child- which she had not even decided on- but the names and faces of all her children's children, and theirs, and so on for half an Age into the fathomless future.

A name from that impossibly distant time-to-be came to her: Kian.

"Kian," she breathed, and it was if all those mirrors abruptly shattered. She staggered to the floor, the world condensing around her, but the floor...

...was now a muddy expanse of open grassland, and all trace of Mirkwall and its inhabitants had disappeared.

The du-luyan warrior staggered to her feet, weighed down by all manner of stained and broken battleware. Two scimitars, one of them chipped and cut away, were clipped in her belt. Her leather armour and clothing beneath were ripped in at least a dozen places. A filmy redness partly suffused her vision in her right eye. Blood, she thought dimly.

My sight is getting worse in that eye. I expect it will fade completely before the day is done.

A human man standing five paces away in the pouring rain was speaking to her. At first she could understand nothing of what he was saying to her. Then, as if she was slowly waking, she began to comprehend.

"Eluren, my Lady, the last gathering have been defeated," he told her. He bowed untidily and almost collapsed in the process. "They were chased into the circle where the earthdreamers waited. We suffered terrible losses ourselves, and one or two others still linger in Dar-moran, but they shall be found and cut down."

"Not by you, Parril," she found herself saying. "You can barely stand. Send others in your place, and get your wounds attended to. I will not lose you to pride when the choragh bastards have failed against you!"

"As my Lady commands." The relief was apparent in the tremble that ran through his words. Parril would never have made such a choice himself, not without her express command. He bowed slightly again, hair and beard dripping in the relentless rain. Then, considering their dialogue complete, he half-turned, about to rise and shamble off to carry out his general's orders, but Eluren spoke up once more. "Now with the middle lands clear we can turn our attention to our remaining struggles and help Vanir's people in the north-west." She looked around, suddenly confused by something that felt like a flicker of sorcery, some presence within her or around her, benign but watchful. What was it? Eluren shook her head and decided to leave the matter for later. Something more important concerned her now. With a tired effort she drove her ruined scimitar into the soft, sodden earth. "A great battle was fought here," she said, "and a great victory against the Dark."

Parril nodded gravely. Blood from his wounds snaked languidly away in the rain.

"And so we will build a great city here, with a mighty castle at its centre," Eluren intoned, "in memory of the victory, earned after so many tenyears, but also in memory of the terrible cost we have had to pay, so that we all may remember this sacrifice, for all time."

Parril bowed his head further. Eluren suspected he wept from relief and exhaustion, or for the countless thousands who had lost their lives in this bitter war, but in the rain it was impossible to tell if he wept at all.

"And its name," she said, walking to her captain-at-arms to kneel with him in the mud, "shall be Mirkwall."

Kian woke suddenly into the darkness of an unwindowed room. For a moment she stared wildly around, not understanding where she was. Then, as the musty, slightly damp smell of the abandoned farmhouse assailed her, she remembered and relaxed a little. For a while afterwards she lay back on the straw mattress, and the details of her dream still lingered as she cast her mind back through her experience.

No, she thought suddenly. *That was no dream. I saw through the eyes of real people. Whatever it was, it happened, I'm sure of it. Who were they? Were they all...*

Kian sat up suddenly and swung her legs over the side of the mattress, putting her boots on as another realisation rushed at her. *They were all ancestors of mine!*

"Eluren had it built," she whispered into the darkness, certain of her statement. "She ordered the creation of Mirkwall."

Kian pondered how strange it was that she, a dim and distant descendant of a fierce warrior-chieftain, had by chance been raised in that same place, by the last man of Mirkwall. Inevitably, thoughts of those creatures that had now made the place their own came to her.

The Dark.

Why did Shimlock linger there for so long? she wondered, *when he could simply have departed, centuries ago, like all the others?*

It was a puzzle- or so she thought, yet its answer came quickly to her, in the form of Eluren's fierce words that grey and sodden day thousands of years ago. *In memory of the victory, earned after so many tenyears, but also in memory of the terrible cost we have had to pay, so that we all may remember this sacrifice, for all time.*

Shimlock had not been alive when those words were uttered, but Kian suspected that they had been handed down through the generations, and perhaps he had chosen Mirkwall to the bitter end, in respect of that distant time when all the Races had stood together against a common enemy, when they had fought alongside one another without question, without prejudice.

Kian blinked back tears, a deep, heavy feeling in her heart. How the world had changed. How its people had slipped from comradeship and common purpose into hate and acrimony. No small wonder then that the Old Dark and Powers knew what else reached out into the world again like a lengthening shadow. Somehow, all the peoples throughout the land had withdrawn into themselves, and judging by Iyoth's impressions of humanity, her own people were far from guiltless in that regard.

Perhaps such unity was never meant to be, she considered blackly. *Perhaps it served only to vanquish the common enemy. Once that was done, the old suspicions, the old prejudices surfaced again.*

She made her way through to the family room, where Iyoth was busy sharpening his array of knives and scimitars. For a moment she stopped and frowned. His name had registered some faint memory from last night's dream, or perhaps another from the past. But the thought fled as quickly as it arrived.

Iyoth did not look up from his task. "The rain has stopped," he said by way of greeting.

Kian went over and peered through the grimy window at the scene outside, where bracken, gorse and other scrub looked almost aglow in the morning sunlight. "Usually we're up and walking before sunrise," she commented. "Did you oversleep?"

Iyoth shrugged. "You were exhausted. We can occasionally sleep a little longer." He gave Kian a cool look as if he dared her to argue the matter.

Kian said nothing for a while. Eventually she asked him, "How far to Mirkwall? Can we reach it today?"

"We pass by it today," he said, "but we won't enter that place."

Kian nodded, turning away so he could not see the look on her face. "I don't need to go in there. I just need to see it," she murmured. "I have respects to pay."

At sunset on Fourthnight, with the sky on fire in the west and banks of mist obscuring most of Mirkwall's waters to the north, Iyoth and Kian drew to a halt and rested where the ground began to slope down into the vast marshland. Neither of them uttered a word. Iyoth found that the place made him as uneasy as ever and returning here accompanied by the woman he had abandoned twenty-two years ago only added to that unease.

Kian silently observed the waters and what little she could see of the vast fortress in the distance. Occasionally the mists would clear in one area or another to reveal a spire or turret, or simply the dark, dank walls of the ancient castle.

As Iyoth remained sitting, face fixed in a scowl, Kian stared intently into Mirkwall's gloom. To Iyoth it seemed as if she could even penetrate and see through it with that stare.

Kian closed her eyes and felt every contour of her former home come back to her, as if she had never been away.

And yet it had changed. As foretold in her dream, some of the corridors, stairwells and rooms, familiar for so long, had now been altered beyond recognition- the work, no doubt, of what Shimlock himself had called the Old Dark. The creatures of a forgotten Age, newly returned along with their masters. What purpose they served by causing such changes Kian had no idea, but they were surely intent on weaving their own powers into what had once been the icon of the Races' eventual triumph, two thousand years ago, over their *choragh* overlords. Kian felt the beginnings of a deep rage stir within her, fury at the abandonment of Mirkwall, at the inability of her own people and others to safeguard the place. She wondered again how it was that Shimlock had remained, yet everyone else had departed many decades earlier. Had it truly been out of some stubborn respect?

The old sorcerer was dead now, and she would never know.

Kian frowned suddenly as her senses picked up a new movement amongst the *choragh*-kin, as if they had separated themselves into two distinct groups. One, she realised after a while, stayed deep within the architecture that her ancestor had brought into being. The other mass headed through Mirkwall, through the narrow apertures, wide corridors, empty stairwells and dusty, forgotten rooms, in a northerly direction. Some soon reached the marshes to the north of the castle perimeter and continued at terrifying speed, silent, flitting like ephemeral shadows through the mist. Kian could feel all of this, and by feeling it she could see it. She wondered with a shudder what it might be like to encounter that unearthly mass of hurrying chaos as it rushed heedlessly past.

"Iyoth," she said, rousing herself with an effort, "which city is it that lies leagues to the north of here? Is it Nisstar?"

"Nisstar is some distance away, more than twenty leagues," Iyoth said, "but yes, that would be the city to the north. Why do you ask?"

"Many creatures have left Mirkwall," Kian said, "and they move directly north. Thousands, perhaps." She frowned and shook her head. "Why would they do that?"

"You ask too many questions," Iyoth told her. "We cannot hope to understand them." He gripped her arm suddenly, almost painfully, and she saw anger flare in his eyes. "Enough of Mirkwall, Kian! It's gone, derelict, *forgotten*, even if it does still stand. We head west now, and out of these lands. Beyond these troubles."

Kian gave the mists and the castle one last lingering glance. "I don't think these troubles *can* be escaped," she said softly, but Iyoth already strode away as if hurrying to catch up with the sunset, heedless to her words.

II

Six days later, a short while before they reached the great stone towers of Cai, Iyoth became certain that trouble lay ahead. When they arrived at a high point in the surrounding moorland and could see in the early morning gloom the vastness of the *du-luyan* settlement, his fears were merely confirmed.

Not even one of the great braziers that marked the corner of each tower had been lit- at least, none of those that faced east. This was unprecedented, but Iyoth knew that there was more wrong here.

He drew to a halt and motioned for Kian to do the same, and they stood motionless in the cold breeze. Dark moorland in which all manner of things might hide loomed for many leagues in each direction. Tough heather and gorse

115

rustled in the wind as if secrets were being carried over the landscape.

Kian had expected a place such as this to be teeming with wildlife even at night, but all the animals she had expected to see or at least hear had inexplicably disappeared. The light available changed moment by moment, as Ildar's bright disc rode the waves of passing clouds, emerging from swathes of darkness only to disappear again.

Iyoth swiftly considered the possibilities. Why might the tower braziers have been extinguished? This had never happened before during his lifetime, and he had never heard of it happening in anyone else's. Through wet and dry, light and dark, they always remained lit, the use of quickpowder making the flames all but unquenchable no matter the weather. Now, Cai appeared to be nothing more than an assortment of vast, cold stones rather than the ancestral home of *du-luyan*, the place to which all wanderers born here eventually returned. *And never a day went by when I did not think of returning here,* he thought. *The more I lived amongst humankind, the more I ached to come back. Why didn't I?*

Had everyone simply left, or vanished? Or even been annihilated? Iyoth found that almost impossible to conceive. Who or what could possibly have overcome his people in their own home? One thing he somehow knew for certain, however, without any need to walk into Cai itself- the place had been deserted and its people were gone.

He began to walk slowly towards the settlement, and Kian followed. Although the night vision of all *du-luyan* was second to none, Iyoth did not trust the thick, oppressive blackness that stared impassively from the windows of the vast towers beyond the outer wall. In the eastern section of that wall itself, the iron gates stood half-open, but not invitingly.

By now the first hints of morning light suffused the sky in the east. In this half-glow, Iyoth and Kian made their way through the gates and observed the emptiness of Cai's courtyards, the cobbles and statues still standing unbroken, the archways and corners free of debris. The grey and black stone, marble and granite interlocked, glimmered faintly in the gathering light, and offered no clue as to what might have happened here. *No signs of bloodshed anywhere,* Iyoth thought. *No signs of a struggle. No footprints. As if they turned to dust in an instant, and the dust was then swept away by the wind, across the moors.*

It was Kian who suddenly realised that they were not alone.

A shiver ran through her, a cold, unpleasant ripple as if something stirred for a moment under her skin. Instantly she knew what that meant. *How could I not have known before now, as we approached this place?* she asked herself grimly. *Are they now able to mask themselves from me?*

Kian caught a glimpse of something long, dark red and glistening, with too many heads and legs, as it dragged itself around a distant inner archway, near to the base of one of the tall black stone fortresses. She did not know the name of this monstrosity, if indeed it had one, but she knew its nature immediately.

"Iyoth," she said softly. "We are not alone."

Almost silently, both his longknives came out into the dawn. "The Old Dark?" he whispered.

"Yes." Kian drew a deep breath. She had no fear of such beings- though she felt certain she would be terrified of an actual *choragh* if ever she saw one- but she loathed them with all her heart, and her dream-visions of Mirkwall's distant heyday and then its founding had only hardened her resolve further.

What should I do? she asked herself. *Destroy the creature and seek out any others of its kind that wander the forsaken streets and passageways of Cai? Do I have such power? Often I thought they feared me, though I never knew why. Will they fear me now? Or were Shimlock and even Mirkwall itself my protectors? Am I now at their mercy?*

She glanced at Iyoth's weapons and resisted the temptation to tell him they might be next to useless against the *choragh-kin.*

"Our people, Kian." Iyoth did not sound in fighting mood. He sounded as if part of him was breaking apart. "Where have they gone? Where have they been *taken?*"

She could find no answer, not knowing whether some immense sorcery had spirited them all away, or they had realised that an end was coming, that they would have to leave Cai or otherwise face certain annihilation.

"Would they have left without fighting to defend this place," she asked, "if they knew that to defend it would hasten their own destruction?"

Iyoth considered that for a moment. "Cai is our spiritual home," he said finally, "and would be defended at almost all costs. But..." He shook his head. "If they left, then even now they must be planning swiftly for a day of bloody vengeance. No move against our people goes unpunished, Kian."

They fell silent. Kian saw, no more than a hundred paces away, the creature that she had sensed before as it walked slowly around the tower. It paused for a moment, several heads raised to the sky and then towards *her*, as if to ascertain her position. Kian held her breath. She had no idea what to do if it rushed towards them, legs clicking and needle-teeth snapping in the chill air. It did not. *This thing is wary,* she realised. *Even now, it prefers not to approach me. It senses that I might harm it.*

"You can, perhaps," Iyoth said, and Kian jumped, startled. She hadn't realised that she had spoken.

"If you feel their presence, if you can touch and even *shape* the Old Dark," Iyoth continued quietly, "then perhaps you *can* harm them."

"There are many others," Kian realised as she stared deeper into the abandoned settlement and allowed her mind's eye to wander into the black archways and windows of other buildings. She could feel the *kin* as they burrowed and nestled amongst the towers and houses they had taken. "Too many."

Iyoth said nothing. In the east, the light grew stronger and as the shadows shrank back, Cai became an even lonelier place to look upon. Kian sensed many of the kin shrink away from the dawn and work their way into the earth, or even into the stone itself as some of them had the ability to do. Here and there she saw or felt a flicker of something- antennae, or a tail, it was too quick to be anywhere near certain- in the vicinity of distant archways. Shivers of revulsion ran through her, each one a helpless reaction to some movement or other by the creatures that now dwelt here. The sensation was all too familiar, yet it sickened her as much as it always had done.

"What do we do?" she whispered eventually.

Iyoth remained silent for so long that Kian thought he might not have even heard her. "We continue westwards," he said eventually, "towards the border and then on into Harn, perhaps. North-west, for we'll be granted no entrance by their Border Guards. Further north, we may find a way through." He glanced at her. "There is nothing we can do here."

Kian uttered a groan of disbelief and leaned against the wall as the thought of travelling even further brought all her exhaustion rushing back. Seeing her reaction, Iyoth turned his calm gaze to her- *too calm,* she thought. "We have no choice, Kian. We cannot remain here. We cannot turn back and wander Aphenhast like desolates. There are *du-luyan* communities in Harn- in fact, with Cai deserted, those settlements are the nearest to us."

She opened her mouth to argue, but he gripped her arm painfully. "*We head north-west.* I will tolerate no argument from you, Kian. I will tie you and carry you over my back if I have to." He looked her up and down, and for a moment a curious look entered his expression, one she could not fathom. "You are a grown woman. It's time you behaved as one."

Kian stared incredulously at him as she rubbed her arm but could think of nothing to say. Over the days they had spent together she had learned when to argue with Iyoth and when not to. *I could leave him,* she thought. *But what then? I don't want to be alone.*

They made a detour around the outer walls of Cai. Kian glanced at the desolation as they strode across the moorland; Iyoth steadfastly avoided looking anywhere but ahead. Behind them, eventually the sun rose and bathed the windswept heath in golden light.

V – The City of Dreams

I

Open land stretched ahead, darker than the sky, yet it could have been the ocean for all Jaana cared. Her entire body ached, and exhaustion had seeped into every pore of her being, yet sleep had proved elusive since their departure from Culvanhem. Worse, sometimes during the small hours before dawn she was further plagued by what sounded like whispers and faint laughter that seemed to come from every direction at the same time. These sounds melted away almost as soon as they announced themselves. Jaana did not tell anyone about them, fearful that some of her companions thought her half-crazed already. Nor did she tell anyone about the small, dark shapes that she occasionally caught a glimpse of from the corner of her eye- apparitions that she could never see properly, faint hints of the *choragh* spies, she thought at one point. *They know I withstood one of their lords, and now they are drawn to me, perhaps to monitor my movements but also to understand how I did what I did.*

Even were they to torture me to breaking point, I could not tell them.

Jaana found herself equally fascinated by these elusive beings that watched her from afar. Behind them lurked something far greater, a vast intelligence as old as the world, insidious and all-pervasive. *Once, in the First Age, they were thought of as Gods,* Jaana remarked to herself as she gazed at the indeterminate landscape before them. *But then they faded as the younger Races began to learn the secrets of the world. The Great War was fought, and then eventually came the Enlightenment.*

That much she understood from what Fistelkarn had mentioned to her over the last few weeks, but for everything she thought she had learned, a dozen or more questions appeared, and Fistelkarn had few answers for those. *It's all but forgotten lore now,* he said, *and it was much the same when I was young. Some of us still know that the* choragh *and all those under them- including the Younger Races back then- waged war against the* marandaal. *We know that later another war was fought, between the* choragh *and the Younger Races. A great war fought over the great powers of Aona. But the detail? The detail has long since turned to dust.*

She wondered what Ludas might know of these myths, but she could not speak with him and doubted that she could have brought herself to in any case.

Ludas, their captive dreamreader and a man she feared and loathed in equal measure, had been silenced by Fistelkarn so that his words could no longer taunt her. He could no longer utter a word without his mouth starting to spasm painfully. The sorcerer had not, however, forced the man's eyes shut, and even in the dark Jaana could often feel his gaze upon her from a distance, drawn helplessly. It felt as if worms crawled all over her, trying to find ways in. *Would I know if he rummaged around in my head?* Jaana wondered as she stared hatefully at him. *And if I did, could I harm him somehow?*

Oh, how she wanted to! But her rational self forbade her. Ludas was essential to the faint hope that Fistelkarn held, the hope that with the dreamreader's help they could convince the powers in the city of Nisstar that the madness and delirium afflicting so many people was a consequence of the *marandaal,* on the verge of reaching into Aona. Before being silenced, he had even claimed he could sense the slow emergence of Gates somewhere within that city. "I dream of them each night," he had said. "Nisstar. That's where they will be. And the dreams grow stronger as they draw nearer. Imagine what that's like for those within the city, those whose minds are being pulled apart."

Jaana remembered he had smiled then, as if he took pleasure from the thought.

I'm not sure I believe it myself, Jaana thought. *No matter how powerful they are, how can these beings and the Gates they supposedly control touch the minds of people here, even before they themselves have even appeared?*

They sound like Gods, she realised, and that was perhaps the most disturbing notion of all. Jaana had no time for religion, but she almost understood why such entities might be thought of in such a way, planting dreams in the minds of the weak, to slowly drown them in a mad sea they could never escape.

Fistelkarn had bought Ludas' freedom from the *crommari* people on condition that neither he nor any of his companions would ever return to the *crommar* city of Culvanhem deep within the Crescents, where Ludas had spent years locked away in darkness. The *crommari* had been suspicious of Fistelkarn and his companions from the outset- as they were of all outsiders- but after the events that had occurred during their stay in that fortress city, they had quickly become hostile and demanded that the companions leave. That Fistelkarn had been able to strike any sort of bargain was testament to his reputation as a sorcerer, a reputation even the *crommari* respected, although they would never like nor welcome him.

Is he even worth hating? Jaana asked herself, glancing sidelong at Ludas, who sat a dozen yards away, head bowed in exhaustion. The dreamreader was a pale shadow of a man, thin and drawn and far older in his appearance than his years. Much of his hair and most of his teeth had been left behind in the cell he had occupied deep in the mountains. *And to think for a moment I pitied him when I first saw him,* she recalled. *Now I would snap the key in the lock and wait for him to rot away.*

Before Fistelkarn had silenced him, Ludas had reluctantly told them about the visions that had come to him- visions, he claimed, of other people's dreams and of people falling into restless yet never-waking states. Jaana had no reason to doubt the man. She had seen some of them herself, in her previous life as a healer before she met Lyya or any of the others. She had been called upon many times to aid such victims. *But I was never able to,* she remembered. *I could sometimes ease their suffering a little, but nothing more than that. There could be no cure, because some higher power held them. Something reached to them from another place, beyond my understanding.*

Gods, she thought, shuddering.

Jaana recalled Ludas' claim that these dreams were the result of two things: the coming of the *marandaal* and the gathering in strength of the *choragh,* the Old Dark. In so saying, he had confirmed Fistelkarn's own fears. "The heartbeat of the world," Ludas had called the *choragh,* to which Fistelkarn had said: "Then Aona has a sick heart." The idea that anything so vile, so utterly abhorrent as the *choragh* could be a part of the world itself was one that Jaana struggled with. Certainly it was not a view with which Ellen would have agreed.

Jaana closed her eyes for a moment and tried to will away the thoughts of her deceased mentor. She turned to look at Lyya. The *luyan* woman sat by her side but had not spoken all evening, which was unlike her, and although she found her presence comforting, Jaana eventually felt the need to break the silence.

"I was thinking about my childhood earlier," she began. Lyya glanced across, her translucent hair shimmering in the firelight. Jaana always found the effect disconcerting as much as fascinating. "Anything in particular?" she asked.

"I always wondered why there was so little I could remember about those years," Jaana said. "I lived in many places- my mother and I moved around almost continuously- but I could never properly remember any of the settlements where we stayed." She frowned. "It was as if a mist hung over everything. But I never really thought about it- until the last few days. Maybe I'm not supposed to remember."

"Would you want to?"

Jaana shrugged. "I'm simply curious, I suppose. I look for answers everywhere. No doubt I'll wish I could forget again, if ever I do recall those times properly." She frowned. "It felt sometimes as if my mother and I were being hunted by something. Even then, before all this... all this *choragh* and *diafagh* and the Powers know what else."

Lyya pondered that for a while and then said, "Could it be that they sought you even when you were a child?"

"If that's so," Jaana reasoned, "then how is it that they could never find me?"

Lyya had no answer to that.

That night, however, Jaana dreamt that they *had* found her, that minions of the *choragh* had indeed been following her for her entire life, drawn by something but unable to walk close to her.

She stood by a window in a cottage, watching the rain pour down. Summer had faded, and the nights began to draw in. Today the light had failed even earlier under the blanket of dark grey clouds. The village road had started to turn to mud in the face of the relentless downpour. Jaana listened to the comforting rhythm of the rain, staring at the collision of earth and water, then noticed that something had stirred within that deluge. Clumps of mud and debris were taking shape.

Human shape.

Peering into the gathering darkness, Jaana lost sight of this mystery for a moment, then she noticed the movement again. Despite the poor visibility, she clearly beheld the bizarre event that then occurred.

The muck and debris- and waste and leavings from outside the huts and cottages- that clung to the surface of the road, as it glistened with rain, moved and grew. Sliding and slipping over the soaking stone and mud, it formed a pile, then joined with other conglomerations to form a larger shape. Powers, it's human, Jaana thought, but even at this young age she knew there could be nothing human about this atrocity.

It stood about six hands high now, with a rounded head and misshapen body of filth. Suddenly, Jaana could smell the creature even from inside the cottage. The stench was nauseating.

It stumbled towards her like a clumsy child, and as it did, parts of the putrid body flaked away in the rain as the heavens opened a little wider and a stream of spiteful sleet hammered down; yet the form of the beast was maintained. An arm reached out almost imploringly, and a fissure opened in the head like a gaping wound or a mouth, as if this creature, at once so laughable and so horrifying, intended to speak.

But it made no further movement towards her, battered perhaps by the rain, and no words issued forth.

"It cannot harm you". Her mother's voice came from directly behind her.

Jaana almost jumped out of her skin and whirled round to face her mother, who held her close. When Jaana turned again to point out the mud-creature, it had disappeared. Maybe it had been washed away by the rain. Jaana knew there and then a spell of some sort had been shattered. She burst into tears, and her mother held her awhile longer, murmuring an old lullaby. Although she was too old for lullabies at that age, the gentle cadence soothed the child and eventually her sobbing ceased.

She glanced up into her mother's eyes, searching for answers. But all she discovered there was a profound, deep sadness. "You'll remember," said Meryse, the greenwitch as the midland folk called her. "But not before time. They cannot harm you, my child, not these dark things of the earth."

"Mother..." Jaana whispered, intent on asking so many questions, but Meryse placed a hand upon her forehead, the touch warm and somehow fluid. Jaana cried out as she felt the memory begin to fade, and she could not fight it any more than she could stop the rainstorm outside.

Jaana woke suddenly into the night. Next to her, Lyya stirred briefly, grunted and then shifted onto her other side before going back to sleep. Of her companions, only Tyrameer was awake, keeping a solitary vigil until dawn.

That was real, she thought numbly. *It happened, when I was a child. It was real.*

"Why now?" she whispered into the darkness. "Why remember now?"

But no answer came.

II

The following evening, as they sat some distance from the others and looked out over the wide Heathwold valley that opened out into the lower lands, Jaana confessed to Lyya, "I can feel Ludas looking at me, even when I turn away. Sometimes I'm sure I can even hear him speak, even though he was silenced." She smiled wanly. "Foolish imaginings."

"Hardly." Lyya flashed the dreamreader a dark look, but the man was already asleep even though dusk had fallen only a short while ago. The journey affected Ludas more than anyone else, no doubt because of his years of incarceration in Culvanhem. Jaana knew little of *crommar* judicial matters but she suspected that their prisoner had seldom been allowed out of his cell. Yet she could feel no sympathy for him; nothing, in fact, except the same ever-bright hatred. "He's a dreamreader," Lyya reminded her unnecessarily, "and every one of their kind is dangerous, even those who may not seek to bring harm to others." She lowered her voice further. "They *attach* themselves to people.

127

They learn their thoughts, their fears and eventually everything they need to know. There's a creature called a *leech*, a scourge in the southern swamplands, which attaches itself to anyone unlucky enough to venture near it. It feasts upon the blood of its victim..."

"Yes." Jaana nodded. "I've heard of it."

"Well, I'd say that dreamreaders are like leeches but worse. They feed upon the part of you that makes you who you *are*." Restlessly she tapped the pommel of her longknife. "I could rid you of Ludas in a moment, Jaana, if only you give me the word."

Jaana swiftly reached out and removed her friend's hand from the weapon. "I can't do that! You know that Fistelkarn brought him from Culvanhem for a reason. If Ludas can somehow show that this is the consequence of..."

"How can such beings affect the dreams of people," Lyya interrupted her, "if they have not yet arrived in the world? That makes no sense at all."

"I don't know, Lyya. I've asked myself the same question. Believe me, if the situation was any different, I would already have slit the man's throat myself given half a chance."

The two women said nothing more for a long while, and watched as Archaon rose, giving a dull light in the east to match the fading scraps of sunlight across the western sky. Stars shyly emerged, first the bright Southern Fire and its attendants, then the members of the Sword. *We call that constellation the Sword,* Jaana remembered, *but the* luyan *call it something else. The Cross, I think.*

"If the *marandaal* are as Fistelkarn described them," Lyya said sometime later, "then who can stand in their way, regardless of what warning is given? Even if the bloodlust is wiped from the eyes of all the Races, even if peace is declared- what then?" She turned and stared intently at Jaana. "What do *you* think? Would you say that anything we do will matter? Or should we hide and run and live what we can of our lives, in the time that remains for us?"

Jaana remained silent for a long while. Finally she said quietly, "I don't know, Lyya. It's not for me to say what we should do. But I think there must be a reason for me being the way I am. There's a part of me that somehow *knows* the creatures of the Old Dark, Lyya. Why would that be if not for some reason, some purpose?"

Lyya looked away, discomforted. "I don't know about such things."

"Something is passed down over many centuries, perhaps for use in these dark times," Jaana continued. "Yet it's the same force, the same as the *choragh...*" She shook her head, confused by her own thoughts. "I fear for the world, if we must unleash this darkness, this magic or whatever it's called, against the *marandaal.*"

"These are things for warmongers to decide," Lyya told her. "Human warmongers."

"The Rising declared war," Jaana reminded her. "Whatever their intentions, whatever wrongs were done, still that declaration makes them warmongers."

"For a just cause," Lyya said, although Jaana could tell that she had no heart for the argument. "Ah, the entire story is a sad one repeated over and over. One injustice gives rise to another, which itself births another several, and the powers that be amongst any race ensure the continuation of the injustice. This has always been the way." She shrugged wearily. "In honesty, Jaana, I would be ashamed to be human in view of everything that humankind has done."

She shook her head in disgust. "Many of them call us *mutants,* as if we are some ill-made branch of humanity. Perhaps it's our translucent hair, or our extra fingers, or our sudden aging, or the fact that we only ever give birth to one child and always know its gender before it's born... who knows?"

"I'd say all of those things and more," Jaana said sadly.

"I am even ashamed of the enmity with the *du-luyan*," Lyya remarked, "but that has always been a strange matter. I was brought up with cautionary tales about their kind, forever reminded of their warlike nature, the anger that shapes them. The *du-luyan* seem to forever strive to prove themselves, and that proof seems always to be linked to bloodshed."

"Everyone does strive to prove themselves, in one way or another." Jaana shook her head. "Fauli does not seem overly angry to me."

"No, well, she is amongst her friends."

"Human friends," Jaana noted with a smile, and allowed herself a little enjoyment at Lyya's expression. "I spent much of my childhood hated by other *humans*, Lyya. I can hardly value them above others- strangers or companions- of other races, who have done me no harm, whatever their reputation."

They sat in silence for a while and watched the sky change. Solemnity draped itself about them once again, a shroud that could never be entirely discarded.

Before they set off the following morning, Fistelkarn called for attention as soon as breakfast was over and done with.

"Not all of us will be heading into Nisstar," he said, and immediately held up his hand as several of the others tried to speak at the same time. "Enough! We all know the situation in Nisstar. Fauli and Lyya, I need you to head to Rockmire and seek out an old friend of mine at the Rising. Her name is Serina. She was once a prominent member in the gathering of earth-mages known as the Circle."

The Circle, Jaana thought. *I've heard of them. Ellen spoke of them occasionally, although not with any great fondness. I thought all those witches had passed away or disappeared many years ago.*

She watched as Lyya and Fauli glanced warily at each other, and she wondered yet again what had originally caused the suspicion and hostility between such closely-related races. She reckoned that neither Lyya nor Fauli would know, if asked. Doubtless it had much to do with the way both had been brought up.

She felt a sudden pit open in her stomach then, as she realised what was about to happen. The group would split, but worse than that, she would be parted from the one companion she felt able to call a true friend. Jaana almost spoke up then, to plead with Fistelkarn, to beg that she ride with Lyya and Fauli to Rockmire.

But she said nothing, because she knew that her plea would change nothing. Fistelkarn had already said he would take personal responsibility for her safety, and given what had happened in recent weeks, she knew also that he would not let her out of his sight. *Damn everything that happened,* she thought angrily.

Finally Lyya spoke up. "If we find her, what then? What message should we give her?"

"There are two things at least, that she needs to know. Remind her of the last message she will have received from me. And whatever it takes, convince her to return with you to Alinnora's Haven, where we will come together once again a tennight from now. I think the Rising has no intention of listening to her appeals for calm and peace, and we may need her help. In fact, I'm certain that we will, given the discoveries we've made."

He glanced at Jaana, who looked down at the ground. She felt the weight of all her companions' gazes, but that of Ludas most of all. *I wish the* crommari *had rejected Fistelkarn's offer,* she thought fervently. *I wish we had left Ludas where we found him, to rot away in darkness forever more.*

Not for the first time, Jaana wondered if she might ever be able to turn her supposed powers to some use against creatures other than *choragh* and their ilk. *Then I could show him what happens if he mocks me,* she told herself savagely, but she dared not look towards him, fearful that if she did then he might gain some insight into her thoughts.

"So," Fistelkarn continued, "will the two of you do as I ask?"

Both women nodded reluctantly. "It's not as if either of us could turn up at the gates of Nisstar to beg entrance," Fauli pointed out lightly.

Fistelkarn turned his attention to the others. "We'll continue into Nisstar. Whatever can be done must be done. War between the Races must be averted. Dangers far greater than our own neighbours face everyone. We know this already. Whatever else we do, we must demonstrate this to the authorities of Nisstar." He stared into the southern distance for a moment. "If we can help to stop this looming bloodshed, then perhaps more of us may remain to fight the true threats to our existence."

"Will they listen?" Tyrameer wondered.

"We will find a way to make them listen. Ludas will help." But although Ludas cringed at the very mention of his name, Fistelkarn sounded neither confident nor even hopeful.

They rode a little further along the southern track, which wound through heath and scrub, until the way divided in two. One path continued south whilst the other headed through more open land in a westerly direction. "This is where we go our separate ways," Fistelkarn announced, as he glanced towards Lyya and Fauli.

Jaana felt a desperate heaviness in her heart as she returned Lyya's fierce hug. "Take care of yourself," Lyya whispered. "It will not be long."

"Too long," Jaana replied miserably. Lyya kissed her on the cheek. "Take this," she said suddenly, and pressed a small, plain copper ring into her palm. Jaana blinked. "A ring?" She smiled uncertainly. "What..."

"A simple token of friendship," Lyya said, "to be returned when we meet again." She smiled at Jaana's confusion. "A *luyan* tradition. Keep it safe until we see each other once more."

A short while later, Fauli and Lyya rode away west, and Jaana felt the despair of watching the only true friend she had ever had slowly disappear.

III

Jaana had been largely silent before Lyya's departure, but now that her friend had been sent away she said nothing at all unless she had to, and lapsed into a state where she only vaguely noticed everything going on around her. She realised it was foolish, knowing what she now knew about the enemies ranged against them- and she knew it was selfish too, although she suspected that if the servants of the Old Dark sought to harm them during their remaining journey, she would know about it even before Fistelkarn.

They'll not reach us in Nisstar though, she thought at one point three days later, as they rode along a wide stony road through farmed land. Icy wind gusted around but she barely felt it. *The cities are the places where the religious gather. The cities are places of light and noise and machines. But most of all, they are places where beliefs are different.*

And belief was important. Even though she scorned the practice of religion and superstition, Jaana knew the importance of belief in shaping people's lives.

Although I have no beliefs myself, she thought with a faint smile, idly wondering if she felt better or worse because of that fact. *None that I hold absolutely, at least.*

Keeping one hand tightly on the reins, she allowed the other to check her trouser pocket for the fourth or fifth time today, to reassure herself that Lyya's parting gift was still there. *I suppose I believe in Lyya,* she thought, her hand pressing against the hard, unyielding shape of the ring. *But*

133

there's a world of difference between believing in friends and being guided by blind faith.

If the world is coming to an end, Jaana considered, *then why should I head towards the place from where that end may come? Does Fistelkarn truly think he can persuade the priesthood of Nisstar that the world they know will end and that they will all be swept away, unless they make peace with the Rising? Does he think they will listen to whatever Ludas can discern from the mad and the fevered?*

Jaana did not know a great deal about the One Church and its hierarchy, but she suspected that the priesthood thought of dreamreaders and their like as possessed in some way, diseased, maddened, to be shunned or at the very least converted to their doctrine in some painful way. *I wonder what they would make of someone who senses the movements of the Old Dark?* she wondered. *Perhaps they simply don't believe in such things. But I suspect we won't be telling them about that anyway. It would be too much for them to believe, coming from the likes of us.*

By late afternoon that day they had reached Nisstar, a low-set walled city with several minor and major gates leading in and out. Impromptu markets had been set up near the ever-widening road that they followed; none stood closer than fifty paces or so from the city's outer wall, and Jaana wondered why they had been placed thus. Glancing up, she saw numerous archers in position on the battlements, many of them with their weapons primed.

Fistelkarn slowed his horse gently to a halt, and called out to one of the traders, a vegetable farmer: "Why is this market being held beyond the city walls?"

The stallholder threw a fearful glance towards those same walls. "Only folk born in Nisstar may trade in the city squares," he said finally, and flinched as if expecting an arrow to come whistling his way.

Fistelkarn shook his head in disgust, and they rode on as far as the outer gates. At their approach, the number of guardsmen nearby almost doubled, and their sergeant, a stocky man with a scarred, tanned face called for the riders to halt with a good six paces remaining between them.

"Wait, wait," he scowled. "Hold up. What business do you folk have in Nisstar?"

"Only good business, sergeant. That much I can assure you." Fistelkarn smiled benignly at them all. "My son and daughter here are eager to volunteer their services to the church. And my younger brother"- he gestured to Ludas- "is dumb. He has long lost the power of speech. We can only hope and pray that a priest of the One God may be able to heal him."

The sergeant looked at each of them in turn. His men meanwhile, having seen nothing that offered either threat or amusement, had already lost interest and a few had wandered off towards the barracks that stood further beyond the wall.

"Two silver crowns each for entrance," he said finally.

"*Two silver...*" Tyrameer began in disbelief, but Fistelkarn spoke up. "Be quiet, son, and hold your tongue. This man is simply doing his duty. We're happy to pay the church. More than happy. I assume most of these collected funds *are* given over to the church, so they may continue to preserve law and order?"

"Of course." The sergeant frowned as if he thought Fistelkarn an imbecile. He motioned for two of the remaining guardsmen to pull open the gates, waited for the four of them to ride into the courtyard area, and then called them to halt again. "No talk of false Gods," he said, gaze moving from one of them to the next. "No relics of forbidden lore. No practice of witchcraft. You will attend whichever church is nearest to you at sunrise on each fourth-day. You will not carry out trade of *any* sort on each fourth-day. Above all else, you will be seen to give praise to the One God, whenever in the presence of a priest of His Church. These are simple laws that anyone can follow. Even a wordless dimwit." He gave Ludas a contemptuous smile. "Stay within the law and your heads stay on your shoulders."

He waved impatiently for them to move on, and the four of them rode slowly through the courtyard and out into the city proper.

As they made their way along the street, navigating their way between throngs of people, carts being pulled by sad-looking mules, and the occasional large chariot that sent everyone scurrying to either side, Jaana surreptitiously watched those they passed by whilst trying not to attract any attention herself. Most of these people did not look happy. They looked like the sort of folk who were desperate to get through the day without being seen to commit some alleged offence against authority. Heads were bowed often; eyes looked furtively. Trade and commerce were conducted not exactly quietly, but without much enthusiasm by either party.

Ah, but not all of them are so downtrodden, she realised after a short while. Soldiers resplendent in the uniform of the City Guard swaggered around, ostensibly keeping an eye on goings-on but making much of each opportunity to take from a stall or shop without payment, or to insult or molest any woman young or attractive enough to catch their eye. Jaana was unsurprised to see only a few women about.

"We'll rest the horses and find somewhere nearby to stay," Fistelkarn called across. "There are stables just up here. At least, they were still standing when I was last here." He pointed to a side-street that led off nearby, and they cautiously made their way over and up the street, which lay covered in shadow from the low afternoon sun.

The stables still stood and happened to be open. Fistelkarn paid the stable hand for three nights' keep for each horse- Jaana wondered how he still had as much silver as he did- and they headed to a nearby tavern to seek rooms where they could stay for the next several nights.

With accommodation bought, they sat in an unoccupied area of the downstairs tap-room. "About the One Church, and what you said..." Tyrameer began in a low voice. Fistelkarn held up his hand quickly. "All to get us in with only minimal questioning, of course. But we may need a similar excuse when we seek audience with the priesthood. Once we have that audience, well- we will say all that needs saying." He glanced at Ludas. "You will need to keep your part of our bargain."

Ludas stared sullenly back at him and pointed to his mouth. "You'll speak soon enough," Fistelkarn told him. "When you need to."

Exhausted and troubled by being in the city, Jaana barely managed to drag herself upstairs to her poky little bedchamber later. With a sigh she placed the lamp she had been given to light her way onto the floor nearby and put it out, then lay on the hard mattress with a groan, wincing at the pain in her lower back and buttocks, surely the result of riding so much over the last few tennights. Nothing could be done about it, and once their business here was done there would more of it to endure. Assuming they left Nisstar at all.

In this city, a place she had once sworn she would never visit, Jaana thought sleep might not be possible. Noises, some of them muffled and some worryingly clear, came from the street outside her window or from the tap-room downstairs, which had still been heaving with drunks when she left.

Eventually however she drifted off into a fitful slumber and woke near first light with rain lashing against her window.

It was also around first light that Ludas woke in his chamber with a sudden start, to find Fistelkarn nearby.

"Come to kill me already?" he whispered hoarsely, and then blinked in astonishment that he could actually speak.

Fistelkarn smiled thinly. "You should know better, Ludas." The dreamreader watched as the other man casually wiped at his cloak and left a red smear just visible in the emerging light. He swallowed and grimaced at the iron taste in his mouth. "What have you..."

"What have I done?" Fistelkarn shrugged. "You cannot be trusted. You and I both know that. So, if you utter a single word you shouldn't- and you know which words those would be- well, that would be unfortunate for you."

"How?" Ludas swallowed again, grimacing in pain.

"Breath would be denied to you. *Breath*- that most basic privilege." Fistelkarn made a swift motion in the air, and the dreamreader's head was pushed suddenly back against the mattress, as if pressed by some unseen heaviness. A small, strangled sound emerged from him. "Be especially careful as to what you choose to say to Jaana," Fistelkarn advised him. He paused, considering. "In fact, it would be best if you said nothing at all to her."

He left the bedroom and closed the door quietly behind him. Gradually, the invisible pressure around Ludas' head and neck became less, and the dreamreader sat up, drawing a pained, ragged breath, so consumed with hate that he could form no coherent thoughts whatsoever.

IV

The largest church in Nisstar stood tall and austere on the summit of the city's only hill of note; all the better, Jaana surmised, to make it look as if it truly touched the limits of the sky.

The companions had waited for almost the entire day in the queue of citizens that had grown along the winding road up to the church in order to petition the brotherhood of priests. Jaana had whiled away much of the time listening to the quietly hopeful conversations of those around her. Some people had come to ask for justice or retribution following some crime or other, while others intending to request that their souls be prayed for, as if guilt or remorse hung heavy upon their shoulders. By and large they remained patient, and those few who showed intolerance with having to wait and occasionally shuffle forward in the chilly wind were quickly hushed and reprimanded by the obedient majority.

Jaana looked occasionally towards the great complex shape of the church, its ramparts, towers and arched windows, where sometimes priests could be seen stopping to watch the tail of human misery that made up the day's petitioners. *They must know the futility of what's being asked of them by many here,* she reasoned. *But they continue anyway. They tighten the noose regardless.*

By the time the companions had reached the outer doors into the main worship hall, the billowing high cloud had dispersed and the last of the afternoon sunlight spilled out over the hill, eerie against the backdrop of dark grey storm clouds to the north. The guards took their weapons from them as they were admitted- normal practice, Fistelkarn had told her- and they were directed forward to a raised dais at the far end of the worship hall where three priests sat in attendance. The archpriest, who sat between the other two, looked aged but severe and strong- cruel, Jaana thought as she took in his look of continuous distaste. The two seated on either side of him were younger, with shaved heads and white and red robes that contrasted sharply with the archpriest's black and grey. Jaana spent only a moment in observation, then cast her eyes to the floor and feigned interest in the black and white marble tiles instead.

"Speak," the priest on the left said sharply, as Fistelkarn stepped forward and motioned for the others to wait. The old man gave a short, untidy bow, which caused a murmur of displeasure amongst the two younger priests even as the same half-hearted gesture elicited a smile of amusement from the archpriest.

"My name is Fistelkarn," he spoke up, "known in the middle lands as Fistelkarn of the Round Tower. You may..."

"Have heard of you?" the archpriest cut across suddenly, leaning forward. "Yes. *Yes*." He peered at Fistelkarn for a moment, then sat back and uttered a dry laugh. "I have. We all have. You're a trickster, a student of past Ages, and a collector of artefacts. You are also a man of considerable insolence, waiting a day to pass these doors and stand before us in wilful ignorance of correct protocol!"

The priest on his left, whose dark, close-set eyes glittered with anger, stood up. "You *will* kneel before His Worship, Archpriest Herath, petitioner. Kneel!"

Jaana could not see anything of Fistelkarn's expression, but it seemed to her that the old man bristled with rage of his own as he slowly acquiesced to the demands of Herath's underling. Herath watched him awhile as he knelt, and finally, perhaps bored with the spectacle, commanded him to rise. Fistelkarn did so, slowly and painfully.

"I grow weary of you already," the archpriest complained. "Speak what you will, creature, then take your lackeys with you and get out."

"Nisstar will fall in days," Fistelkarn told him. "If you value your lives- more so, if you value the lives of your people- then you have to listen to me."

"You *threaten* the One Church?" The archpriest looked understandably aghast.

"You must do two things. Firstly, peace must somehow be made with the Rising, and reparations made for the injustices against the *luyan* and other Races who were forced to flee Nisstar or become slaves. Secondly, this city must be abandoned. Indeed, the city must be abandoned regardless of your feud with other Races."

All three men stared at him incredulously. Finally, even as his underlings laughed and shook their heads, encouraging the surrounding guardsmen to do likewise, Herath stared grimly at Fistelkarn. "You dare to mock me, you pitiful hermit? You dare to mock this bastion of civilised people?"

"No. I am telling you only what will come to pass." Fistelkarn looked slowly around at the multitude of swordsmen and archers lining the shadowy edges of the worship hall. Dozens of arrows remained aimed directly towards him. "Your people must love you greatly," he remarked, "for you to keep your guardsmen lurking wherever I look. If you would do one thing for the masses, do this: heed my words. Make peace, but even if peace cannot be made, abandon Nisstar."

Herath blinked in bewilderment, and then looked left and right. "Fistelkarn's army has us surrounded!" he exclaimed, eliciting polite laughter from some of the guardsmen.

"Perhaps a quarter of the people within these city walls are, as we speak, lying in a state of everlasting sleep or of walking madness," Fistelkarn remarked, and the archpriest's contemptuous smile faded as the sorcerer continued quietly, "Would you care to know the cause?"

"I would care to know your theory," Herath said, and motioned for him to continue.

Jaana listened as Fistelkarn proceeded to methodically tell what he knew of the *marandaal,* of the time in the First Age when they had found their way to Aona, and a decades-long war had ensued. He told the story well; even Herath's two minions grew serious and contemplative as he spoke of the events leading up to that invasion, of lunacy, disease and chaos. *They are listening,* Jaana thought, hardly daring to believe her eyes. *They're not dismissing it out of hand.*

"There is every likelihood that Gates shall form and *open* somewhere within Nisstar," Fistelkarn said finally, "and when they do, the *marandaal* reach out into the land. As before, it will take all the Races, united, to defeat them."

He's missing part of the tale, Jaana thought suddenly, *and I think he's missing it deliberately.* From what Fistelkarn had told her and the others previously, the Races were still blood-slaves to the *choragh* during that distant time. Only centuries afterwards did they overthrow their masters.

So in truth, legions of choragh *and their kin led the war against the* marandaal, Jaana reminded herself, recalling Fistelkarn's words during their journey to Nisstar. *But that tale would do no good if it were told here.*

Fistelkarn's story had caused a ripple of unease throughout the worship hall. Jaana had hoped it would, having suspected that these people, like everyone else she had come across, could not even begin to fathom the reason for what had happened to so many of their folk. *The priests have surely blamed it on evil spirits,* she thought, *but they think they can defeat them. They think their One-God will give them powers to do so.*

"An interesting tale," Herath admitted, "and I'll admit there may be a grain of truth in the legend. But we are not about to break bread with outlaws and abandon this great city simply because an old man from the hills has come down here to tell us a good story."

"Then what will it take you?" Fistelkarn asked bluntly.

"Such action requires proof. How will you supply it?"

Fistelkarn turned and motioned to Ludas, who reluctantly shuffled forward, keeping his eyes steadfastly upon the polished marble floor. "This man can read the dreams of those who are lost in unending sleep," he said, which caused an even louder murmur of consternation to ripple through everyone gathered in the hall. "He may even be able to entice them to speak of what they see, to describe what they *feel* as they drift helplessly. If they speak of *marandaal* or the Great Light, or Gates..." Fistelkarn stared up at the archpriest. "Will you listen then?"

Herath took a moment to consider. "Priests Arin and Jon"- he indicated the two priests to either side in turn- "will stand in attendance whilst you attempt to show such evidence. A messenger will come to you with details of where you are to do this." He turned to the other priests. "Attend and observe," he said simply. "If such things as this man has described are mentioned, you will document everything that you see, everything that you hear, and then let me know with all due haste."

He turned back to Fistelkarn. "Be gone, all of you. A messenger will come to you tomorrow."

"We are staying at..." Fistelkarn began, but Herath cut him off. "I know where you are staying. You've been watched since you made your way through the city gates."

V

Even before they set out into Nisstar's streets the morning after the message arrived for them from Herath, Jaana felt the need to pull down the hood of her cloak so that when she bowed her head, very little could be seen of her face. It was not the fear of being seen that moved her to do this, but the continuously oppressive feeling she had had ever since the four of them had entered the city. This was a place, she reckoned, where all it might take for someone to attack them would be a glance in the wrong direction at the wrong man. Many of the folk in this city seemed to be restless, listless, and possessed of an underlying fear and frustration that might easily boil over into violence.

And all this despite their Church overlords having banished luyan *and other races from the city,* she thought, *which was by some accounts a decision favoured by most of*

143

these people. What more do they want? They worship at the altars of the Church, the Church preaches piety and goodwill- on the face of it- and yet there's a quiet malevolence to this entire place. It runs in the veins of the populace; it seeps through the walls of their buildings.

She shuddered and took a few deep breaths of the cold air to calm herself, standing back and rubbing her hands together as Tyrameer helped saddle her horse outside the stable. Jaana was still at best an average rider and reckoned she would never feel completely at ease on horseback. She watched with envy as Tyrameer prepared her mount with the greatest of ease. He barely appeared to look at what he was doing and still managed to do a fine job as far as she could tell.

"There!" he exclaimed with a grin, which faded as he glanced at her. "We'll not wait for long in this place, Jaana. Fistelkarn wants to leave as much as we do. But we have to try and show these priests that those afflicted..." He shrugged. "Well, we all know why we're here. But we'll be gone once we've..."

"Once we've failed," Jaana said quietly. Despite Herath's words the other day, she felt despondent about their chances.

Tyrameer helped lead her horse outside into the paddock. "We'll at least try," he said. "And then, either way, we'll be gone."

If we make it to Alinnora's Haven, Jaana thought as Tyrameer helped her into the saddle, *and we are reunited with Lyya and Fauli- what then for us? If these* marandaal *are returning, if the Old Dark is rising, what future can there be?*

She considered the options. They could flee to some remote part of the land, perhaps, or another part of the world entirely, somewhere that had yet to be touched by this evil...

Jaana smiled humourlessly to herself. That was the only option she could think of. To flee; to find somewhere so remote that even the vast reach of war could not find her.

You're a coward, a voice within taunted her. *You have a talent that others can't even comprehend, but you fear it and you'd rather do anything than use or even try to understand it.*

It's a meaningless defence against marandaal, she silently rejoined. *Useless!*

"Are you all right, Jaana?" Tyrameer enquired.

Jaana almost jumped. She had not been aware that he still stood nearby. "I will be," she said, "once we leave this city."

Their morning journey was a slow one. Jaana was glad that her horse had shown herself to be a calm and patient beast even amongst the throng of people that threaded their way along the streets and criss-crossed the squares and marketplaces. She was also relieved that they had elected to ride to the infirmary. Although she could never feel safe here, she felt a little calmer on horseback than she would have done on foot.

Jaana did her best to keep her eyes averted and her concentration solely on the way ahead but found several times that her gaze was drawn to macabre or odd sights, such as a low, grey building with many windows, all of which looked dark with grease and condensation, as if they were sweating. Yet this was no place of industry; no steam emerged from the array of chimneys. At first she had no idea what function the building might perform, until she saw the emaciated remains of a body on a makeshift stretcher being delivered to a side entrance of the place.

"The quiet dying," Fistelkarn said from near her side. Jaana thought of asking him what he meant, but instead just asked herself. The *quiet dying?* Those who simply fell asleep and failed to wake, perhaps. The body she had seen looked half-rotted, as if it had lain somewhere for days before discovery.

Further along the way, they encountered men or women who had seemingly singled out their group for attention. They stared from a distance, stumbled nearer, reached out their hands- Jaana could not tell if they were begging or trying to grasp at them, for the gestures looked like both at once- and all the while these people had about them the heat of fever and a wild, unknowable look in their eyes. One woman bared her teeth and snapped at the air when Tyrameer kicked away her outstretched arm with his boot. *"Starlight, starlight,"* she sang after him as they hastened onwards. *"Starlight, death light, death light..."* And then even that cracked yet strident voice thankfully became lost in the babble of the crowd.

The infirmary was a squat, ugly building of dark grey stone and few windows, built in an area of cleared land near the centre of the city. Arin waited in the courtyard with three guardsmen. He looked restless and impatient, and after their horses had been led to the stables nearby, he took them through the main entrance and into the building at a pace that did nothing to conceal his wish to be elsewhere. The guardsmen marched along behind, boots echoing harshly in the narrow hallways through which they passed.

"To the far end," Ludas whispered as they walked along. Fistelkarn caught his arm and turned the dreamreader half around, eliciting a mutter of annoyance from Arin as everyone had to stop. "You're certain?"

"As certain as I can be. Many of those here are fading. Others burn brightly. One burns brighter than the others." Ludas turned his head slowly to look down the passageway. "Inside, he's like a human torch. His mind burns so brightly." Jaana saw a look upon his face which might have been mistaken for longing.

The priest stared at Ludas and then looked to Fistelkarn for an answer. "What is he talking about?"

"One of those who were brought here." Fistelkarn motioned for the priest to continue down the corridor. "Whoever it is, they will make a good subject for Ludas' talent."

Eventually they reached a part of the infirmary where the doors to the rooms had been daubed with splashes of black paint. "Those who have become violent are kept here," the priest explained as he saw them taking in the sight. "Some of them have lost their minds entirely..."

"Would it not be a mercy to put them to peaceful death?" Jaana asked coldly, then bit her lip; she ought to have thought before speaking.

"Murder is not God's way." Arin's lips smiled at her; his eyes looked full of contempt that she could propose such a thing.

They turned down a side passage and then another. Jaana could not tell whether or not their passing by agitated the patients in their cells, but many of them stirred as the eight visitors walked by; she heard a woman cry out, a man run into the door as if he had no idea it was even there, and worst of all, someone whose gender or age she could not even hope to guess at, a lost creature whose low moans became a ululating shriek of utter despair in the time it took her to walk five or six steps.

Sitting outside one of the cells on a wooden box was the other priest Jaana recognised from the previous day: Jon. He sat with shaven head bowed slightly and hands pressed palm to palm with fingers raised towards the mildew-marked ceiling, in silent supplication to his God.

The other priest stood and waited until Jon raised his head and turned to beckon them nearer. "Forgive me," he said, "but as you can see, they've come as bidden, to..."

"To mock us in the eyes of God. Yes." Jon smiled humourlessly at Fistelkarn. "Are you ready to have your minion perform his trickery, old man? It will make an interesting sight."

"In one thing, then, we are agreed." Fistelkarn turned to Ludas. "Are we near?"

Ludas pointed to the door opposite the one nearest to where Jon had been sitting. His hand trembled violently. "There," he said. "In there. He burns so brightly inside..."

Jon walked across and peered through the bars of the grille. "This one? He's one of the sleepers."

"I know." Ludas waited with visible agitation as Jon unlocked the door and pushed it open. Muck and rust scraped over the floor. A stale odour pervaded the room into which the companions walked.

As Ludas moved forward, Fistelkarn grabbed his arm and said something to him in a low voice. Jaana could not be entirely sure what was spoken, but it sounded like: *You had better... or I'll make you suffer.* Whatever it might have been, Ludas averted his eyes and said nothing in response. At Fistelkarn's command he walked to the patient's bedside. Jaana glanced at Jon and Arin, who stood near the foot of the bed and fixed their attention on Ludas. *Either they believe nothing about dreamreaders,* Jaana thought, *or they think of them as tricksters or sorcerers. But that's exactly what we expected.*

Ludas, meanwhile, saw none of this, for his attention had become fixed upon the old, frail form lying on the bed. After a moment he reached out his right hand and placed it just a fingernail's length above the fevered forehead. Then, he closed his eyes and bowed his head.

He remained thus for what felt like an age. No one in the room so much as moved a muscle: not even the priests.

Then something extraordinary and terrifying happened. The air in the bedchamber somehow became *thinner,* and for a short while it was almost impossible to breathe. Jaana gasped as colours and shapes swarmed around at the perimeter of her vision. *I can't survive this,* the thought shrieked over and over in her mind, as her legs started to buckle.

Abruptly everything returned to normal, as if all the air that had been somehow spirited from the room came rushing back in a single instant. Everyone gave a gasp of relief. Arin, who looked about to stagger over and pull Ludas away from the patient, threw a furious glance at Fistelkarn as if it might have been his doing.

Ludas had now collapsed so that his head lay upon the stomach of the bedridden man, while his right hand lay flat and trembling upon his forehead. The patient had neither stirred nor uttered so much as a whisper, yet his mouth now hung wide open, and Jaana fancied that he had somehow, just for that brief period, spirited away a proportion of the air in the room. *That can't be so,* she told herself, but a voice inside her countered those words immediately: *Have you not already seen things that were just as incredible? Will you now disbelieve them as well?*

A low, barely audible hum started up; Jaana could not tell if it emanated from Ludas, the man on the bed or somewhere between the two of them, as if a new, shared voice had been created. Listening to it, Jaana felt certain that it constituted fragmented images and words, ideas and concepts. *Dreams,* she thought suddenly, *but also much more than dreams. It's like a thousand rhythms playing at the same time...*

"From the other side of the Existence," she whispered, but no one heard her.

The man on the bed suddenly sat bolt upright, without using any support from his arms. It was as if he had been pulled to a sitting position by unseen rope. His mouth opened even wider, so much so that Jaana thought his jaw might break.

"To cleanse all places of the life that came before," the patient murmured. *"The path has been found. The path has been found."* Blood began to flow from his eyes and made red tears that gleamed in the lantern light.

"Enough! This is possession!" Jon shouted, and as Ludas suddenly roused himself, the patient slumped back with a sigh. Mercifully he said nothing more.

Beneath the terror that the man's monotonous words had stirred within her, Jaana found herself sickened by the entire scene. What were they hoping to achieve through this? The priesthood would not, could not be swayed in their view; the man could have floated half a dozen hands above his sickbed and the priests would have called it possession, or trickery, or sorcery, or more than likely all three.

Perhaps it is a kind of possession, she thought, *but not the sort they could ever understand.*

"*If* this man suffers some intrusion by a spirit, we shall tear it from him," Jon continued more quietly. "I cannot be certain, however, whether or not this is simply trickery." He turned to Fistelkarn, perhaps more confident now that the patient had fallen back onto his bed. "I have heard about you, old man. For decades you have meddled and tricked and involved yourself in matters that are the domain of *only* the legal authorities..."

"It's no trickery," Ludas murmured as he staggered to his feet. "Your talk of spirits is nonsense..."

"Silence him," Jon said to the nearest of the guardsmen, who strode over and struck Ludas on the head with the flat of his shortsword. The blow was hard enough to make a resounding crack, and the dreamreader sagged to the floor, blood dripping between his fingers as he held his head in his hands.

"Arrest these people," Jon said to the guardsmen.

As the three guardsmen reached for Ludas, and then Fistelkarn, Tyrameer drew his sword, but he failed to see the younger priest move at his side and stab him in the ribs with a small, jagged knife. Tyrameer gasped and stumbled. Fistelkarn shouted something, and suddenly the lantern light in the room was extinguished.

In the utter darkness, Jaana heard the clashing of blades, punches being thrown, gasps of pain. She could smell blood, but something else too: something bitter, pungent, acrid. *Poison,* she thought dully.

Survive, Jaana told herself over and over as she backed away into the nearest corner, which she already knew was just a few paces behind her. She held her hands over her face, fearful of a blade suddenly arcing through the air to cut her to ribbons.

The chaos persisted only for a short while. Finally, Jaana heard one man only, painfully dragging himself across the floor, gasping in pain. She could not say who it was, for the room remained lightless.

She heard him reach the door, stagger to his feet and pull at the door handle, then fall to the floor.

Then everything became still, and utterly silent.

Jaana waited a while longer as panic-stricken thoughts rushed around in her mind. Finally she moved from the corner on her hands and knees for fear of tripping over a body. All the while, questions chased one another through her mind: *Is everyone dead? How can that be? Will I be able to open the door? What if I'm locked in here until someone comes to check on the priests and the guards?*

What if Tyrameer and Fistelkarn are dead?

A numbing fear and a need to be out of this place overwhelmed all other thoughts. She reached a body, flinched and cried out as her hand touched a wet, open wound, and then she stood up and felt her way along the wall until she found the door and then the door handle.

Please, by all the powers that are, let me out of here...

She pulled, and the door opened slowly, protesting. Light poured through. Once her eyes had adjusted, Jaana opened the door further, and then, despite her fears about what she might see, she looked down and around her.

The body by her feet was that of one of the guardsmen. Further into the room, Jaana saw the bodies of

Tyrameer and Fistelkarn, the other guardsmen and the two priests. Blood spattered the floor in places.

Jaana walked a little closer and knelt by Tyrameer. His neck had been slashed. The amount of blood around him made her feel faint. She swallowed and turned away, tears brimming in her eyes, then stared in wordless horror at Fistelkarn, who had been disembowelled.

Dead, she thought numbly. *All dead. I'm on my own now.*

A sudden, discomforting thought occurred to her. Where was Ludas? She couldn't see his body anywhere, but he couldn't simply have melted through the wall, so where was he?

As she stared into the dim furthest recesses of the cell, someone moved from under the bed. Jaana took a step back towards the doorway as she saw Ludas emerge from his hiding place, wide-eyed and trembling.

"Jaana," he whimpered imploringly as she took another step back.

"You have to help me," he said, as if that was the only choice left to her. Jaana stared at him. *I should have known he would survive,* she thought. *I should have known.*

Ludas managed to sit up. Rivulets of blood dripped down one side of his head. Jaana backed all the way out of the cell and saw a look of utter dismay upon his face. "Help me," he murmured, and reached out an arm. "We only have each other..."

"I have no one," she said, and pulled the door closed, leaving him shut in with darkness and death his companions. The dreamreader uttered a shriek of rage, and she heard him scramble in desperation towards the door. Swiftly she put the thick metal bar in place to prevent his escape.

Then, not wishing to hear his fury nor indeed anything from him ever again, she turned and ran.

VI – The Last Light Burning

I

Nia had no doubt that this remained the grandest sight in the world.

Less than a half-league away stood the great city of Luudhoq, a sprawling expanse marked with vast towers, turrets and fortresses of all shapes and sizes. The city extended all around the bay, into which the wide Fhaarluy River passed, under a multitude of bridges, each one different in design and build to its neighbours. Luudhoq in its entirety sparkled in the morning sun almost as brightly as the ocean, and Nia smiled broadly, taking a deep breath of salt air as she drank in the sight of home.

"Welcome to Luudhoq," she said, glancing around at her companions. "Is this not the most beautiful place you have ever seen?" Without waiting for their response, she strode on, eager to be inside the city walls.

They reached the east-facing gates with the sun still climbing in the sky. After a short delay during which Nia's identity was checked with another of the star-shaped objects, they were admitted, and with the day still relatively young they found themselves in the heart of the Cobbles. This area, just to the east of Luudhoq's centre, was where most of the Guilds were situated as well as the imposing fortress known as the Sanctum where the Watchers and the Seven resided. Nia reckoned it to be her favourite part of the city. Today, as she glanced up at the vast walls of the Sanctum, which towered over the area, she was reminded once again of the prize she had brought, a prize for which she would surely be handsomely rewarded. *Kelandra is a harsh taskmaster but a fair one,* she reasoned. *She can make the discovery her own and be rewarded by her own masters.*

153

Prior to their arrival, Nia had spent some time deciding which of the local taverns her companions should stay at. She had opted for the *Anchor and Spyglass* at the edge of the Cobbles. It was suitably large, comfortable and not too expensive, but more important than that, she knew the innkeeper, Marc, who owed her a favour in return for her choosing not to report certain illegal dealings that had taken place in his establishment. Of course, Nia had ensured that she had Kelandra's blessing before she engaged in this blackmail- "He can be of great use to us from time to time," she had pointed out, "for if you look at the list of crimes he has allowed to take place- the man has smuggled and distributed almost everything criminal that he could- he could easily spend the rest of his years in the Sanctum dungeons. He knows that if he puts a foot wrong, we have the evidence to condemn him."

Kelandra had agreed, for she knew perfectly well that it was often much better to use and extort rather than simply arrest and be done with the matter.

And one such favour will be called imminently, Nia thought as she glanced across at Alexia, who had already been distracted by the vast array of market stalls on each side of the street. *Look on and be dazzled,* Nia silently invited her, *because soon I will be rid of you.*

They took their time reaching the *Anchor and Spyglass;* Nia was happy enough to wait patiently as the other three allowed themselves to be distracted by the multitude of wares for sale along the way. At one point she took the opportunity to purchase a few small items, making sure as she did so that none of her companions looked her way.

When they arrived at the tavern later that afternoon, Nia made her excuses once they had found a table and went around to the rear of the building in the knowledge that she would be likely to find Marc in the gaming room. She paused briefly, remembering her appearance. *I'll be a colleague of Nia's,* she thought with a smile. *Another blackmailer.*

"A word or two, if you please," she said politely, opening the door to the room once she heard Marc's voice from within. "An official matter," she added, for effect.

Marc hurriedly sent the three other fellows on their way and closed the door behind them. He waited until certain that they had departed the inn, then turned reluctantly to face her. "What's this about? You used the exact same words as..."

"Nia? Of course I did. I know the same things about you that she does. I work closely with her." Nia grinned at him.

"Have I displeased your mistress Kelandra in some way? I've done nothing to attract her attention, to my knowledge." He tried to appear nonchalant, but Nia had already noticed beads of perspiration on his forehead and under his eyes.

"Believe me, you would already know if you had displeased her," she reminded him, which was true. "You've done nothing you need worry about. But I do need a small favour from you."

"Of course." He relaxed a little.

Nia sat down and motioned for him to do the same. Once he was seated, she leaned forward and said quietly, "I've brought three companions with me today. They are sitting in the front bar-room right now. A man and his young daughter, and a woman roughly my age. Shortish black hair, badly cut. When you go in there, which will be after I've finished talking to you, you will see them. Pay particular attention to the woman, without her noticing you of course. I need her to be..." Nia frowned, choosing her words carefully. "I need her to be moved to another part of the city altogether. This is how you will do it."

She delved into her belt pouch and pulled out a small packet containing a brown powder. "You will sprinkle a little of this- no more than a sprinkle, so *this* much"- she picked a little between finger and thumb to show him- "into each glass of wine she drinks this evening. I will purchase each of these drinks myself- they haven't a silver star between them. You will indicate to me the glass to which this powder has been added, each time. Now, you must add only a *little* whenever you do so- just a pinch- because that will make her sleep heavily later, rather than fall asleep at the table. We *do not* want it to appear as if she has been affected in any extraordinary way. Perhaps she'll be a little more tired than usual, but then we have been travelling for a long time, so that would hardly be out of the ordinary. Do you understand me so far?"

He nodded his head quickly.

"Good. Now, wait for a while after the four of us have retired to our chambers. Then, making as little sound as possible, use your key to her chamber and with the help of one of your men, pick her up, take her outside through the back way and through the yard to the alley beyond. Choose someone strong who can work deftly enough and not be clumsy about the task, and who *will* keep his mouth shut. At the end of the alley- the Spiral Street end- a horse and cart will be waiting. You need only pass her to the men who will be with the cart." Nia sat back, arms folded.

Marc blinked, running a hand through his thinning hair. "That's it?"

"That is it." Nia smiled. "It is, as I said, only a small favour, and according to Nia such a task is well within your capabilities- wouldn't you say?"

He bobbed his head in agreement. As Nia suspected, his relief at having only such a minor task to perform had lent a certain enthusiasm for it.

She left the tavern a little later, having explained to her companions that she was going to organise a day for Yui to be seen by her physician friend- *As if I'm friends with physicians,* she thought with a smile- and made her way across the city towards one of the less salubrious establishments in Luudhoq, a guest-house called the *Spear,* which in fact served as the front for a brothel. Nia knew the madam of the place, a woman by the name of Mirram, and she had traded information with her several times. Mirram had often turned out to be brimful of useful knowledge, particularly concerning the West Square area which bordered the infamous Shallows district, and Nia suspected she would be glad to receive a form of payment for services rendered in the past.

Before she arrived at the brothel, Nia slipped into the darkness of an abandoned outhouse and *shifted,* shivering in the damp cold as she quickly dressed afterwards and headed on. Marc was a fearful man who could be coerced by someone claiming to be a comrade of Nia's. The same would not work with Mirram, who simply refused to entertain the thought of business with any man, whoever he claimed to be, unless he had come to relieve his desired with one of her girls. *I doubt I'd even get past the front gates unless I was a client,* Nia thought.

"I have a new girl for you," she said as soon as they were seated together in one of Mirram's private chambers with a glass of white wine each.

Mirram merely nodded, but the look in her eyes gave her away. A new girl was always a good way to drum up interest. A new girl could be priced more highly.

"She is Hastian," Nia continued, and saw the price to her clients increase further in the brothel madam's eyes. For a moment she considered telling her about Alexia's unusual heritage; Harn had no royal or ruling family of course, and never had, but the very novelty of Alexia's upbringing might make her more exotic in the eyes of men- and some women. But she decided against saying any more on the matter. *This time, a little is enough,* she reasoned.

"What do you want in return?" Mirram said bluntly, remembering her common sense.

"Nothing." Nia spread her hands expansively. "I simply want to reward you for previous services."

Mirram smiled thinly. "I know you too well, Nia. You give nothing freely unless you must. We've dealt honestly for years- I ask you not to treat me as a fool."

Nia held up a hand to apologise. "You're right, Mirram. We do know each other better. Well, the truth is I'm not sure what I do want. I only returned to Luudhoq yesterday. No doubt my mistress will have a mountain of tasks for me, and I'm sure some will require your help. But I can't yet say what these might be."

Mirram nodded. "Then explain why you are giving me this girl."

"Truthfully, she's a thorn in my side, someone who cannot be allowed to interfere with another task of mine. I was hoping that I could have her delivered to you late tonight. I'll need you to spare a few of your servants and a cart, to have her brought here. She will be taken from the *Anchor and Spyglass,* to the end of the alleyway just near the tavern, which joins with Spiral Street." Nia calculated silently for a moment. "At Ildar-rise, if you can. The night should be clear. Do with her as you wish, but whatever you do, make sure that she can't escape. Can you do that?"

Mirram thought, but only for a moment. "I can. But you already knew that." Observing Nia briefly, she added, "You realise, of course, that many of the men who come here have..." A flicker of a smile crossed her features. "They have *particular* needs. This girl may find life here difficult to adjust to."

"Indeed she may," Nia agreed, "but her welfare is not my concern. I have more pressing issues to deal with."

They discussed other matters briefly. Odd things were happening in the Shallows; forbidden witchcraft, Mirram thought. The Guild had finally appointed a successor to the deceased arch-principal Charin, but the man chosen was not the favoured candidate amongst the Watchers and the Seven. Mirram thought he might last a week or two before he met a curious end. Elsewhere, rumours were circulating of a gathering of rebellious forces in the town of Waylorn, but Nia paid little attention to that. Rumours of rebellion were stirred up all the time as a reminder to the general population that although the South lived in peace and harmony, malevolent influences still clung to the shadows and plotted against the might of the Seven.

If such revolutionaries truly existed, Nia thought, which they might, then they were perhaps more delusional than malevolent. No one plotted against the Seven and then carried through with their plan; no one in the civilised South, anyway. Certain things were certain for all time, and the Seven was one of them.

Are seven of them, she corrected herself with a smile.

Nia left a short while later and made her way back to the *Anchor and Spyglass* as afternoon became evening and the street lanterns were lit. The weather had worsened, and cold rain slanted across the market square as she hurried across to the brightness and laughter of the tavern, male once again. Despite the unusual chill in the air, Nia barely noticed these inclement conditions; this time tomorrow, she would have dealt with her remaining problem and told Kelandra all about the prize she had brought back with her from Darkenhelm.

II

"Wake up!"

Alexia heard that word as if from the bottom of a deep well; its utterance pulled her half-out of some murky, insubstantial dream. Then it came again, harsher this time, insistent, impatient.

Her eyelids fluttered open. For a while she lay on the bed in silent confusion, trying to work out where she was. This room looked different to the one she had retired to. *I*

159

went to bed, she recalled, *but I'm sure it was not this bed, not even this room. Or did I wander into the wrong room by mistake? Maybe, if it had been left unlocked. Gods, how much did I drink?!*

Footsteps sounded from somewhere near the foot of the bed. She managed to lift her head enough to see a plain, dumpy little woman appraising her. Suddenly Alexia realised that she was lying on top of the bed without a shred of clothing on, and swiftly moved her hands to cover what she could.

"Well," the woman said flatly, just as Alexia opened her mouth to apologise, "you've been thoroughly inspected and you seem clean enough."

Alexia stared at her in stupefaction.

"And a virgin too- at your age!" the woman exclaimed, then folded her arms and shook her head as if in remonstration. "You're pretty enough, although your hair will need some attention. I cannot think any man would find it attractive. Tell me, how old *are* you?"

She moved to the side of the bed and repeated the question when Alexia just stared at her.

"I... I'm twenty-three." Alexia swallowed, trying to keep herself calm. "Look, I think I must have slept in the wrong bedchamber. Is this yours? If so, I can only apologise, I have no idea how I wandered in here..."

Her voice trailed away as the woman looked her up and down from tip to toe. Alexia felt even more heat rise to her cheeks and tried again to place one hand and one forearm strategically, which seemed to amuse the woman. "You've no reason to be coy with me, girl. You've been inspected thoroughly already, as I said. Of course, you'll be coy and childish with the men if they demand it, but only if and when. My name is Mirram, by the way. I suspect we will get to know each other very well over the coming weeks."

"Mirram." Alexia shook her head, utterly confused. "Wait... what do you mean? What men are you talking about?"

"Hush and listen. You should know the rules of my house, the most important of which are these: firstly, you always obey me. Secondly, whatever a client should happen to want, you give. If you perform well, you will be given enough food and drink. Perhaps even *kyush,* should you wish it. Do you smoke it at all?"

Alexia shook her head again. *I'm dreaming,* she thought. *This is all some mad dream.*

"You may want to consider the habit," Mirram advised. "Many of my women swear by it. Now to the third rule, although you may think of it more as a promise. If you are difficult or unhelpful in any way, if you disappoint a client..." She shrugged. "Well, the first time, I suppose you'll get off quite lightly. You'll be given a good beating. But the second time, I'm afraid you will lose something. A finger, perhaps. Something you could live without. But the third time, your loss will be significant. A hand, a breast, or even an eye. And so on. Do you understand?"

Alexia stared at her in wordless horror.

"I don't care for those who play dumb to my questions, girl. So I'll ask you again- do you understand?"

"Yes," Alexia whispered, and then: "Where am I?"

"This is my whorehouse," Mirram told her, "and you belong to me."

III

A thousand instruments shimmered, ticked or oscillated as Kelandra made her way unhurriedly through the Hall of Measurement and into the large, tiered chamber where a few of her colleagues had already gathered. They were waiting to be admitted into the Sunset Ceremony which took place every tennight without fail, but most looked distracted by other matters.

Of course, Kelandra reminded herself, such distraction was only to be expected- the truth was that everyone's thoughts *were* on other matters. Routine, order and discipline, the cornerstones of the Watchers' hierarchy, remained constant as ever, but thoughts strayed as never before. Those who had been in the Hall of Measurement or nearby when the *new disturbance* happened had probably pondered little else during these last few days. Calculations had been made, discussions had sparked other discussions, and a couple of debates about the nature of the forces involved had already sprung up.

Kelandra glanced back briefly at those instruments which had been broken, many of them irreparably. Even now as she observed, a few Watchers valiantly attempted to fix the unfixable surrounded by hundreds of diverse components, many of which had melted or fused. A few had even been made dangerously unpredictable and had been placed within special containers, which themselves had been borne away to more secure areas for research.

Who was it that first sensed the shifting? she mused. *Louden, I believe. And he has disappeared now; nobody knows where he has gone. But the Keys did nothing at that point. No, the shock, the ripple, arrived much later. Yet Louden sensed it before it arrived, somehow, as did three others.*

She frowned and wondered what that must have been like, then where Louden might be, but only briefly. Neither his whereabouts nor his welfare was any concern of hers.

A darkness touched us even here, Kelandra thought. Something reached out from the void, having found Aona at long last. It reached into Luudhoq- unthinkable!- and in that moment, everyone present here in the Sanctum must have recognised that long, familiar shadow. We can never forget the marandaal, *and they will never forget us.*

Although, she noted, *some Watchers had forgotten the name entirely, and have had to be reminded.* She frowned, curious for a moment as to why that might be.

Kelandra had not been one of those lucky or unlucky enough to witness that movement of forces- she had been on her way back from an assignment in the region next to the Shallows district when this had happened, and therefore still on the other side of the city- but like everyone else within the Sanctum she had heard of almost nothing but that reverberation since. It had also made her aware of something new, namely that some of the devices in the Hall of Measurement had originally been made specifically for such an event as this, although as such an event was impossible to conjure up, to *replicate,* no one could have known precisely the effect it would have.

It was, apparently, something that had not been common knowledge previously, which itself had become another topic of argument.

But the Seven persist forever, she reminded herself. *They are truly immortal. So they may have taken the view that sooner or later, the* marandaal *would come. The laws of numbers dictated it.*

In the meantime, the human population outside the walls of the Watchers' fortress knew nothing of this, had not felt even the slightest hint of it. That amused Kelandra but in a strange way it also frustrated her. Their blissful ignorance, their inability to feel the subtle weaves that held together the world they all thought they knew, was a measure of the vast gulf between Watchers and those they watched over. The city folk continued with their largely humdrum lives as they always had, at least since the Seven and the High Watchers had arrived in Harn more than a thousand years ago to shine the light of civilisation upon them. She suspected that uppermost in their minds at the moment was the unseasonal chilly weather. Luudhoq's winters were normally short, mild and wet and swiftly gave way to a long, warm spring, but this year winter had arrived early and with unexpected bitterness. Sleet had even fallen on a few days.

Kelandra took a seat in one of the upper tiers of the antechamber and listened for a while to the debate on the central floor. Juran was reasoning that once enough events such as the *new disturbance* had occurred- for it was undoubtedly a sign of Gates and what lay beyond them- it would be possible to pinpoint the time and the location of the next one with a certain degree of accuracy, by observing the ways in which the elemental forces reacted to the first such event. With a small but deft weave, he had drawn diagrams in the air before him, a skilful act with which she would normally have been as fascinated as her colleagues in the lower tiers. It went without saying that such a display of logic and reasoning, backed up with evidence, ought to command the attention of everyone who had gathered here today.

Yet her thoughts drifted elsewhere, as they had done since the event that had sparked this hitherto unparalleled level of discussion and worry.

Great plans had, it was said, already been devised in response to the *new disturbance,* the surest sign yet that *marandaal* had somehow found a pathway to Aona. The Seven had conferred; the High Watchers had spoken of the *marandaal* and what might be done to defeat them, though in little detail. Kelandra knew her history and therefore knew that more than three thousand Aonan years had passed since her race and the *marandaal* had last fought. *Last time, we were defeated and were chased and hounded across the Existence,* she thought, as she recalled passages she had learned from *Journeys.*

And the pursuit has never truly ended. It never will until one side is destroyed for all time.

164

News of what had started to happen in Aphenhast had reached the remaining Watchers. Sooner or later a version of that same news might be released to the populace of Luudhoq, but that would be later and only if and when necessary. That news would of course be wrapped in a proclamation about what would be done to ensure the safety of Harn.

The very thought of *marandaal* being so near chilled Kelandra to her core. Watchers, she reminded herself, did not- *could* not- feel outright fear as humans did. Except that was not exactly true.

Kelandra wondered briefly where others of her kind might be, somewhere in the incomprehensible vastness of the Existence. Had they come to places such as this, or were they still wandering, lost? Had the *marandaal* found them already and annihilated them? *Journeys* and the other texts with which she had been fascinated for years had little to say on the matter. Kelandra judged that the Seven and the High Watchers had been far too busy fleeing from world to world- for although the Seven could not be killed, certainly they could be harmed by the *marandaal*- to spend time detailing the horrors of *marandaal* pursuit.

She sensed that almost every Watcher was certain they *could* defeat the *marandaal* if necessary- and surely it would be necessary at some point, when their enemies firstly forced their way into Aphenhast and inevitably turned their collective gaze westwards to Harn. Any fear they felt was of the *marandaal* themselves, their enemies since before time itself had been measured.

Marandaal, on the other hand, did not and could not feel fear or emotion of any kind, from the little she knew of them.

Kelandra did not entirely share the confidence of her people, or rather the confidence with which the High Watchers spoke to those below them. Although she would not admit it to anyone- to do so could make her very existence forfeit- she did not even think victory likely as matters stood. No doubt the High Watchers had been told by the Seven that victory was inevitable, and no doubt they believed that supposed inevitability. No one cast doubt upon any statement made by the Seven, and the High Watchers, after all, had been the ones who had travelled with the Seven to this world over a thousand years ago.

But how can it be certain? How can it even be possible?

She thought back again to some of the historical books she had read. Books that even mentioned the *marandaal* in passing were few and far between, but Kelandra's passion for history and patience in looking for scarce information had eventually provided her with more information about the *marandaal* than she had wanted to find.

Everything that she had read about them, usually late into the night in one of the seldom-used archival chambers, essentially retold the same grim tale. An army of frighteningly powerful beings that roamed the Existence. A gathering of creatures dedicated to the destruction of everything else that lived. A disease within the heart of the Existence itself- but placed there by what? A God?

Were the *marandaal* themselves a race of Gods? A race that had nearly extinguished her own? Or simply the manifestation of a relentless force created by some power outside of the entire Existence? Why did the *marandaal* exist and how had they come to be? Every document she read that stretched its ideas this far drifted inevitably into conjecture, and Kelandra knew nothing of Gods or how the Existence had come to be. As far as she was aware, not even the Seven knew such things.

The Watchers were more than a force to be reckoned with, and the Seven wielded sorcery far beyond her comprehension, far beyond the understanding of any Watchers. They had, after all, used Gates in order to reach

Aona. Kelandra had not even heard of anyone else who had so much as seen those brief events when Gates appeared for an instant. There were rumours of such people in other lands, but they remained rumours.

And yet all my kind were brought from out of such portals, she reminded herself, *in the years and centuries after the Seven arrived. We were all rescued, each one of us, from some dark journey through the Existence, located and pulled somehow into this world through the sorcery of the Seven.*

She recalled the first thing she had been asked, ten years ago when first she opened her eyes.

What do you remember?

I remember nothing, she had answered as she closed her eyes against a blinding light, feeling the presence of the Seven all around her, standing in a circle, as if to welcome her into the world.

Welcome, a soft voice had murmured in her ear, as she staggered to her knees in that chamber of intense light and glass.

And as far as she knew, none of those who had been brought here recalled anything of their previous lives, their journeys. By all accounts that was just as well.

But despite the great powers of the Seven, the harsh and never-spoken truth was that their law extended only through the south of Harn. A traveller who headed further north than Mornkastle would find little evidence that either Watchers or their sorcerous overlords ruled at all. Beyond that grey stone city lay land that Kelandra and all her kind knew only by ancient maps or the uncertain works of the few minions they had sent into the region who had also returned. These were the dark places of wild magic and superstition, of old ways that clung to the time before the Enlightenment. Blood feuds. Witchery. Sacrifice.

The people of the north- though Kelandra could barely think of them as people at all- were their enemies, and had been so since the Seven and the High Watchers had come to Aona. For many centuries an uneasy truce had existed between the civilised south and the tribal leaders and warlocks of the dark north- a truce that occasionally broke down with blood spilled on either side, but which had otherwise stayed resolutely in place. It had done so because- much as Kelandra and every other Watcher hated to admit it- those who dwelt in the unknown hinterlands were ruled over by power as great as their own. That was one of the few things they knew for certain about life in those places- that fearful witches and warlocks and nightmarish creatures held sway over the Races. It was a land of madness, depravity and senseless bloodshed, and thinking about it made Kelandra almost tremble with hatred.

More than eight hundred years ago, one of the High Watchers had put forward the idea of building a vast wall across Harn, all the way from the Daymorn Peaks in the east to the Bay of Bones in the west, to shut out the practitioners of forbidden arts, the crazed worshippers of bloodthirsty powers. The wall had never been built, perhaps because the Seven had never completely given up hope of capturing the north.

And so, Harn remained as far from united as any land could be. When the *marandaal* roamed as far as their borders, soon they would see the division and suspicion of a land easy to overcome.

This was why Kelandra knew the apparent certainty of victory for what it was: blind arrogance.

She wondered suddenly if it might be possible for a pact to be formed, if only for the purpose of uniting Harn against the *marandaal*. The thought itself sickened her, yet it was persuasive. She had already learned that a few in the north already knew of the dangers faced. Might they even agree to such a pact?

That man who made a speech in Mornkastle a while back, Kelandra thought suddenly. *Ruhal Dalmorn. That was his name. We have kept eyes upon him for a long time; he has influence in that region, and he knows some of the Northern sorcerers. He must do, or he would never have spoken of* imminent threats, *as he called them, even if he did not name them.*

Kelandra found the whole idea of a pact difficult to imagine. Even if it were somehow agreed in principle, surely such an alliance would be unworkable in practice.

With an effort she put all such thoughts aside. Were she to even suggest such a thing, she would be put to trial and executed shortly afterwards, probably somewhere deep within the Sanctum where only the Seven and a few chosen High Watchers were permitted to tread.

But Luudhoq must prevail at all costs.

Luudhoq was, after all, the cradle of civilisation. Their history taught that this had been one of the few places where the Races had learned to exist in a state of order and balance, with the guidance of the Seven and the High Watchers. Little enough had been documented of the time before the coming of the Seven, and the histories were scant on detail, but the fact of the matter held regardless. Kelandra imagined it almost as a citadel fashioned from light, a physical embodiment of enlightenment itself, pushing back the darkness of what some called the First Age, and others called the Unravelling or the Time of Blood.

Kelandra found thoughts of her imagined pact creeping back. Would enough of those who held sway in the north even consider such an idea? Perhaps. Some of them knew about the *marandaal.* But how could she reach them to begin with, to find out?

A strength that many Watchers had in common, albeit to vastly different degrees, was their intricate network of agents, spies and information-gatherers, their eyes and ears in the places that required observation and monitoring. This web of knowledge became more fragmented north of Waylorn and barely existed at all beyond Mornkastle, the city about which surely everyone in Harn agreed in one respect: it was the place where north met south.

Mornkastle. Of those who served her, who might go there and exist unhindered long enough to make contact with those they judged to be receptive to her idea? Kelandra swiftly ran through some names. Pitrar was capable enough, but deeply entrenched amongst the nomads of the Wistledge in the far west. He was not reachable; not in time, at any rate. Nia was more than capable, but as far as she could gather, Nia had just a few days ago returned from Aphenhast- doing what? Kelandra sighed. Giving her finest spy such relative freedom had been like clutching a two-edged blade, but she had had little choice, save imprisoning the girl, and where would that have left her? Blind in one eye, or as good as.

All her other agents were useful only for missions within the confines of the southlands, for they lacked any sort of ability to mingle seamlessly with the people of Mornkastle, and more importantly, those from the north who ventured there. Kelandra sighed inwardly. If only she had the influence and web of spies that some other Watchers boasted!

And if I were to choose Nia, how could I be certain about her? How could I ensure her absolute loyalty to me?

The answer came swiftly. *Because Nia is the one who needs to guard her secret at all costs. She is the one who will do anything to safeguard that secret and avoid being imprisoned and tortured as a freak, a harbourer of forbidden powers.*

Kelandra smiled. She would at least would have a messenger who could be relief upon, who would do as bidden and tell no one of her plan, particularly if she made it known to Nia that she knew her secret.

So I can at least see if this pact may be formed, Kelandra thought, *and perhaps do so without risk of being discovered dabbling in such perceived treachery.*

The Watcher looked up, suddenly aware that everyone else had already left the antechamber. Whatever debate had taken place had long finished, and somehow those taking part and those watching had departed without her even knowing. The great archway leading into the Hall of Measurement revealed that theatre to be empty as well. Had everyone left for the Sunset Ceremony, or had that too finished? Could she have spent half the night sitting here and pondering?

Kelandra sighed, the sound harsh in the enveloping silence. Eventually she also left, wrapped in her forbidden thoughts.

IV

For the next two days, Kelandra's thoughts wandered endlessly. She carried out her tasks without concentrating on them any more than necessary, although fortunately for her these were the sort of mundane chores that barely required any attention. She spent time organising the arrest of petty thieves; she mulled over paperwork relating to import taxes for products from the South Ocean Islands; she attended discussions about the *eastern concern* as it had by consensus been named, although even then she did so only to see if anyone had anything to say that might hint at her own worries.

In the event, no one did, although she noticed that Alturus, a coldly withdrawn Watcher of few words with whom she had shared missions in the past, seemed deep in thought during a few of the meetings where she saw him. More than usual, even for him, Kelandra reckoned.

Perhaps he has misgivings, Kelandra decided, *and where there is one, there will be more. There are nigh on five hundred of us.*

But she could not speak to anyone about her own fears. It was too early for that. *I need some hold over anyone*

171

I choose to approach, she thought on the second evening after the Sunset Ceremony, as she lit lanterns around each of her chambers.

The lighting of the lanterns dealt with, Kelandra stood before her full-length mirror and stared at her reflection. The Watchers' Mantra leapt unbidden to her mind; as ever she was glad of its comfort.

I am a Watcher. I am the guardian of law and order. Reason and logic shall be preserved at all costs. The dark shall be beaten back. For thousands of years, we have provided the guidance that sets humankind against their worse selves. We have constrained the evil in their hearts. We are the light of all their worlds, wherever they may be.

To an untrained observer, Kelandra might look human herself at a casual glance. But a second, longer look would swiftly reveal the curious lustre to her eyes- sometimes violet, sometimes an orange hue- the hardness of her features, and although nothing specifically could reveal her as being something other than human, still she gave no impression of humanity.

Slowly she stretched out an arm and stared down at it. Had anyone been watching her in that moment, they might have seen her eyes change colour, become lighter and then darker as the pupils suddenly dilated.

Every day without fail, Kelandra would stare into her arm once the day's work was done and she was shut away in the privacy of her chambers. Her inner workings, visible and tangible, were an endless source of fascination. Tonight as ever she gazed, utterly self-absorbed, at the intricate channels of flesh, nerves, bones and metal, held together in a mesh of beautiful silver threads. *Another part should be written into the Mantra,* she thought. *We are the perfect marriage of flesh and pure, mechanical sorcery, a beauty created out of the need for order.*

In that short space of time, she knew the speed at which her blood flowed around the construct of that limb, she knew the tensile strength of the fist she suddenly made and uncurled. She knew a thousand other things, some important and some useless. A wave of information about that moment in her body's life coursed through her mind.

Kelandra finally drew herself from that gods-eye view and remained sitting with head bowed, arms now resting at her sides. Her eyes closed; her head slumped forward slightly. She drifted into a lower state of consciousness.

But she did not sleep. Watchers never slept. They had no need for it.

The night wore on. The brightest of the stars shimmered uncertainly above Luudhoq's glow, and Ildar's face came and went in a smooth white arc, briefly illuminating the Watcher as it passed through the night sky. Kelandra remained perfectly still except for the slight rise and fall of her chest as she breathed long and slow through the small quiet hours.

The following morning, she received word that Nia was at the outer gates, pleading for audience with her. Kelandra readily allowed it, keen to learn more about what her spy and daggersmaid had been up to in the distant east.

The first thing Kelandra noticed when Nia was ushered into her study was her look of quiet self-satisfaction, in place of the careful neutrality that she almost always wore like a cloak. Immediately she knew that Nia had done something she was proud of and was desperate to tell her. Or *thought* she had, anyway. What would it be? Kelandra had been impressed before with Nia's quiet resourcefulness. *That's why she's my best, she reminded herself,* though of course she retained her usual distant look as she cordially bade the girl be seated.

Nia could not help herself. Unbidden, she burst out: "I have some important news, Kelandra. Well, to be more precise, I've brought someone back with me from Aphenhast.

Someone who will be of immense interest to the Seven. And that will itself be of great benefit to you."

Her insolence is breathtaking, Kelandra marvelled as she gazed coldly back at her spy. "*I* will be the judge of that, Nia. Rein in your presumptions. And tell me, what exactly *were* you doing in Aphenhast? Word reached me that you were on some errand- some *death-errand* to be exact about it- for their Council of Priests."

Nia blinked as if taken aback, though surely she would have known of Kelandra's curiosity regarding her sudden request to spend time in the eastern land. "True enough," she said after a moment. "Although you *did* give me leave to do so."

"Did I? Perhaps," Kelandra commented, recalling that moment clearly.

"Life is strange, I've found," Nia remarked. "I expected to be paid well, but I had to leave Darkenhelm in something of a hurry, without payment. Still, had I not done so, I would never have made this discovery."

Kelandra shrugged. "We live and learn. To the matter at hand: who is this, and why would he or she be of such interest?"

"She's a child of perhaps nine years," Nia said, "with a special gift. She has visions, which..." Kelandra had never before seen her so lost for words; Nia was clearly struggling to describe what and who she had found. Kelandra found her interest in her spy's Hastian sojourn growing markedly. As ever though, she feigned politeness to the point of indifference, waiting for Nia to speak.

"They felt real," Nia said finally, her voice oddly distant. "She was speaking of real places, real events, that she never could have seen, which *I* had never seen, yet I knew they were somehow real, they were happening or about to happen in some place, near or distant..." Nia took a deep breath and blinked as if in an effort to pull herself back into the present. "I'm certain of one thing. She was seeing *Gates,*

Kelandra- coming from out of nothing, appearing, moving even..."

"*Moving?*" It was Kelandra's turn to be rendered speechless.

"Other things too- dark things. Shadows, or places without light, or... I don't know what they were."

Kelandra struggled to retain her composure. "Be certain, Nia, before you answer me. Are you sure that what you saw- what she caused you to see- were Gates? Can you be absolutely certain?"

"Yes," Nia said without any hesitation, staring boldly back at her. The girl's hands trembled, and she pressed them together to calm herself. "On my life, Kelandra. I could not be *more* certain. Ask me how, though, and..." She shrugged helplessly.

Kelandra fell into deep thought. If all of this was true, then this child's visions might be of help when the *marandaal* turned their attention westwards. *And*, she mused, *it could reaffirm my own resourcefulness and integrity in the eyes of the High Watchers and the Seven. That makes me a far less likely traitor, does it not?*

And if it was not true, if Nia was lying or simply mistaken- well, she would die a lingering death in one of the Sanctum's deepest cells.

"Her name is Yui," Nia ventured after a while. "Her father travelled with her from Darkenhelm. He can, I'm sure, provide further information- and perhaps encourage her, if she's to be interrogated."

Kelandra nodded. "Tell me where they are and I shall arrange everything else."

"They're staying at the *Anchor and Spyglass*, just off the Square," Nia told her.

"And would you say they are likely to put up any kind of resistance?"

"Hardly. They're tired and they know nothing of Luudhoq. In fact they're expecting someone to visit them, claiming to be able to take them to a healer. I briefed them myself. I'm sure that anyone you send could ask them politely to come along and they would. All the way into the Sanctum without a second thought."

"Good." Kelandra allowed herself a smile. "You have done well, Nia. Better than even I expected of you, which is some achievement." She watched as the girl's expression became one of stupefaction and finally broad delight, before she collected her emotions with visible effort. "Thank you, Kelandra."

"You may go now." Kelandra waited until Nia had reached the door, and then spoke up again. "One more thing. I have something else I need to speak with you about in two days' time. Come to me then, at noon. Until then, stay here in Luudhoq."

"As you wish." Nia turned, gave a little bow and left.

Kelandra sat back in her chair, and then, suddenly restless, she wandered over to the window where she had a view over the inner courtyard of the Watchers' Halls. Could matters be about to fall into place? Nia's discovery might have been happy coincidence, something that Kelandra normally believed in unless she had an overwhelming reason not to, but this- if it was all true, and it *felt* true- was a handy piece of luck to say the least.

If this girl...

Kelandra removed contemplation of the possibilities from her thoughts. *One cautious step at a time, no matter the urgency,* she reminded herself as she watched the comings and goings two hundred feet below in the courtyard, comforted by the ebb and flow, the routine of another morning passing uneventfully. *Gather what knowledge you can, choose wisely those with whom you speak.*

One step, with which any journey must start.

V

She left a message in Alturus' chambers the next day. The message only indicated that she needed to talk with him on a matter of some urgency, and that no one else should know about the matter. He was to be under the Middle Guild Bridge, on the western side of the river where it reached the shore, at the same moment as Archaon touched the bridge span above on its nightly travel.

Kelandra had quite deliberately chosen this area for a reason. One of her specialist areas of expertise was the use of water-mirrors, devices that many of her kind struggled to use effectively. Nevertheless, some *could* use them, and so she had chosen a place where she knew they could not be used for scrying. The fast-flowing waters of the Fhaarluy, rushing on towards the ocean, coupled with *something*- Kelandra did not know what- inside the framework of the bridge, created a sort of dissonance that interrupted the water-mirrors to the point that conversations held here could not be heard through them. Nor could anything that happened here be seen through them. This area therefore made as safe a place as possible to have the conversation she intended to have.

Of course, the risk remained great. She could not know if Alturus shared her beliefs or could be convinced of them. She could only suspect, strong though that suspicion was. It was worth the risk, she told herself, even as her own reason repeatedly told her that it was not.

Alturus arrived a moment after she came to stand on the shore under the bridge. Kelandra suspected that he had been nearby for a short while already, waiting to see if she appeared.

The great red moon cast a faint glow, dimmer than the hundred thousand torch-lights and lanterns of Luudhoq. The two Watchers glanced up at its grim face; Archaon was in position above the nearest bridge span.

"Why here?" Alturus said brusquely by way of greeting.

"Why not?" Kelandra rejoined. "It's as good a place as any." She pointed to the multiple parts of the bridge silhouetted against the sky. "Time may be measured with precision."

Alturus regarded the river in silence, waiting for her to explain why she had requested his presence in this place.

"I need to speak with you regarding a matter of great importance," Kelandra said after a while. "It concerns the matter of these *marandaal,* and the appearance of Gates in places to the east." Her voice remained smooth, steady. She might have been remarking upon the mathematics of the bridge architecture, or the speed of the river water.

"What do you need to say about them that has not already been said?"

Had she heard a hint of wariness in his voice? Kelandra silently wondered. At the same time, she closed her eyes briefly and gave her other senses free rein over the entire area. As she had already known, no one of any importance lurked nearby. Three hundred paces back from the shore, a vagrant stumbled through an alleyway. Almost all the way across the bridge, an old woman had begun the long journey towards this side. She moved slowly, deliberately. Concentrating, Kelandra heard the human's short, laboured breath, and listened to her slow steps. They had plenty of time, and she knew that no one, near or otherwise, would catch the detail of their conversation, much less understand it.

"I think a disunited land will fall against their might," she said, and left those words hanging in the air for him to ponder.

Alturus stared fixedly ahead. "Are you saying," he said eventually, "that in *your* estimation, the Seven, the Watchers and the massed armies of the entire South cannot overcome them?"

"Have you read *Journeys?*" Kelandra asked him.

"A few passages. The distant past has never concerned me."

Kelandra glanced at him, a cold little smile upon her face. "It *will* concern you. It will concern us all. The Seven and the High Watchers..." She dropped her voice even further, so that even Alturus had to strain to hear. "...were pursued by these foes, from world to world, across the vastness of the Existence."

The other Watcher did not deign to respond. Kelandra continued, "It's an unspoken truth that beyond the Never-Built Wall, powers as great as the Seven hold sway. If there were not, the Seven would have dominion over the entire land."

Alturus stared at her. "Unspoken for a reason, Kelandra. Have you lost all sense?"

"If Harn remains as it is, I am certain it will fall." She paused and regarded him for a moment. "What do *you* believe? Given that our own race, and the Seven themselves, fled before the *marandaal?* Given that a divided land is twice as easy to conquer, if not more so?"

"What do you suggest?"

"There are a number of others, in the North, who believe the same," Kelandra told him. "I suggest that discussions are held with them, at the earliest opportunity."

Alturus shook his head and took a step back as if her dangerous ideas might be contagious. "This is madness. The Seven would never agree to this. You would be hanged for even suggesting it."

Then he looked at her again. "Now I understand. You have even greater lunacy planned."

"I need allies," Kelandra said, "even if they number only a few. Whoever is willing to take part in this with me would need to keep their involvement an absolute secret. I am certain that those in the North- the man I intend to contact, and his own close allies- would need to take the same risks."

"And together you intend to convince the powers on both sides of the Wall that only a united Harn can withstand the *marandaal*." Alturus shook his head.

"What do you believe?" she asked him.

"I believe you are correct." He rose to his feet and looked around as if expecting the shadows of listening Watchers to fall around him. "But it will never happen. The Seven will never allow such union."

So saying, he left.

Kelandra sat by the shore for hours. Archaon sank ponderously over the jagged south-western skyline. Clouds moved north to south bearing rain, and after a short while a steady rhythm began to beat down upon the ramparts of the bridge. To the silent Watcher who sat under it, the sound of the rain was like a continuous percussion roll at an execution. *Her* execution.

I should have spoken to no one, she thought, but knew that sooner or later she would have had to. *I misjudged him,* she thought then. *I saw something I wanted to see. I made the worst of errors. I should be hanged for my stupidity as much as anything else.*

Briefly she wondered if Alturus would tell the High Watchers about her treacherous thoughts. *He has no proof,* she reasoned, *and I could as easily say the same about him. But what then? Might we both hang? Even to voice such a suspicion could be enough.*

She returned to the Sanctum around dawn, pensive and listless and wishing that one way or another, the matter would be swiftly dealt with and done with.

A note had been pushed under her door. *Ah,* Kelandra thought, picking it up and carefully unfolding it. *He has decided to bribe me.*

But the note gave no indication of such action. It read simply:

There will be one more, at least. Two days from now, at the same time and place.

Kelandra crushed the note before burning it over a candle once inside her chambers. Then, and only then, did she allow herself the briefest of smiles.

VI

The following morning, Kelandra sent five senior guardsmen to the *Anchor and Spyglass* to bring back the girl and her father and have them sent directly to the High Watchers. She doubted that that as many as five would be needed but wanted to be as certain as possible that they would not resist or even evade arrest. Whilst they were gone, she carefully penned a note which she passed to the first High Watcher she found. "This concerns two people who will arrive shortly," she said politely, averting her eyes as custom dictated. "You will find their interrogation... productive."

A little later, she watched from one of the ramparts of the Sanctum's inner walls as the girl and her father were marched through the inner square towards the High Watchers' courts. They looked confused. Kelandra wondered if around now the truth might be dawning on them- that they had not in fact been brought here for the child to be healed. The girl was a thin, sorry-looking creature who stumbled wearily along, and her father cast bewildered glances to either side. At one point he stopped and appeared to ask one of the guardsmen a question but was firmly ushered onwards.

At noon, Nia returned as bidden, escorted by two of the Sanctum guardsmen. Kelandra dismissed them, and cordially ushered her spy into her inner chambers, ensuring that no one could be near enough to hear the conversation they were about to have.

181

"I will come immediately to the point," she said as soon as Nia was seated. "I have an important task with which only you can be trusted."

A flicker of amusement crossed Nia's lips, just for a moment. No doubt she thought that such an elevation in status was the result of her lucky find. Kelandra paid no mind to that and continued, "There is a man by the name of Ruhal Dalmorn, who lives in Mordenglen forest in the far north but sometimes travels to Mornkastle and the towns between the two. He is well known throughout that lawless region. Indeed you may know the name already- he is on the list of known Enemies and has been for twenty years or more."

"I have heard the name," Nia remarked, "but little of the man's reputation."

"Some tennights ago now," Kelandra told her, "he made a speech in the city of Mornkastle, in which he spoke of a desire for one land, a people united. What do you think he might have been speaking of, in truth?"

"Others have said similar things. I expect that like most of them, he dreams of invasion, of turning the South over to the warlocks and outlaws."

"Certainly those sentiments are widely felt amongst such people," Kelandra agreed, "but something about what this man said intrigued me. He has a colourful history. He has even made enemies amongst some of his own people, in part for speaking against many of their more violent and primitive practices. In short, he appears to be a voice of relative reason amongst the frothing babble of superstition and sacrifice.

"So, I decided to find out more about this Ruhal, using what limited resources I could bring together in Mornkastle. I would have liked to involve you, Nia, but of course you were in Aphenhast assassinating soldiers at that point. Regardless, with some perseverance I found out a little more about this man. He knows about Gates, but more importantly, I am certain that he knows about the coming of the *marandaal.* That must mean he holds sway with some of the witches and warlocks of that region. They would be the only folk who could know such things for certain. We must assume that there are people of power in the North who are equally aware of the threat from the east.

"It seems that he has spoken several times about a need for a common, united Harn to prepare for the inevitable war against the *marandaal,* although few have taken those words as seriously as they ought." Kelandra sat back and placed her hands together. "This is something in which I also believe."

Nia blinked, struggling to take in everything she had been told. "The... the *what*? The coming of the *marandaal*? I have no idea..."

"Of course you don't." Kelandra watched her for a moment. "I expect there are wielders of one power or another in the east lands who know about them, but here in Harn's civilised south, only the Seven and the Watchers know the name."

"What are they?"

Kelandra smiled at that unwittingly excellent question. "They are the light at the end of time, the destructive unseen face of the Existence," she said, thinking: *They are many things, but that description will do for Nia. Anything more would be wasted on a human.*

Nia looked uncomfortable. "This has something to do with Gates? Something to do with Yui's visions?"

"I would say so, yes." Carefully Kelandra gauged Nia's response, which was one of dumbstruck silence. Finally the girl, ever concerned primarily with her own survival, said quietly but urgently, "I should not be hearing this! If anyone knew that I..."

Suddenly her expression changed, and although even now she was too quick-witted to say anything, still Kelandra knew exactly what she was thinking. With a predatory smile she leaned forward. "And if anyone knew that *I* had spoken to you about such things as the *marandaal*- or that *I* planned or even entertained thoughts about such treachery- well, I'm sure you can imagine what would happen to me."

"I would never betray you," Nia said quickly. "Upon my life, I would not." She looked horrified and trapped in turn.

"Upon your life. An apt turn of phrase." Kelandra gave her an intent look. "You have always been a faithful woman, Nia. And occasionally a faithful man."

She sat back and did not hide her satisfaction as the remaining colour drained from Nia's face. Panic flared in her eyes, and Kelandra knew in that instant that she had the better of her- that she would from hereon *always* have the better of her.

In an instant, Nia leapt up and ran straight for the door. Kelandra marvelled at her speed- although she still could have been waiting for her at the door if need be. She did not bother to react. In fact, she had half-expected the illogical, so-*human* response. *Panic,* she thought. *Panic is the ugliest of things to behold.*

She did wince slightly however, as Nia's hand grasped the doorknob and a flash of white light enveloped her for a moment, before throwing her violently back onto the floor. There she remained for a short while, shivering involuntarily as her pleading eyes stared up at the ceiling.

"It feels cold, doesn't it?" Kelandra said casually. "As if your innards themselves are turning to ice. You can try again if you wish, but I suspect the next time your hand will remain stuck to the door whilst the rest of you ends up exactly where you are now. That would be a... *shattering* experience for you."

Nia stared hatefully up at her. Kelandra waited until she deemed Nia able to move without aid- she was not going to get up and assist her- and then motioned for the girl to be seated once again.

"How did you find out?" Nia asked, after what seemed an age. She sat slumped in her seat like a frightened, defeated child.

"A simple enough scrying with use of the water-mirrors. I must admit it involved some luck. A moment or two either earlier or later and I might never have known. The *farseeing* is difficult to use and even more difficult to control. I was curious about your whereabouts, nothing more than that. But when I saw... well, I realised how special you were, of course. Unique, even."

"Who else knows about this?"

"No one else knows, and no one need *ever* know, if you do exactly as I say, and if you *never* speak of the tasks I now have for you." Kelandra looked her up and down. "No one in Luudhoq is aware of any natural shapechangers. There have been none for many centuries. Think of what would happen if you were... *revealed*, so to speak. Think of the interest that the Seven would have in you."

Nia stared directly ahead, at nothing.

"I was almost tempted to explore your talent myself, to find out what I could," Kelandra confessed. "But to hide such a find and keep you to myself..." She shrugged. "That would have been treachery, wouldn't it?"

Nia had nothing to say to that either, though she gave a brief, unhappy smile.

"Your secret is safe," Kelandra told her, "and will remain safe for as long as you remain utterly loyal to me. If ever anyone discovers anything about what we have discussed here today, well- as I'm dragged away for questioning, you can imagine the first thing I'll be telling my captors. And you can be sure that whatever *my* fate, yours would be far worse."

She handed Nia a small scroll sealed along its length with dark wax. The girl held the object as if it might turn into a snake at any moment.

"This must reach Ruhal Dalmorn," Kelandra said. "You will ensure that that happens, and you will remain in Mornkastle until either word comes by return from that man, or until I send for you."

Nia stared at her. "That's it?"

Kelandra leaned forward. "Make sure that you succeed in this task, Nia. To do anything less..." She shrugged. "Use your imagination."

Nia left a short while later, sunken-eyed and defeated. Kelandra watched the sun set over the rooftops from her window. *Now I wait, and work with due diligence as ever*, she thought, *and hope above hope that she brings me agreement from this man.*

She did not remember *lapsing* later but stirred sometime in the small hours of the night to find herself standing by the north-facing window, eyes fixed upon the unseen horizon. For the briefest moment, she imagined that some great horror had been brought into being through her actions, and that all she knew, all light and civilisation, would be swept away into unimaginable chaos.

The moment passed, as Kelandra knew it would. She was a creature born of reason and enlightenment, not given to fevered imagination, and so she turned from the window and whatever waited in the dark distance.

VII

Kelandra made a point of paying a visit to the spot by the river during the daylight hours. She did not expect Alturus to turn against her- what evidence did he have?- but it could do no harm to be thorough. She walked around and through the area, noted everything she saw and searched for anything that might be out of place. She returned to the Sanctum and briefly sought out that same area with the water mirrors. The mask over sight and sound remained.

186

Satisfied, Kelandra returned to the riverside earlier than she needed to, partly to ready herself but also to see if Alturus or whoever he had brought with him might arrive early.

The red moon rose. Stars swiftly emerged as the last light of day failed. Kelandra watched as Archaon made its ascent. It had still not touched the arch of the bridge when she heard sounds of approach.

She was taken aback when *four* other Watchers appeared with Alturus from the end of the trail where waste ground met buildings. *Four,* Kelandra thought. Something was wrong. He could not possibly have convinced that many. She would have found even three suspicious. Energy coursed through her veins, and she took in the minute details of her environment once again, working out a course of action that would somehow ensure her survival.

"Kelandra," Alturus called softly, his voice barely more than a whisper carried in the breeze. "Be at ease. We are with you."

Still the urge to flee remained strong, as they walked nearer. With an effort, Kelandra quashed it. She recognised each of the Watchers who accompanied Alturus.

Kal-Myrran was known as much for her arrogance as her ability, and for her feared reputation as a Questioner within the Sanctum. Dozens of human men, women and children had died or been rendered insane at her hands, Kelandra reckoned. Even if Kal-Myrran believed in her cause, she was not certain that she wanted her to be a part of it. *If we ever get to that distant point,* she thought, *we will have to deal with the humans who hold the reins of power in the hated North. How will she be able to do that?*

Kunas was a minor Watcher, brought from the void perhaps six years ago. Smooth-complexioned and silver-eyed, he nevertheless looked more human than most of their kind, although such an observation would never be voiced. Kelandra could not recall having ever spoken with him.

Aylin stood a little shorter than most Watchers, and broader. Kelandra recalled that his skills lay in cartography and architecture, but he too had studied his histories, if not for as long or as diligently as she had.

Ildoron had been in Luudhoq longer than any of them: a hundred years or so, Kelandra had heard. Watchers barely aged at all, and when they did, it was in a subtle way. Ildoron had a certain greyness to him, but not in the same way as a human would; certainly not a human of the same age. Kelandra had shared missions with him before; his experience was vast and his intellect formidable. If he was with them, then he would make a most useful ally. Perhaps he would even be able to control Kal-Myrran's sadistic tendencies.

And it was Kal-Myrran who spoke first, her dark eyes glittering. To Kelandra, she looked every inch the torturer, almost gleeful at the discovery she had made. "So, Kelandra," she murmured. "Who would have thought it? *You*, unremarkable in all ways, neither the best servant of the Seven nor the worst. But then, one might say that your anonymity makes you an excellent traitor."

Kelandra stared back at her. "I stand for Luudhoq, for the Seven, for the light of civilisation." Buoyed by her own words, she continued, "I propose the unthinkable for one reason only- through unity, through a pact with the forces of the North, we may defeat the *marandaal*. I loathe them as much as any of you, these worshipers of darkness and depravity, these enemies of everything we defend. But there are some even amongst their ranks who have recognised the need for a united Harn. I have sent one of my people with a request to meet a man who is possibly a leader amongst them..."

"Wait. You sent a *human* with this knowledge?" Aylin frowned.

"She can be trusted absolutely," Kelandra smiled. "I would not have sent her otherwise. She is to contact him and ascertain whether he and his followers are open to the forming of a pact. The message she carries may only be read by him after it is first opened. If anyone else even opens it, the message cannot be read. Once opened, it can be read only by those he *allows* to read it, and no others."

"Ah. You tied it in a naming spell of some sort," Ildoron noted.

"He may have many enemies amongst his own people," Alturus pointed out.

"Undoubtedly he has," Kelandra concurred, "for most of them loathe and fear us. Certainly, they fear any words that suggest reaching out to the South. But they allow him to speak what he will, for the moment. That's often their way- allow the indiscretion and find a way to deal with it afterwards."

"You speak of this great land as it were one half, calling it *south*," Kal-Myrran said coldly.

"But it is half a land," Kelandra told her, without even looking in the Watcher's direction. "I can only suggest you relearn your geography, Kal-Myrran, if you think otherwise."

Ildoron spoke up again. "Suppose that somehow such a pact is formed, against considerable odds. What then do we become, aside from a demonstration that two irreconcilable sides can stand together?"

Kelandra thought for a moment. It was a good question. If she could not find an answer worthy of it, she could at least give a bluntly honest reply. "The fact itself is the lesson," she said finally. "Of course, the risk is enormous. We may fail, and if we do then still we may be named as traitors here in Luudhoq. But if enough on either side of the Wall see that we *can* stand together, if only to face the *marandaal,* then they may stand with us. This is about convincing the people of all Harn, through our actions."

"We could say that we never heard any of this," Kunas said suddenly, and they turned to him as he continued, "The Seven are the greatest power in all the Existence. They *brought* us here, from the depths of the void. They travelled between the stars at will. They are immortal and all-powerful. Together, the Seven, the Watchers, and the humans and other races will stand against the *marandaal*."

"And perish," Kelandra stated.

Kunas stepped nearer to her. Instinctively Kelandra's hands moved in a swift motion, the air rippling before her, somehow *thickening,* to slow any physical assault. Kunas approached no further and raised a hand in half-hearted apology. "Think," he said, still addressing them all. "Can we risk such a venture? We will withstand the *marandaal* and anything else that emerges from whatever Gates form, and we will do so without doing deals with the agents of madness and darkness."

"Luudhoq must stand regardless. Civilisation must survive regardless. Are we agreed?" Kelandra said coolly, regarding each of them in turn. When they murmured agreement, she continued, "I have read a book by the name of *Journeys.* Alturus has also read a little of it. The book tells of the flight from the *marandaal,* that took place thousands of years ago. There are other texts also, if only a few, that mention them. Always, they are spoken of as too powerful to be resisted by whichever force defended whichever world the *marandaal* had found. Confrontation is followed by flight. Wherever the Seven are mentioned, they are *fleeing* these beings."

"Outnumbered," Aylin pointed out. "They were outnumbered. I read a little of that book."

"Outnumbered," Kelandra repeated. "And so, not all-powerful."

They fell into silent contemplation. Eventually Kelandra spoke up again. "I have read more about the *marandaal* than any of you. I would wager my own existence upon that. Why face them as half a land, when the knowledge and powers of the witches and warlocks of the North could *double* our strength?"

"What do you think will happen," Alturus asked her, "if, as you say, we face the enemy, and they hound us all the way back to Luudhoq, turning the land to ash?"

Kelandra felt a cold certainty sweep through her as she considered that. "The Seven will leave Aona to its fate," she said quietly. And then, without having any idea why, she added, "This place cannot be left to die. How many other worlds might the *marandaal* have already destroyed? What if this, *this* place where we stand, is the only one remaining? The last light burning in the void?"

VII – A Quiet Malevolence

I

After a brief, inexplicable thaw during which time the snow that had lain for weeks all but disappeared, winter had returned to Ruan-Tor with a spiteful vengeance as if to make up for its lapse. Two days after conditions had deteriorated, Rocan made his way to the Lord Protector's fortress in order to submit a report on town provisions, which had become a greater concern than ever. *Although what can be done about that, only the Gods know,* he thought. *The strong and the healthy will live; the weak and the very old or very young will perish.*

Amid winter's iron grip, the town had all but shut down. No one ventured outside unless they had to. So bitterly cold had it become that even the usual scene from years gone by of children building snowmen or having snowball fights had been entirely absent, for their parents kept them indoors. That said, likely they would have kept them indoors anyway given the massacre, not to mention the reports of what had happened to other Plains settlements less able to defend themselves. The number of defenders at the territory fences remained woefully inadequate, but even Rocan had not been able to keep as many men on patrol as he wanted. Guard posts stood at six places around the perimeter fence, but conditions had become so cold at night that they could no longer be manned.

Other problems abounded. At least two dozen townspeople had perished, and horses had frozen to death in their stables. The stocks of firewood had dwindled, even though there could not be a single citizen of Ruan-Tor who remained unaware of the need to preserve it as far as possible. The autumn hunts had been poor this year and, as

Rocan intended to report, food supplies had run worryingly low.

As Rocan stepped out onto Low Road, the snowfall miraculously eased. The previous day's fall had frozen hard in the night, which made walking treacherous. Keeping his gaze lowered as much as possible in order to watch the surface, Rocan pressed on up the road, listening to the crunch of hardened snow under his boots. Even with two cloaks wrapped tightly over his leather armour, he felt the chill in his bones as he walked up the hill towards the Lord Protector's fortress. *Keep yourself busy, keep yourself sane,* he told himself, and tried to concentrate on the mountain of challenges that faced the town in the weeks and months ahead. It was more important now than ever that he be vigilant.

The new Lord Protector, Amos Relf, had been an almost anonymous presence since being sworn in a day after Vothangrane had been laid to rest. Reports and accounts had been left unread, important decisions left unmade, and the elected Council had made the decisions in his absence much of the time. That said, Rocan could not remember when the last decision had been made by anyone at all, with the town having fallen into uneasy slumber.

Someone must remain aware, he thought as he walked over the icy snow. *Someone must remain in control. Without guidance and control, chaos comes swiftly.* Right now, the commander-in-arms of Ruan-Tor's militia felt that he might need to be that man. *The task should not be mine,* he thought. *I'm a soldier and a leader of soldiers, nothing more than that. But if the leaders of my people are transfixed by winter and can't fathom what to do, then I'll raise the best of my men from their beds and we'll do what needs to be done ourselves. Men with strength of will and common sense will make a better town than fearful politicians, with winter closed in around us all. And yet, we all need to do more.*

He shivered violently and gathered his cloak more firmly about himself. He could not remember a worse winter than this, and everyone older than him swore it was the worst *they* could remember, but this time of year was always hard in Ruan-Tor, so he could think of no excuse for the ineptitude- the *silence-* that emanated from the Lord Protector's Fortress. The season had arrived early, but not entirely unexpected.

Another worrying fact was that some of the fortress staff had left their positions, if not in droves then certainly in a quiet stream, giving notice and returning to their homes. Of course, there was little enough for them to do during this season, but Rocan recalled that in previous winters those employed by the ruling Council had always remained within the fortress along with their families if they so chose, where as a benefit of their employment they were kept fed and bedded, and warm. For them to steal away in the night in this manner was unheard of.

But much that happened recently was previously unheard of, Rocan considered. He paused for a moment to get his breath back before trudging onwards again. Already his calves and thighs ached deeply from his cautious walk over the compressed snow, and his face had become utterly numb from the cold.

A blizzard had started by the time he arrived at the outer gates of the fortress. The gates themselves had been shut, but they were neither locked nor barred. A long, partly rusted chain hung loosely on one of them, trailing down as far as the snow. Rocan pushed one of the gates open with some effort and mentally added their unlocked and unguarded state to his list of points to discuss.

Smooth snow many feet thick covered the courtyard, and no boot prints or even impressions made by birds or other creatures could be seen; the fall was utterly smooth, undisturbed. No light issued from any of the windows that dotted each floor and tower. Rocan stared in wonderment at the scene of desolation. The drab grey walls rose out of the snowdrifts as if in bewilderment at the season, like half-erased sketches against the thick, swirling snow that had now become relentless.

This doesn't even feel real, he thought suddenly, recalling a long-ago dream in which he had taken this exact journey to this spot in the same conditions, and gazed upon the abandoned fortress. *Now I'm staring into that dream, and my dream is staring back at me...*

For a moment, Rocan was overwhelmed by such a sense of foreboding that he reached under his leathers and grabbed at the holy star symbol of his necklace, holding it tightly enough for a starpoint to break his skin. Almost silently he whispered a quick prayer to the sky God, Thawnfar. So numb was his mouth that he struggled with many of the words. After a short while he roused himself with an effort, finally a little calmer, and struggled across the courtyard to the inner gates. They screeched in rusty protest against the buried courtyard surface as he pulled them open and then forced open the double entrance doors beyond.

The entrance hall gaped in austere silence. Statues of past Lord Protectors and other high dignitaries within the Council, or important figures from times gone by, gazed severely from their long-held places in each corner and along the back wall, as if to say: *How could you allow this?*

Rocan crossed the hall, his boots making a harsh echoing sound on the marble floor and walked slowly down one of the passageways into the heart of the fortress.

A while had passed by when eventually he found one of the servants, a boy of sixteen or so who stood facing a door at the base of a wide spiral staircase. Rocan noticed a feather duster in his hand, but it was obvious that the boy's cleaning duties had been abandoned in favour of staring slackly at the door. He did not move except to sway slightly, and the door did not open. As he passed by, Rocan caught a deep stench of excrement coming from the servant. With a chill in his heart, he made his way onwards.

Rocan found several more people during his walk through the corridors, as he headed for the Lord Protector's chambers. None were in any way lucid. One guardsman shrank back in fear at his approach and pressed himself into a corner as if the walls on either side might move to protect him. He could offer nothing but wordless sobs in response to Rocan's questions. Elsewhere, next to the passageway that led off towards the kitchens, a young maid stood slumped against the wall, a fevered sweat upon her brow despite the deathly chill that permeated the entire fortress. She whispered something to herself over and over but stopped as soon as Rocan drew near. Yet she would respond to nothing he said.

Rocan wondered how long it had been since any of the great hearths that lined the larger halls had been lit. Days? As he came near enough to see the other side of the girl's face, he shrank back despite himself. Someone or something- or possibly the girl herself- had picked at her left cheek until the skin had started to come apart in slivers. Rocan stared at her wordlessly. *Should I help? Can I?* he wondered. *What has happened to her? What has happened to them all?*

The girl stared directly ahead and gave no indication that she even knew he was there. Rocan finally turned and walked away, but when he *felt* the slow turn of her head and then heard her languid, almost wistful voice, his legs nearly gave way altogether.

"*Light and dark. Light and dark. The ever-spinning stone.*"

He did not turn, fearing what he might see. After a moment he continued around the corner, and for a while he walked much more swiftly than before. Nothing followed him; at least, nothing he could see.

As he reached the flight of marble steps that led up to the Lord Protector's chambers, Rocan stopped suddenly, aware of a change in the air, a peculiar ripple of warmth that had a bitter tang to it. Involuntarily he took a couple of steps back, confused. *This has the feel of sorcery,* he thought. Grimly he tried once again to take a step forward, but an inexplicable fear gripped him. A moment later he found that he stood even further back, one hand curled around his cold necklace again.

"Do you feel it?" a voice whispered from behind him. Rocan whirled round to behold- of all people- Ulan, the Chief Guardsman. He stood maybe six paces away and trembled like a cur about to be punished.

As the initial shock faded, it occurred to Rocan that he had not seen the Chief Guardsman for almost as long as the Lord Protector. Ulan's appearance bore a worrying similarity to that of the various servants he had encountered along his way. Dull, dark eyes glimmered faintly in their sockets as if only a dim spark of life remained. A thick glaze of sweat and dirt covered his face except where a straggly beard spread from his chin, unkempt and matted with something glistening and pink-hued. Rocan realised after a moment that it was raw meat.

"What has happened here?" he demanded. "I have seen only half a dozen servants and one of your guardsmen. Where is everyone else? Where is the Lord Protector? When did the Council last meet in session?"

Ulan responded by staring in one direction and then another. He moved his head almost like a twitching bird. Finally he opened his mouth in what looked almost like an apologetic smile. Rocan stared in fascinated horror at the man's teeth, which seemed to have grown inordinately large on one side. For a moment he thought he could see several small tongues darting around in Ulan's mouth, deep red and furtive. But Rocan fancied that that must have been his imagination, because Ulan opened his mouth wider a moment later and picked something- more raw meat by the look of it- from a single and human, if desperately unhealthy, tongue.

"Times are hard," Ulan told him, as if that might be an acceptable excuse.

"Answer my questions, Chief Guardsman, and if you fail to do so this time, or if your answers do not satisfy me, I will draw from you an answer that does. I trust you understand me even in your fevered state. Any trickery and I will cut you down."

Panic lit up in Ulan's eyes for a moment, and he shrank back as if he expected Rocan to leap at him regardless of the answers he gave. Rocan judged that the Chief Guardsman was searching the recesses of his mind for a suitable response. *Choose wisely,* Rocan thought grimly, although at the same time a dark voice whispered within his mind: *If you do cut him, what might you find inside?*

"We can't face the other ones alone," Ulan whispered finally, as if the *other ones-* whatever they might be- could very well be eavesdropping on them. "This always been this way. It was this way before, is now, and will be again. The Old Ones, the Earth Lords, aid us in our time of need." His voice dropped so much that Rocan could barely hear him at all even in the otherwise absolute silence of the corridor.

"Have you found new gods to worship, Ulan? Is that what this is about?" Rocan shook his head. "How does that explain all that I've seen here? A fortress more than half-deserted, its last remaining occupants having succumbed to madness? How does *that* aid us against anyone? Where are the Councillors? Where is the Lord Protector? I must speak with him."

Ulan said nothing, but a thin rim of fresh, bright blood appeared at the edges of his right eye. He blinked slowly, and from one corner of that eye a thick red drop emerged, and trickled part of the way down his cheek.

"One of the halls still has a fire in the hearth," Ulan said suddenly. "Let me take you there. It's warm. So much warmer." Another drop of blood made languid progress down his cheek, as if the very thought of warmth made him weep.

"Tell me about these *Earth Lords* first. Then we can go." Rocan allowed one hand to stray to the pommel of his sword, where it remained. The name meant nothing to him, or so he thought, yet it had a peculiar resonance to it, as if he somehow *ought* to know what it meant. Had such things been mentioned by people in the outlying settlements from time to time? He thought they might.

Ulan's response was both disturbing and strangely pathetic. He reached out an arm imploringly, a look of desperation in his eyes. "Please, Rocan." His voice sounded different again now, almost childlike. "*Let me take you.*" He took a faltering step forward, and Rocan half-drew his sword, never taking his eyes off the Chief Guardsman. "No further, Ulan, or you die. I'll not warn you again."

Ulan grinned savagely, and Rocan noticed with shock that his mouth was now filled with many more teeth, and the squirming redness behind them was not a tongue or even many tongues; it was something he had never seen anything like before.

Abruptly, Ulan turned and fled down the corridor. He moved with a strangely fluid action and laughed as he went. Rocan watched until both the Chief Guardsman and the echoes of his mirth had gone, and only then did he allow himself to relax a little. A little was all he could allow. He felt as if a hundred unseen enemies hovered nearby, ready to sink their teeth into him.

Rocan did not head upstairs to the Lord Protector's chambers, fearing that air of menace and what might happen if he persisted in fighting his way through it. *I won't become like Ulan,* he told himself, although he had no idea what Ulan had become. *I won't.*

Instead he made his way along another corridor, having decided that even one of the few remaining servants might be of more use than Ulan in helping him piece together what had happened here. He kept one hand on his sword hilt, but its familiarity failed to comfort him. *Because it will do little to protect me,* he told himself, before angrily banishing that voice of despair.

What happened to Ulan? he wondered. *What was that... creature inside him? Was it a creature at all, or just some illusion or glamour, an effect of whatever sorcery has been let loose within these walls?*

From time to time he passed close to windows that looked out on the wintry scene outside and noticed that the sky had swiftly darkened and the snowfall had become thicker than ever. With a sinking heart, Rocan realised that he would likely have to spend the night here, and perhaps the next depending on conditions tomorrow.

I'd rather die frozen in the snow, facing the sky, he thought savagely, but he had no idea if he meant it.

Rocan encountered no one as he walked through one passageway after another and looked cautiously into abandoned rooms and halls. Each of his laboured breaths hung in the icy air. His right hand began to feel almost lifeless, nothing more than part of the sword hilt he continuously held. More than once he stumbled, and several times he failed to remember a line or even an entire verse in the long prayer he iterated, the *Virtue of Spring.* The spring season might have been an eternity away or a myth from long ago, but this was the only prayer he could remember now.

Full darkness had fallen outside when finally he came upon a hall with a roaring fire in the hearth set into the far wall. Perhaps it was the one that Ulan had so desperately promised him. The great flames danced as reflections in the windows, as if strange cousins of theirs had somehow lit themselves outside. A moment after he saw these, Rocan noticed the man kneeling by the fire, and wondered why he had not noticed him before anything else in this place.

He walked cautiously into the hall a little way, sword drawn, and as he did, the man who sat at the hearth turned to face him.

Had the sword not been so firmly stuck to his hand, Rocan might well have dropped it in his shock.

Arrko Neam, his father, once commander-in-chief of Ruan-Tor's fighting men, gone for twenty years, beheld him calmly with a faint smile upon his face. "Rocan, my son," he said quietly, looking him up and down. Dark brown eyes gazed implacably. "It has been too long."

Rocan struggled to speak. For a moment he even struggled to stand. "You... I thought... I thought you..."

"...had gone forever? I expect you did." His father patted the rug sprawled near the fire, part of which he was sitting on. "Come. Sit with me and I'll endeavour to explain. I have quite a story to tell."

Fatigue and confusion had shredded Rocan's resolve. He knelt by the hearth with a faint sigh and stretched his hands towards the fire. Soon he felt the familiar prickling and pain as blood began to flow through his fingers again. Meanwhile, his father remained silent, perhaps considering something. Eventually he said, "I feel I must apologise for the actions of the Chief Guardsman. He has not handled his responsibilities well, unfortunately."

Suddenly Rocan decided that all of this- his father, the fire, even the whole damned fortress- was itself nothing more than a sorcerous glamour, the purpose of which was to destroy him. He moved suddenly, intending nothing more than to get to his feet and scramble away into the surrounding cold darkness. Arrko reached out his hand, however, and grasped Rocan's wrist. *He's lost none of his iron strength,* Rocan thought wildly, still striving for the exit. *If this is him.*

"I can assure you that I'm every bit as real as you," his father said softly. The steely gaze met Rocan's, and the knight-commander suddenly realised the truth of those words. "I can tell you anything about yourself, Rocan. Until you reached eighteen summers, at least. I shouldn't have left, but I did, and there's the fact of it. I have heard of your more recent exploits second hand, which shames me."

Rocan sat down again, staring at the shadows of flames dancing madly upon the walls. *Something is wrong throughout this place*, he thought, *yet here he is after all these years, amid this madness. Why has he returned? And...*

"Why did you mention Ulan?" he asked suddenly. "Why would you apologise for him?"

Arrko smiled. "I'm sorry, Rocan. I failed to explain myself. I have returned in order to help prepare Ruan-Tor for the war to come. You could say that *I* am now the Lord Protector, although that title no longer has meaning or relevance."

Rocan stared at him. "I understand none of this. Who made you Lord Protector? There's been no meeting of the Council for weeks as far as I can gather, and such decisions may *only* be made by the Council. How did you travel here, when everywhere surrounding Ruan-Tor is snowbound? And what has happened to this place? What has happened to the people here in the fortress?"

Arrko raised a hand as if to placate his son. "These are all good questions, Rocan. I will answer them, and I'll do so truthfully, but first you must be made aware of one thing- you may not like the truth. You may hate and fear it."

"Nevertheless, it's the truth I must have from you," Rocan told him. "Leave nothing unsaid."

"As you wish." Arrko turned to the fire, as if to include it in the discussion, and presently he began to speak. By the time he had finished, the world of certainty that Rocan knew had fallen apart entirely.

"As I said, you may soon wish never to have heard what you're about to learn. You are entitled, I suppose, to react in such a way to the unknown." Arrko gazed levelly at him then and shook his head, a ghost of a smile upon his face. "If I had remained here, I could have told you this years ago, Rocan. Instead, I left- but *you,* you've become blinded by your own piety. It's therefore harder for you to comprehend. But let me assure you of one thing for certain. The Age in which you and I were born, the one we know, is at an end. The Existence itself is dotted with the beginnings and endings of things, and yet the Existence itself never truly ends. What we are witnessing, what we are a *part* of, is the closure of one way and the opening of another. Even the stars are not forever, my son. They are like people; they burn brightly for a while, and then they fade, and new stars take their place."

"How can you know such things?"

"Be patient. I have a story to tell you. Of a sorcerer who became weary, angry and unworthy of the gift granted to him. Of Aona itself rising against those invaders that would defile it. You have heard of Morthanien, of course."

Rocan nodded. "The old warlock. Who has not heard of him? What gives him the right to persist for centuries, using forbidden powers, when others are born, struggle to live and then perish?"

"Well, there we are." His father seemed amused by something. "You unearthed something of the truth all by yourself, Rocan. What indeed gives him such a right? His talents were considerable, but still they were nothing but a gift bestowed upon him by powers far greater than he."

"You say *were*. Has something become of him?"

Arrko's smile widened further. "Indeed it has. Morthanien is no more." He leaned forward slightly, and when he next spoke, his voice sounded quite different, delivered in a slightly higher pitch. The words he uttered

spilled forth with urgency, almost as if he had remembered
something soon to be forgotten again, like a half-remembered
dream that had rushed back into sharp but only temporary
focus.

"We came from the forgotten cracks in the world,
deep within the Pinnacles, the unwalked places where the
ice lies forever. We ran through the valleys, fast, eager,
racing over hardened snow. We felt a gathering of power in
the air. The time fast approached for *taking it back*." Arrko
nodded grimly. "Yes, time for the warlock to relinquish his
loan from the ancient powers of Aona itself, the loan he no
doubt always thought a gift from his distant younger days. Is
it not always the way? These shapers of forces believe
themselves to be the centre, the creator of the force, the
source of the powers.

"That evening, as soon as the sun had set Archaon
rose slowly in the east. By red light we formed a circle
around Morthanien's stone borders, a circle even he would
never have seen."

"How so?" Rocan asked, but Arrko explained nothing
and pressed relentlessly on, stretching out his arms on either
side almost like wings as he continued: "Each one of us
remained linked to those others nearest on either side. The
heartbeat of the earth belongs to no one, yet at that moment
it felt almost as if it belonged to all of us. I could see
everything. Upon the ground, the minute detail of life. Rising
in the sky, each mountain and valley of the great red desert
moon. It *is* a desert, you know. I knew it in that moment,
Rocan; I could taste the dust upon its surface. In the sky, I
knew the places where each star would emerge, and even the
distance to each one of them." His eyes flickered quickly and
fixed on his son for a moment. "Can you imagine that? Can
you imagine what it felt like? A window to every secret,
opening for an instant?"

Rocan shook his head numbly. He felt more terrified
now than he had ever felt in his life.

"Now, Morthanien had over centuries made his holdfast the very centre of his power, so much so that there came a time when he no longer left that place, fearful that his supposedly innate talents had diminished, somehow fled into the walls of his home. Madness, perhaps, but I suspect there might have been some truth to it.

"So, by planting in his mind a most persuasive thought, we brought him forth from his fortress. You see, days earlier he had been visited by that miscreant and vagrant Vornen Starbrook, and Vornen warned him of the coming of the *marandaal,* the starspawn as some old texts refer to them..."

"Starbrook." Rocan spat the name. "If I could find him, I'd hang the man without trial. He's a traitor and a murderer."

"Is he?" Arrko smiled at that. "If you say so. But we digress. Those of us who dwelt near to Morthanien's domain sensed the shifting of his thoughts after he sent Vornen away..."

"You could have killed Starbrook there and then," Rocan said bitterly.

"Why? He is nothing to us, and in fact, because of nothing more than simple luck, he struck an important blow in the first battle against the *marandaal.*"

"I don't understand. What are these *marandaal?*"

"You'll find that out in time. But enough of Vornen; soon his part in these matters will be done. We brought Morthanien from his safe abode with whispered promises of alliance- not with ourselves of course, but with the *others-* those of the First Race who separated from the Earth Lords millennia ago. We call them the Forgotten now; it's the only name they deserve. In time, he emerged, and walked into the Pinnacles.

"He did not find the Forgotten. Why would he? They are long gone from the world that you and I know. They have *faded,* for want of a better word. And he died amongst *us* instead, confused and in agony, barely able to recall who and what he once was. His powers- still considerable, though he no longer thought them to be- were…" Arrko, paused, trying to find the right turn of phrase. "We feasted upon them," he said finally.

Even then, as Rocan struggled to comprehend any part of what his father had just said, the hall was not a silent place. The fire now roared in the hearth more fiercely than ever, as if Arrko's telling of his story had stirred it into joyous celebration. Outside, snow fell gently onto the many feet already fallen, but Rocan imagined he could hear the soft descent of every single flake as it sighed through the air and came to rest. *Gods,* he thought miserably. *Gods save me! I am becoming like Ulan. Should that happen and I finally succumb to madness, what then? Will I still retain the wits to…*

With an effort, he abruptly ceased that train of thought. Self-murder was self-murder, no matter what the circumstances. *If only this were a nightmare,* he thought. *One long nightmare from which I could wake into summer and find I spent the entire winter ill, delirious, as some others in the town were…*

"You have heard of the Earth Lords," Arrko stated. Rocan found himself pulled back into the terrible dream. Finally some dim recollection came to him: *The name was mentioned by some of the plainsfolk further west. Nothing was thought of it.* He ventured, as he remembered a little more, "Some call them the Blood Lords, or by their ancient name- the *choragh*. If they are now your masters, then truly your soul is no longer your own."

"Soul? Is that what you call the essence of life?" Arrko laughed contemptuously. "Our lives are *not* our own, my son. We are all a part of something greater, part of the world itself. That may not be what your idiot church teaches its fearful followers, but nonetheless it is true, and will forever be true."

He reached out his hand and grabbed Rocan's wrist. The flames in the hearth roared and leapt further in approval. "You are stronger than most, Rocan," he said, "and if you direct that strength to our cause, you will be rewarded. You will become as I am."

"And what are you?" his son demanded. "A renegade sorcerer, dealing in all things dark?"

"Nothing of that sort. I'm only a dedicated follower, the eyes and ears to the Earth Lords amongst those of my own kind." Arrko's grip tightened. Rocan could feel his pulse resonate with the crackle of logs and the insistent, supposedly inaudible patter of the snow outside.

"Forsake your old beliefs," his father said, "for they can't help you and they never could. I can ensure that whatever now happens, you will not share Ulan's fate."

"And why *did* Ulan endure such a fate?"

"He was weak. Soon, he will wither away, his usefulness at an end. But Ulan and his like are not our concern. Our concern is the guardianship of Aona- this precious world- against the *marandaal*. I can assure you of one thing in that regard: nothing is more important. *Nothing.* Do you understand?"

In that moment, Rocan almost *did* understand. He thought also that he understood the feverish look in his father's eyes, his words about Aona, about the night that Morthanien had been borne on the wings of a false, whispered promise to a cold end.

"I see that you still don't entirely comprehend," Arrko said flatly after a while. "But you will."

"When?" Rocan found every utterance a vast effort now. His mouth would barely open. His head felt as heavy as iron.

Arrko reached forth and, by way of answer, closed both hands around Rocan's.

Rocan decided that some mysterious strength or protective force had passed from his father to himself, for when a short while later they stepped out into the snowbound courtyard, he felt as warm as if they were still sitting near the fire in the abandoned hall. He closed his eyes, and when he did so he could feel the heat of the fire itself, hear the logs snap and burn, even smell the wood smoke. *He has taken a little of it with us,* Rocan thought as he stared at Arrko, who stood to his left, face tilted gently towards the snowfall. His father's lips moved but uttered nothing that Rocan could hear.

For a long time the two men stood in the freshly-fallen snow without speaking. Rocan could sense every snowflake as it swirled to meet its brethren, as if it were a boulder hurtling through the close sky. An invisible and unfathomable blanket of warmth wrapped itself about him. His vision swam and blurred almost to a smear, then suddenly cleared. He even fancied that he could see the stars of the sky, although that was impossible; low, thick cloud hung over the town.

I have become something fell, Rocan despaired. *Despite everything, I have followed my father's footsteps. There's a taint running through my veins. What hope for me now?*

He reflected that Ruan-Tor would likely fall anyway; to the *marandaal* perhaps, or to his father's Earth Lords. *It's a battlefield,* he considered, *but my people are nothing but mud on that battlefield, to be trodden underfoot.*

It occurred to him that the hell that followed self-murder might be preferable to his continued existence, for in that moment, as Arrko breathed in the night air and smiled into the darkness as if he shared secrets with it, Rocan realised numbly that Ruan-Tor belonged to his father now, and through him his father's masters. *Damned whichever path I choose,* Rocan thought savagely, and silently he mouthed a final, desperate prayer to the Gods he knew, who had abandoned him, and abandoned his people.

Neither salvation nor any sign came. All he could see and hear now were a thousand elemental instruments playing the Earth Lords' symphony.

VIII - Threads in the Earth

I

Dawn light crept ever closer from the east, pale blue etched with faint gold where the silhouettes of distant hills met the sky. Leaves sighed in the chill breeze. The air seemed full of unseen things, moving as the night faded.

Lyya woke suddenly into such a scene, confounded by it, for she had just dreamed of sitting exactly where she sat now, watching shadows and listening to sounds in the depths of the forest, to the odd poetry of their motion and sound. She had been about to get up and wander across the encampment, to see and hear these things more closely, to catch a glimpse and a whisper.

Dream and reality, she thought with a shiver, and wrapped her blanket tightly around herself. *Sometimes I can barely tell the two apart, here. Why do they so often seem the same, since we came to this place? Is this something conjured by Ilumor and those who cleave to him?*

Fauli was already awake and sitting cross-legged on the ground, head bowed and eyes half-closed in that disconcerting way that was peculiar to her, a flicker of sclera just visible. Lyya almost felt tempted to cast some tired insult her way- Powers knew they had traded plenty of those during their tempestuous and occasionally violent journey to Rockmire- but she lacked the strength and spirit at this early hour. In fact, she was beginning to feel that her strength and spirit were being quietly carried away bit by bit as she slept each night. *Perhaps into the depths of the forest along with my dreams,* she thought moodily. In any case, the *du-luyan* woman was ill-tempered at the best of times, and Lyya had no stomach for a fight.

She had a fair idea of what Fauli was doing and did not entirely begrudge her the exercise. Her companion was not praying exactly, for the *luyan* and *du-luyan* Races did not pray as humans did, to invisible and intangible deities. It was more a call to the elements themselves, to the life force of the earth, a cry for strength and hope. Lyya understood that well enough, although the calls and chants of her people differed markedly from those of the *du-luyan*. She had felt an urge to recite her own calls ever since they had entered the sprawl of tents and temporary shacks that made up the Rising encampment. But she had been disturbed to find that she could no longer recall them exactly. It had, she thought ruefully, been a long time since she had spent time amongst her own people, other than those gathered here in the Rising.

And no matter what the elders say, about us never being strangers to one another, Lyya reflected, *that's no longer true. I spoke with these people, but they themselves spoke only of vengeance, or acts that went far beyond vengeance. They had nothing else to say. Their past, their families, none of those things meant anything as far as I could tell.*

They look one way, towards Nisstar. They lust for one thing: the blood of humankind.

She wondered briefly if the others had reached Nisstar yet. Idly she caressed a ring in the pocket of her trousers. Its twin was in Jaana's hands. *Will I see her again?* Lyya wondered. *She will find Nisstar a terrible place. By all the Powers I hope she survives it, and that we meet again in Alinnora's Haven.*

Lyya sighed. She had never expected to meet someone like Jaana and being here in Rockmire with only Fauli for company made that loss feel even more acute.

Not loss, she told herself angrily. *Fistelkarn will look after her. I'm sure of it.*

"Bad dream?" Fauli enquired softly, without making any discernible movement. Lyya cursed herself for jumping, though every little sound or movement was apt to make her do just that.

Fauli slowly raised her head and stared at her companion. Lyya returned the almost feral, yellow-eyed gaze. She noticed that Fauli had tied three more tight knots in her hair, another protective warding favoured by the *duluyan*, although Lyya doubted that it would do much good here.

"Dreams seem to take on an aspect of our waking moments here," she said eventually, keeping her voice low. "I can't help but dread the possibility of the two becoming indistinguishable. Yes, I realise how mad that sounds." She smirked humourlessly. "You could say I had a bad dream, yes."

Fauli moved lithely to sit next to her and placed her hands together palm-first as if in contemplation. A hundred paces or so away, where some of the Rising's foot soldiers had made camp, a few had struggled from their tents either to relieve themselves or help with the preparations for breakfast. The two women watched the unfolding scene in silence for a while.

Eventually Fauli turned to her and said, "Every day and night we spend here takes us further from our path. A few days more, and I feel sure we would become helpless pawns, foot soldiers in this pointless and bloody enterprise, no matter what our feelings are on the matter. I too no longer feel that my dreams or even my thoughts are entirely my own. When I talk with those who have gathered here, preparing for war, I somehow *feel* their rage course through their veins. I've never felt anything like that before. If it's sorcery, then it's subtle- almost a heightened empathy. A presence of some sort weaves itself around them and into them." She shook her head. "I have no wish to empathise with their urges. But I feel also that something has stirred them up into an even more vengeful state."

Lyya was startled and disturbed at that insight. "Perhaps. Certainly it's as if there is some... some *spell* to this place."

"We must convince Serina to come with us to Alinnora's Haven," Fauli reminded her. "But I cannot figure how we do that. She still seems to believe that by remaining within the Rising she can somehow affect its outcome. I don't believe that's possible."

"Then we speak again with her today and no later. This morning, if we can." Lyya recalled the conversation they had both had with Serina yesterday when conveying Fistelkarn's message to her. The woman had been terse and tight-lipped and had eventually sent them both away, although she had at least firstly told them of the man who seemed to be the true leader of the entire Rising- incredibly, a *human* man, or part-human. "His name is Ilumor," Serina had told them, "and you had better hope beyond hope that you fail to attract his attention." Then she had muttered something about Fistelkarn being an old fool for sending people to her, that it was already too late for such pleas.

Lyya had caught a glimpse of Ilumor later, or someone who could have been him based on Serina's description; a tall, slim man with black hair and dark eyes. She had swiftly turned away, fearful that she might attract his attention as Serina had warned, but his likeness remained in her mind- that smooth, oddly ageless countenance, and the discomforting feeling that he was human only in shape.

Lyya continued, "It won't be easy. She's intent on staying here: she fears Ilumor. Still, we must try."

"And if she chooses to remain here, and will not be swayed," Fauli said, "then we leave anyway, with whatever information and knowledge about the Rising she can pass to us. I won't be a blood-pawn to whatever vileness presides over this gathering. One way or another, we must return to Alinnora's Haven to wait for the others. I suggest we leave today. If Serina is not with us, we can only say that we've done our best."

Lyya nodded. "For once, Fauli, I think we're in complete agreement about something."

They watched and waited through the morning and observed all that went on in the various camps dotted about the area. Occasionally they wandered between them and gathered what information they could by listening to the words of those around them and watching training exercises and briefings by the commanders of each group. Lyya and Fauli remained astonished that the Rising had held together for this long with nothing but the singular purpose of attacking the city of Nisstar holding it together. As far as they could tell, there was little else to the plan except the attack itself, the intention to take the city by sheer force of numbers.

They noticed several self-styled officers of the Rising poring over maps of the land between Rockmire and the city, occasionally pointing at various villages that were unfortunate enough to lie in the way. Lyya wondered if the people of those settlements knew the extent of the danger they were in- she had already heard outlandish boasts about the number of Hastian peasants and smallholders they would butcher as they passed through. *What of the land-lords?* she wondered. *Some of them are powerful enough to have their own armies, small though they may be. Would they allow the Rising to simply rampage through their territories? Or have they opted to simply defend their mansion houses and inner lands, and to the under-earth with those who till their fields for them?*

They also observed Serina's tent that stood on the other side of their clearing and watched to see if and when Ilumor made an appearance. They saw him briefly, talking with a couple of fierce-looking *crommari* men. Eventually he left the area on horseback with one of them, heading east along a broad trail. The two women watched him ride away, waited awhile and then made their way over to Serina's tent.

Fauli called softly to her and a moment later she bade them enter.

The witch was combing her hair in front of a mirror balanced on a chair. Sunlight on the outside surface of the tent cast a warm glow within. Even Serina's drab hair looked alive with light, Lyya noticed. The huge grey wolf Gaan lay at the back of the tent. His eyes flickered open as the women entered the tent, and he raised his head. Lyya paused, her heart almost skipping a beat, but the creature gave them nothing more than a contemptuous look before he settled again.

Serina did not turn, but continued brushing her hair, perhaps a little more fiercely. "What may I do for you both now?" she asked brusquely. "Haven't we exchanged enough words already?"

"We leave Rockmire today," Fauli said, her voice low. She turned and glanced outside the tent, fearful of Ilumor's sudden return.

Serina looked round and waved a hand impatiently. "You'll not be eavesdropped upon here- there's a spell woven into the fabric, or the other way round to be more truthful. Say what else you have to say, and then be gone. You shouldn't have come here at all."

"You have already learned of Jaana, through the message that Fistelkarn sent to you, which you showed to us," Fauli said. "He wrote that Jaana could in time, with mentoring, become powerful enough to withstand the *choragh* and even protect others from their kind. He said also that for many years you had sought out others like her."

Serina grimaced. "Yes, I showed you the old fool's message. But what of it? Nothing came of such efforts. I have done many things, some of them shameful, to find others like her. I *knew* deep within myself that they existed but finding them was an altogether different matter."

"Fistelkarn appears to have found one for you," Lyya pointed out, "and there will be others like Jaana."

"My place is here now." Serina stared coldly at her.

"Your *place*?" Fauli shook her head. "From all I've heard, Serina, your place was once amongst the Circle. They answered to no one."

Serina said nothing for a long time. Lyya thought that she might suddenly shout at them to leave her alone and ride out of Rockmire if that was what they wanted. *If she commands us to leave,* she thought, *then I'll do just that, and drag Fauli with me if I must. Not that I expect she'll need much persuasion.*

But the witch-woman did no such thing. Finally she laid down her hairbrush and sighed deeply. She looked suddenly older, as if a memory of defeat occupied her mind.

"Yes. Once there was the Circle," she said quietly. "But it's been gone for many years now. It grieves me still, that some of those amongst us betrayed the ways that we had led for so long- for the Circle had existed, in one way or another, for eight hundred years before my time, and not always by the same name. Betrayal broke it; conflict and bloodshed. Those few of us who survived became scattered, the Circle and all it stood for eventually forgotten. Perhaps it was too painful for us to remake all that we once had. We could not continue once the trust had been broken. But I've long wished to create something, unhindered by events of the past... a new Circle, if you will, but stronger.

"So I searched for many years, trying to locate those who might have the potential to form a gathering like the Circle again, and make it able to withstand more than ever before, so strong that there cannot be any betrayal."

"You would bind people to it?" Fauli frowned.
Serina shrugged. "If necessary. Such a Circle would need to be unbreakable. I have made attempts to find those who even *might* have that potential. And in recent months..." Serina turned and leaned forward intently. "In recent months, as I learned more about the *marandaal* and the *choragh*, I realised that there existed a much more

important reason for the Circle to be formed again. So little else stands between the Races and their annihilation, either at the hands of their hate-filled leaders, or the minions of the *choragh*, or the *marandaal* themselves. The odds are stacked against our survival. But since the Age of Blood, there have been individuals amongst the younger Races who possess the talent to shape and control the old powers. Above all else, the *choragh* hate and even fear the potential that some amongst the younger Races have- that precious ability to shape and change the world itself. *That* is what gave rise to the Enlightenment. *That* is what caused the fading of the *choragh,* the end of that Age."

Serina sighed and bowed her head. "Of course, one such person is known to you already. Jaana." She looked at them both in turn. "I suspect you've seen something of her powers already."

"A little," Fauli said guardedly.

The fearful look flooded back into Serina's eyes. "In other times, I would accompany you without a second thought, if only to see this girl for myself. But of course, Fistelkarn knew nothing of the situation in which I now find myself. He only knew that I had joined the Rising as a voice of reason, to try and prevent the bloodshed they have planned. I had intended to do this even before... before *him.*"

"You can do no good here, given that the Rising will march on Nisstar regardless," Lyya said. "Surely you can do more if you come with us. You cannot preach peace to a restless army bent on vengeance. They will leave the cover of the forest soon and head across the open land, pillaging their way towards the city- and what then? Will you stay with them and be a part of it?"

"Even if I leave," Serina whispered, leaning forward and glancing swiftly about as if Ilumor might suddenly loom from out of the shadows, "*diafagh* and others will be sent after me. I am certain of it. One I might destroy, but with an entire horde of them on my trail- on *our* trail- our chances of ever reaching Alinnora's Haven vanish altogether. Can you not see that for yourselves?"

"And if you *don't*," Fauli said quietly, "then how can this new Circle ever be formed? How can any of these witchlings you speak of, who you have been trying to find, ever reach their potential, leaderless and scattered? They know nothing of each other, and never will. Is this how you choose to end your days, Serina? Half-maddened by your dreams, your body and mind a plaything for the *choragh*-worshipping creature you call Ilumor?"

Lyya stared in shock at her companion, but Fauli's words seemed to have had an effect of some sort. Human and *du-luyan* stared at each other for what seemed an age. During that time, it was Lyya's turn to fear the return of Ilumor. She opened the tent flap a little and peered out, but thankfully he failed to appear. Perhaps he wandered the deepest reaches of the forest again, chanting or singing, as she had heard people say he liked to do. *Communing*, Lyya thought to herself with a shudder. *Is that what he does? Talk to the earth? That's a* luyan *way, but so different...*

Finally Serina said quietly: "What you propose is madness. Suicide."

Fauli folded her arms and stared implacably back at her. Lyya knew that look of grim determination. The *du-luyan* woman would not back away now. *What are we doing?* Lyya thought in a moment of sudden panic. *We're out of our depth. What will Ilumor do? What kind of horrors will he send after us? Maybe Serina is right- we will never reach Alinnora's Haven if we leave and she comes with us.*

She almost opened her mouth to argue against this sudden move by Fauli, and drag her outside if she had to, but did not. For a long time afterwards, she would bitterly regret her silence.

"The alternative is unthinkable, Serina," Fauli said, "and if you are to ever see the Circle or anything like it made again, you must leave with us."

Until the last Ildarian month or so, Lyya had yearned for adventure. Now she was finding the grim, frightening reality of it wholly unlike the enthusiastic notions from her youth.

Of the three, Serina was the best rider. She rode a good twenty paces in front of Lyya and Fauli, hurtling down the broad East Road. The great wolf Gaan appeared sometimes, a faint blur alongside Serina. Then he would leave them awhile and either run ahead or drop back, perhaps on the lookout for their enemies, however they might manifest themselves. *They will follow,* Serina had reminded them. *Not Ilumor himself, but he will send others. He will not rest. He wants me by his side, to eventually be broken. And if he cannot have that, then he will destroy me.*

Then, she had grimly added: *This girl had better be worth the trouble.* Lyya had hated her for that. If Jaana was ever trouble, then certainly it was not her own doing. As far as she could tell, Jaana detested the power that dwelt within her, and bitterly wished it would vanish. She had never asked for it. Lyya had no love for humankind, but there were people of all Races who stood out from those amongst them, and Jaana was surely one of them. *Who could have thought I would feel that way?* Lyya reflected. *And yet I sought her out, before any of this happened, all because I wished to learn the ways of witchcraft. That never happened. In fact, I'd rather know nothing about it now.*

Soon it became too dark for them to continue safely on horseback. They made camp a few dozen paces from the road, where they could see and hear any travellers that might pass by and yet remain hidden from them- aside from whoever or whatever Ilumor sent after them of course. *Anyone travelling by night in these parts will be of ill will,* Lyya thought morosely, *and are most likely Ilumor's minions.*

Shortly after they had settled, Gaan returned. The unearthly grey beast loomed over them, red-hued eyes glittering by Ildar's light, and Lyya's right hand stole instinctively nearer to the hilt of her longknife. With a concerted effort- and noticing Serina's sharp look in her direction- she relaxed. Giving the creature an excuse to tear her to shreds would hardly be the wisest move. *Powers, I hope we make it to Alinnora's Haven,* she thought fervently. *Let us just make it that far and reunite with the others a few days from now. Maybe Jaana will be able to do something about whatever Ilumor sends after us. Maybe Fistelkarn will.*

Serina stared morosely into the distance. By the time she finally spoke, the red moon Archaon had risen high into the sky, and Ildar had sunk beneath the tree line in the west.

"We are damned now," she said, "and all for a favour returned."

"A favour returned?" Fauli repeated, frowning.

"To Fistelkarn. He found Jaana, or to be exact, you brought her to him. But it will take far more than one foundling to remake the Circle." Serina shook her head. "I have thought about it again throughout the day, and in honesty I'm not sure it should be made again. *Once broken, forever broken,* was one of our old sayings about our alliance. Because in many ways it was built on trust, and eventually that trust was betrayed."

Serina spat upon the ground as if trying to excise the memory. "Yet I cannot resist the *idea.* It's like a poison that can never be purged. That's why I sent..." She stopped abruptly. "Never mind."

"Why was the Circle formed at all?" Lyya asked her. "In order to govern and rule over those who practised witchcraft?"

Serina gave her a derisive look. "Hardly! If anything, we had two reasons- for those of repute to link together and share their knowledge, and to seek those with potential, so that they might be brought under our wing, and guided. Protected, where necessary."

"From what?" Fauli asked.

"Many things." Serina's expression grew even grimmer. "Persecution by those who are fearful and superstitious, or those in the cities and towns who follow the teachings of the various Churches, to whom sorcery of any sort is anathema. Loss of control over their own abilities. Some start to harm themselves or others. Madness. Murder. There are always people who, when they unlock the powers within themselves cannot resist the urge to use them for wrongdoings. Need I go on?"

Lyya and Fauli exchanged glances. "Does this happen often?" Lyya asked.

"Often enough. Through guidance, they can usually be helped. But we live in different times now. All those who possess any such potential would in peaceful times be found and brought together, not only for their own protection but because the Old Powers have two sides, a light and a dark for want of better words. Always the *choragh* have resented the younger Races' acquisition of the talent, the wielding, that once they had to themselves. Now, as they grow strong once again, they will reach out to all those in whom the Old Powers run, seeking to corrupt them, bend them and reshape them as one would a tool. The forces themselves are growing strong- the forces that govern this world. They have awakened in the form of the *choragh*, but also in the form of those such as Jaana- and there will be others- who are finding more to themselves than they ever feared existed."

Serina shook her head as if in self-disgust. "The Circle cannot be simply made anew. I realise that now. All those with the potential for greatness must be nurtured, trained, taught to master their talent. But that would normally take many years. We do not even have many tennights, I suspect." Serina sighed. "Therefore, I would instead have to hurry them along the path. To do that carries great risk."

"And aside from you, who might teach them in any case?" Fauli added.

"Well, indeed. They are in distant places, and the nearest would likely be in Harn. I know of none in Aphenhast except Morthanien, and he also is far from here. I even heard a rumour that he perished."

Serina smiled thinly. "In my own way, I have been searching for these... *witchlings* as some would call them, for a very long time. Some part of me wanted to find them and protect them. All my adult life I was a part of the Circle, until its breaking, so the habit is hard to break. But they're not easily found. I used any method I could..." Her voice trailed away, and a curious, hard look flashed in her eyes.

I have no doubt of that, Lyya thought as she stared up at the starlit heavens. *But what do you truly want, Serina? To help guide those who otherwise would remain alone and afraid of themselves- or to help yourself become the leader of a new Circle, despite your protestations that it should never again exist?*

III

Ilumor's first reaction when he learned of Serina's disappearance would have astounded the three women who had fled from his gathering. He simply shrugged his shoulders. Serina would have continued to be a useful vessel, he considered, powerful but still controllable, and he had enjoyed the irony of manipulating the woman who had summoned him from his half-aware wanderings within the twilit other-place of the Silver Road. Of course, it would have been impossible to trust her, but hadn't it always been so? Being human, she possessed an odd faith in the younger Races. *You cannot protect them,* he had told her. *You can only use them. See how I use you?*

She had not listened of course. In her mind, she had still tried to fight against him. She still believed that the younger Races possessed some Powers-given *right* to the secrets of the world. But then, she would. She was one of them. She had never crossed over and seen the things that *he* had seen.

It occurred to him soon enough, however, that Serina might have left for reasons other than her difference of opinion with his masters. The more he dwelt on this possibility, the more it troubled him. The *luyan* and *du-luyan* women evidently knew her, and they too had departed. Why?

Abruptly, Ilumor decided to have them all destroyed.

That same evening, under the cover of darkness, he had three foot soldiers slain. The deeds were carried out by a sloe-eyed *crommar* knifeman who had already shown not only unswerving loyalty whatever might be asked of him, but a definite penchant for murder. One of the three victims was a human renegade who sought vengeance on his entire race. The second was a *luyan* female who had been showing signs of insanity and was therefore not likely to be of use for much longer, and the third was a particularly violent *du-luyan* man who Ilumor had seen brawling on several occasions.

He had the bodies brought to a clearing half a league from the Rising encampment. It would not do if anyone beheld the ceremony he was about to carry out. After all, the overwhelming majority of those amongst the Rising felt that they were on the same side as the *light,* or the *good*, no matter how much they bragged about the number of humans they would butcher on their triumphant march to Nisstar.

Ilumor waited for his *crommar* helper to leave, which he did without so much as a word. Then he undressed and arranged the bodies in the middle of the clearing so that their heads touched one another. Finally he removed his own clothing, noting with amusement his intense state of arousal. He crouched by the dead and began an ancient ceremony known in the old tongue as the *diafagh caiin,* the making of vessels.

From each of the bodies he drank a little blood. Then he daubed symbols upon his skin using more of their blood, each one to represent one of the elements. Then he cut out the hearts of each, and ate them, squatting in the grass and breathing in the harsh odour of blood as his teeth tore at the tough flesh. In the distant east, Archaon rose slowly into the night sky.

Finally he began a low, guttural chant, and the few animals that remained nearby that night turned and fled at the sound. If Ilumor's *crommar* henchman had remained behind to spy on his master, he would have seen an odd shimmer in the air, as if heat rose from the ruined bodies. He would have seen Ilumor's arms raised over them, suddenly longer and leaner than they ought to be, hands outstretched like claws. He would have seen the vertebrae in Ilumor's naked back jut out like barbs.

But the *crommar* man had sensibly long fled the scene, and so he did not hear Ilumor's chanting grow faster and lower at the same time, until it blurred into a continuous bestial growl.

Finally the bodies twitched, and as if tugged at by an invisible puppeteer they staggered lopsidedly to their feet. Ilumor sagged visibly and the noise that emanated from him died away. He uttered a long drawn out sigh, and something emerged into the night from that exhalation. It had the appearance of red smoke, and the taint of iron and earth. This release signalled the end of the ceremony.

Ilumor rose unsteadily and smiled as the three *diafagh* stood slack-jawed and glass-eyed before him. *Will Serina and her young ladies see the irony of being hunted and slain by one of each kind- human, luyan and du-luyan?* he wondered. *I would like to think so.*

From a glass vial in his discarded belt pouch Ilumor poured some of Serina's blood into his palm. He had had it for a long while, the product of what had seemed an innocent handshake, back when she had thought him malleable. *The arrogance,* he thought. *Even after she brought me back, once she recovered from her initial fear, she thought I might be hers, and dance to her tune.*

He smeared some of the blood upon the lips of each *diafagh* and observed as they thirsted for more. The *duluyan* once-man snapped at the air; the *luyan* bit its own lip and tore at the flesh. The human stretched out a hand imploringly.

"This is the taint of the human witch, Serina, once of the Circle," Ilumor intoned. "Seek her, and the two women she is with. Slay them. Do not rest until they are all dead."

No *diafagh* was capable of understanding anything beyond simple orders; they were vessels for a higher purpose and nothing more. None showed any comprehension of his order, but as they turned and stumbled away across the clearing, heading east under the red moon's muted light, Ilumor knew they would not rest until Serina and those with her had been destroyed.

And thus will die the last of the Circle, he thought with a smile. *It should have happened long ago. Still, better now than never. Did I not tell you, Serina? Whilst upon the Silver Road I learned that every other member of your laughable coven had perished, most of them at the hands of the Earth Lords. Yes, their reach grows with each passing day. And yes, the Silver Road is not the safe place you thought it to be.*

Ilumor laughed out loud, tired but happy with his night's work. Then he dressed and began the long walk back to the camp. After a while his strength returned, and he broke into a run. As the forest became a blur around him, Ilumor broke into a chant-song, ancient and terrible, and it seemed to him as he hurtled through the night that Rockmire itself sang back.

IV

The last scrap of sunlight fell below the horizon just as Amethyst and Ileana reached the eastern edge of Alinnora's Haven. In the gathering dusk, bats flitted about near to the woodland that spread towards the south of the village. A slight breeze sighed through the grass.

The village before them looked an oasis of calm, nestled amongst fruit-tree arbours and meadows, built around tracks that ran east-west and north-south to meet at a central crossroads. Smoke curled lazily up into the cool evening air from some of the house chimneys. The scene was peaceful, but Amethyst's thoughts were not.

"This is the place, isn't it?" Ileana spoke up softly. "This is the village where the witch lives." She shivered. "I saw it many times in my dreams. Often I dreamed that I couldn't escape from here. I dreamed that nothing existed outside the village lamplights except endless darkness."

Amethyst said nothing. She had suffered many dreams of her brief time in Alinnora's Haven but had no desire to mention them.

They paused by the side of the road as Amethyst gathered her thoughts, and she reflected on the bitter, painful circle she had travelled, away from and back to this quiet place over the last few months. "At this moment," she said to Ileana, "I feel almost too exhausted to hate. But when I see her again..." An almost savage smile crossed her lips, until she saw Ileana looking wide-eyed at her. "Don't do anything to make it worse," the girl pleaded.

Amethyst could think of nothing to say to that, nor could she to Ileana's next words: "Remember, I'm the one who will suffer at her hands, once you're gone."

They made their way down the main track into the village. A short while later they arrived at the witch's dwelling, a narrow, ramshackle place that almost leaned against the adjacent Haven Inn as if attempting to draw sustenance from its walls. Neither light nor sound issued from within. The two women regarded it in silence before Ileana asked softly, "When you hand me over to her, will you then be free?"

Amethyst blinked in surprise at the torrent of emotion that the question caused. "Yes. At least, I hope beyond hope that I will." She glanced at her companion. "None of this is your fault, Ileana."

The girl shrugged. "I would have done the same, were I you."

"It looks as if the witch-woman isn't at home," Amethyst remarked after they had watched the house a while longer, "although I suppose we should check."

She felt deeply reluctant. The notion suddenly occurred to her of abandoning this course of action entirely. *I could escape with Ileana*, she mused. *It might even be possible. After all, didn't the agonies vanish as soon as I found Ileana? Perhaps all I need do is keep her with me, and that would be easily done. I've had worse travelling companions. If we manage to get to Darkenhelm, surely we'll be safe from witchcraft behind the city walls. Won't we? Do witch-women have allies in Darkenhelm?*

Was it worth the risk? Amethyst stood by the house in the gathering darkness and tried to weigh both sides. For much of her life she had been an impetuous risk-taker by nature, but events had changed her since she had left home. She was beginning to realise just how much she had changed.

The witch could still find us, she considered. *Would she pursue us in search of her quarry? Of course she would, if Ileana means this much to her. And yes, it's just possible that she might have allies in Darkenhelm. Whereas although I have a few favours to call, none of them are for powerful people. I have never known any powerful people.*

And that course of action might place my family in danger. I couldn't live with myself, if I returned only to heap misfortune upon them.

"Well, we can do no good standing here and getting cold," she said abruptly, having made her decision. "I suggest we pay for a room at the Haven Inn here, and find out when she might return, if we can. And if she *is* lurking in her lightless hovel, well"- Amethyst shrugged- "I'm sure she will know where to find us. After all, I felt the hag's eyes in the back of my head for months."

Ileana nodded tiredly. She looked about ready to drop.

Amethyst gave the house one more glance and shuddered. The influence that witches could bring to bear was reputed to spread far and wide across the world. She recalled her father once describing them as spiders, with webs everywhere, hung out and waiting for people to touch and spread ripples through them. It was, Amethyst thought, more than likely an unpleasant truth. Might the witch have fed Ileana's dreams in some way?

The tavern turned out to be pleasantly warm and bright, more so than Amethyst remembered from the previous occasion she had been here. A multitude of lanterns pushed back the shadows, and in the hearth set into the back wall a great fire roared, stoked up every so often by an old man who appeared to be one of the servants. The innkeeper, a young but prematurely balding man with long sinewy arms, looked up as Amethyst and Ileana made their way over to the bar. For a moment he frowned, as if he might have remembered Amethyst from the last occasion she had come here.

"The house just next to us," she said. "There were two..." She paused, considering for a moment. The word *witch,* she had discovered, was best used rarely and with extreme caution in these middle lands- a far cry from in Darkenhelm, where it was no more than a common insult thrown at conniving old women. "We were hoping to meet with a woman who lives there, but we could see no lanterns lit in her cottage."

He looked them both up and down. "Are you friends of hers?" The look in his eyes made it clear he believed them to be nothing of the sort.

"We need to speak with her," Amethyst said. She was not prepared to share anything further with this man. Ileana had to be delivered safely, and the less people she told about the reasons for this, the better.

"Well, Serina has gone away." He returned his attention to the barrels and bottles behind the bar and continued over his shoulder, "She left here some days ago in the company of a man I'd not seen before. Strange fellow as I recall. I can't say I liked the look of him much. They seemed to be in quite a hurry to leave."

"Do you know when she might return?"

"Soon, I expect. Often she disappears for a time. That's her way. Here and there and everywhere. She's a healer, so she has business in many places."

Amethyst ground her teeth in frustration. What more could she do now? She had brought Ileana here, as commanded, in the hope of then being freed. *Some assumption,* she thought. Should she simply leave her here? Or might Serina return in the next few days? For a moment, she began to think again about her reckless but persuasive idea of simply leaving with Ileana in tow and making all haste to Darkenhelm.

"Perhaps we could stay here and wait for her," Ileana said. "We've travelled a long way and we're very tired." To Amethyst she sounded ready to burst into tears.

"Well, we have a room available. A small one, but it's clean and tidy. It's a copper crown per night, which includes your water from the well out the back yard, but any food you pay extra for." He laughed suddenly, humourlessly. "They'll not be calling them crowns for much longer, I expect."

"What do you mean?" Amethyst frowned, and he gaped at her. "Where have you been, lady? Haven't you heard?" He shook his head as if she was the twentieth simpleton he had had to deal with today. "The Queen and her family were usurped by a regiment of the army down in Darkenhelm. I expect the Council of Priests will start minting its own coinage soon. Some say such coins are already in circulation, though I've yet to see them myself."

Amethyst stared in bemusement. "We've been... away in the north for a long while. I'd heard nothing about this."

"Well, they presume to follow different laws entirely, north of the Crescents. Those that follow any rule of law at all. I expect the news meant a lot less in those parts even if it did reach them. I won't even pretend to know the reasons behind what I've heard, lady- we're far from such goings-on here- but I'd make a guess and say greed, grievance and opportunity must have joined together and made it happen. I heard it was bloody. Very bloody. But that's not all." He leaned forward and glanced at both in turn. "A month later, soldiers from the Council of Priests in Emberton marched on Darkenhelm and retook the citadel. Still, the Queen's family are gone. All of them. Massacred."

"What about the people of the city? Are there many dead?" Amethyst asked, trying to keep her voice steady.

He shrugged. "I've not heard of any *other* massacre. I expect it all happened within the walls of the palace."

Gods, I wish I knew if Mother and Father were safe and well, Amethyst found herself thinking. *And Lona too. Had she left Darkenhelm in time? I remember she intended to head east. Mother never truly forgave me for making her want to travel and explore. But maybe she'll be far from such troubles by now...*

"A copper crown per night. In advance." The innkeeper extended his hand in expectation. "Or two if you'd like a meal each. Looks as if you could do with it. We've fresh lamb and vegetable broth tonight."

"Thank you." Amethyst handed over two copper crowns, and they made their way to the back of the bar room to sit down. Within a moment of sitting at the table, Ileana had fallen into a light slumber, head bowed forward slightly. Every now and then her lips moved, and she frowned, as if she was protested something or someone in her dream.

Later, after they had had their meals, the two of them made their way up to their chamber. After placing her lantern on the mantelpiece, Ileana flung herself onto the large straw-stuffed mattress with a tired groan. "I could hardly remember what a bed felt like!" she exclaimed.

Amethyst smiled distractedly, her mind on other matters. What were they to do? How long should they remain here? Should they even attempt to head further west and seek out Serina? If so, how might they find her?

Ileana grabbed the jug of water Amethyst had brought up and took a long draught from it. She wiped spillage from around her mouth and then said something that confounded Amethyst.

"I never thanked you," the girl told her shyly.

"*Thanked* me?" Amethyst blinked.

"For taking me from Ethanalin Tur-morn. From my prison." Ileana shuddered and gazed solemnly at Amethyst. Her pale blue eyes glazed over for a moment. "I would have starved to death there," she declared, "with nothing but frozen corpses for company. So I'm glad you found me. I thought I'd end my days in that place."

Amethyst overcame her surprise enough to give her a smile and a hug.

"But if we find the witch," Ileana pointed out, "you'll still hand me over to her. Because you have to."

And in so doing I lose another companion, Amethyst thought sadly. *But perhaps I can bargain with Serina. Perhaps I can stay with Ileana, watch over her, try and make sure no harm befalls her, though how I'm to do that I have no idea. But to walk away and leave her in the hands of a woman capable of torture would be much harder. What should I do? And what will I do?*

"If I can, I will stay with you," she said eventually. "After all, we *are* friends now, aren't we?"

"I suppose we are." Ileana smiled to herself. "I think I'd like that."

Later, as they began to drift off to sleep, Ileana had more to say. "Do you miss Vornen?"

Amethyst's heart almost skipped a beat. She was glad her expression could not be read by the rapidly failing lamplight. "I suppose I do," she said eventually. "But he had to go his own way. He had no choice."

"You liked him a lot," Ileana observed. "I could tell."

Amethyst turned away on her side as tears suddenly welled up. She said nothing, knowing that if she did it would only emerge as a sob. "Maybe we'll see him again," Ileana said encouragingly.

"I don't think so, Ileana," she answered eventually, more roughly than she intended to. "As you said before, the damned Gates will take him, if they haven't already."

Everyone goes away, Amethyst thought bleakly in the darkness. Then her exhaustion got the better of her and moments later she had already fallen into a deep and dreamless sleep.

By the morning, which dawned with mist and drizzle- just as it had when Amethyst had first travelled through this place- even her lingering thoughts of Vornen were pushed to one side. As they finished their breakfast downstairs, the witch-woman returned.

Through the window next to their table, Amethyst saw three riders pull up nearby. When she saw that one of them was Serina, her heart pounded madly for a moment and a quiet rage began to stir within her. The woman untied and shook out her iron-grey hair and gazed grimly about for a short while, then turned to speak with her companions.

Despite the fear and anger that swirled within her, Amethyst's attention was diverted for a moment when she glanced at the witch's companions- a young *du-luyan* girl who looked slender and graceful, until she tried to dismount and did so in truly ungainly fashion- and a *luyan* female who was possibly even younger, though she couldn't be certain.

I wonder what made those two choose to be travelling companions, Amethyst mused as she recalled what she knew of the cool relations between the two races. *Perhaps Serina has forced them to ride with her, much as she forced me to wander through the snowbound lands.*

She glanced at Ileana, who had now also seen the three of them and was watching as they fed and watered the horses at the nearby stable. Even the stable boy seemed to be deferential towards the witch, going as far as to doff his cap at least three times during the brief conversation between the four of them. Amethyst's lip curled in disgust. Was that all it took to be an esteemed elder amongst people in such far-flung places as this? Dabbling and meddling in the sorcerous arts and bending people to your will in so doing?

Ileana pushed her breakfast plate to one side, looking paler than ever. "That's her, isn't it? The old woman with the grey hair."

"Indeed it is." Amethyst found herself wondering madly if she might be able to fling one of her blades at Serina and kill her with a single strike- perhaps from an upstairs chamber facing the stables. She would need to be deadly accurate. Anything less and both she and Ileana would surely be faced with a dire situation. She thought about it a little longer, wondering at the same time if she was serious or not about such an undertaking, before she finally dismissed the idea. It was not because of lack of faith in her own ability- if there was one thing she could do it was use daggers and throwing-knives to devastating effect- but because of what would happen- what would *surely* happen if by some faint chance she failed to embed one of her blades in the witch's head. There were Serina's companions to be considered too, and they both looked more than capable of looking after themselves.

Amethyst noticed the wet gleam in the Ileana's eyes. "Remember what I said last night," she said quietly, "I will stay with you if at all possible."

"You don't have to risk your life for me," the girl said despondently. Amethyst smiled and squeezed her hand. "We've been through a great deal since we met," she said. "I don't want to turn and leave you, Ileana. Not after all that's happened."

The look of gratitude in the girl's eyes was humbling; to stop herself from welling up, Amethyst quickly decided they should go and meet Serina and her friends. "Come on. We've both finished. No need to wait any longer."

They made their way outside and waited for Serina to notice them. When she did, Amethyst smiled inwardly at the momentary look of shock on the old woman's face. "Serina, I believe," she said, "although I never had the pleasure of learning your name when we first met. Still, few days passed in the last few months when I failed to be constantly reminded of you, and your... what should I call them? *Methods*."

The witch's companions bristled with suspicion and youthful impatience as if they simply waited for Serina to give the word, so they could exercise their fighting skills after time in the saddle. Amethyst gave them both a warning stare and folded her arms as Serina gazed at Ileana.

"You found her," the witch-woman said finally. "Tell me, *where* did you find her?"

"Ethanalin Tur-morn," Ileana blurted out before Amethyst could get a word in. "Amethyst said that you had forced her to find out where I was, so that I could be brought to you.”

“Whatever you intend to do with Ileana,” Amethyst spoke up, “I hope for your sake it involves no harm to her. I intend to stay with her, to ensure that that is so.”

“Well, well.” Serina smiled humourlessly. “First I have to bind you to your task, and now, when you’re free to walk away without a further care, you decide to remain and play the big sister.”

The *du-luyan* girl, who had been staring continuously at Amethyst as if she yearned to pick a fight with her, turned to the witch-woman, yellowish eyes glittering. “Serina, who are these two?”

Before Serina could reply, Amethyst did so for her. “Had Ileana not mentioned my name, I doubt Serina would even know or care who I am. After all, she saw fit to curse me.” So saying, she met Serina’s cool, dispassionate stare, and considered it a minor victory when the witch turned to her two companions. “We have perhaps a day, I think, before we must be on the move again. Maybe less.”

“A day?” The *luyan* girl frowned. “You think we’ve hidden our trail that well?”

“Not at all. I simply know that if Ilumor has sent after us what I expect him to, they are hampered by daylight travel in open land. They will keep to the shadows and move more slowly. But that gives us only perhaps a day’s grace, no more. When on the move, they are tireless.”

“What about the others? We were supposed to wait for them!”

“I’ll leave a message. There’s nothing else to be done.” Serina began to make her way towards her dwelling, then looked back and added sardonically, “Perhaps the four of you should sit and become acquainted in the tavern. I have some belongings to bring with us which I need to find. I will not be long.”

After they had seated themselves inside, the *luyan* girl introduced herself, extending her hand in greeting. "If we're to travel together, let's be civil. My name is Lyya."

"I'm Amethyst, and this is Ileana," Amethyst said warily. She shook the *luyan's* hand and tried not to stare at her extra fingers. "But you know our names already." She glanced at the *du-luyan* woman. "And you?"

"Fauli." With some reluctance, Fauli leaned forward and shook hands with both Amethyst and Ileana, who stared at her for a moment before saying, "I saw a *du-luyan* man once. He came to Ethanalin Tur-morn. I saw him in the tavern where I lived, in the bar-room."

"So," Amethyst said to Fauli and Lyya, "from what Serina said, the three of you are running from someone or something?"

Neither of them looked eager to reply. Finally Lyya said quietly, "Have you heard of the Rising?"

Amethyst nodded. "A movement against the laws that were passed in Nisstar? Yes, of course. The priests who rule that place shame all humankind."

"The Rising is not everything it appears to be," Fauli said quietly, "Certain forces have disrupted and infiltrated it. For the moment, they share with the Rising the common purpose of marching against Nisstar- in fact the march may have already begun- but their purpose is simply to enslave *all* the Races."

"All life," Lyya echoed.

Suddenly the door of the tavern flew open, and as the four of them jumped at the sound and turned towards the doorway, they saw Serina silhouetted in the morning sunlight.

"Something is wrong," Fauli whispered, even before the witch collapsed against the table nearest the doorway, heaving and shaking. They rushed over, along with the innkeeper who had abandoned his morning tasks to try and tend to her.

Serina's hands shook and veins jutted from her careworn hands. Her eyes bulged obscenely, blood trickling from their corners. Specks of what looked like black dust mingled with her blood. Her mouth opened and closed as if she desperately sought to convey some message which pain and paralysis prevented her from saying.

"What happened?" Fauli demanded. "What happened, Serina? Are they here?! Powers, how can they be here already?!"

Somehow the witch-woman managed to speak, though she sounded as if she had begun to choke on her own blood. "Too... late... head north-west..."

"What happened?" Fauli demanded again, but Serina gripped her arm with sudden, vicious force, causing her to cry out. "To Harn. *Now.* Take... take from... *go...* GO!"

Her head jerked back suddenly, and blood trickled from her mouth, where something indeterminate moved and *gleamed.* The witch's mouth opened wider and her jaw bone snapped. Finally, her body became still.

The four women stumbled outside into the morning sunlight, spattered with Serina's blood.

It was Amethyst who saw the *diafagh* first.

V

She stood transfixed and stared in horror at the three creatures- corpses pulled upright, bone visibly gleaming in places. The morning sun lit half their putrid bodies as they stood crookedly in the main street, watching them all with sallow eyes.

"It's *them,*" she breathed.

"*Diafagh,*" Ileana echoed faintly.

Despite their rotting appearance, still Amethyst could discern that they were-or had been- human, *luyan* and *du-luyan. Like Serina, Lyya and Fauli,* she thought, although the notion seemed crazed.

The three *diafagh* stumbled towards them. The once-human one snapped at the air, revealing teeth stained with blood and a mouth part-filled with gore, which it spat onto the ground. *Part of Serina,* Amethyst thought, her thoughts and her sight swimming amid this nightmare.

The *diafagh* had almost reached Lyya and Fauli, who desperately prepared to defend themselves, when the creatures stopped suddenly, and with curiously slow movements, turned their attention to Ileana. Helplessly they stared- with what remained of their eyes- in the direction of the girl, who gazed just as helplessly back.

"Kill them!" Amethyst shouted, but Ileana could not. She could only hold them, and thus the nightmare continued. Ileana stood and swayed, blood now dripping from her nose, and the three *diafagh* remained rooted to the spot.

Fauli was the first to move. Moving in a smooth arc, one of her longknives sliced through the neck of the once-*duluyan and* severed the head completely. The body swayed but did not fall; incredibly, it remained standing, blood oozing- not spurting, Amethyst noted absently- from the neck and down the torso in a languid shower. Fauli stepped back and watched in open-mouthed horror as the creature reached out its wasted arms to claw at the air, at once ridiculous and horrifying.

Then Ileana slumped to the ground, her strength gone, and chaos ensued.

The *diafagh* lurched forwards, though more slowly than before, and Fauli and Lyya both stumbled back, hacking furiously at them but to dismal effect. Even the headless *diafagh* staggered relentlessly onwards. Amethyst felt a chill rise in her stomach. She knew that ordinary weapons had little if any effect on these atrocities. "We have to *go!*" she shouted. Not waiting to see if they had even heard her, she hauled a barely conscious Ileana to her feet and retreated towards the stables.

By now, villagers poured from their homes in increasing numbers. Some merely stared in speechless horror, others bore weapons but dared not use them, and still others took one look and fled the scene, many of them screaming. Children clutched at their mothers' skirts and whimpered in fear. The *diafagh*, meanwhile, cared nothing for any of this, nor indeed did they seem intent on attacking Amethyst or even Ileana- they had only one purpose, which was to kill Fauli and Lyya as they had killed Serina.

Finally Fauli and Lyya beat a hasty retreat towards the stables to join Amethyst and Ileana. There was no time for saddling properly. They slung their packs into saddlebags on the horses and a few moments later they burst forth from the building. The horse bearing Amethyst and Ileana was unfortunate enough to emerge nearest to the *diafagh* as they approached the stable door, and shied violently away, almost unseating his riders. Amethyst grimly held Ileana around the waist with one hand and the reins with the other and prayed that they would not be thrown to the ground. Drops of blood fell from Ileana's nose, some of them onto Amethyst's hand. *Gods, I hope she survives this,* Amethyst thought fervently as they hurtled down the main street and out of the village, heading along the north-west route. *If this happens whenever she encounters these creatures, sooner or later she will perish. She even said so herself.*

Almost without thinking she tightened her grip a little around Ileana as the four of them slowed the horses a fraction. *Not yet,* she thought. *We are nowhere near done yet.* She glanced back, half-expecting to see three lurching forms in the distance, but instead she saw only the dust they themselves had raised.

They rode on in grim silence until the horses began to tire after a half-league or so. Lyya called out, suggesting that they stop, and they drew to a halt near the edge of a pasture through which a narrow stream ran. Everyone dismounted, and Amethyst felt her legs almost buckle as she landed on the grass and helped a barely conscious Ileana down from the saddle.

The riders and their horses drank thirstily, and Amethyst took the opportunity to fill her water flask. Ileana stirred as Amethyst made her sip some water from her flask. "Too strong," she murmured as her eyes opened. *She must be talking about the* diafagh, Amethyst thought, setting the flask down.

Dazedly Ileana managed to raise her head a little and glance around. "Where are we?"

"As far from Alinnora's Haven as we could get without crippling the horses." Fauli stared across at her from where she was sitting on the stream's bank, feet and ankles in the water. "It seems that you *do* have some hold over them."

"Barely a hold," Ileana whispered, paling visibly. "I couldn't stop them." She struggled to a sitting position and stared at the *du-luyan* woman. "They were too strong," she told her. "They were made by someone who wants to destroy you. Both you and Lyya. They will just carry on until they succeed, or until *they* are destroyed. And I can't destroy them. They're not like the others."

Lyya, who had taken the opportunity to arrange the saddles properly on each of the horses, threw a glance in Fauli's direction. "Maybe it's because Ilumor sent them."

Fauli nodded glumly. "It must be."

"Who is Ilumor?" Amethyst asked.

Fauli smiled humourlessly. "Insidiously, he controls the Rising. He and the forces with which he surrounds himself... they have infiltrated and poisoned it utterly."

Amethyst drew a deep breath. "And he controls those *diafagh?*"

"I would say so, yes. I cannot say how, but I'm certain of it. They are creatures of the Old Dark. And so, without doubt, is Ilumor."

And what future can there be for Ileana, Amethyst considered, *now that Serina is no more? Who can teach her to master or even control these powers inside her, to stop them from consuming her entirely? I certainly can't. Nothing I do can harm those who wish to bring harm to her.*

Angrily she kicked at a loose stone in the dusty track and watched as it tumbled away into a shallow ditch on the other side. *Must I lose everyone I care about?* she asked herself morosely. *I cannot protect Ileana from evil like this. I cannot even fight it myself.*

For perhaps the thousandth time in recent months she wished she had never left Darkenhelm, despite the stories she had heard about events there recently. *If only,* she thought tiredly. *Didn't I once promise myself not to keep saying that?*

As they sat and rested a little longer, with the horses tethered to a nearby tree and grazing nearby, Fauli reminded them, "Serina spoke of fleeing to Harn just before we arrived in the village."

"They will follow us regardless," Lyya said tiredly. "Did you not hear what Ileana told us? And what of Fistelkarn, Tyrameer and Jaana? Are you saying we should abandon them?"

Fauli said nothing, suddenly considering, but Amethyst spoke up. "Why would the witch have mentioned Harn? She must have had a good reason." She paused and wondered whether to press on with what she had been about to say. Finally she continued, "I was in the far northern town of Ethanalin Tur-morn not so long ago. Well, both Ileana and I were. I saw a Gate open on the hill. I saw things I could scarcely believe. A struggle, in the sky, between light and darkness. I saw... I saw *marandaal* coming from out of the Gate."

As soon as she looked up from the stream, into which she had been gazing, Amethyst knew that somehow they not only knew the word but also what it meant. Both Lyya and

Fauli stared at her in mute shock. "How do you know about them? How do you even know the name?" Fauli demanded eventually.

"I could ask you the same question," Amethyst retorted, "but in any case, it was only through poor luck that I even found myself in that place. I was travelling through Alinnora's Haven months ago and was unfortunate enough to meet that witch. Serina. She placed some sort of curse on me." Amethyst shuddered at the memory and feared for a moment that even dwelling on that tortuous time might somehow trigger the return of that malign presence, even though the woman who had instigated it was dead. "I was forced... in a particular direction. North, then east. I couldn't walk in any other direction except that demanded by the *thing* that Serina had somehow placed in my head. And that continued until I met Ileana."

"Now I begin to understand," Fauli said, frowning. She glanced at Lyya. "So, Gates have already opened. One at least. Perhaps others." She turned back to Amethyst. "But how do you know the *name?*"

"A man we travelled with knew of such things. He knew of the Gate, even before it appeared. And he knew the name of the beings that would try to break through into the world from whatever lay beyond it." Amethyst considered saying more but decided against it. *I'd rather try and forget about Vornen's helpless march to his death,* she thought.

"To Harn, then," Fauli said, but Lyya shook her head. "I can't abandon Jaana. I as good as promised that we'd meet again at Alinnora's Haven. That was the *plan,* Fauli."

"You think I wish to abandon Tyrameer and Fistelkarn?" Fauli snapped. "What choice do we have in the matter, you stupid woman?! If you wish to turn and head back, then do so. I have no doubt you'll meet the *diafagh* along the way, and they'll rip you apart. *I* intend to survive, and our friends would urge us to do just that, if they knew what followed us!" She leapt to her feet and stared into the east as if she expected the *diafagh* to come lurching out of the cover, snapping hungrily at the icy air, urged on by their unstoppable thirst for destruction.

"We should go," Fauli said uneasily, and she turned to Amethyst and Ileana. "Are you with me?"

Amethyst thought for a moment. Heading into the north-west was the best way to stay as far as possible from the *diafagh* that were doubtless still on their trail, now that they had fled this way. *Although they're not hunting us,* she remembered, and glanced at Ileana. *What should I do with her? Serina is gone, nothing ties me to this girl, but I can't just leave her to fend for herself. She's not old enough to survive the world on her own. And if matters become worse across Aphenhast, or even across the whole world, I'd prefer not to be on my own. I suspect she feels the same way. Ileana and I could head south, towards Darkenhelm.*

"We aim to head south..." she began, but Fauli shook her head immediately. "Have you forgotten about the Rising? They may have already begun their march across the middle lands. Heading that way would be madness."

Amethyst opened her mouth again to argue but stopped herself. The *du-luyan* woman was correct. And apart from anything else, she had almost run out of money. Getting all the way to Darkenhelm would be a tall order to say the least.

"We'll come with you," Amethyst said finally.

Fauli untied her horse from a tree a short distance away. "What about you, Lyya?" she called back. "Death or survival? I'd say the choice is plain."

Lyya scowled and said nothing but got up and stalked over to her horse. Amethyst watched her and could see that the *luyan* woman was visibly upset. *As would I be,* she thought, *if I had friends to leave behind.*

Within a short while they set off again and headed over shrub and bracken-covered upland, towards the fast-setting sun.

That night, they made camp in a sheltered valley that ran east to west between two wooded hills. They had finished their meal and were sitting around the fire when a low, mournful howl rose up somewhere behind them, towards the east.

"Gaan," Lyya whispered.

"It could be any wolf," Fauli rejoined, but she looked unsettled. Amethyst stared questioningly from one to the other, and Lyya explained, "Gaan is Serina's wolf. I didn't think to wonder where he was, back in Alinnora's Haven..."

"Maybe she sent him away," Fauli suggested, turning and staring along the track they had followed through the valley. "But I don't see why..."

A while passed. Fauli was the first to see the lithe, silver form that headed slowly towards them, but by then Gaan had almost reached the companions. He stopped half a dozen paces away and sat, brooding and silent.

"Dead or not," Fauli said, as they stared at the silent creature, "this is Serina's doing."

IX – Treachery

I

The roads of Harn, Nia had long observed, became gradually worse as one travelled further north. The journey from Luudhoq to Waylorn had been smooth enough, but the road between Waylorn and Mornkastle deteriorated markedly over the three days she had travelled the route.

Nia had always held mixed feelings about Mornkastle, a city of uneasy peace that the so-named Unseen Wall or Never-Built Wall ran through. As the name suggested, this was an arbitrary line seen only on maps that dissected Harn east to west, and so divided the land into South and North. The Watchers' rule of law still held there, though barely- much of the day to day running of the town had been handed over to local wardens under the appointed overseer.

To the north of Mornkastle, the Watchers' influence was almost non-existent. The rural boroughs and villages were ruled over by local landowners and their militia, although in truth the powerbrokers of this altogether different Harn were the shadowy witches and warlocks, practitioners of sorcery that had long since been outlawed in the South. Luudhoqians had many names for the people of the North and their sorcerous masters, none of them complimentary. Likewise, they had just as many names for the powers wielded by these sorcerers: the Old Dark, the Blood Lore, the Forbidden, and many more.

Mornkastle was effectively the front line of the truce, a city ruled in name by the Watchers, or at least those appointed by them, but where the agents of the North's powers also observed from the shadows and gathered information.

Nia had to admit that the city made an ideal place for locating those who might know associates of this Ruhal Dalmorn, whom Kelandra was so intent on finding.

Not that I expect he and his allies would trust a word of her proposal, Nia thought. *I'm wasting my time.*

But of course, that didn't matter. She had no choice but to do as bidden. Anything less than utter obedience and complete honesty and Kelandra would reveal her secret to her masters.

Nia stared out at the passing countryside and pondered. She could think of no way out of her predicament other than revealing Kelandra as a traitor, and that would only land her in an even worse situation. She would be revealed either way.

And that must never happen, she thought. *Never.*

Sighing, she leaned back against the hard, wooden headboard in the carriage and closed her eyes. She would be in Mornkastle later today, perhaps in time for supper. At least then she would have a task in hand to concentrate on.

But fears of being revealed continued to gnaw away at her. Could Kelandra prove it, she wondered? Quite possibly, if torture was used. Nia felt darkly certain that if the right *conditions* were met- extreme agony in other words- then the *shifting* would happen of its own accord.

And then I would have lost control for a final time, she thought, watching as the vehicle passed a group of labourers toiling in the nearby fields, picking a late harvest of root vegetables. *But if I continue to be useful, I'll be spared that fate. If I can find a way of remaining useful to Kelandra for the rest of my life. Unless...*

Thoughts of escape rushed through her- escape into the mad North, where the further she trod the less likely her capture and return to Luudhoq. *But Kelandra would have thought of that,* she reasoned. *And would I fare any better, a lackey of the Watchers wandering alone in the North? I doubt it.*

Nia nodded off after a while, although the sleep she managed was shallow and fitful. She woke with a start when the carriage came to a sudden halt and the driver rapped loudly on the roof to rouse her.

Darkness had fallen. Nia peered out and saw that they had stopped in the busy cobbled circle in the middle of Mornkastle. Oil lamps had been lit throughout the area. Nearby, a couple of horses were being led to the stables set just down one of the streets. Further down one of the wider roads, Nia heard sounds of revelry, perhaps even a celebration of some sort. A song started up, accompanied by some sort of string instrument and a drum.

Nia had a few contacts in Mornkastle, some more reliable than others. She paid the coachman the remainder for her journey and wandered slowly up the street, considering each of these people in turn.

Serran was a footpad and occasional informer, a nervous little man who had every right to be nervous, for he constantly played one side against the other, trading information almost in the manner that other men traded gambling chips. Quite why he played out this unusual and dangerous drama, Nia had no idea. He had occasionally been useful, but he certainly could not be trusted. If she so much as mentioned Ruhal or anyone connected to him, she felt certain that the overseer or town wardens would hear of it soon enough, and then so would the Watchers.

I must take the path of least risk, Nia reminded herself, although at the same time she feared that that path would be least likely to lead to success.

If not Serran, then perhaps Maiina would do.

Maiina was an altogether different creature. The only thing she had in common with the likes of Serran was her interest in the two forces that manoeuvred either side of the Never-Built Wall. Maiina was a secretive, retiring type, something of an archivist and historian. Nia wasn't sure how old she was. Forty, perhaps, but with her ever-present *kyush* pipe and greying hair, not to mention her somewhat dry interests, she seemed older.

Kelandra had not told Nia how many days she had in which to gather her information and contact a trusted associate of Ruhal, but Nia judged that it was a little too late to call on Maiina now in any case. She would do so tomorrow.

She stopped outside a brightly-lit tavern called *The Line And Anchor*. She had been here a few times before, and on each occasion the seemingly odd name had reminded her of its own origins. The inn had been built perhaps three hundred years ago, during a time when actual war had almost flared up on several occasions. According to the history that Nia had read, the line referred to the invisible line that threaded through Mornkastle- the Never-Built Wall in other words. The anchor, meanwhile, referred to the collective weight on the townspeople, situated as they were amid a truce which at that point in history could have snapped at a moment's notice.

It struck her as odd that such a concept had been applied to a common-house where folk gathered to drink themselves under the tables, abandon all reserve and protocol and lose their hard-earned wages gambling. Not to mention lose a few teeth fighting.

Nia wondered briefly if Kelandra's machinations would themselves pull the entire land into such a war. *That would be an irony worthy of note in history,* she reckoned, *if she sought to unite the territories and instead plunged them into violence.*

She wandered inside and inquired about a room for the night. The Mornkastle accent, with its slightly harsher and deeper inflections than its Luudhoqian equivalent, came to her easily enough. She had quietly practiced it during her journey north. A room was available, the young barkeeper informed her, but it was small, the ceiling was low and a problem with mould in the corner had yet to be dealt with. Nia felt a little tired to traipse around the city at this time in hope of finding accommodation elsewhere, so she paid him a silver star, bought a glass of wine as well- ale was too filling for this time of night- and afterwards, enjoying the warmth in her empty stomach, she retired to bed.

On an impulse, Nia removed her clothing and *shifted* in front of the mildew-spotted mirror in the room, having ensured her door was bolted and secure. When she opened her eyes, she felt that familiar small tremor of shock at the sight of her new reflection. *Nia's twin brother,* she thought, and then added sardonically: *But no- that can't be. Remember, poor Nia doesn't have any family and never did.*

Looking herself, or *himself* up and down, she wondered what it might be like if somehow she could become *two* people- her natural, female self, and also this curious mirage staring back at her, a male who had never been born, who had no name except whichever she happened to give him. As she stared into the eyes of her mirror-self, Nia felt a sudden stab of fear and looked quickly away.

A sudden thought occurred to her. Kelandra had seen her in this form, but perhaps she had caught only a brief glimpse. Nia knew next to nothing about the water-mirrors and the sorcery that powered them, but felt certain that Kelandra used those devices sparingly, perhaps cautious of some hitherto unknown reaction or result. She remembered Kelandra saying one time that they were volatile and unpredictable.

But despite her reticence, might the Watcher have used them to locate her in the last few days?

Nia sighed. She might well have done. And if she was going to pick a time to do so, it would be around now, with her leashed spy in Mornkastle and engaged in unarguably the most important mission of her life.

It didn't matter where she turned; she was caught.

Nia lay down on the mattress. *Do what must be done,* she reminded herself, *because that's all you can do. Worry* about other predicaments afterwards, if and when the work is done and you still have your freedom.

She shifted back, and exhaled softly, infinitely more comfortable in her natural skin. *Come what may,* she thought fiercely, *I can never let myself be handed over to the Seven. Never.*

Nia drifted off to sleep and dreamed of sailing down a wide river. The waters became wider still, until eventually she reached a nameless ocean that spread out before her, sparkling and limitless. Carried by a stiff breeze, her craft carried her further and further from land, until a great distance and a vast depth lay between her and all her enemies.

II

She woke with a start, certain that she had heard someone trying to quietly unlock and open her door. Quietly she padded over and listened carefully but heard nothing. Perhaps it had been one of the other doors nearby.

It was already light, so Nia dressed and made her way downstairs where breakfast was being served. The night's rest had improved her appetite. She wolfed down hunks of fresh bread with roast pork, washed down with cold water, and then set her mind to the task ahead. She would go and see Maiina, and perhaps explain that she hoped to research some of the more influential figures of the North. In order that the eyes of law and order could be kept trained upon them, she would say, which would fit perfectly with her usual reasons for journeying to Mornkastle.

Maiina's dwelling was much like the woman herself, set apart somewhat from the main hustle and bustle of Mornkastle. Her house stood amid a warren of twisting little streets that all looked much the same, and although Nia had been there before it still took her a while to find the place. Maiina's house had become a little more covered in ivy and other vegetation than she remembered, and perhaps the walls had cracked a little more, but otherwise it was still the same quiet shambles she had expected.

As she made her way down the path to the house, Nia remained mindful of brambles and other plants that reached out tendrils as if in a vain attempt to thwart her progress. *It's very overgrown,* she noted. *More so than at first it appeared.* That thought led to another, more worrying one. *What if she no longer lives here? What if she moved away, or died? It must have been almost a year since I was last here. I should have had someone keep an eye on her movements somehow.*

Beset by these doubts, Nia pressed on regardless, and rapped on the door using the heavy and rusted iron ball on a chain which had been left for that purpose. She waited, her patience diminishing as it became less and less evident that her call would be answered.

Then the door flew open.

Nia opened her mouth to speak, but the words died in her throat.

Maiina looked older than Nia had expected; much older. Her sunken, grey eyes almost crept back into her sallow countenance at the sight of the startled girl on her doorstep. *She's ill,* Nia noted. *Something ails her.* Aloud she said, "Maiina? I hope you remember me. My name is Nia. We've met several times before. I..."

"Nia. Yes." Maiina's suspicious glare softened a little. "I remember you."

Nia wondered if she really did, looking at the confusion in the woman's eyes. Maiina ushered her inside, and through into a cramped little room festooned with all manner of ornaments and trinkets. *Was it like this before?* she wondered. She suspected not.

Maiina drew back the curtains at the far window to allow the drab wintry daylight to pour into the room. Seating herself, she gestured for Nia to do likewise, and then asked: "What can I do for you?"

"I'm researching a number of the more influential figures in the North," Nia said directly. "I hoped that you might be able to assist." She smiled. "It's just some simple information I'm after, nothing more than that."

Maiina nodded. "Anyone in particular?"

Nia paused for a moment, giving the appearance of someone trying to recollect a list of names. "Someone- a man by the name of Ruhal Dalmorn. Or specifically, I'm interested in knowing about allies of his, rather than the man himself. Allies who might be found here in Mornkastle sometimes." She shrugged. "It's not especially important."

Maiina frowned and lapsed into thought. "The name is not familiar to me," she said finally. "I don't think I can help you."

She's lying, Nia thought immediately, and somehow knew that for certain. Briefly she recalled the way Maiina had looked at her when she had opened the door. *Something has indeed happened to her, and it's no simple illness.*

She glanced again at Maiina and nodded as if in reluctant understanding, and then a chill ran through her. For the briefest moment, she felt sure that the woman's eyes had become both darker and slightly larger. She averted her gaze and willed herself to remain calm, but as she looked slightly away and tried to fix her attention on the window behind Maiina- anything but the woman herself, who still stared directly at her- she heard a faint snapping sound that repeated itself several times. *Like the protest of joints being stretched,* she thought, but from the corner of her eye she saw that Maiina had not moved a muscle.

"Well," Nia managed eventually, "I apologise for my intrusion. Perhaps someone else will be able to help me."

"Perhaps." Maiina did not move. Nia could even have sworn that the woman's lips remained tightly closed. She rose and waited to see if Maiina got up to see her out. But she remained seated, utterly still.

Nia turned and left. Only when she had safely navigated the thorny path and made her way back down the street did she allow herself a sigh of relief and drew a sharp breath of cool air.

This is not working out well for me, Nia thought blackly a little later, as she sat on one of the little stone walls that ran through the town marketplace. The loud hum and cacophony of trade usually put her at ease wherever she might be, but nothing could do that today. *Why would Maiina lie?* she wondered. *Has she been threatened in some way, for passing information to the likes of me in the past?*

But Nia knew that more lurked behind what she had seen and heard. Something inexplicable had happened to Maiina; something that Nia could not understand beyond her fear that dark sorcery of some kind lay at the root of it.

Powers, I'm tired, she thought, and realised suddenly that her head had slumped forward a little and her eyelids drooped. With an effort she roused herself- *Don't fall asleep in a crowded marketplace, you fool!* she thought sharply- and looked around. She had enough money for at least the next five or six days. *I can afford some lunch then,* she reasoned, eyeing up a small bakery set just off from the market a little way.

She rose, and promptly collapsed to her knees.

How can I be this exhausted? she wondered desperately, staggering to her feet only to fall again. All the strength had drained from her legs. A few traders and hawkers nearby even ceased their chatter and stared curiously at the invalid who had suddenly appeared nearby. Several folk stopped in mid-purchase and looked at her either in concern or mild amusement. "Is she drunk?" Nia heard one man ask.

"Not at all!" someone called out cheerfully from a little further back, threading his way casually towards her.

"She's my sister. I'm afraid she's not very well at the moment- I've been looking for her all morning, thank the Powers she's here..."

Nia's head felt like lead or stone as she forced herself to look up at the man who had now reached her. She could see very little of him beyond his shape, silhouetted against the midday sun. She tried to open her mouth in protest and could utter only a faint groan. Her head slumped forward, and a moment later a hand cupped her chin. For an instant her eyes flickered open, and she saw a little more of him. His expression was lean, almost hungry. It was almost like gazing into the eyes of a wolf.

Nia's eyes closed, and the sounds around her faded.

III

She woke with a violent start, into utter darkness. Rope had been used to tie her wrists and ankles, so she could barely move them. She lay on a bed or stretcher of some sort; it creaked slightly as she tried to move from side to side.

Nia swallowed, her heart hammering madly. *There I was, thinking matters couldn't get any worse,* she thought blackly, *but they always seem to find a way.*

Once the initial panic faded somewhat, she tried to calm herself with reason. *I'm still alive, so whoever they are, they must need something from me.*

The darkness around her was total, so her eyes failed to adjust to it. As far as she knew, the walls of this chamber could be ten paces away, or a hundred. *Am I somewhere underground?* she wondered. *What do they want with me? Is it something to do with Maiina?*

A while passed. Nia had no idea how long she lay in silence on the cold stone floor. Her thoughts drifted. At one point she began to quietly sob, and then she angrily forced herself to stop, thinking, *What good will crying like a weakling do?*

She waited, not knowing what she waited for, and wondered why she had shown any emotion at all, even in her own company. Emotion had got the better of her in recent times, and she told herself there was no excuse for it. *Make yourself as cold as stone, you stupid woman,* she thought. *What happened to Kelandra's finest servant?*

Then, just as she was about to drift into unconsciousness again, a lit candle suddenly appeared, perhaps ten paces to her left. Sitting cross-legged next to it she saw a middle-aged man with a short growth of grey beard, dressed in a thin hoodless cloak. *He must have been here the whole time,* Nia thought, *unless he somehow spirited himself to this place.*

"So," he murmured. "A servant of the Black Citadel comes to us, looking for Ruhal Dalmorn and his friends."

Nia said nothing, thinking it likely to be the safest option.

"Your name is Nia," he continued softly. "The Watchers are your masters. So, your presence here is not entirely unexpected."

Nia cleared her throat, and spoke up hoarsely: "I need to speak with him or with someone who is a trusted friend of his..."

"Trusted friend? He has few of those." The man took a small object from one of his robe pockets and held it up for her to see. With a sinking feeling Nia knew it to be the scroll with which Kelandra had entrusted her. The wax seal remained intact as far as she could tell, but for how long? Would he open it now, and reveal her real reasons for being in Mornkastle? What might happen if he did that? Had Kelandra placed some protective weave about it?

His eyes remained fixed intently upon her. "Should I break open the seal, I wonder?"

"I don't know," said Nia, truthfully.

The man said nothing to that at first; he looked from side to side, then above him, as if he expected someone or something to materialise from out of the gloom. Nia stared at him. Finally he nodded, as if in agreement with some unseen companion, and to her surprise he tossed the scroll over to her. Nia flinched despite herself as it landed at her side.

"Interesting," he whispered, a faint smile upon his face. He raised a hand and turned away. Abruptly the candle light was snuffed out. Nia heard measured footsteps fade into the backcloth of silence, and eventually the distant, faint sound of a door opening and closing.

Somehow, despite the torrent of questions that rushed through her mind, Nia soon lapsed into a slumber. She woke sometime later to the sensation of her ankles and wrists being untied. Once that task was complete she was hauled to her feet. "Bring the scroll. She will need it," a woman's voice called out, and she was marched along, someone grasping each arm. She could tell nothing about the people who surrounded her and imagined what they might look like. Maiina's visage loomed in her thoughts, and panic threatened to overwhelm her. *Be calm,* she told herself grimly. *They are people and nothing more.*

So saying, she tried desperately to ignore the iron, cold grip in which they held her, and the fact that she could hear their footsteps but not even the slightest breath from her captors.

They stopped abruptly. A door swiftly opened, and Nia cried out as light poured forth, intense and painful, stabbing into her like hot needles. She screwed her eyes shut as they bore her along a flagstoned surface and then roughly seated her in a hard, wooden chair.

Nia felt her panic ebb away somewhat as her guides let go of her and walked away. After a short while she dared open her eyes a little, and then a little more, affording herself a view of her surroundings by painful increments.

The chair in which she had been seated stood next to a circular wooden table in a closed courtyard. The light came from a high noon sun. Across from her, a woman not unlike

Maiina in appearance stared at her. Nia noticed at that exact moment that the high courtyard walls had neither doors nor archways, nor any other visible way in or out. *Then where have those who brought me here gone?* she wondered and tried to picture them simply melting into the wall. She looked over the walls in each direction, then noted with relief that she was at least still somewhere in Mornkastle, for she recognised some of the taller towers and fortresses of the town, whose spires reached even higher than these walls.

Nia's scroll lay upon the table, directly between the two of them. Nia glanced at it and then looked away. "This interests me," the woman told her as she pointed to it. "The contents remain shrouded. Some Watcher-made cleverness, no doubt."

"It must be given to Ruhal Dalmorn, or to someone who can be trusted to deliver it to him," Nia said. Managing to pluck a little courage from somewhere she added, "It's for viewing by him alone."

"And what then?" the woman rejoined coolly. "What happens if it's delivered?"

"I wait for a message by return," Nia said.

The woman gazed at the scroll for a while and then said, "It will be taken to someone who can in turn deliver it to him."

"Can you be sure?" Nia asked.

She smiled at that. "No. Nothing is certain in Mornkastle except uncertainty itself. You will simply have to wait and be patient." Leaning forward, she added, "My name is Elarin. This is my home. And this is where you will wait until a response comes from Dalmorn's messenger."

"Oh, well that's very kind," Nia said hastily, "but you see, I already have a room paid for at a tavern, and..."

"This is where you will stay," Elarin cut across her. "I am no friend of the man myself, but some others are, and for the sake of the truce I would rather that he *not* meet some untimely end at the hands of some Watcher-driven sorcery, particularly if that can be traced to my household. There are factions that would perceive and take advantage of such misfortune. Therefore, if you seek to deliver harm into the Free Territories, harm will come to you. Swiftly."

"I can assure you, that's the furthest thing from the mind of my mistress..." Nia said, and suddenly stopped, for she knew that to say more could be the worst thing of all.

"And so, you will wait here," Elarin continued patiently. "If you mean no harm, then you have nothing to fear. Dalmorn may open the scroll, if it's given to him, or he may choose not to. If he does, presumably he will be able to read its contents, and perhaps a message will find its way back to you. Perhaps not. As I said, if he is harmed in any way then of course we will learn about it, and you will pay in kind for the harm inflicted. If he is wounded fatally, then..." Elarin shrugged. "Then you will be also."

Even as Nia nodded, her eyes quickly took in the view of the walls around the two of them once again. Were there any handholds? Might she be able to scramble up to the top of one of the walls, and over? She would need to grab the scroll from the table first...

Elarin missed nothing, however. "Try, if you wish. You'll be punished for it. Try a second time, and we'll break your legs. Broken legs that fail to attract the attention of a physician would be quite a painful prospect. Wouldn't you agree?"

Not only that, but she has servants who can seemingly walk through walls, Nia reminded herself. "I agree," she said.

"Good. Then you'll be our house guest for a little while. You'll be kept fed and watered. Why, I expect we'll all find you quite interesting. The tales you'll be able to tell us of life within the Black Citadel!" Elarin reached out and clasped her hand, a predatory gleam in her eyes. "I am really quite looking forward to the next tennight or so- aren't you?"

IV

When he observed the daily lives of Darkbrook's people, Ruhal often found himself considering that in some ways, little had changed since the end of the bitter, centuries-long war between the younger Races and the *choragh*-led hordes, more than a millennium ago. He had not witnessed those events of course- he was thirty-eight summers old, not a thousand and thirty-eight- but in common with almost everyone else born and raised north of Mornkastle, he had been fed the tales of that time from infancy.

Ruhal was pragmatic enough not to believe all the embellishments such tales carried with them, but he understood the underlying truth they possessed, the importance of the struggle and the sacrifices made by those who had fought and perished so that today the Races might live in peace and enlightenment.

Yet in many ways these settlements clung to the old ways. It was evident in their fervent, irrational fear of witches and warlocks, who they would do anything to appease. It was evident in the scores of bizarre superstitions to which they clung, generation after generation. In a few of the further-flung places- the undusted corners of the world, as Ruhal's long-gone father would have said- there were rumours that sacrifices to the *choragh* were still being made. If that was true, Ruhal reflected grimly, then it was little wonder that their shadow had never completely left the north of Harn, or that the same shadow now lengthened once again, to reach into the hearts of those who still knew the ancient stories of their masters from a distant Age.

Darkbrook was cast in twilight, the last traces of sunset about to melt into the surrounding night sky. Ruhal sat by the old roundstone well in the middle of the town circle and pondered these and other gloomy thoughts. Everywhere had about it an uneasy stirring these days, and it filled him with a foreboding of what might come. Rumours

259

and tales had trickled into Harn from Aphenhast to the east, none of them good. As ever, some were probably false and others had been added to with each telling, but if even a few held some truth then there remained reasonable cause for worry. Ruhal knew several witches and warlocks who had all, in their different ways, spoken to him of their fears that *marandaal* had returned to the east lands. He knew better than to repeat that word to all and sundry, although few knew its meaning after so many long centuries. But he had tentatively spoken of the need for a lasting peace and even a form of unity between North and South, in the light of the threat of war from the eastern lands.

Not that many had listened to him.

The people of Darkbrook did not step outside their doors after sundown as a rule, but to anyone who might have passed casually by, Ruhal looked unassuming enough, a muscular but bedraggled warrior or mercenary they might guess, whose clothing and equipment had seen better days, whose dull brown hair was greying and whose left cheek wore a pronounced scar along its length. He was, however, more than that, and even in Darkbrook a few people would have recognised him had he arrived with the sun still hanging in the west.

Ruhal's calling was in distant Mordenglen, the forest vastness many leagues to the east. There they called him *protector, ranger, woodlock* and even festooned him with other, more unusual titles. *Protector* he liked best- he had made it his duty to help protect the place from those who wished it harm, including those miscreant sorcerers who might attempt to tap into the strange and barely known powers of Mordenglen for nefarious purposes.

Woodlock he was not. Ruhal had learned a few minor chants and incantations but he was certainly no sorcerer. *Many still believe such talents are passed down without fail between parents and children,* he recalled. *But I have none of my mother's powers, nor do I wish for them.*

He sighed, realising how tired he was. *Travelling seems to be all I do now, as I try to gather information,* he thought.

The sound of hooves thudding dully on the muddy dirt track that led into Darkbrook caused Ruhal to turn. A moment later he relaxed a little, recognising the newcomer as Sarros. The spy and one-time pilferer leapt down from his horse, swiftly tethered it to a worn post near the well and tipped his battered old hat in greeting as he sauntered over.

"You are early," Ruhal remarked.

Sarros peered up at Ildar's half-face, which tonight darted in and out of high, fast-moving cloud, then nodded as if by its position he might have figured the exact time. "A curious matter has come to my attention," he said. Ruhal had never quite become used to the man's lilting Wistledge accent. "Most curious in fact, if it is indeed genuine." He paused and peered into the night in all directions. Ruhal could hear nothing but the breeze sighing in the fields nearby, and a few crickets here and there. Sarros, however, could probably hear a pin drop a league away.

"Good. No one is around," Sarros said finally, and sat next to Ruhal on the wide stone edge of the well. For the first time, Ruhal noticed how nervous- and oddly perplexed- his friend looked. "Well?"

Sarros looked lost in contemplation for a short while. Then he turned to face him and whispered, "Word has come to me from the South, of certain powers that seek an alliance. This much came to me from Edryn of Steepleford..."

"The apothecary?" Ruhal was not impressed.

"Apothecary *and* spy," Sarros corrected him. "This is the story as far as I can make out. He was approached by someone from Mornkastle who asked that a message be passed to you from some Southern girl. Of course, that means it was passed to me, as we agreed years ago."

Ruhal was not much given to exclamations of any kind, and merely raised an eyebrow at this strange news. He placed his hands together and leaned forward slightly in mute contemplation. Finally he said, "Was she a Watcher?"

"Edryn asked the messenger, who asserted that she was not." Sarros smiled. "That would have been more than unusual. Such delicate matters have only ever been dealt with through their minions."

"Indeed," Ruhal noted.

"But this is where the tale turns peculiar, Ruhal. Edryn was told that the message was from her employer- and her employer *is* a Watcher. One who *apparently* seeks an alliance with us. It seems that somehow, word of your talk about unification, of one land to face the enemy, may have caught the attention of one or two within the Black Citadel."

"Such words should never have been spoken, even in Mornkastle." Ruhal shook his head. "That was rash of me, even if I did not specifically *name* the enemy. We must prepare for whatever comes out of the East, but there are better ways."

Sarros grinned at him, obviously relishing the twists and turns of his story, and handed Ruhal a tightly-rolled scroll, which had been sealed with dark wax and stamped with an intricate symbol that showed three city gates within one another.

Ruhal eyed it with suspicion. "Did you check it in any way?"

Sarros sighed. "It's for you alone, it would seem, so I suspected something unpleasant might happen if I opened it. Edryn and Hallith both checked it as far as they were able to, but... it's shrouded in some way."

Ruhal carefully broke the seal and rolled the parchment open. Sarros helpfully struck his tinderbox and held the wan flame close enough for Ruhal to read by, although to Sarros the parchment appeared entirely blank.

Mordenglen's protector sat and read the entire message, slowly and deliberately, then read it a second time. Finally he passed it to Sarros. "Here. Read it," he said.

"There's nothing to read that I can see," Sarros pointed out, but as he looked down he saw the intricate script of the message swim into sight, as if ink that had faded entirely away was being refreshed.

Ruhal sat in expressionless silence as his friend read the message. Sarros was a better reader than Ruhal; he had only to scan through it to understand its meaning and detail. Finally he extinguished his flame and waited restlessly for Ruhal to speak. But, unable to hold his own silence for longer than a moment, he soon ventured, "I think it must be a ploy, although the language used is persuasive. It makes sense, as a good trick must."

Ruhal said nothing.

"They are devious, one must give them that," Sarros mused. "Often I think the Wall should have been built all those centuries ago, when we resisted their attempt to turn all Harn to their ways and put the free people in chains."

"Simple walls do not keep Watchers out, and especially not their eyes-and-ears," Ruhal told him.

They fell silent again. Sarros noted presently that Ruhal had fallen into deep contemplation. Wisely, he remained as still and quiet as he could until eventually Ruhal spoke up.

"If this is a ploy, Sarros, then so be it. I think, however, that it is not. Yes, the words are persuasive; they are persuasive because, as you say, they make sense. True, a Watcher's trap might be equally so. But I don't think this is such a thing. I have pondered and spoken about the fate of Harn, of what may happen if a divided land is attacked. Little wonder that some amongst the Black Citadel heard those words and even discussed them. And we *are* divided, Sarros. We have been for a thousand years. Is it so unreasonable to think that they too have been considering the fate of Harn?"

"Division was the price we paid for half the land remaining free of their tyranny," Sarros reminded him. "A price I myself have always thought worth paying. The tales speak of a great army led by the warlocks of that time, the descendants of the First, who defended the free North."

"I'm not disagreeing with you, friend. But the reality remains that Harn's divisions- and there are many beyond the more obvious- make it an easier land to conquer. You have heard the news from the east. Powers know I've mentioned it to you more than a few times."

"I have heard many stories from out of the Gods-fearing land, this past month," Sarros remarked. "Risings against human cities, apparently fuelled and poisoned by *choragh* influence- I never thought I'd say that- and those disturbances in the far north that you told me about. *Gates,* you said."

"That's what I was told, by someone I have no reason to doubt," Ruhal said grimly. "Much of what we hear from Aphenhast may well be true. Whatever is happening there may spread here."

"This Watcher," Sarros said, "presents the notion of an alliance with which to defend Harn against such an invasion. If that could be achieved, it would indeed be a mighty force. Yet I don't believe such an agreement could ever work. A thousand years of enmity would take at least a hundred to end, I'd say."

"If I at least try, are you with me?" Ruhal asked suddenly, turning to him, and Sarros' mouth fell open in astonishment. "Be careful how you answer, if indeed you do," Ruhal warned, "because what I intend to do is to simply meet with these Watchers, as this Kelandra asks, and to even *think* of doing that is straightforward treachery in the minds of the great and good of the Free Territories. If you were to involve yourself in this, then you too become tarred as a traitor. I can already picture Inerdyr's wrath if he should discover that any conversation took place- if it ever does."

Sarros shivered and cast a quick glance about, although he would have heard anyone approach from more than a hundred paces away. Inerdyr, much-feared warlock and one of the most powerful men in the north, would move swiftly to punish any such treachery. Although the appointed Warden of Mornkastle and his elected men presided over that city in name, most people knew well enough that Inerdyr had considerable influence over what happened in that place as well as the vast lands to the north of Mornkastle. It was said that Inerdyr had made his home there, on a hill overlooking the city from the north, in order to defend the Free Territories against the tyranny of Luudhoq's overlords. Inerdyr's hatred of the Watchers and their mysterious masters the Seven was legendary, and Sarros had no doubt that Ruhal's suffering would be too, should the great warlock discover his intentions.

And mine, he added ruefully, *if I follow Ruhal in this.*

"I have always trusted your judgement, Ruhal," he said after a while, "and I trust it now. But the price we would pay, if we were to be found out..."

"...is nothing compared with the price *Harn* pays if we cannot mend this broken land." Ruhal gave him a forbidding stare. "We could all be overrun as we squabble and spy and mistrust, ever hateful of the foes we have been *brought up* to hate. Are you with me, Sarros?"

The little spy nodded wearily, reluctantly. "I am. But your damned heroism fills me with fear, Ruhal."

"I'm no hero, friend. I simply love this land, and I will do whatever it takes for it to survive. If that means I must become a traitor, then so be it. It may come to nothing, and our names will be spat as curses for decades to come. But we must try."

He then added, "We need to send word to this Watcher's apprentice, or whatever she is. I will meet with Jahar later and ask him to use a binding for the message, so the contents cannot be understood by anyone other than this Watcher, if opened. Tomorrow morning, pass our message to Edryn, sealed. Ask him to find the messenger from Mornkastle. No doubt she is still in the town, waiting."

"And our message is?"

"We agree to meet with the Watchers who sent her, in the designated place, a tennight from now, at the meeting of the moons."

"Just you and I? But the message mentioned six Watchers!"

"If the worst should happen," Ruhal said with a thin smile, "then being labelled as a traitor will no longer be a worry for me, nor indeed for you. But no, I will call for Jahar and Lura as well. I need those I can trust around me for this. The old brotherhood as you liked to call it years ago."

"Lura?" Sarros brightened visibly at the mention of that name. "It will be good to see her again."

"No doubt she will feel the same." Ruhal's tone was sardonic. "But we have words to write first."

V

Nia had thought herself quite familiar with Mornkastle and many of its inhabitants, but in the days that followed her conversation with Elarin she began to discover that she had previously only scraped the surface of the place.

I ought to have realised, she thought more than once, *that such a place as this- effectively a precarious balance between not just two halves of a land but two separate and irreconcilable worlds- must have secrets that I could not even hope to guess at.*

Ruled in name by a Warden and a small group of men appointed by Watchers, it was in fact presided over by a council whose members were taken from various walks of life, but more importantly from both sides of the Never-Built Wall. Not that any of them were open enforcers of Southern law, nor did any of them seem to be affiliated with warlocks, hedgewitches and other shadowy folk who were known to lurk in the north of the city. They consulted with the Warden's men; they advised, they influenced, and it seemed to Nia that if they wanted something to happen badly enough, it usually did.

"They distrust one another, of course," Olin, the chief guardsman and member of the household who had been entrusted with her welfare, told her one day as they sat by a window in the study playing hardstone on a marble board and listening to the insistent patter of rain outside. "Oh, there are times when they would rather slide a dagger between the ribs than work out some measure of compromise or even agreement. But it's been this way for a *very* long time and has stood firm against stern tests. Always the protagonists take the required steps back from the precipice. It takes men and women of character to do that."

He gave her a considering look. "Maybe you can ask your mistress for more details of our town's ways, should you return to her of course. But she'll tell you nothing of it, I expect. As far as I know, even Watchers choose not to speak about this arrangement unless they have to."

Nia smiled faintly, still a little bewildered by what Olin had been telling her. Part of her tried to believe that he was simply spun tales to pass the time and to mock her- Powers knew she had seen some strange things since being brought here, and a few of them she still couldn't quite bring herself to believe- but she knew deep within herself that he spoke the truth. From the little she knew about him, he was a straightforward man and not given to mockery.

"I had never even heard rumours of such a Council," she remarked, moving one of her white stones two marks forward only to watch in dismay as he deftly countered with a black and a grey.

"Of course not." Olin met her gaze, his steely eyes seeming amused. Nia found herself wondering once again how old he was. Somehow, she found it impossible to tell. She wondered if he might have *luyan* blood. "It does not officially exist," he continued. "It meets in a different place every time. Meetings are arranged with barely a day's notice. The whole purpose is to ensure that the balance is always kept. Remember that the people of Mornkastle are not exactly of the South or the North, but the powers that preside over them are of *both*. The Council has held subtle sway over the people since..." He shrugged. "In one way or another, since Harn became a divided land. Keeping the peace, which of course means preserving the balance."

Nia frowned at the board. It was difficult to concentrate on the game and Olin's ongoing revelations at the same time. "I'm surprised you tell me such things," she remarked, "unless of course I'm to be kept here forever and never have the chance to tell someone."

"I can assure you of one thing, Nia- you won't be kept here forever," Olin told her. "If you have delivered harm into the heart of the north, I expect you'll be executed and your remains sent back to Luudhoq for your mistress to ponder over."

"I've delivered nothing of the sort." Nia thought about that statement. "Of course, someone could quite easily exchange the scroll that Elarin took from me for another, if they wished harm to come to this man Ruhal." She smiled wanly. "There's nothing I can do about that."

"The scroll that Elarin took will be delivered as requested. It may already be in his hands." Olin frowned and shook his head. "Elarin is no friend of Ruhal's, but neither is she his enemy. As to the matter of the Council- who would you tell? There's no evidence that such a thing even exists. Have I named you any names? I could have made the entire idea up. Powers know this is a day for such idle pursuits. You're losing, by the way."

"Where else could such an arrangement exist but here?" Nia mused, and looked up at him. "*Does* it exist anywhere else?"

"The invisible council was formed out of necessity and the need for the truce to be maintained. As you said, where else but here could such an arrangement exist? I would wager my life that Mornkastle is quite unique in that regard."

He glanced out of the window and then looked appraisingly at her. "I think you have secrets of your own to worry about, Nia. That a servant of the Watchers comes here but not to spy and upset the balance, well..."

He left the sentence unfinished, and they lapsed into silence. Finally both players appeared to concentrate fully on the game on the table between them, but Nia's mind raced. *Could it be that Elarin is a member of this hidden Council?* she wondered. *That might explain a few things. But why would she have agreed for the message from Kelandra to be delivered? Unless...*

Unless she has guessed that it contains some proposal for unity and agrees with it.

Days passed. Soon enough a whole tennight passed. Nia's mood changed by the day, and after the sixth day she reasoned that the scroll must have reached its destination by now, and that whoever had delivered it had witnessed that it bore no harm within. By the eighth day, she found herself increasingly restless, wondering how long it might take for a reply to be written and for that message to be relayed back from wherever it had been sent. Would a reply even make its way back to her? She even sat down to mentally calculate how long it might take, based on the distance to various towns she knew of in the north, but soon enough she gave up in frustration. It was pointless. She had no idea where Ruhal or those who answered for him might be. Certainly it seemed that no one in Elarin's household knew.

By noon on the tenth day, she began to wonder how long she would be allowed to wait here, indeed how long she would be forced to wait. Perhaps Kelandra had wanted her to remain in Mornkastle until she received the answers she wanted, but the matter was urgent and Nia also doubted that Elarin and her household would permit her to stay with them indefinitely, regardless of whether or not any answer came from out of the wild north. In any case she longed to be away from them. They made enough effort to be cordial, but none of them aside from Olin showed any degree of friendliness, and a few were outwardly suspicious of her every movement.

Late in the afternoon, sleet began to fall, and for a while even became snow that lingered awhile on the ground before it melted as the deluge reverted to sleet and then cold, stinging rain. Nia watched from a window on the first floor and observed the changing scene. *When was the last time I saw snow fall?* she mused. *It must have been on high ground near the Dianaar Hills, years ago...*

Nia shivered. She was used to Luudhoqian winters which from what she knew of the season in more northern climes, were barely worthy of the name; they were rainy and mild and hurried along quickly to make way for the spring. But this winter had been unseasonably harsh everywhere- she recalled that conditions had been much the same in Darkenhelm.

The world is changing, she thought, and suddenly she recalled the day when Yui and Phyqor had been delivered to the authorities of the Sanctum. *All for the greater good,* she mentally added, and wondered why that memory had suddenly re-emerged. *All for the greater good. But I did it only to please Kelandra, and Kelandra gratefully accepted that piece of good fortune as it made her seem ever the loyal servant of the Seven, seeking out and finding useful weapons in the coming war.*

The greater good had nothing to do with it. It never does.

Nia noticed that the guardsmen at the small watchtower by the gate that led into the front courtyard had emerged from the cover of the tower and were pulling the gates open for a rider. Nia could not see who the rider was with the hood of their robe pulled forward and the head bowed against the inclement weather, although the bulky, solid build indicated a man. He rode slowly on and into the courtyard, out of her sight, slumped forward as if exhausted by his journey.

Nia sat back in her chair, stared at the fire burning low in the hearth on the other side of the room, and pondered what she had seen. Might that have been the messenger she was waiting for? He was due or overdue.

The wind gained in strength outside; dusk fell, and with it Nia's hopes. She was about to wander over to the bookcase and select something to read over by the lantern, if only to distract herself awhile, when the door opened and Elarin walked into the room.

Nia was unsure whether to remain seated or stand, to say anything or remain silent. It was perhaps only the third or fourth time she had seen the woman since their first meeting. She hesitated and was about to stand when Elarin motioned for her to remain seated.

"A message has been delivered for your superior," she said without further ado.

Nia swallowed. Her mouth felt suddenly dry. "What does it..."

"Say? I have no idea. The contents are not my concern. But I have been told to instruct you thus: only the originator of *your* message, that we delivered, may safely open this one." She took a small scroll from an inner pocket of her robe. "Here. I expect you will want to keep it safe, and resist any urge to open it."

"I expect so." Nia gingerly took it and held it lightly in both hands. *And what would happen if I did try to break the seal and read its contents?* she wondered. *Would I fall dead before I could read a single word?*

Then another thought occurred to her. *What if Kelandra opens it, and some terrible witchery is released? What if this Ruhal and his people have decided to use this as an opportunity to strike against Luudhoq, even strike at the heart of the Seven themselves?*

I could be taking a nightmare back with me.

"As I say, I have no idea what message it may contain," Elarin said, observing her. With that, she turned and walked back towards the door.

"Wait," Nia said suddenly. "What happens to me now? May I leave?"

"Leave now if you wish, in the darkness and the rain," Elarin said, seeming amused, "or you could wait for the morning. I think the worst of this weather will have passed by then."

"Thank you." Nia sat back in her chair and placed the scroll carefully on the small table in front of her. Only once Elarin had left did she allow herself a heartfelt sigh of relief, her task now at least half-done, and her temporary fears about the scroll allayed. After all, she reasoned, why would Ruhal of all people risk destroying the delicate truce between south and north?

The following morning dawned brightly, the clouds borne away by the continuing stiff breeze. After she had risen and dressed, Nia was taken down to the front courtyard by Olin. The scroll had been carefully placed in a pocket on the inside of her robe, which she had then crudely sewn up. She was determined that having at least achieved this much, she would not allow her entire task to be unravelled by a pickpocket.

"Farewell, Nia," the guardsman said as the gates were opened a little to allow her to pass through. "You've made for interesting company."

Nia blinked at that. "I have?"

He smiled. "Take care." Then he turned and made his back across the flagstones. Nia watched him for a moment, and then turned and walked away, down the sloping street that led towards the main transport area.

She took the next wagon to Luudhoq that had a spare seat. This time, as she leaned back and watched the countryside gradually roll past, she barely noticed the jarring of the cart or the lack of room to stretch her legs out. For the first time since Kelandra had set her upon this journey, Nia felt that matters might finally be working out for her.

X – All Swept Away

I

Vornen woke into a fog of pain and confusion.

He rolled to one side and closed his eyes until the pain ebbed somewhat, then opened them again. It took a moment for him to remember where he was- a grim, chilly guesthouse in the north of Nisstar, where the rooms were a copper crown a night.

He had arrived in Nisstar the previous day, had somehow been granted entrance on the premise of applying to join the city's army- quite possibly the last thing he would have considered doing, but he had seemed earnest enough and perhaps stupid enough- and had wandered aimlessly for a while, trying to fathom...

Fathom what? He sat up, and allowed himself a groan as thick, dull pain shifted from one side of his head to the other. For a moment he thought he might vomit.

As he sat slumped forward and breathed in the damp, still air, the memory eventually came to him. *The point of the Gates moved,* he recalled. *One moment I could tell precisely where it was, or would be, and the next... the next moment, it became vague, impossible to pinpoint, as if that point might itself be moving.*

That fact itself would have been enough to give him a pounding headache even if he had not spent all of yesterday evening drinking foul white ale. A point that might indicate where multiple Gates would imminently form, yet that point itself moved as if on an axis.

Throughout his journey as far as Nisstar's north-facing wall, Vornen had felt the irresistible pull of the Gates. He even fancied that he could see them in his mind, three of them, empowered by one another, each one a dark abyss whose promise lurked somewhere within the city walls even though they had not precisely *arrived* yet. They had even somehow given him the illusion that his journey towards Nisstar was being speeded up, as if he headed directly towards the centre of a vast maelstrom. The three days of travel after he had left Amethyst and Ileana had amounted to what felt like a single day.

Vornen had found it impossible to recall anything from those three days with any clarity, and wondered blackly if that was a new symptom, that he would gradually lose all track of his life, of the sequence of events and chapters that had made up the patchwork of his existence. *Maybe in the fullness of time I would simply unravel*, he thought, *the memories that have held me together floating oblivious to time, ready to drift away entirely.*

That was the notion Vornen found more frightening than anything else. It frightened him more than death, which like an elusive friend had promised to call many times.

He closed his eyes for a moment and banished the spiral of black thoughts with an effort. But when he opened them, his vision swayed, and nausea overcame him. He leaned forward a little more and this time he vomited over the side of the mattress. The pungent fluid burned his throat; he coughed and spat several times to try and rid his mouth of the taste.

I could warn anyone who might listen, he thought a little later, as he sat downstairs and shivered in the early morning chill. He drank a few sips from a flagon of water. *I could thread my way through the streets, staggering and odorous like the homeless wretch I am. I could stop anyone who looked as if they might neither flee nor fight and tell them to get out of this place whilst they can. And keep running.*

For the rest of their lives, he added, setting aside the water jug. He made his way out into the dull light of morning and slung his pack over his shoulder. As he reached the corner of the street, sleet began to fall. Vornen wandered as far as the sloping overhang of a small church that stood nearby and rested against one of the pillars as the downpour intensified.

I could do with a smoke, he thought vaguely and dug through his pockets for a few scraps of *kyush,* which he eventually found. *I shouldn't have purchased it,* he gently admonished himself, *but where's the sense in abstention when your life's about to end?*

In the distance he could see one of the main thoroughfares teeming with people intent on being elsewhere, nothing but their journeys and their own survival on their minds. They looked more downtrodden than ever, he thought, as the dust and dirt began to turn to mud. The people of Nisstar had grown ever more suspicious of anyone from outside their walls, Vornen recalled from his wandering the streets yesterday, even if they were human men and women who had come from villages only a league away to sell fruit and farm stock. Substantiated reports of the mass gathering in Rockmire had been seized upon by the Church in order to whip this suspicion into a frenzy of hostility. He had seen priests speak at street corners, expounding upon the evils committed by the Rising and urging the "good people of Nisstar" to be vigilant, report any wrongdoings, and of course give praise to the One God.

And so the close-knit paranoia grew apace.

Vornen had felt suspicious or even hostile stares that followed him wherever he went in the city, no matter how low a profile he tried to keep. It was, he had reflected sourly, a little like being back in Ruan-Tor. But when he had briefly caught a glimpse of his own reflection in the sluggish waters of the River Niss, he understood. He looked hunted, haunted and not at all unlike the mad, shambling folk who wandered endlessly through the city's streets and squares, wild-eyed and chanting.

Ruan-Tor, he thought, having finally lit his *kyush* pipe. *Will Rocan swear to the townsfolk that he'll hunt me down for the rest of his days? They'd like that, I'm sure.*

A man less vengeful than Rocan might put his energies towards more urgent matters. That place had far worse problems to contend with than a recently returned vagrant-turned-murderer, no matter what the knight-commander said or thought.

Yes- murderer, he reminded himself, recalling the young guardsman he had killed in Lord Vothangrane's chambers, and wishing that memory would fade. *I wonder what Amethyst might have made of that?*

We'll never know.

Vornen had often wondered if the black sword's reaction to the Gate and the *marandaal* on Tur-morn Hill had helped save Ruan-Tor and the other northern settlements, or at least buy them time. If it had, he decided, perhaps he should one day tell Rocan about that, just to see if the stony knight believed even a small fragment of his story. If one day ever came, that was. Then again, if it did, he might not have a chance to tell that marvellous tale before Rocan slit his throat from ear to ear.

It's a fanciful idea regardless, he reminded himself. *You'll never return there, no matter what happens anywhere else in the world.*

The faint smile vanished from his lips. He no longer had that sword, which ought to have been a relief given its malevolent nature, but he could feel no relief. Suli had taken it, and by now it had almost certainly destroyed her.

Vornen felt a weight of despair in his stomach that a hard, trembling pull on his *kyush* pipe could only partly blur. Hers had been a wretched life, more so than his, and he had been unable to help her, unable to alleviate her growing confusion and pain. The fact that no one could have helped her did nothing to lift that despair.

But she left you many years ago, he reasoned with himself. *Yes, you met her again, but she never came back to you. She was simply drawn to the Gate on Tur-morn Hill. Everything else was simply cruel coincidence.*

This was not the only one of life's closed doors that Vornen meditated on as he sat and half-listened to the insistent drumming of sleet on the shelter-roof above. He still wished fervently that he could have travelled with Amethyst and Ileana to their destination, but sooner or later he would have been drawn into Nisstar, particularly as the murmur of the Gates became something more akin to a crescendo. *I couldn't have headed further away from them,* he thought, and recalled with a shudder the agony that had caused him to collapse on the path.

If they opened- or *when* they opened- and the *marandaal* poured through, then the entire city and eventually the entire land would crumble.

And here I am, he reflected bitterly, *drawn near again, without even so much as a* choragh-*sword in my possession.*

For a moment, anger flared; anger at Suli mostly, for having taken that blade. But it turned swiftly to anguish. However muddled her thoughts, however crazed her mind, she had- in part, at least- taken the blade to save him from the oblivion that would eventually come from that cursed artefact.

But she must have known also that I would be drawn here, he thought, *and likely face oblivion anyway. Or would she have even thought that far ahead?*

Vornen sighed and inhaled another fierce drag of *kyush.* His vision swayed, though not unpleasantly. *I somehow retained enough wits to be sitting down first,* he thought, and just about stopped himself from barking out a sharp, senseless laugh. He sat back against the coolness of the pillar, pushed back his lank hair and watched the last few people seek shelter from the downpour across the way.

Suddenly the sound and feel of the Gates, like a waterfall and a heartbeat thundering through his mind, quietened to an almost imperceptible murmur. *It's even less,* he thought in wonder, so shocked that he almost dropped his pipe. *It's there, but it's less now. Quieter... further away? I can't tell. What does it mean?*

A sudden thought occurred to him, and with it came not fear but a strange exhilaration, a hope that his time might finally be at an end: *Is it happening now?*

The deluge softened to a half-hearted drizzle. A dozen hardier souls who had sought cover across the street under the canopy of a shop decided to brave the elements and scurried on their way through the muddy streets. Vornen watched, waited and listened.

The end did not come.

II

As morning wore into afternoon, Vornen finally roused himself and got to his feet, wincing at the pain in his knees and using the pillar to support himself. He had almost fallen asleep and was on the verge of going for a wander to see where he might be able to do that without being disturbed, when he noticed that for the first time since he had sensed the imminence of the Gates back in Ethanalin Tur-morn, *he could not feel their pull at all.*

"This can't be," he whispered. "It can't be."

The possibility occurred to him that the Gates had somehow vanished or moved to some distant place, but after a moment of standing there in silence he knew that that could not be so. Such a thing had never happened before, and surely if they moved to some other place, he would have felt that new pull even if faintly and would sooner or later have been compelled to stumble like a condemned man after them.

A second possibility occurred to him, one that he did not, could not dare to believe.

Have I lost the sense entirely? he wondered. *Have I lost the ability to...*

The thought drifted away as he closed his eyes, to try and sense anything of smaller, more distant Gates, or of the constant, unyielding lines of force that criss-crossed the world. He had *always* been able to see where they were- in the darkness behind his eyes they emerged as bright lines, scything straight through buildings, through rivers and mountains, forests and lakes, unstoppable, and for most people, unknowable and hidden.

They had vanished.

Except, he knew, they had *not* vanished. They could not. They were as constant as the world itself, or even the stars and sun.

"It's me," he said out loud, which caused a passing farmer with a cartload of hay to stare suspiciously at him as his vehicle trundled past. "It's me!" And he favoured the man with a sudden broad smile that had him urging the horse on so he could be away from the weed-addled madman standing under the church shelter.

Vornen repeated the same thought over and over in his mind: *It's all gone. The Gatesight, the sense of the lines of power... all of it, gone. I can't touch any of it now, even if I want to.*

He made his way back to the guesthouse in a stupor and was just about to shuffle inside- having firmly decided to only drink wine tonight- when he stopped and thought.

This changes nothing in the wider world. My sense of these things has been snapped, but the Gates will still appear into the world sooner or later. Nisstar is still doomed. Perhaps all Aona. Everything is as it was.

And now I can run. I can turn away, free from their pull, and keep running.

He looked around. The sky had cleared finally, although by now the light had begun to fail, stores and market stalls had already given up for the day, and the streets were emptying. An insistent, cold breeze buffeted him and crept under his clothing. Vornen shivered and pondered his choice of action one more time.

Music began to play in a tavern across the street, accompanied by singing and clapping. Vornen gazed across at the enticing scene. *Perhaps a few cups of wine to celebrate,* he thought, and made his way across the road. *Just a few, and then I'll be on my way.*

III

At around the same time as Vornen headed slowly back to his guest-house, yet to be enticed by thoughts of flight, Jaana made her way swiftly through the back streets. She headed towards the city's north-facing gate, her cloak dripping wet from the deluge that had just passed. Her thoughts were frantic. She barely noticed the people and places she walked past, beyond making sure she didn't bump into anyone.

They'll find the priests soon enough, she thought. *Herath will send others to search for them. And they'll open the cell and see the carnage... and what then? They'll see Ludas cowering there. He will have prepared lies for them as he waited there. He'll say I killed them all or something like that. But who will they believe?*

Jaana tried to reason. As far as anyone here knew, she was simply a companion of a now-deceased country sorcerer. She was no one of note. But Ludas was known to Herath, known to all those who had been gathered in the church when Fistelkarn told them what he was. They had paid attention to Fistelkarn's words about him. No doubt they had spread rumours about Ludas, some of them true and some of them outlandish. Surely they would be more interested in him. Certainly they could not let him go.

He's a heretic in their eyes, Jaana reminded herself, *and they'll more than likely burn or execute him. An example will be made.*

281

To her surprise, the thought filled her with no pleasure, but she did feel relief. All she had to do, she told herself, was leave the city, find transport of some sort to Alinnora's Haven, and Ludas would be gone from her life forever.

Just like Fistelkarn and Tyrameer, she thought suddenly, and stopped to lean against a nearby wall, blinking back tears. Her companions had died pointlessly, trying to persuade two unmovable priests of a hideous faith that the growing number of sick and deranged within the city was the result of the *marandaal* reaching out through the very fabric of the Existence, somehow able to touch the world and its people without being physically here.

I'm not sure I believe it myself, no matter what I saw, she thought, and willed herself to trudge along the street a little faster. Drizzle had started to fall again. *Nobody can know for sure.*

Dusk approached, and visibility became worse still as a cold, miserable fog descended. Jaana cursed under her breath as she stopped at a crossroads of narrow little streets, no longer certain which way north was. *Straight on?* she wondered. *Perhaps, although that way bends to the right after a short while. Left? To the west?*

She took the turning to the west, not wishing to look a fool- or worse than that, a fool ripe for robbing- as she stood there in the rain.

The road twisted and turned, sometimes narrowing almost to the width of an alleyway. Jaana had encountered no one for a while now, which in a way she felt grateful for, although the fact also made her uneasy. Several times she stopped and looked back, for a moment unable to decide whether she ought to press on or double back. Each time she took a deep breath and hurried on along the street, vaguely aware that she walked a little faster than before. The sounds of her dull, damp footsteps on the cobbles and her breath could be the only noises left in the world, and she the only individual left in the world to make any noise.

Her imagination began to take over. *Would it be so inconceivable,* she mused, *for the* marandaal *to spirit people away entirely? If I walk all night and lose myself in this damned fog, when it eventually lifts and morning comes, will I find myself in a deserted city?*

Jaana smiled at her flight of fancy, turned a sharp corner in the road, and almost tripped over the body sprawled across the flagstones.

As she stumbled away from it, an unpleasant thought occurred to her. Might this man- who had evidently been a down-and-out judging by his appearance- have any coins on him? Even in Nisstar, surely a few people tossed coins to beggars?

Jaana gingerly searched through the pockets of his trousers and of the goatskin jerkin that he wore and tried to ignore the stench of the man. She found two silver crowns, which was more than she expected, and pocketed them, then stood up and glanced down almost apologetically at her unknowing victim.

"They're no good to you," she said, "but they could be everything to me."

Wondering if they might get her as far as Alinnora's Haven, she hurried on.

Daylight had faded by the time she finally arrived at a wider road where a few hooded lanterns had been lit. A few folk wandered along the road. Jaana saw one man make his way into a tavern called *The Stone and Feather,* and as she passed by that place she paused, her hand touching the coins in her pocket. *I've nowhere to stay and I'm cold,* she reminded herself. *I can't wander the streets all night or sleep in some corner. I might never wake.*

She enquired within about a room for the night but was told that none were available. "We've a stable, mind you," the barkeeper suggested. "It's warm enough. Silver crown for the night."

To Jaana that sounded like far too much, but she had no stomach for an argument. She was ready to drop, and reluctantly agreed.

The stable, which was situated just behind the tavern, was at least warmer and drier than outside. Jaana was shown to a stall where fresh hay had been piled. "Saddles and bridles are kept elsewhere, and these horses will all cause havoc if you try to steal one," the barkeeper informed her with a friendly smile, holding his lantern out to illuminate the area better whilst she arranged hay for bedding.

"I've no intention of stealing anything, let alone a horse," Jaana promised him with a tired smile. "I can barely ride anyway."

"Just letting you know, miss." He nodded, turned and left the stable. Jaana lay back with a sigh as she listened to his footfall over the flagstones of the paddock, then the sound of the back door to the tavern as it opened and closed. A moment after that, she was asleep.

IV

Sudden light pouring through the doorway pulled Jaana from her slumber. Shielding her eyes against the brilliance, she sat up and peered at the silhouette in the opened doorway. "Begging your pardon, miss," a young voice mumbled, "but I need to see to the horses."

As the stable lad went about his business, Jaana got to her feet and brushed away loose bits of hay that had stuck to her, and then stumbled out into the bright morning. *At least I know which way to head now,* she thought, and set off once again towards the northern gates of the city, wishing that she could ignore the gnawing emptiness in her stomach.

284

A wagon stop was usefully located near to the exit gateway, and when she reached it later that morning, Jaana found one that was headed towards Alinnora's Haven. The only other passenger waiting for the wagon to depart was a man with shoulder-length brown hair and bedraggled appearance, who grinned at her as she glanced in his direction. Jaana silently cursed to herself- *Won't it be just my luck if he's a dreamer,* she thought- and looked away from him, but he spoke up anyway. "Headed for Alinnora's Haven?"

"Apparently," Jaana said without looking at him.

"Should be there in two days, I reckon," he continued, oblivious to her lack of interest, then walked up and extended a hand in greeting. "My name is Vornen."

Reluctantly she shook hands with him, then frowned as she caught the odour of wine on his breath. Had he been drinking at this early hour? "I'm Jaana." Immediately she wished she hadn't given her real name, but it was too late to worry about that. *Damn it, I want to be away from here now,* she thought, and watched pensively as the coachman chatted with someone across the square. *Why must we wait any longer?*

Soon enough however, they were on their way. The only check the guards at the outer gates made was to ensure that the coachman had collected the fares from his passengers. *A healthy proportion of which will no doubt head straight into the church coffers,* Jaana mused, but as they left Nisstar and headed across open grassland she put such thoughts to one side, relieved simply to be outside the city walls.

Vornen, who sat across from her inside the coach, seemed determined to converse. Jaana was not sure what to make of his bright mood but decided she might as well be polite. In her limited experience, drunkards who felt ignored became angry drunkards.

"Do you have friends or family in Alinnora's Haven?" he asked.

"I'm to meet a couple of friends there," she said, thinking, *What should I tell Lyya and Fauli? It all sounds scarcely believable. With Fistelkarn and Tyrameer gone, what are we to do?*

"That's exactly my reason too, if I'm lucky enough to find them," he said. Then he leaned forward and added in a low voice, "To tell you the truth, Jaana, I never thought I'd leave Nisstar alive."

"Why not?" she asked despite herself.

He smiled faintly. "Well, that's a story that would take some telling. But I will say one thing: the further away you are from that place, the better. Once you've met with your friends, I suggest you keep going. Get as far away from Nisstar as you can."

Jaana felt suddenly uneasy. *Why would he say that?* she wondered. *What does he know? Or does he simply hate the place?*

"Why should we keep going?" she asked quietly.

Vornen's happy mood seemed to have faded entirely now. His expression had become one of fear and a strange, desperate sadness.

"Nisstar will be destroyed," he said finally. "It will be nothing but rubble, perhaps only days from now. A hole will open and a nightmare you cannot even begin to imagine will emerge from it. It will spread, and possibly consume the world in time. If I were you, Jaana, I'd seek out the company of friends, and if you can, do whatever you've always wanted to do in the time remaining."

He smiled at the expression of shock on her face. "Of course, I must be quite mad. I must be in the thrall of senseless dreams about light. I expect a fever will come upon me sooner or later. You must have seen many others like me, during your time in the city."

Jaana had no idea what to say to that. She looked out of the window at the countryside. They passed near a hamlet of six houses and a farmstead set on the gentle slope of a wooded hill. Smoke drifted lazily upwards from a few of the chimneys. Two men and a woman had gathered to talk by the edge of the dirt track that threaded between the buildings. Near to them, a child played, making signs and shapes in the dirt with a stick.

All this and so much more, Jaana thought. *All of it swept up into darkness. The world changed forever. But how does Vornen know about all this? Did he have the same dreams and visions as all these others, but then somehow recover? I've never heard of anyone who recovered from them.*

She decided it would be best to say nothing more on the subject.

As light began to fail later that day, clouds swept in from the north-east and the weather turned foul. Rain began to patter down and made a harsh sound on the roof of the coach. Jaana felt sorry for the coachman, perched up there in the darkness and peering ahead into the dank darkness of the country night.

Briefly she wondered how far they could get tonight. Would the coach become stuck in the road, as often happened during the rainy winters of the middle lands? What then? They would walk, she supposed. Perhaps there was a village between here- wherever *here* was- and Alinnora's Haven. *But I have no money left,* she thought suddenly. *What will I do?*

For a moment, sheer desperation threatened to overwhelm her. She took a deep breath. *You must be strong,* she told herself. *You must survive, whatever happens.*

A muffled thud suddenly sounded from above them; Vornen frowned and drew his longknife. *That sounded as if the coachman had slumped over or something fell on the roof,* Jaana thought. A short while later the coach drew to a lurching halt.

"Robbers," Vornen muttered as he glanced out on either side. But the relentless rainfall remained the only sound they could hear, and nothing of note could be seen amidst the gloom of the surrounding countryside.

The air, which had been chilly even inside the coach, suddenly became much warmer, or so Jaana imagined. It smelled of earth and salt and iron.

What followed happened so fast that it was over almost before either of them had any time to react. The door of the coach flew open, and it was as if a storm rushed in; Vornen was thrown backwards by the sudden blast of air, and at the same time Jaana turned and stood up, staring out into the night.

I know what this is, she thought. *I know it well now. This is the work of* choragh, *or at least their minions.*

Her eyes, Vornen thought wildly as he stared at her. *Her eyes have changed colour.*

But it was more than that. Something- some fluid or essence- swam in her eyes, itself changing colour continuously. Jaana stretched her arm out towards the source of the howling gale, which threatened to fling the coach over onto its side, and from somewhere in the chaos outside, a sound like a scream of rage rose up, as if unseen foes had been thwarted in some effort to destroy her.

For a moment, the wind intensified; it lashed against one side of the coach and then the other and circled like a raging, uncontainable animal.

Then, abruptly the storm abated, and Jaana fell back into her seat, ashen-faced.

Vornen dared not move. He listened intently, but the night had become eerily silent. The rain had eased off and the air was utterly still and damp.

Suddenly the door of the coach creaked and moved slightly, and Vornen's grip on his longknife grew tighter than ever. The blade shook and gleamed faintly in the remaining light. As the door became still again, and Vornen began to hope that whatever had visited them had gone away or even been banished, he stole a quick glance at Jaana, who still gazed out through the doorway, intent on something that he could not see.

Whatever that was, he decided, *it has something to do with her. I'd wager anything on it.*

For a moment, a memory of Ileana came to him- Ileana holding back the *diafagh* in the Crescents. She had halted them in their tracks and turned them to dust, unmaking them entirely.

"Jaana," he whispered a while later, thinking that perhaps now it might be safe to speak. She turned her head slowly so that her eyes stared into his. Nothing looked unusual about them. Perhaps they were a little darker than before, perhaps not. Vornen was already finding it difficult to distinguish between what he had seen and what he might have seen.

"Has it gone?" he whispered, his attention briefly upon the door once again as a hint of breeze made it move and creak. *Because it was something evil,* he reasoned. *It wasn't simply a small dust-devil whirling through the night.*

She nodded. "I think so. But maybe others will come."

Did she simply banish it or destroy it? he wondered. *And what was it anyway? Does she even know?*

"Then we'll not stay here and wait," he said as he peered out into the dusk. "There's a little light left. We're near Riversreach, I reckon. I passed along this same track for a while when I headed into Nisstar. The village is a little north of here. We can get there if we set off now."

Without waiting for an answer, he stepped out of the coach onto a waterlogged track thick with mud. The coach horses, he noticed, were nowhere to be seen, but something long and glistening from inside one of them could be seen where they would have stood. He glanced up at the coachman's slumped body and wished immediately that he had not. The top half of the man's head was missing. A forest eagle which had been pecking at the exposed brain-flesh shrieked angrily at the interruption and flew away.

Vornen glanced back into the coach. Jaana had sat up and was inching her way towards the door. He held out an arm, and reluctantly she allowed herself to be helped down from the coach.

"Whatever it was, somehow it took the horses," Vornen whispered, but Jaana said nothing.

The two of them headed on along the muddy track under the hastening dusk. The rain did not return but the air remained damp and cold. They made their way as swiftly as they could along the muddy, undulating track and kept their eyes on the way ahead. Vornen saw and heard nothing to cause any alarm, and suspected that Jaana didn't either, for she remained tight-lipped and silent.

Who or what is she? he wondered. *Clearly someone with certain powers, though I can't fathom what they might be. Something to do with the* choragh, *perhaps?*

Was Jaana like Ileana in some way? Vornen wondered how many people in the world could withstand the creatures of the Old Dark in that way, or perhaps even banish them.

Or turn them to cold dust as Ileana did.

If we get to Riversreach, he decided, *then I'll ask her what she knows of such things. If she lies or denies that she knows anything, then so be it. I'd like to at least ask the question.*

As they walked on along the gently winding track the clouds began to disperse, enough for Ildar's light to shine upon them. The white moon was only half-full, but the illumination made it possible to walk a little more safely through what had become full night. Vornen shivered and drew his cloak more tightly about himself. He thought back once again to their encounter in the Crescents. Had those creatures come for Ileana, desperate to stop her reaching the witch who sought her out, or had they simply been after the *choragh*-sword? He had no idea and was resigned to never knowing.

I hope they'll still be in Alinnora's Haven, he thought. *Will they? Will Amethyst have left Ileana with the witch, or might that woman have bound her to some other task?*

Or has something utterly unforeseen happened?

Vornen shook his head, smiling tiredly at the pointless conjecture.

They arrived at Riversreach a while later. As its name suggested, the village stood huddled near one bank of a river, a tributary of the River Niss. They had to walk over a stone bridge that spanned that river to reach it. Vornen glanced at Ildar's rippling reflection in the fast-flowing waters, and a cold feeling rushed through him for a moment, for he fancied he could see a pair of eyes upon that likeness, black-centred and red-rimmed.

Jaana, however, saw none of this. Espying the lights of the village no more than a stone's throw away, she marched with even greater purpose over the bridge, and Vornen hurried after her, averting his eyes from the river and the tricks it might or might not be playing.

XI - Possession

I

Alexia had long feared the *act of love* as some referred to it, to the point of steering clear of any potential suitors that her family tried to arrange for her. As she passed out of her teenage years they gave up altogether, considering her a lost cause who loved books more than she would love any man. Alexia's only response had been to give a heartfelt sigh of relief and immerse herself in her studies with renewed energy.

In many of the quiet studious hours since then, she had put aside her work and stared beyond her reading light, idly wondering what her first time might be like, if she ever let it happen. But she had never, even in her darkest hours, imagined that it would be with a fat, stinking man in a brothel in Luudhoq.

She walked slowly over to her bedroom window where the air was a little fresher, wincing in pain. *Today is better than yesterday,* she tried to remind herself. *But then, yesterday was the worst of nightmares.*

The grotesque bald man who had broken her maidenhead had whispered in her ear as he lay squirming on top of her: *I paid extra for you, so don't just lie there with your face turned from me!*

So she had turned her face to him, gritting her teeth at the savage pain in her womb, but he remained unsatisfied and said as much to Mirram after he had dressed and left her chamber, pausing only to spit in her face. Alexia had expected a beating there and then, but instead Mirram instructed her to clean herself up and then ushered another man through shortly afterwards.

The second man had brutally sodomised her, laughing every time she screamed in agony. When he had finished, leaving her bleeding and almost unconscious with the pain, Mirram came in and inspected her, then said, "I think I'll spare you your thrashing."

She helped Alexia downstairs to the outside privy, and watched expressionlessly as she squatted and expelled her breakfast and the man's leavings, sobbing loudly at the pain and humiliation.

That was yesterday, Alexia reminded herself again, holding the bars in her window with both hands.

Today no men wanted to see her, so she had had time to think about her circumstances and how she had come to be here. Alexia concluded that she must have been kidnapped while she was asleep- but who would do such a thing, and why? Could it have been the authorities in Aphenhast? No, they would have simply had her taken back to Darkenhelm. Whoever it was, why would they have sold her or given her to the madam of a brothel?

Someone wanted me out of the way, she had reasoned. *And it must have had something to do with Yui and Phyqor. It must be Narin.*

Alexia had been suspicious of that man ever since setting eyes upon him. *I always wondered why Narin had gone to the trouble of taking Yui and Phyqor out of Darkenhelm and all the way here,* she thought. *It had something to do with Yui's unusual talents, that much is certain. And the story about helping her, healing her, was just that- nothing but a convenient lie. I can't prove it, but I know it.*

Alexia's grip on the window bars tightened as cold rage rushed through her. *The way he looked at me the other evening as we sat in the tavern. That look makes sense now. Oh, he tried to hide it, but I could see it plainly enough. I just didn't think he would move against me so quickly.*

If I ever see that man again, I'll put a knife through him.

She had felt helpless many times before in her life, but this was surely the worst time of all. Yui and Phyqor were no doubt suffering while she stood here, a prisoner looking out in anger across the city. *I must rescue them somehow,* she thought over and over, but she knew that such a feat would more than likely be impossible even if she still had her freedom.

From her window she could see that this part of the city seemed muted tonight. Aside from a few revellers in various alehouses and one or two stores that remained open in the hope of extra trade, few people were around. Alexia watched as a grubby-looking lamp man began his round, and recalled watching similar scenes years ago in Darkenhelm, though from the comfort of a palace window.

The lamp man tripped on a loose cobble and earned himself a few jeers from a small crowd of drinkers on their way between taverns. Alexia watched them for a moment, then allowed her gaze to wander further. Her room faced east, and in the distance, she could see the vast fortress that Narin had called the Sanctum. Its spires and turrets were surely easily recognisable from almost any distance within the citadel walls, black needles dotted with points of light where illumination poured forth from windows and rose into the swiftly darkening sky.

The centre of the civilised world, Narin had proudly called it. *This is the great castle of the Seven, and of the Watchers.*

As she looked towards that place, Alexia suddenly felt as if she was being observed- which she knew was a mad thought. Abruptly she looked away and her gaze fell a little nearer. Aromas of evening meals being prepared, *kyush* smoke and other, less fathomable flavours emanated from tavern doors and windows and drifted up into the evening air, along with the occasional odours of refuse and sewage trickling short distances to the cess-holes. All these smells took turns to assail her senses. Alexia had not thought a city with more baffling sights and smells than Darkenhelm could be possible, yet evidently it was.

At least they have a decent drainage system here, she mused, but the thought led her to an occasion- not so long ago, yet it seemed so now- when she had been part of a small audience gathered in a palace antechamber to listen to a detailed proposal for such a system for Darkenhelm. The proposal had been created and voiced by Phyqor.

Phyqor and Yui put their trust in Narin, and I suspect they are now prisoners just like me. I wonder how much gold that bastard pocketed from all of this?!

Drizzle started to fall from the moonless sky. The lamps fizzed and spat, casting greasy yellow light across the road. Alexia wondered if she would eventually be released. *Perhaps if I don't prove to be popular, Mirram will let me go,* she thought hopefully, but her mind issued an altogether darker riposte: *If you don't prove to be popular, she'll have your throat slit and your body thrown into the river.*

There must be a way, she thought. *But I can't see what it might be. I've no friends here, no one I can turn to, no one who might pay Mirram enough gold to let me go.*

A truly mad thought leapt up. It was nonsense and she dismissed it as such, but it nevertheless caused her heart to pound urgently. *I could kill her. I don't know how, but I could kill her. If I hit her in the right place. Will the other women come to her aid? Perhaps, perhaps not.*

Alexia shook her head. Some of them, she knew from listening to their talk, were here because it was safer for them to be housed in this place than to wander the streets where they could quite easily be murdered, or worse, kidnapped and kept as playthings to be tortured and beaten and raped until their minds snapped or their bodies simply gave up.

I can't act against Mirram, even if I somehow had the opportunity, she realised. *As much as I hate her for keeping me here, she provides a place for women who have nothing and no one, even if she earns a living from their situations. I can't take what little safety they have away from them.*

Tiredly she made her way over to her mattress and lay down to sleep.

II

The high round tower loomed over much of the city. Had it been possible, Yui would have stared at the scene of Luudhoq displayed before her for many hours, soaking up the sights and sounds; the multitude of other towers, ramparts and fortresses that jostled with lesser but no less fantastic structures, the sun glittering on the windows, the people far below as they meandered along the thoroughfares and winding, narrow cobbleways.

Instead, she was thrown to the floor of this dusty upper chamber by something invisible, whilst the two tall, cold-eyed men watched her. She remained crouched there and listened to the breeze as it sighed around the tower and the panicked thump of her heart as the cold stone pressed against her cheek. *The wind,* she thought. *The wind and the sunlight on the stones of the tower. The light and the sounds of the afternoon.*

And suddenly in her mind's eye she was outside her round prison, hovering somewhere near one of the windows, able to see the faint muscular contortions in the necks and shoulders of her torturers as they pressed their invisible wall against her as if to crush her bones into dust.

In this moment Yui could see herself as well, the frail, pathetic child curled up on itself against the stone, eyes tight shut, chest rising and falling frantically as it breathed in what it could of the cold air. *That's not me,* she thought spitefully. *I can move outside of myself. I can see the backs of these men. If only I could make daggers out of air just like they make walls!*

296

Inevitably she had to return to her body as the pressure, the torture, ebbed and ceased. To Yui it felt like a prison within a prison. *If they kill me, do I stay as a ghost?* she wondered. *Will I always be up here?*

She knew that the men tortured her in order to make her tell them where the black gateways were forming out in the world, or at least describe the places where they were made- she could describe each such place perfectly, although she would never tell them- but they didn't know that she could move outside of herself, and stare down at the situation in which she was trapped. They didn't know that the more they tortured her, the easier it became for her to step out of her body for a fleeting moment. *And when I'm outside of myself, I no longer feel the pain,* she reminded herself.

She might have smiled then, at the thought of that precious secret, but one of the men kicked her into the centre of the room, and then footsteps sounded. As on previous occasions, they began to walk around her in opposing directions. Yui knew that this circling was significant in some way, though she could not fathom how. Even without looking at them- which she dared not do- she could tell when their circular paths met, twice during each revolution, for the nagging pain in her head became, for that brief duration, crushing agony, so much that she felt her brains might be squeezed out in thin rivulets through her eyes, nose and ears.

Each time that this torture subsided, she almost sobbed with relief, but many days of this treatment had conditioned her against making any such sound or conveying any emotion. The worst part of it was not the pain so much as the fact that for some reason, when they employed this tactic, she could not leap out of herself.

At the very core of her being, Yui's desire to find her father and escape this place burned more strongly than ever. But she had no hope of doing so without the aid of other people. She knew that Alexia had also been imprisoned somewhere, so for the moment she couldn't help- but there were others somewhere out in the city, to whom she had managed to reach out, sometimes without knowing or being in control of what she was doing. They too were part of her desperate plan; somehow, in her mind's wanderings, she had found them, weak and pliable. She could bend them to her will on occasion, something about which Yui felt great shame, because she knew it was wrong. Yet her need to survive, to escape, overrode everything else. Sooner or later her captors would tire of her resistance, or she would snap like a twig under their continuous torture.

Yui recalled brief moments from the journey that she, Phyqor, Alexia and Narin had taken, from Darkenhelm to Luudhoq. She had spent some of that journey in a delirium, but could remember certain things nonetheless- the coolness of country rain, the sun as it rose at their backs each morning, the sights of distant forests, and other scenes taken from her more lucid moments.

I want to see the world, she thought fiercely. *I want to see every corner of it.* She remembered her father had told her that in the more distant parts of the world the air smelt different; colder, clearer, sharper, sweeter. This was just one of many nuggets of information that Yui had stored away in her short life, glimpses of a world wholly unlike the one she inhabited.

In her fevered imagination, Yui breathed in this vital air when the footsteps stopped and made herself believe that its inhalation might serve to heal her. Finally she dared to raise her head, for she knew that the two men had already spirited themselves away without a sound. Every time they left her alone for a while, the intense relief and even gratitude overwhelmed her.

As on every other such occasion, Yui crawled over to the wall directly under one of the arched windows, curled herself up into a ball and sobbed for an age. Finally, exhausted, she fell into a light slumber from which she later woke with a frightened start, convinced that her torturers had returned.

But they had not, and the child sat with her back against the wall to think about the strange objects and paths, the *gateways* about which she dreamed. She knew them intimately without knowing what they were. She could describe their locations in perfect detail. She even knew *when* they would open, or change, or disappear.

This knowledge baffled and frightened her, and the *things* that she caught glimpses of beyond the gateways and the deep, vast holes in the ground frightened her even more. But she knew one thing for certain- that all these things were important to her captors. So important, in fact, that each day they spent vast amounts of time and effort trying to torture her into giving them that information. That was enough for Yui to be utterly determined that she would never give them the answers they needed.

Her hands tightened into fists as she sat in the gloom of her remote cell, a look of icy hatred upon her face. *Never,* she thought again, for good measure. *Never, ever, ever!*

For a moment Yui's eyes became near to black in colour, her hands unclenched without her even being aware, and she heard a low murmur of sound rise around her, as if all the people of Luudhoq milled around just outside the tower, engaged in a thousand separate conversations. It was always like this whenever she *reached* in this way. *Their talk is like a river,* she thought, and she stepped into that river.

I need to find Alexia. I know she can't help now, but maybe she can escape, and maybe then she can find a way of helping us.

It was a desperate thought and she knew it.

After a short while Yui's eyes closed and her head slumped forward. She swam, in her mind, past the chatter of thousands, the vast and overwhelming chorus, until eventually she found who she was looking for.

Moments after hearing what sounded like the frightened whispers of a child in her head, Alexia stood by the window, staring out at what little she could see of the city, and the vast array of stars in the sky.

It was Yui trying to talk to me, she thought, but knew that it could not have been. If she had such a talent, would she not have tried to talk to her before, back when she and Phyqor had been captured? It made no sense. Yet Alexia also somehow knew beyond doubt that it *was* her. The words had been distant, indistinct, and somehow she felt that Yui had known that; she had caught a measure of the child's frustration.

I can do nothing for you now, Alexia thought miserably, although Yui had long gone, pulled back to wherever she was imprisoned. *I'm a prisoner too, powerless and unable to help. But if I ever see Narin again, I will kill him for you. I know he handed you over to the Watchers. Everything that happens to you now, happens because of him.*

Alexia did not sleep that night. The next day, as afternoon became evening and the higher buildings basked in the last of the day's sunlight, she lay down on her bed, and wished once again that she could sleep. *How could Yui have spoken to me?* she mused. *How could it be? Is she able to reach across distances, into people's minds?* She hardly dared to believe it might be possible, and yet part of her was certain that it was.

Yui's voice came to her suddenly, stronger and clearer. *Alexia. Can you hear me?*

Despite her exhaustion, Alexia almost jumped up, and crossed to the window as if she expected to see Yui down in the street below. Instead she saw only a couple of lampmen working their way up the street, lighting lanterns as they did so, and a shopkeeper shutting his premises for the day and trying to ignore the mumbled imploration of a beggar who loomed nearby.

"Yes," she whispered, as she continued to watch the scene below but taking none of it in. The shopkeeper turned the key in the door. The wheels of the lampmen's cart squeaked in protest as they slowly proceeded up the cobbled hill. The beggar found a more strident, angry voice as the shopkeeper turned and walked away. Somewhere further into the distance, raucous laughter rose into the air for a moment.

"I can hear you." She traced a finger across the window sill. "But even now I think I must be dreaming."

No immediate response came, and for a moment Alexia felt truly adrift, as if she had been tricked by her own mind. But then the child's reply came to her, simultaneously joyous and desperate at the same time. *I found you!*

Alexia heard faintly the sounds of distant sobs and felt something of the girl's desperation. *Oh Gods, Yui- I wish I could help you!*

"Where are you? How are you being treated?" she asked and felt the knot in her stomach tighten a little further when Yui failed to respond to the question but instead whispered, *Please help us, Alexia-* as if the evening breeze was already started to carry her away.

At a loss as to what to say, Alexia could utter nothing, and presently Yui's voice returned. *Maybe I can...*

Abruptly, Alexia felt a *loosening* around her mind, a sensation of sudden release and emptiness, and realised that the connection with the child had gone. Whether this was through something she had done, or some accident, or some interruption by those who held her prisoner she could not tell.

Tears rolled down her cheeks as Alexia moved to sit on the edge of her bed, and hours passed by. She barely noticed. She could not remember feeling more wretched than this at any point in her life. Even the aftermath of her family's massacre somehow paled into insignificance now; she had barely thought about it in recent weeks anyway.

I must help Yui and Phyqor, she thought miserably. But even if she somehow escaped this place- and she had no idea how she might do that- she remained alone and friendless in a city that she still struggled to understand. Here in Luudhoq she was no one of consequence. *I'm even less now,* she told herself, and glanced at her barred window. *I'm a low whore.*

Looking down at her still-trembling hands, Alexia smiled wanly. She could barely raise an arm in anger at the moment.

The once-princess did not lie down to sleep that night. As the small hours crept towards dawn, she sought inspiration, ideas, anything that might help her friends in some way, but nothing came to her. The morning light found her slumped forward in a light slumber, from which she was awakened by the bell sounding the morning call to breakfast.

By midday, however, another violent change had left its mark upon her. Not for the first time, Alexia's life was about to take a sharp, terrifying turn.

IV

The man stood near the doorway to her room, a look of utter confusion on his face. His mouth hung open, and the look in his eyes was no look at all.

There's something wrong with him, Alexia decided as a pit opened in her stomach. *He'll be worse than the rest. What will he do to me?*

From somewhere she summoned the courage and the good sense to behave as she knew she ought. After all, what else could she do, imprisoned and unarmed? Smiling, she opened her legs and beckoned him nearer. A faint part of her remained embarrassed, aware of the clumsiness of her movements, but Alexia's thoughts were on one thing only:

what might be done to her, by this man whose mind seemed to be damaged.

Had I not given up all hope though? she asked herself. *Isn't it about time I was done with this misery?*

He didn't undress. He didn't even move. For a moment his lips worked wordlessly, and his eyes blinked as if he had just woken up. Alexia wondered suddenly if he might be almost as frightened as she was.

And then: "Come with me," he said. The words formed a slow struggle, as if he could not quite believe or even comprehend what he said.

"I..." Alexia shook her head, not sure how she ought to react. *Should I ring the bell to bring Mirram and the guards?* she thought suddenly, and glanced for a moment at the rope that hung from a narrow aperture in the ceiling, near to her bed. All the women who worked here had one in their rooms, supposedly for raising the alarm should a visitor threaten murder. Of course, almost every other atrocity was permitted.

"I can't," she said eventually. "The madam of the house forbids such things. I can't come with you." She wondered if the man was a simpleton. Did he really expect to convince the whores he slept with to go with him, willingly or otherwise? She didn't know whether to feel afraid or sorry for him.

"She'll have no choice."

In the silence that followed, the possibilities raced through Alexia's mind. Might it be possible for her to escape? Could he somehow fight his way past Mirram and her guardsmen? He looked strong enough, young enough. Was he armed? And if they escaped, what then? What would become of her? Would she be set free or would he try to make her his? What were his reasons for this lunacy?

"Get dressed and come over to the door," he said.

He waited in expressionless silence as Alexia hurriedly dressed. *What am I doing?* she asked herself over and over. But she had already agreed to his mad plan.

He held her forearm tightly as they made their way downstairs. Down the hallway at the bottom of the three flights of steps, Mirram's grubby little reception area stood. The woman herself sat there, staring at some papers with a deep frown upon her face as if she might be working out her accounts or figuring out a particularly challenging puzzle.

When she saw them coming towards her, the brothel madam's eyes widened in disbelief. "She's not yours, Daril. Have I not told you before about trying to take my girls from me? I won't have it. But I will have a finger or two from you for your insolence, and perhaps something else of yours. After all, you seem to favour theft over fornication. You'll not miss it, I expect."

So saying, she brought a wicked-looking longknife from behind her desk and moved to block their way, formidable and grim as she stared directly at Alexia's would-be rescuer. Lanternlight flickered in the brackets on the walls and deeply shadowed her eyes.

The man she had called Daril stopped suddenly. Alexia waited for him to pull a weapon of some sort from an inner pocket of his coat. Surely he had come here armed, if he intended to steal a whore from directly under Mirram's nose? *Please, let this be finished soon one way or another,* she pleaded silently.

Daril simply walked down the last few steps into the corridor, as Mirram stared incredulously at them. "Last chance, boy," she hissed. "What's the matter with you?"

Alexia wanted to hang back out of harm's way, but Daril's grip was like iron, and he forced her along by his side. Mirram laughed as if she could still not quite believe the man's audacity, and swung the knife, aiming for his neck.

Daril's hand reached out and caught the blade. Unbelievably, it drew no blood. At the same time, something dark and indistinct appeared to leap from his hand, down the blade and along Mirram's arm, and then vanished.

Several things then happened at the same time.

The lanterns set along the corridor flared suddenly as if in mutual reaction to some invisible presence, and then their light was snuffed out in an instant. Mirram collapsed to the side of the corridor. Her knife clattered to the floor. Alexia willed herself not utter a sound, even as panic threatened to overwhelm her and her blood pounded in her ears. Suddenly she wanted nothing more than to be back upstairs, a prisoner but at least *alive*.

She could hear rain begin to fall outside. It sounded far louder than it ought, as if the raindrops were nails being hurled upon the rooftops of Luudhoq. Daril's hand retained its vice-like grip around her forearm as he walked on along the passageway. Alexia could see nothing at all as she was borne along by her captor; her eyes remained unable to adjust to the darkness. *Something happened,* she thought as she stumbled along. *Witchcraft.*

By the time they reached the front hallway and had stepped outside into the rain, Alexia's thoughts had turned to the guardsmen that Mirram employed. There were always two of them. She had seen them from one window or another on occasion, on either side of the gated entrance to the house. They would attack Daril as soon as they saw him, and they might even attack her as well.

But Daril walked her calmly down to the front gates, and as she stared to one side and then the other, Alexia realised numbly that the guards would not be putting up any sort of fight. Both had had their throats slit almost from ear to ear. Even now, blood seeped from their wounds to mingle with the hard rain.

Alexia's only, horrified thought was: *He's a killer. I have to get away from him.*

She tried to remove his hand from her forearm, but he shook his head, and set off down the narrow little street and pulled her with him. Alexia shivered as her soaked clothing began to cling tightly to her skin. She stumbled along in his wake and desperately looked around to see if there might be anyone nearby she could call to for help, but the two of them were alone with nothing but the hiss of rain on the flagstones for the company.

The afternoon became a grey blur. Daril led her along a multitude of narrow, twisting little streets and kept only to the more obscure routes where houses, storage buildings and abandoned shells that might have served some purpose long ago leaned and crumbled, providing scant respite from the rain which had now started to turn to sleet. Alexia collapsed to her knees at one point, exhausted, but he hauled her to her feet and strode grimly on, albeit more slowly.

Finally they arrived at a narrow alleyway with a wooden door at the end that led into the dark interior of a storehouse. The lock had been broken, and Daril ushered her inside. By the fading daylight that seeped through, Alexia saw boxes and sacks and could smell, amongst other things, grain and cured meats.

She turned and saw that Daril remained in the doorway, sleet angling across his face. He sighed and leaned against the doorpost. Alexia watched him for a moment. *I have to know what happens now,* she thought, and asked him: "Will you let me go? Please?"

Daril did not answer. It was as if he had fallen asleep as he leaned against the doorpost. Alexia waited pensively, but moments passed and still he did not move a muscle. The sleet intensified. It looked as if it might even tear holes in his clothes.

Then, just as she was about to speak again, he raised his head to look at her, and even before he spoke, Alexia stepped backwards, shocked. She felt certain that something *different* now lurked behind those eyes. The same thing, perhaps, that had killed Mirram and brought an impenetrable darkness to the brothel.

"Please..." she began, her voice shaking, but then he spoke, and Alexia forgot everything about Mirram and her whorehouse, everything but the instant in which she heard these words.

"You'll be safe here for a little while," Daril said softly.

But it was not Daril who spoke.

It was *Yui*.

V

Father, wake up.

Phyqor's eyes flickered open and he sat up, certain for a moment that his daughter was somewhere in the prison cell with him. But the moment passed; dull realisation set in and he leaned back against the roughly-hewn stone wall.

I may as well be back in Darkenhelm, he reflected, *except that would have been better. Yui was still with me then.*

The knowledge that she was imprisoned in a separate place so he could not even see what had happenedto her and how she was being treated, was an agony that persisted and became worse day after day. His captors could not have visited a worse torture upon him if they had tried- but the irony was that they had *not* tortured him. Instead they had held him in a spacious, clean cell that even had its own privy. He had not been shackled to the wall; he was free to pace around, which he did frequently, ever restless and ever tormented.

Phyqor guessed that they had decided to treat him this way because they thought that Yui could somehow sense his condition, and they might therefore coax out of her whatever it was that they wanted. He had already decided

307

that their journey to Harn and their subsequent arrest in Luudhoq had something to do with Yui's dreams and visions.

The authorities did not even know who Narin was, he recalled. *I described him, but they seemed to have no idea. And then, when they claimed to know nothing of the healing that had been promised, and we tried to leave...*

He felt as if part of him had been entirely torn away. They had always been close, in part because of the unfortunate events that had marred Yui's life. Her mother had died in childbirth, and Phyqor's world had descended into a maelstrom of confusion; unutterable grief accompanied by the singular joy that the healthy baby girl had given him. In time, as the grief subsided to a dull, continuous ache, he had dedicated himself to bringing up the infant as best he could. Staff worked within the Palace in Darkenhelm who were able and willing to help in some ways, but it had been Alexia, as she grew older, who helped most.

Phyqor smiled weakly as he remembered the occasions when Alexia had helped teach Yui her reading and writing and her numbers. Alexia had had no time for her own family and they certainly cared nothing for her, but in her awkward, bookish way she had grown attached to Yui.

And I grew attached to Alexia, he reminded himself, thinking back on how complicated matters might have become if the world and its troubles had not caused their comfortable lives to cave in around them.

Father, listen to me!

Startled, he looked around, certain for a moment that he had heard his daughter's voice. *Now I'm imagining things,* he thought miserably, but as if to prove him wrong Yui's voice spoke up again in his mind, even more urgently.

Please tell me you can hear me!

"I can hear you," Phyqor whispered, and thought that perhaps he could hear his daughter utter a sigh of relief. *It really is her,* he thought, utterly bewildered. *How did she learn to do this? Do the Watchers and the Seven know about it?*

"Where are they holding you?" he whispered. "What are they doing to you?" He feared hearing the answer to that question, and those fears multiplied when she failed to answer but instead said: *I'm going to get you out of there.*

"Wait!" Abruptly he remembered to speak in a whisper again. A few of the other cells nearby were occupied. "I need to know where you are. I'll find a way to..."

His voice trailed away as he realised the stupidity of his words. What difference would it make if he knew where Yui was being held captive, when he was a prisoner with no hope of escape?

She had gone. The realisation that he had just spoken with his daughter, only for her to leave again, filled Phyqor with a terrible, wretched grief. He sat with his head bowed and rocked back and forth, weeping.

Eventually he raised his head, for he had heard a key turning in the lock of his cell door.

The man who stood before him wore the uniform of a senior jailer, but Phyqor did not recognise him. As he stared at the jailer, he wondered why he simply stood in the doorway, saying and doing nothing.

"You will come with me," the newcomer said eventually, and Phyqor could see no expression at all on the man's face, nor any trace of intelligence behind his eyes.

XII – In Motion

I

Aside from the meeting to which he had now agreed, Ruhal Dalmorn had another task that loomed large, one that filled him with almost as much trepidation as his forthcoming rendezvous with the Watchers. He would need to attend to it before the meeting, he decided, for it was equally important.

Eighteen years ago, Ruhal had been involved in a task about which he remembered almost nothing. A group of men, himself included, had been charged with watching over an infant and taking her from the depths of the unnamed, forested hills beyond the distant north-west of Harn, to Mordenglen, where he had only just become apprentice to Falvor, the Guardian of Mordenglen.

His memories of the journey there and back had about them a loose, disjointed quality, as if they were simply vague dreams that chased each other swiftly through the few hours before an awakening. Whatever lay between those journeys, during which time they had presumably been handed the infant for safe carrying to Mordenglen, Ruhal had no conscious memory of whatsoever.

Ruhal was a man of instinct and intuition, unused to working through puzzles as knotted as this, but he had continued to dwell on the matter from time to time over the years. As commanded by Falvor, he had never visited the infant after handing her over to her new guardians, and neither had any of the other men as far as he knew. They too had been forbidden from doing so.

But several months after that journey, Falvor had told him that one day he would need to visit her and take her away from her guardians who had raised her as their own. *Not for many years*, he had said, *but one day*.

Ruhal had pressed him for more information- *Take her where, by all the Powers?* he had demanded in frustration several times- but years passed before his master told him anything else on the matter. When he did, the young ranger almost immediately wished he had never asked.

In all likelihood, you will need to be a Protector of far more than Mordenglen, Falvor had grimly warned him, after laying before him the truth of the journey as they sat fishing on the riverbank one morning. It had been summer and unusually warm even for the season, but Ruhal had felt a chill nestle within him for days afterwards.

Why could I not have been told all this before? he had asked.

It would have distracted you from your training, had been the reply, *and it was a condition of those whom you met, that you and your companions should remember nothing of the destination and little enough of the journey. And Ruhal, you have seen far more of the hidden world now- your mother has shown you that as much as I have. Perhaps now you can bring yourself to believe the truth of this weight upon your shoulders.*

But what will I do, after I take her from her guardians? he had asked then, repeating his question from years before.

You will know when you need to know, Falvor had told him, which to Ruhal felt like no answer at all.

He had asked his mother what she knew of this on countless occasions, but she had said nothing on the matter. She had been close to Falvor, but perhaps this mystery was something he had held back from her, or he had held her to secrecy. Ruhal supposed that he had his reasons, unfathomable though they were.

In the ensuing years, he had dwelt on the mystery as much as he had time to, but even to the time of his passing Falvor had refused to say anything more on the subject.

Almost without thinking about it, Ruhal rummaged in the small leather bag he always carried about his waist. It contained some coins, a couple of gemstones whose value he remained unsure of- he had forgotten to ask Sarros the other night- and a small, perfectly ovoid pebble engraved with a complex sigil that, years ago, he had been told by Falvor to look out for. When that strange stone had arrived, left outside his hut deep in Mordenglen by an unknown visitor whose tracks even he could find no trace of, Ruhal had puzzled over it at first before finally its significance had dawned upon him.

How long did that take me? he thought. *Two days?* He smiled ruefully. As his mother often liked to remind him, he tended to be far quicker in action than in considered thought.

As the pebble's deliverer had been impossible to track- something that impressed Ruhal greatly- he conjectured that perhaps a bird or some other flying creature had deposited it, although deep within himself he felt that his visitor had hidden their trail by sorcerous means. Despite this, and despite having some knowledge of such matters handed down by his mother, he could not even begin to guess what that might be.

He traced his fingers over the elaborate, curved sigil on the smooth stone, then abruptly took his hand away, discomforted once again by the thought of what he would have to do, what he had *sworn* to do- take this young woman from her guardians without so much as an explanation, and then await whatever message or command arrived next from the mysterious, seemingly invisible and unknowable powers with whom this girl was entangled.

Still, he considered, *at least she is a child no more. That would have been harsher still. But what do I do, when I have her with me? I don't even know what to do with her, where to go, whom to seek out. There is no next step.*

The matter troubled him greatly. *The things I will have to tell her,* he thought bleakly as he recalled the same things that Falvor had made him memorise and repeat all those years ago on that summer day by the river. *Will she believe such words, when I can't be sure I believe them myself even now?*

Once again he had become a cog in a machine he could not understand. Forbidden talks with the ancient enemies of his people were one matter, and enough to warrant him being hunted and hanged, but he had also to contend with this reawakening of a chapter he had thought dormant.

That it should happen now of all times, he cursed, and wondered suddenly if the two matters were truly unrelated after all.

With an effort he put these matters to one side, but finding himself restless, he paced the length and breadth of the forest hut where he awaited his friends, thinking instead about the matter of the Watchers. *I might have set something terrible in motion,* he thought. *But are they not also risking much? Are they not also about to act against the law that they've spent centuries upholding?*

Ruhal did not want to think about what might happen to him, and to Sarros, Jahar and Lura, if his intentions were discovered by the powers in all the towns of the Free Territories, but more importantly by the sorcerer Inerdyr, whose ire he had already drawn by speaking on the matter of unity in Mornkastle.

Well, Inerdyr never did like me, Ruhal thought, *but if he discovers this plan before we can raise support for our cause, he'll more than likely raise an army of his own against me.*

Ruhal sighed. Inerdyr was the worst man to make an enemy of: unpredictable, and capable of holding a grudge for all eternity.

Someone approached. Ruhal ceased his pacing and listened. No, three people. A short while later he heard familiar voices, opened the door to the hut and watched with a smile as his friends approached.

They made an odd group, Ruhal thought. Jahar, the quiet and morose sorcerer and student of all things strange; Sarros, the laughing thief, spy and trickster; and Lura, a fiercely proud woman and the best swordsmistress he had ever known. *How have we all remained friends for this long?* he asked himself, for perhaps the hundredth time.

"You are late," he observed.

"*You* are just impatient," Lura said with a smile.

Ruhal embraced them each in turn and ushered them into the hut, thinking: *So, Sarros has had the good sense not to mention the reason for this meeting, judging by Lura's good mood. Of course, that will not last.*

He said nothing, but took Kelandra's scroll from his pocket and handed it to Jahar and Lura, then stood by as they read it in silence.

Lura was the first one to speak. "What is this, Ruhal? Have the overlords of the Black Citadel lost their minds entirely?" She gave the message a cursory glance once again. "Is this some trickery? I'd put nothing past those creatures..."

"I believe it's genuine." As they all stared at him, Ruhal continued, "Even in Luudhoq, consensus cannot be absolute. In all places, there are those who question the judgement of their lords and masters, even if they do so in silence. This Watcher has already risked much by sending this message, and I've risked as much myself by sending one in return."

"You *replied*?" Lura gaped at him as if he had grown a second head. "Powers, Ruhal! What did you write?"

"I arranged to meet with this Watcher and her comrades. I also said that the three of you would accompany me."

Utter silence followed. Lura looked helplessly at Jahar, who as usual said nothing, and then at Sarros. "Did *you* know about this?!"

"I..." Sarros smiled weakly. "Ruhal did discuss it with me..."

Lura turned her attention to Ruhal, fury in her eyes. "You expect me to come with you? You expect me to become a comrade-in-arms with *Watchers*?!"

Ruhal gazed steadily back at her. "I don't expect you to, Lura. But I do want you with me. I want all three of you at my side. You listened to my speech. You know about the growing threat in the east. You know my beliefs concerning a union of all the territories. You *agreed* with them..."

"Oh, I want a unified land," Lura hissed. "I want us to build an army and march on the Black Citadel. I want us to raze that place to the ground and destroy every last Watcher we can find. I want nothing more than an end to the Seven. I want a free Harn. They're our *enemies*, Ruhal, and they will *always* be our enemies. They would enslave the Free Territories if they could."

"Raising an army to march on Luudhoq would simply hasten our annihilation," Ruhal said quietly. "It would *weaken* Harn. This Watcher speaks the truth, Lura, whether you like that truth or not. Recall what I said to you all only a tennight ago: all the signs are that the *marandaal* have found Aona. I have seen and heard *choragh-kin* abroad in the more distant regions. There are even tales of one or two mingling with smaller communities, taking convenient shapes and gaining trust. You know the stories as well as I do..."

"Stories are all they are," Lura said, but she sounded tired, defeated. Ruhal moved to stand next to her and put a hand on her shoulder, as she looked down at the floor as tears brimmed in her eyes. "No vengeance can ever bring him back," he said softly. "You know that."

Lura said nothing.

"Will you join with me?" Ruhal asked. "Of course I cannot trust them, and I'll ask no one else to. But I'll need you with me."

The swordswoman still said nothing, but she wandered over to the other side of the cabin to stare out of the window.

"Jahar- are you with us?" Ruhal turned to the sorcerer, who frowned pensively before he spoke. "Inerdyr will hear of this soon enough, Ruhal, if you intend to spread the word of unity and attempt to rally people to your cause. He will not like what he hears."

"Inerdyr has never liked what he hears from me," Ruhal rejoined.

"It will be difficult to guess his reaction," Jahar continued. "If he raises a force against us, we risk division of the Free Territories. We risk needless bloodshed." He sighed. "But I see no alternative. I agree about the signs. Hope lies in unity, and no unity can be achieved without risk."

Ruhal nodded, relieved and grateful in equal measure. "Thank you, friend." He glanced at Sarros, who was leaning against the back wall of the cabin, the brim of his hat all but covering his face. "You've not changed your mind, have you?"

Sarros adjusted his hat, looked up and shrugged wearily. "It's a little late for me, I think. If Jahar and Lura are with you, then so am I."

"Good. We'll meet here again in seven days' time, at sunrise, and then ride out to Anrith. I intend for us to be there just as the moons appear to touch. The Watchers study the movements in the sky; they will know when to be there."

Lura turned away from the view of the forest outside. "I hope by all the Powers that this doesn't end badly, Ruhal."

Ruhal smiled. "It won't, if we are all determined."

But inside, he felt a chill settle in his stomach, and there it remained.

A day later, Sarros arrived at the one and only guest-house in the village of Southbirch, five leagues to the west of Mordenglen. He tethered his horse to a post at the edge of the village square- he did not intend to stay here any longer than necessary- and waited awhile at the door of the guest house, looking in every available direction, silent and laconically observant. If anyone had been following him, he would have known long ago- his skills in that area were legendary, and he knew it. But he nevertheless stayed awhile by the door and listened to the sighing of the breeze and the house sign as it creaked above him, and watched the clouds roll by above.

Finally he made his way through into the guest house, and through to a back room where he sat at a wooden gaming table with a heavy sigh and an even heavier heart. *I do this for the best of reasons,* he thought, but he still could not entirely convince himself.

Ayvin Tarn, Inerdyr's chief guardsman and adviser, stared across at him, tapping a fingernail on the worn surface of the table. "I thought perhaps you might have thought twice," Ayvin commented. "That would not have been a wise choice of action."

"I had much to think about."

"But now your thinking is done and your mind is settled."

Sarros smiled unhappily at that. His mind was anything but settled. "It is," he agreed.

"Then tell me, so we may put a stop to this foolishness: are they intent on meeting the renegade Watchers?"

Sarros nodded. "At Anrith, six days from now, when the moons appear to touch."

Ayvin's thin lips pursed in what might have been a smile. "Anrith. A good choice." He leaned back and nodded, apparently satisfied. "Ruhal Dalmorn has been a thorn in the side of the Free Territories for too long. My lord Inerdyr tries to guide us all, in his wisdom, but Ruhal consistently undermines such efforts, firstly to the point of making inflammatory speeches, and now by consorting with our enemies. He's a common mercenary who believes he need bow to no law save his own..."

"He is not a mercenary," Sarros said uncomfortably, but he knew what was coming next.

"The disaster at Wistport, five years ago," Ayvin said quietly. "Clearly I need to remind you of the detail. Rather than await instruction from the correct authorities, Ruhal took it upon himself to do battle with the Rannikian pirates, accompanied by his motley band of renegades and, even worse, *orkar* beasts who saw fit to plunder the town, rape and kill the women and children..."

"They are not beasts," Sarros said quietly, "and that is not what happened."

"A hundred or more witnesses came forward in the aftermath. How many more might persuade you?" Ayvin surveyed him coldly. "Ruhal was stripped of all rank save the guardianship of his beloved forest. He was lucky. He could and should have been hanged for what happened in Wistport."

Sarros shook his head tiredly. "You were not there to see the madness of Wistport for yourself, Ayvin, but I've no stomach for argument on the matter. I need to know what will happen to them all."

"Oh, you'll meet as planned. Even in Anrith they might be expecting some sort of ambush, and in any case we want you all to go about your treacherous ways for a little while. No, it will happen a little later, I expect." Ayvin smiled suddenly. "Fear not, Sarros. Your comrades will be spared their lives. Inerdyr has given his word. And *you* will remain a free man."

Sarros leaned forward. "I ask that no harm comes to Ruhal, Lura or Jahar. Ruhal bears no ill will to the Free Territories. He's simply misguided, in dealing with Watchers."

"An example must be made," Ayvin told him, "but as I said, their lives will be spared. In truth, that's more than they deserve."

A short while later, Sarros rode east, under a cloud and full of misgivings. He had no love for Inerdyr and his cohorts, but he knew for a certainty that Ruhal's plan could never work. Perhaps the offer the Watchers had made was genuine, perhaps not, but it didn't matter. The plan was doomed to failure, and better that it failed soon, before it had the chance to sow the seeds of rebellion and divide the Free Territories.

In some parts of the distant far north, Ruhal was a more popular man than Inerdyr. But, Sarros reasoned as the cold wind drew tears from his eyes, Ruhal was simply a nature-guardian. No longer could he truly call himself a warrior. And how, even with whatever unfathomable talents Watchers might possess, could he hope to stand against a man of Inerdyr's immense power and formidable intellect?

Of course, it would have been impossible to reason with Ruhal on the matter; he had made up his mind weeks ago, at the time of the first murmurings of *marandaal* and the Powers knew what else stepping from the void, in Aphenhast. *All your ideas can do,* Sarros had wanted to say to him, *is make you more enemies than any one man or even an army can handle. Would you truly stand against not only the* marandaal, *but also the Black Citadel and the Seven, and even Inerdyr? What can you hope to gain?*

So it was better that this madness be stopped in its infancy and his comrades be spared their lives, than it be allowed to become a rebellion, the rebels to be cut down and reviled as traitors through all history.

XIII – The Heavens Burst

I

Under Ildar's bright light and with a multitude of banners flowing in the night breeze, the Rising marched steadily eastwards. Long forewarned of this rampage, the human settlements in their way had been abandoned weeks ago. Little remained for pillaging and so the bloodthirsty mass pressed on towards the city of Nisstar with nothing to distract them. They would reach it by dawn, for they made swift progress across open grassland.

They numbered perhaps fifty thousand; *luyan, duluyan, crommari* and a smaller number of humans and once-humans. Even their presence in this strange army was not questioned; however they were given a wide berth.

Some had arrived, silent and stumbling, just before the great march out of Rockmire had commenced. But many others, some of whom defied adequate description, had appeared later from out of the south, a seething chaos from which the foot soldiers of the Rising shrank back. A few of these newcomers to the cause bore a certain resemblance to Ilumor.

These creatures obeyed Ilumor alone. Most of them could not speak. They had need of neither water nor food. Their bodies moved, but as some amongst the Rising whispered, their insides were still and cold as Ildar itself.

Ilumor, who dimly remembered being a mere human man once, rode near the head of the vast army. His thoughts, oddly disturbed fragments for the most part, formed two distinct threads. The lesser of these concerned Serina. He was confident that the fresh *diafagh* would find her and tear her apart, but he would have preferred to see some part of

320

her brought back- a bone for him to look at, a dead-eyed head for him to toss aside, anything tangible.

I should have commanded that too, he thought, but it was pointless to give more than one instruction at a time to *diafagh.* The smear of her blood across their dead lips was a command to find and ruin, but anything more than that would have been asking too much. *Theirs is a simple spark,* he reminded himself, *dim in radiance and dimmer still in intellect. Not all tools need to be sharp.*

The other strand of thought, which occupied him more and more as they drew nearer to Nisstar, concerned the Great Enemy, the *marandaal* to those who remembered the name at all. They would emerge in Nisstar as the Earth Lords had foretold, and they would burst forth like white light.

The true test, for which we were all made, he thought. *This is the greatest challenge any of us can face.*

The smile that adorned his lips now, wide and blissful, had the appearance of a dark crack. His eyes, like hard black jewels, gleamed in Ildar's light. For a moment he recalled an occasion that mirrored this one, another long march over open ground under the same moon, over two thousand years ago. It seemed more recent than that, but Ilumor had spent much of the time since then dead to the world, in curious limbo, wandering the places that witches and their like sought to explore.

His name roughly translated from the Old Tongue as *that which seeps from the depths.* And he had seeped from the depths, coaxed forth from the bitter darkness of the earth and the sterile eternity of the Silver Road, by Serina of all people.

I knelt by her that night, he recalled, *and I kissed her even as she recoiled at what she had done. The sense of sudden freedom addled my very being. How else could I have felt something almost akin to love?*

Ilumor shook his head. She should have known that he answered only to his own lords, to the world itself, and not her shallow attempts to capture and contain powers for her own brief use. *Like all your kind, you think yourself a shaper,* he had told her. *But you are simply a shape.* By now Serina had surely been snapped apart and was missing even the marrow from her bones, so that was another chapter to close away.

Ilumor had lived for a very long time, one way or another, but he was not in the habit of reminiscing.

The presence of the once-humans, once-*luyan* and others that the Rising creatures feared and shunned, intrigued Ilumor in an absent-minded way. Perhaps they really had once been human- even he had been once, though he could remember almost nothing of that time- and perhaps some of them were pure shapings, but either way their flesh, their very essence, was the dominion of the Earth Lords now, the blood that coursed through their veins in tune with the ancient masters of the world.

If blood courses through their veins at all.

Ilumor's smile widened into a savage grin as the touch of his masters moved like a dark, roiling wave within him, as if to remind him of their eternal, immortal presence. It had always been this way. Whenever he pondered their power, it moved within him, the thought and the answering reminder the one and the same.

For a moment his free hand strayed to the hilt of the black-bladed sword that one of these followers had gifted him with. *Not a sword,* the once-woman had said blankly, even though her lips remained still. *But it will serve as one when you need it to.*

When he held it for the first time, testing the exquisite balance, the beautiful, *total* blackness of it, he had known exactly what it was- a versatile and fluid tool, one of the most powerful of all *choragh* tools. Hefting that great blade, he also knew its purpose in an instant- nothing less than the destruction of the *marandaal*, the burning away of their entrances to this world. Truly this was a precious gift.

Where did you get this? he had asked the once-woman.

I do not remember, she had answered, *but one of the Highest returned it to me, after I had given it myself, that I might bestow it upon you.*

I am blessed, she had added, and a black liquid seeped from her eyes.

Ilumor had been intrigued by the possible stories behind the device, but not enough to ask. The history of the object was of no importance. Its power and its imminent use undoubtedly were.

The once-woman, dead-eyed and ruined as she was, nevertheless had become a source of amusement to Ilumor throughout their long ride east. Each night he had lain with her, waiting for Archaon's ponderous rise- a habit he had had for as long as he could remember- before he slid his entire arm into her from between her still and pale legs, exploring her internal putrefaction as the light of the red moon bathed them, before replacing his gore-stained limb with his engorged member. *She could have been beautiful years ago,* he had surmised one evening as he looked down upon her unresponsive face. He caressed the marble-hued skin as he spilled his ancient, useless seed deep inside her. *Might she once have had a story to tell?*

But if she had then it was gone forever like those of the other once-humans. *Ah, if only you were more than a vessel,* Ilumor had thought as he stared into the pools of her eyes. *If only you could still sense, and feel, and fear.*

As Serina could.

Disquieted by that thought, for he had no idea what it truly meant or where it could lead, he had detached himself and wandered away from the encampment. Suddenly his desires had felt almost like a blasphemy, a contradiction.

Ilumor stared across at the once-woman now, his gaze drawn to her withered right arm, and the side of her face where she had been touched by an Earth Lord. She stared only ahead, an empty husk fixed only upon their destination, their goal.

Yes, Ilumor decided, not without a tinge of sadness. *I should have kept Serina with me. I should have bound her tightly to me. She would have been my companion, and in time she would have turned. She would have seen and felt for herself the pulse of the world. Yet she chose to leave. She chose her destiny.*

It would all soon be forgotten, he knew. Years passed by faster with time, so it seemed, and therefore one day even Serina would be a name he struggled to remember.

II

To the south of Nisstar's centre lay a large area of waste ground, overrun with a vast tangle of weeds and undergrowth. Here stood the remains of buildings that had fallen into disrepair long ago and that no city administration had done anything with. This stark and unpleasant landscape occasionally made a useful location for rape and murder, situated ideally for such opportunities. It had also long been the home of outcasts and the dregs of society, neither the presence nor absence of whom was noted.

One such outcast, whose name had once been Emeth, spent much of his sorry existence here, untroubled by the better-to-do of the city. He had once been a silversmith of some repute, but poor choices and ill luck had combined and within months he had found himself here, largely forgotten.

He stumbled around near an abandoned warehouse that had become home to him, drunk on stolen liquor. He vaguely wondered to himself why it felt so warm today, when it had been bitterly cold for so long. "Winter's done with.

Finished!" he mumbled to himself, but even he knew that many more weeks remained to be endured.

Various pieces of metal and wooden junk died a slow, rusty death in the long grass. One of them snagged the string he had used to tie one of his boots and he went sprawling. He cursed and laughed at the same time, got to his feet with as much dignity as he could muster- as if someone might be watching- and walked on.

As ever, his home- an abandoned warehouse- stood silent, derelict, ruinous and faintly brooding. The building rose higher than the other few nearby, built up of five floors laid on top of one another- a hideous construct, yet it kept him dry when the rains came, and a little warmer than he would otherwise be when the winds howled around this wasteland.

Most of the windows had been either shattered or boarded up, and the front entrance through which Emeth staggered was a dark doorless space. The melancholic silence of the forbidding and grey hallway into which he walked somehow felt peaceful. Smells of mould and of faecal matter- much of it his own- assailed him, but he barely noticed. The walls, coated in a bewildering array of signatures, squiggles, threats and pictures made with paint or stains long ago, leered at him. Not even the steps of the stairway that led up from the hall had escaped the attention of these forgotten colorists. In the dim light, the chaotic map of nonsense- chronicles of depravity and boredom for the most part- looked vaguely sinister, like a mass of hideous worms, jagged and writhing on the cold, cracking walls.

But it's my home, he reminded himself. *It's safer here. The people I sometimes see out in the wasteland seldom come in.*

Emeth took a deep breath and began to make his way up the stairs. His weak heart already protested at the threat of exercise. *Should have made my room just here,* he thought as ever. *But then someone might come and slit my throat.*

Emeth had a strong if irrational fear that his bad luck had been caused by malicious forces which still roamed the city in order to finish him off. He had convinced himself that by living in one of the higher floors of this building, he would see and hear the approach of these forces and thus be better able to defend himself against them.

The painted decorations became more lurid and fantastic, in a low and sickening way, as he walked up flight after flight of steps. He paused in the hallways on each floor to spit and draw breath. Late afternoon light seeped in through the grimy windows. *Dark soon,* he reminded himself, and wondered how many cries of pain and terror he might hear from out in the wasteland tonight, how many times he would be dragged from his sleep, his heart leaping in panic as he listened to the dreadful sounds of unspeakable acts being committed.

The forgotten silversmith pushed open the door into the chamber he had made into his home and sank down amongst his few belongings and the foul-smelling blanket that served as his bed. Each morning and evening he counted his remaining belongings, a bundle of worthless curios held in an old cloth sack. Perhaps it was a way for him to remind himself of his continued existence, miserable blur though it was. He insisted on maintaining the routine without fail, in the belief that it bound him a little tighter to sanity.

Yet despite that imposed order, day after day he still felt that grip loosen a little further, as the violent, blood-filled dreams of savage light and burning pain that tore through him every night began to creep into his waking moments.

Emeth was therefore terrified but not entirely surprised when the building began to shake and rumble. He moaned to himself and rushed back down the flight of stairs he had ascended, tumbling down some of them more than once. Finally he reached the ground floor and lurched on into the surrounding undergrowth, then stopped suddenly as he realised that it was not simply the building that shook.

It was the entire area.

Shrubs and undergrowth moved madly. Cracks appeared in the ground. Parts of the walls began to fall from the warehouse and the other buildings nearby. As he stared in each direction, Emeth recalled some persistent, ominous words from a dream he might have had last night or the night before: *The light shall pour forth. Everything disappears into the light.*

He was thrown to the ground by a particularly violent tremor. When he eventually managed to stagger to his feet, a long and narrow crack had opened in the earth, threading through the waste ground and towards the centre of the city where tall fortresses loomed. Bright white light shone from it, and Emeth nodded as if the fulfilment of the promise in his dreams was entirely expected.

Other cracks appeared. A low humming sound filled the air; Emeth felt the pressure increase around him until he thought his eardrums would rupture. He retreated to the doorway of the place he called home, oblivious to the tumbling stonework, and curled himself up into a ball as from all around him came the horrific sounds of that maddening hum, and of the earth itself snapping open.

The sounds and vibrations went on for hours. Finally, Emeth, still crying softly to himself and uttering a lullaby from his childhood as if it might also be a protective spell, raised his head and saw that he was no longer alone.

A human-shaped figure stood in the doorway, almost entirely a black silhouette against the blinding light that had gathered in intensity outside. Emeth dimly noticed that his ragged clothing had started to melt onto his skin, which had blistered and peeled back to reveal glistening flesh and then white bone. The agony and the light became one and the same, an inescapable intensity that hastened his descent into madness in a moment.

Emeth's remains dragged their way through the doorway one final time, leaving a faint trail of pungent gore. The *marandaal,* still no more than a silhouette or a human-shaped burn in the air, observed as Emeth crawled, convinced now that he ascended a vast mountain to the kingdom of the afterlife as he scrabbled around in the tangled undergrowth. It followed him and watched as scraps of flesh lost their grip upon the man's bones. It savoured each spasmodic movement, the action of many dying nerves.

Finally the *marandaal* crushed his head underfoot and into the scorched, cracked earth. White skull dust mingled with baked-dry earth. Emeth's body twitched in the blood-spattered undergrowth a while longer, and then lay still forever.

The *marandaal* turned, and with a dozen others like it, headed directly towards the heart of the city, moving in perfect silence.

III

It took a mere moment, that bright winter morning, for Nisstar to descend into utter chaos.

As the *marandaal* moved swiftly towards the centre of the city, Ilumor gave the order for the Rising to take the western wall and pour through the remains.

The city militia that guarded the wall might have resisted the attempts to breach the defences had it not been for the swiftly mounting mayhem that spread from the middle of the city. The Rising had only makeshift ladders with which to breach the walls, and at first, Nisstar's heavily-armed guardsmen cut down their attempts with ease. But even as the bodies of *luyan, crommari* and many others began to litter the ground, news of utter destruction came from further east into Nisstar. In fact the militia

328

guarding the west of the city need not have heeded such news. All they had to do was turn their heads eastwards, where a brilliant, savage light cut through the morning. An intense humming filled the air. It burned eyes and throats and caused mouths to bleed. Arteries burst, fingernails came free, skin began to wither and peel.

All these were signs of the *marandaal* coming, not that the terrified populace of Nisstar could have known. The *marandaal* slaughtered all in their path, until they reached the western edge of the city, where, as they clashed with *choragh*-tainted night, chaos became cataclysm.

Ilumor lifted the sword towards the sky and closed his eyes. When he opened them again, great slivers of darkness poured from the blade and shimmered in the air, then rose higher and higher to circle over the ruins of Nisstar's west-facing walls. As the first of the *marandaal* became visible, they darted down at incredible speed and writhed around the glowing beings. At the same time, the first ranks of the Rising moved forward. Ilumor watched their fear, their uncertainty, entirely unconcerned by it. They were fodder, nothing more. If they died for the cause, then so much the better for the cause. The sinking of their blood into the earth would only strengthen the *kin* further; it was the *kin* who would carry the fight to the *marandaal*.

The *kin* could feel no fear. They felt only a dim, voracious hunger, and they knew only that the *marandaal* were the Great Enemy. The force that had fashioned them now compelled the *kin*, urging them towards their foes. They rushed, or walked, or stumbled, but however they moved it was in one direction only, and that was towards the light.

As he stared at the *marandaal,* Ilumor began to understand why so many had dreamed of them, had gone entirely mad dreaming of their arrival in this world, had even thought of them as Gods. They made a mesmerising sight. From one angle, in one moment, they might have been fashioned entirely from light, but an instant later they took on a solid appearance, which at the same time looked entirely fluid. *Mercury,* Ilumor thought distantly. *They could be made from mercury, or water, held together by some unseen force. They change shape at will. They are whatever they wish to be.*

He marvelled at whatever sorcery it was that had created these beings. For one mad moment he wondered what it might be like to converse with one, to understand it inside and out.

But that could never be possible; they had one purpose only, and that was the utter destruction of all other life.

For hours the struggle continued, a continuous swirl of light and darkness centred around the fallen walls from which the *marandaal* continually tried to press on and out of the city. The *luyan, crommari* and humans that had made the bulk of the Rising either lay dead upon the charred and cracked ground, or they had fled. Ilumor did not care either way. But eventually, even the *kin* were slowly pushed back from the edge of the city, despite their savage efforts.

As the day grew darker, Ilumor found himself faced with a decision to make. No *choragh* would come to their aid in this hour. He did not expect them to, and it made no sense for them to. They watched, of course, from some great distance, scrying or farseeing in the way that only they could. They would plan and move according to whatever happened here.

Abruptly, Ilumor issued a silent call to all the *kin,* and ordered them to fall back, as swiftly as possible. They could move quickly when needed, quicker than the lumbering masses that had formed the bulk of the Rising, and they swiftly moved away from what little remained of the city walls, to melt back into the dusk as commanded.

The *marandaal* appeared almost like simple points of light as he looked back from a thousand paces further away. Ilumor thought for a moment that they looked like especially bright stars glowing malevolently in the gloom. *Odd that they should seem like stars,* he remarked to himself, *given that they are the destroyers of those worlds that the stars carry with them on their journeys through the Existence.*

They were not pursued into the open land. Perhaps, as Ilumor suspected, they knew that should they do that, the *choragh* themselves might be stirred into a response, or it might simply be that they preferred to destroy Nisstar utterly, leaving nothing alive within its tumbled walls.

In the gloom, one of the *kin* appeared at his side, a creature shaped like a man but which might, looking at its face, have once been some kind of feral dog or wolf.

We flee? it asked.

"Our lords do not ask us to sacrifice ourselves unnecessarily," Ilumor told the creature. Smiling, he added "What do you think the Rising was for?"

The *kin*-beast stared dumbly at him. Ilumor sent it away and rode a little distance further west before dismounting from his horse. He stepped into the close darkness of a copse set at the edge of a long, sloping meadow, and discarded his shirt.

Archaon appeared from the distant east, a bloody fingernail climbing ponderously over the broken horizon. Ilumor congratulated himself on his timing and walked further into the press of thorn and tangle. Pain too savage to be entirely natural flared up as the unyielding vegetation tore at his skin, until he stopped, arms outstretched, a thick bramble wrapped twice about his neck and a thin branch of blackthorn scraping slowly across his midriff.

There are more than we suspected, my Lords, he said mentally, and watched through the gaps in the thorns and bushes as something that might have been a shadow, but was not, drifted across the lush grass of the meadow.

Three Gates formed, came the sighing answer. Ilumor felt the undergrowth tremble slightly at those words, as if it might be uprooted or cut down.

Three? In one place? Ilumor did not know what to make of that. He had never heard of such control being possible. If they could do that, then...

They shall be contained for now. Take the kin *and whatever else of use you may find. We shall call for you.*

"Where shall we go?" Ilumor jumped as soon as he had said that. He had not meant to speak aloud. The thorns and brambles attached to his flesh dug a little further in, perhaps a reflection of the *choragh's* sudden ire.

Mirkwall. It is ours once again. Many of those who fought with you today emerged from that place.

Abruptly the hold upon him ceased. As he staggered out into the meadow, it seemed that even the blades of grass moved slightly away from him. Ilumor idly wiped blood from his wounds over his arms and chest, observed the red moon struggle into the sky, and took a deep breath of the cold air.

Mirkwall, he mused, raising his fingers to his mouth to taste the sourness of his blood. *Ours entirely now. How the First must be turning in their graves at the thought of that!*

The *marandaal* had taken Nisstar, but that place was of no consequence, a huddle of stones and dumb humanity ruled over by the priesthood and, so they believed, their One-God.

Ilumor's smile widened. The first skirmish was done with, but the war had still to be fought. It would be a war to cast the *marandaal* out of this world for all time, to send them hurtling into the emptiness that lay between the stars.

And Aona itself would then be made anew in the image of his masters.

XIV – A Path Inside the Pain

I

No sooner had Nia arrived through the great northern archway into Luudhoq than Kelandra sent for her. She eagerly made her way straight to the Watcher's chambers, keen to unburden herself of the scroll, although she wondered briefly what Ruhal's response had been and whether she would be rewarded at all if Kelandra was displeased with it.

Well, either way I'd rather know sooner than later, she reasoned, as one of Kelandra's servants admitted her into the Watcher's study.

Kelandra looked restless, as Nia had expected. Carefully she undid the stitching that held the scroll securely in place within her robe and handed the scroll to her. Kelandra held it for a moment and said nothing. For a moment, she closed her eyes and bowed her head slightly. Then she nodded, and with a deft gesture slit open the seal and unravelled the scroll.

Nia waited nervously as her mistress read the document and finally rolled it up again, melting and sealing the wax with no more than a touch of her hand. "You have done well, Nia," she remarked. "I shall arrange for you to be well rewarded."

Nia made a little bow, although it was a formality that Kelandra sometimes frowned upon. "Is there anything you need me to do in the meantime?" she asked politely and managed to stifle a groan of disgust for prompting her mistress in such a way.

Kelandra thought for a moment, or at least she gave the appearance of doing so. "Not for now. I expect you need some rest. I would take the opportunity, were I you. I will send for you again three days from now."

Nia left the Watcher's chambers wondering what to make of that conversation, and eventually decided to make nothing at all of it. As Kelandra had pointed out, now would be a good time to take the opportunity to rest, and so she did, returning to her modest little dwelling deep in the crowded northern residential quarter of the city.

Kelandra, meanwhile, located her co-conspirators and arranged to meet that same evening at the riverside, in the same place where they had met previously.

After they had all arrived, she checked that the cloaking was still in place- if anything, it was less penetrable than ever- and wasted little time in getting to the point. "It has been agreed," she said, and unravelled the scroll, then showed it to her companions. The other Watchers read it in turn, as Kelandra stood and observed them in silence. She herself had read the message only once but had committed the words to memory- an easy task for her.

I agree that the time of enmity and uneasy truce must end. I also agree that if there is truth to the rumours I have heard from Aphenhast in the east, then Harn must stand as one united territory in the war to come.

The people of the Free Territories are themselves divided. There are some who think as I do. Others think of the people of the Black Citadel as foes and perhaps always will. But there are very few who know the truth of matters in Aphenhast. Soon enough they will.

As you know, a day will soon come when Ildar and Archaon will appear to touch in the sky, just after Archaon rises. I suggest we meet on this day and at that time.

A ruined village by the name of Anrith is situated ten leagues directly east of Mornkastle. A road leads there but this road is never used. According to popular superstition, the place is cursed. In fact it has long been avoided by everyone, and left to fall into ruin for nigh on a hundred years.

I trust that you hold superstition in the same cool regard as I do, and I therefore propose that Anrith shall be the place where we meet.

R.D

She kept her entire attention on the other Watchers and observed their reactions in silence as they read the message. At the same time she listened to the sound of the river, of the water as it lapped against the bridge, the resonance of this place. Partly this was because she enjoyed that aural pattern, the complexity of it, but she did so also to ensure once again that the cloaking- or to be more precise, the *blankness-* located here remained intact.

The same as ever, Kelandra thought, satisfied, but she continued to listen anyway, and suddenly she felt something else amidst the pattern of the natural cloaking. It was a quiet, barely detectable dissonance, something that surely ought not to matter, for the cloaking remained in place and as strong as ever, but something about it was *wrong,* and Kelandra focussed her attention upon it, without her expression changing in any way.

She remained dimly aware of the quiet conversation now taking place between Alturus and Ildoron, of Kalmyrran muttering to herself that this was sheer folly, and that this forest warlock or whatever he was could not be trusted at all. She absorbed and could still have recited back all that they said. But her thoughts were channelled towards the pattern of the cloaking and how it was being changed in some subtle way by this unknown other force. It was as if some thread was being gently tugged and pulled by it, the tiniest ripples expanding outwards like the effect of a tiny spider near the centre of a vast web.

Someone or something is trying to find its way in, Kelandra thought suddenly. *But how? How could it know this exact spot? The water-mirrors cannot locate anything here; they have always remained clouded.*

There was only one possibility, and it chilled her to her core.

Abruptly she snapped her link with the cloaking force and returned her attention fully to what lay physically around her.

One of us has brought something here that they should not have, she thought, as she glanced at each Watcher in turn. Outwardly she remained as calm as ever, but her insides crackled with energy as she scanned each of her companions. *One of them, or more than one, will be different in some way to how they were before,* she told herself. *Something will have changed. They will have brought something with them, something to disturb the resonance of this area, or to allow some form of communication. They will be carrying something or may even have something inside themselves. A device of some considerable power.*

The traitors themselves have a traitor in their midst.

Kelandra took a deep breath as an anomaly reared up in her mind. One of them *was* different. She could tell this not because of anything they carried or hid, but rather because the cloaking force was slightly weaker around that Watcher. She almost smiled at the revelation.

Aylin should have considered how well I know this force, how intimately I feel it. I have been here and studied it for far longer than he knows.

"What do you think?" she asked brightly, and pointed to the opened scroll which Ildoron held at the moment. A moment later, before anyone could even respond, she leapt at Aylin and pinning him to the ground. *Give him no quarter,* she thought. *Kill him, and the proof will be somewhere with him, or inside him.*

She had to destroy him quickly. With every ounce of strength she could muster, Kelandra tightened her grip on his neck and sank her fingers into it. Dimly she was aware of the others shouting at her, of someone trying to pull her

336

away. Aylin's body shook as he fell back and Kelandra was dragged away from him. "He has something," she said breathlessly. "Something tuned to a scrying device. Search him!" In the same moment, she reached out into the cloaking lattice again, and knew for certain that she had identified him correctly. The cloaking was once again smooth and undisturbed.

Aylin's neck lay gashed and open. Amidst the ooze of blood staining the riverbank, metallic bone gleamed. The savage wound would have already killed a human; for a Watcher, it was survivable. "Search him," Kelandra continued coldly.

Alturus gave her an unfathomable look and ripped the clothing from Aylin's body, as Ildoron held him down. Kal-myrran and Kunas stood by. "You have lost the power of rational thought," Kal-myrran said to her. "If you think for a moment that we..."

"Be quiet," Kelandra retorted. She knelt down and allowed her gaze to slowly travel the length and breadth of Aylin's naked form. His body looked almost like translucent marble in the moonlight, smooth and hairless as were the bodies of all Watchers.

"He has no such device," Ildoron said, and turned to look at her. "You have attacked and tried to kill one of our own, Kelandra." As Ildoron spoke, Aylin's baleful eyes turned and fixed themselves upon her own.

Then, as she studied him again, she saw it- a faintly glistening object hidden in the complex darkness of his body.

"His right arm," she said. "Slit it open."

Ildoron stared at her as if Kal-myrran was right and she had lost the power of rational thought. "Do it," she said icily, "and there will be your proof."

Alturus knelt, took his knife and made a deep incision down from just below Aylin's shoulder to his wrist, and then opened up the deep, vast wound. Aylin said nothing, but a small smile upon his lips became wider as

Alturus peered at the bared flesh, then reached forth and plucked something from it. As he held it up, the other Watchers moved a little closer to observe. The object was a small, metallic ball which trembled slightly in Alturus' grip. A moment later it glowed yellow suddenly, and he dropped it to the ground, crushing it underfoot.

Aylin's mouth opened in a silent laugh, and then he whispered: "You're too late. They're already on their way. They know who you are."

Alturus stepped forth and crushed what remained of Aylin's neck. For a moment the gleam of light in Aylin's eyes flared up as if in some final defiance. Then his head dropped to one side, and his eyes became dark, seeing nothing, only reflecting.

Ildoron turned grimly to face Kelandra. "Our own kind are on their way to seize us. We have perhaps just moments..."

"We'll head to the north-east tower gate," Kelandra said abruptly. "That's the closest way out of the city. We'll get horses along the way." She stared at each of them in turn. "Well? Do you expect any mercy when they arrive here?"

A short while later, five Watchers arrived on horseback at the north-east tower gate. The guardsmen there had been told nothing of the events that had brought them and even if they had had instructions not to allow them through, they would have failed.

As they rushed through the gates and into open country, Kelandra reflected that if she had not detected Aylin's treachery when she did then a small army of Watchers- with High Watchers amongst them, no doubt- would have descended upon the six of them as they stood by the riverside, arguing over the message and its originator.

Ruhal, you and your allies had better be worth this, she thought grimly.

She called them to a halt near a river-crossing later that evening and watched pensively as Ildoron put in place a cloaking of an altogether different kind, one designed to confuse and mislead those who might follow them. Kelandra had no idea if it would work. To her knowledge, no Watchers had ever had to construct such a defence to avoid pursuit by others of their kind.

To be thorough, Ildoron would repeat the exercise three more times during the night. Kelandra, whose eyes remained open through the darkness, did not look back. The glow and heat of Luudhoq would still be detectable to them even from here, and she had no desire to look upon or feel anything related to the city.

She had abandoned and committed treason against her city, her own kind and the Seven, for the sake of Harn and all the light and reason in the world.

II

Nia woke up late the following morning and lay in bed for a while. She contemplated a job done well, a satisfied employer, and the possibility of ample reward.

Her thoughts turned, however, to the gloomier expectation that whatever ample reward she might have earned would be tempered by ever more challenging tasks. A step up that would more than likely be accompanied by a step further in.

I can succeed many times and maintain my life as it is, she thought, *or I can fail once and watch it change for the worse, forever.*

She wandered into the Square, the main trading area of the city around midday. The place felt subdued, even more so when soft rain began to fall from the gloomy sky. *Two more days,* Nia thought restlessly as she leaned against the wall of a storehouse and watched the muted activity. *Sometimes I think I should find myself some other*

*employment, to tide me over during the times when Kelandra
sends me away for days on end.*

Nia bought herself lunch from a bakery just a little
way into the Cobbles, which she tended to frequent at times
like these for no other reason than force of habit. Munching
her way through a meat pasty, she stood at a street corner
and watched people as they wandered back and forth about
their daily business. Afterwards, brushing crumbs from
herself, she decided to wander through the south Cobbles. A
good long stroll would help her sleep better that night. It was
not often that Nia had free time, and she reckoned it might
as well be used up doing *something* even if it was simply
walking the streets.

The afternoon wore on and eventually darkened. Nia
walked along streets that all seemed vaguely familiar,
although she could properly remember only one or two of
them. Here and there little shops stood, most of which had
been converted from the terraced cottages that lined many of
the narrow, winding roads. Many of these stores had already
shut for the day, and a few looked as if they might have
closed permanently some time ago.

The drizzle came down endlessly, but the air felt
milder today than it had been in the last few days and Nia
found that she almost enjoyed the light fall. *When I get back
home,* she mused, *I'll heat myself some buckets of water for a
bath. I deserve that much. I haven't washed myself properly
since my stay in Mornkastle.*

Dusk had fallen when she stopped at a fork in the
road and suddenly realised exactly where she was. It was not
a pleasant revelation.

She peered up the left hand road a little way, and
saw the building, disused for years now. Its glassless
windows stared out into the street, and its doorway gaped
like a hole.

"The orphanage," Nia whispered to herself, and a
tumult of emotion almost overwhelmed her: rage, fear,

misery, and the overpowering wish that she could kick down the walls of that place and grind it all into dust, so that it could be erased forever.

She wanted desperately to turn and head swiftly back, but instead she remained and stared at the building as dusk came. *How I hate it still,* she thought. *How I hated everyone there, the wardens, the officials, even the other children. What could I possibly have done, to deserve everything that happened in that place?*

There was no one there now of course, except maybe vagrants seeking shelter and peace. Nia wondered how many of them would sleep under that roof if they knew all the things that had happened there. *Maybe they wouldn't care,* she reasoned after a moment. *They're probably wrapped up too tightly in their own woes to think of anything else, even if something from the past lurks there even now.*

Angry and unable to bear just standing there stupidly in the rain, Nia turned and walked back. After only a short while she broke into a run, as if a spell over her had been suddenly broken. Eager to be back in an area she found more recently familiar, she ran on and stopped only when she reached a turreted manor house that she recognised. She was near the west Cobbles now, and would soon be back in the Square.

A short while later Nia cut through the Square, the Sanctum to her right. *Two days,* she thought, and looked towards the fortress, the vastness and height of its towers, and the multitude of windows, some lit and others dark, barely visible at all.

The rain came down a little harder, and Nia put the hood of her cloak up, although her hair was already soaked from hours spent wandering. *You'll catch a chill,* she scolded herself, *and all for what? A walk in the rain and being reunited with... that place? Next time know exactly where you're going, you stupid woman!*

She reached the far side of the Square and made her way down the steep and winding Apothecary Hill, idly watching the gleam of lamplight on the wet cobbles. Her thoughts were unhappy ones.

I'll forever be at Kelandra's beck and call, she reasoned, *unless I can find a way out of the situation somehow. But I can't fathom a way. Powers know I spent long enough racking my brains about it, on the way back from Mornkastle.*

But if she leaves Luudhoq, what then for me? Perhaps I'll be free of her then, although...

She stopped, frowning. Surely if Kelandra left Luudhoq, she would have no more work for her. *Unless she plans to take me with her,* Nia thought worriedly. *How can I avoid that? I've no desire to be any more a part of...*

The cloaked and hooded men, who suddenly appeared, one to each side of her, seemed to emerge from the ground itself. Nia had no time at all to react as she was grabbed firmly, her hands tied tightly behind her back and a sackcloth placed over her head. She tried to struggle, and one of them landed a sharp blow to the side of her head. Within a moment she could feel sticky wetness trickling down past her ear. "Any more of that," a voice whispered, "and your resistance will be noted, your punishment increased. Say nothing. Do nothing. The moment you make a sound, you will want it to be the last sound you ever make. *Obey.*"

With each of her arms held, she was forced to march; a boot kicked her in the backside to help send her on her way.

I should have seen them coming, Nia thought numbly as she was half-pulled along through the empty streets, knowing that she was headed for the Sanctum without needing to see it.

Then a dark and truly insane notion came to her: *I should have hidden in the old orphanage. I should have stayed there and made it my home. That's the last place anyone would expect to find me...*

III

A sharp blow to the head sent her flying sideways. The chair to which she had been tied toppled over, and Nia fell, hitting her head on the stone floor.

She opened her eyes after a moment and blinked in bewilderment. Candlelight danced upon the wall in front of her. *What was the last thing that happened?* she wondered. *I remember being arrested and taken to the Sanctum, and then...*

And then, nothing.

Someone hauled her up off the floor and set the chair back in place. A cold hand cupped her chin and forced Nia to look at the face in front of her. She almost lost control of herself completely when she saw who- or rather, *what-* shared this room with her.

"Well," the High Watcher murmured, and a chilly smile spread across its lips. "Our understanding is that Kelandra held you in high regard. Yet she deserted you, as she deserted all her people, and fled to the North. What do you think of that, I wonder?"

Nia could not speak. She remained frozen with fear. She had never had the misfortune of encountering a High Watcher before, but she had glimpsed them occasionally from a distance. The horror of being so close to one, being *touched* by one, threatened to overwhelm her completely. She managed to open her mouth but could issue no words. She could barely breathe.

In a certain light and from a distance, Kelandra and indeed most of the lower Watchers could have been mistaken for humans. The same could not be said of the High Watchers. This one, as it regarded her with eyes that could have been cut from glass, truly *did* have the look of a marble statue.

Nia looked away, towards the multitude of candles set upon the table on her left, near the corner of the room.

"When I talk to you, look at me," the High Watcher said softly. With an effort, she did so. Despite the chill that stirred within her stomach, Nia found herself utterly, helplessly fascinated. The candlelight came from the left only and bathed exactly half the strangely androgynous face. The other half remained dark and the eye deep blue, even as the candlelit one appeared almost on fire.

"I will now ask you some questions," it said. The tone was measured and calm, the voice itself neither male nor female. "You can choose to answer them truthfully, or you can choose to lie. You also have a third choice- to say nothing. I would advise you to choose the first option. Nod if you agree."

Nia nodded. She tried to keep her expression neutral, but her mind swiftly considered all her options. The High Watcher was right, of course. She should tell it everything she knew of Kelandra's scheme. If she lied, she would be found out. There could be no doubt about that. If she did anything except answer the questions truthfully, she would be tortured until she sobbed and begged for her life. Until, perhaps, her mind snapped under the agony.

And if I do everything that's asked of me, what then? she wondered. *Will they let me go? Perhaps, but probably not. But if I don't, then I have no chance. And whatever I tell the authorities, it hardly matters to Kelandra now that she and her co-traitors have fled Luudhoq.*

"The renegade Watchers, of which your mistress is one: who are they meeting with, and where?"

"They intend to meet with a man by the name of Ruhal Dalmorn," Nia said, the words spilling from her mouth more than willingly. "But I don't know the location.

Kelandra did not tell me. In fact, she told me to go home and wait until she called for me in three days' time."

"What task was it that she would have had you do in three days' time?"

"I have no idea. She said only that she would summon me."

"What do you know of this man, Ruhal?"

"He's a figure of some influence in the North, from what I can tell." Nia paused and considered her words before she continued. "I think he may be some sort of warlock, or perhaps not..." She shrugged. "I honestly know very little about him. Kelandra chose to contact him because of his views on the unification of Harn. Somehow, he too knows of the *marandaal*."

The High Watcher seemed coldly amused. "You know of the *marandaal*."

"Only what Kelandra told me." Nia shrugged wearily. "I can't pretend to have understood much of what she said."

The High Watcher nodded. "Kelandra and her fellow traitors will be captured and brought to face the justice of the Seven. A Watcher cannot err. An example must be made. You, however, are human. It is natural for you to fail, to make errors. You will spend the remainder of your life here in the Sanctum. More specifically, in one of the prison cells."

A pit opened in Nia's stomach. "Please..." she whispered. "I want only to serve the Watchers and the Seven. I *never* agreed with Kelandra's plans. But I *had* to obey her. That was my duty as a Watcher's servant. What choice did I have?"

"Of course, you had no choice, and you made a dutiful servant." The High Watcher stood and began to stroll around the room, each pace perfectly even. "One might say you were unfortunate."

"I was her *best* servant," Nia said earnestly. Her voice shook with emotion. "I can be of great use to you. I would willingly serve another Watcher. I want only to protect and serve Luudhoq, under the Watchers and the Seven. I beg you..."

It motioned for her to be silent. "That might have been one option," it agreed, "but for the things that you know. A certain *word* that you know. The city shall learn soon enough of Kelandra's treachery, but it must *not* hear of matters such as the *marandaal*. Not at this time."

"And I would never tell anyone!" Nia cried.

"You will never have the chance," the High Watcher told her, and a sudden pain flared up in Nia's head. She felt her consciousness ebb away, and then she slumped forward.

The last objects to fade from her vision were the candle flames, each one diffuse and oddly distant as if she were on some dark river, floating away from the light of life like flotsam, set loose from pain at last.

IV

Old blood lingered on the walls, the faded stains barely noticeable in the wan light, but Nia could smell blood nonetheless. Some of it was hers. She had been beaten and cut in places by one of the jailers. When she closed her eyes, she could still see him now, eyes bright with gleeful lust, rancid breath laced with liquor, hand-knife glinting as lantern light caught the blade.

He had promised to return sooner than his tasks demanded, and Nia was sure he would. This, she had realised, was a man who had gone beyond the casual, bored violence with which all jailers went about their daily duties. His mission was to harm and terrorise, and he took immense pleasure in that mission.

The wild fury that had coursed through her when she had first woken up in this prison cell had long gone, replaced by dull acceptance of her fate and mild curiosity as to when she would eventually be hanged.

Or is hanging too good for me? she had wondered on more than one occasion. *Is it not the nobility and the well-to-do who get to be hanged, if they find themselves on the wrong side of the Watchers? If that's so, how do the rest of us meet our ends? Why do they keep us here at all, and not put an end to us as soon as we are deemed guilty of something? Some pointless legality, perhaps?*

Nia grimaced in pain as she shifted position a little, her back pressed against the dank, cold wall. She idly wondered what would happen to Kelandra and her cohorts and was surprised to discover that she no longer felt any animosity towards the Watcher, despite her own dire situation. *What will become of her when she's caught?* Nian wondered. *Too late for me to ever find out. I imagine they'll get rid of me soon enough. After all, I am taking up space in one of their best cells.*

She laughed a little at that, then gasped as agony gripped her. She felt sure that a few of her ribs had been fractured.

It's all my fault, she reasoned. *If I had left the city as soon as I'd delivered the message to Kelandra... or did the authorities already know my role in all this? If so, then I could never have escaped. How long had they known?*

The Sanctum had about it an air of silent, crawling malice that would have made sleep all but impossible even if her entire body hadn't been gripped by pain. Large parts of these dungeons were nothing more than an area for holding the guilty until their execution. The air stank of their leavings. Nia herself had squatted in one of the corners, crying out in pain as she relieved herself. She had looked back in dull realisation as she saw blood and perhaps *other* matter that glistened amongst her faeces. *I need a physician,* she had thought miserably at the time, but no physician ever found his way down here. After all, why waste time treating those condemned to execution?

If there is to be an execution, she reminded herself. *Maybe I'll simply be kicked to death right here in the darkness and left to rot away next to my own shit.*

She fell into a light slumber. After a while, a dream, or perhaps the beginnings of one, formed. Yui was in the dream, but the child had become something fearsome and indescribable, even though she looked the same as she had before. Nia fled from her, down a street that became narrower and narrower, bordered by mouldy brick walls that came ever nearer to each other across the close and darkening passage. Yui, who seemed to be getting bigger and older every time Nia glanced back, followed at a casual walk, and no matter how fast Nia ran, Yui remained close behind, each step confident and measured.

Finally no way forward remained, for the brick walls had met each other. Nia turned and pleaded with Yui to stop, to let her go on her way. *You don't know which way to go,* Yui said, taunting her, and Nia realised it was true. She would be running away forever but would never find anywhere to run *to*.

The sound of a key turning in the lock of the iron door to her cell pulled her from one nightmare back into another. Even before the great old lock had finished its harsh protest and the door was shoved open, Nia knew that her familiar old friend had returned. This time he was by himself. Nia's heart thumped painfully.

The jailer had a different look about him this time, she noticed as he set his lantern on the floor and sat for a moment regarding her. Hungry, eager but not mad with the need to hurt. Relief and dread mingled as one within her as she averted her gaze. It meant, perhaps, that she would not be kicked to death or cut to ribbons today, but an even more humiliating fate awaited her.

He pulled at her shirt and tugged at her trousers, motioning for her to remove them. When she failed to move quickly enough, he cuffed her on the side of her head. Nia yelped in pain and removed her garments, trembling, and averted her eyes as he unbuttoned his trousers. All she could hear was his coarse, urgent breath. As he roughly pulled her legs wide open, and clumsily positioned himself between them, Nia wondered for a moment what kind of a madman this was, who would commit such an act in a place like this with the stench of shit and death and disease lingering like a pall.

She screamed out loud as he entered her, a scream she repeated as he pawed, pulled and scratched at her breasts.

Nia closed her eyes and wished by all the Powers for this violation to make an end of her.

Instead, to her astonishment and horror, it began a *shifting*.

No, she thought, and panicked as the rippling, the sense of dissociation, of being unmade and made again, gathered pace. *No, not now... they'll keep me alive for longer, torture me, experiment with me... let me die! Please let me die!*

Instead, she heard a gasp of agony from the jailer. His eyes bulged and he stared in disbelief at what he saw. His hands shook and clutched desperately at her shoulders, then a low, agonised moan escaped his lips as he fell away from her to one side and let go of her entirely. Nia, barely conscious, stared at the remains of his groin, where a gleaming mass of tissue bled gouts onto the dirt floor. His mouth opened and close in mute astonishment and crippling pain. Yet even now one hand fumbled with his belt knife, determined to make an end of her. His ruination must mean hers. Not having the strength to strike him hard enough to kill him, Nia instead stabbed her hand into the ruined remains of his groin. She tore at the wound with all her remaining strength and pulled at the mess of tissue. He convulsed several times, uttered a hoarse, agonised cry, and fell back against the wall.

Nia tried to sit up. The unlocked door beckoned from across the cell. *Powers give me the strength,* she pleaded, and tried again. This time, despite her vision blurring and her legs both swaying, she managed to sit up. She swayed to one side, then caught sight of the man's water canteen and belt pouch, she drank some of the water and rummaged around in his pouch and pockets. She found only a few sugared biscuits, but they were better than nothing.

Nia staggered to her feet. *I am female again,* she thought, looking down at herself. *I must have shifted back a moment ago, but I don't remember it happening.* She trod on something on the floor, and recoiled in disgust as she saw the jailer's severed penis lying in the dirt. Her body must have expelled it as it changed back to its natural form.

I could not control myself, she thought numbly. *What is happening to me? Could this happen again, when I least expect it?*

Perhaps the *shifting* had been triggered in order to save her. For the moment at least, it had.

Thoughts of escape came to her as she clumsily dressed, even though she knew that escape in the wider sense was impossible. She could leave her cell, but how could she possibly escape the vastness of the stone warrens that made up the Sanctum? She remained a prisoner, and the only difference now was that she had a better choice as to where exactly to curl up and die in this miserable stone fortress.

With sudden rage, she pulled the man's knife from his belt, and in a moment of savagery that lent her strength, drove it straight through his left eye and upwards into his brain, where she left it lodged.

Nia gasped in pain as she made her way over to the door. She bent to pick up the jailer's lantern, then slipped through the door and somehow managed to close it after her. With an effort she turned the key in the lock and then struck it hard with the flat of her hand so that it snapped.

The passageway in which she stood disappeared into darkness in both directions. Nia chose to head left, though she no longer had her special coin for making snap decisions- *those were the days,* she thought for a moment, and smiled wanly in the gloom. She turned and dragged herself painfully down the tunnel.

After a while she came to a door which she managed to pull open. It opened out into a spiral staircase. To her left, the steps curved upwards for half a dozen paces and came to an abrupt halt at an iron door dotted with rivets.

Nia's heart sank even before she tried to pull and push the door to open it. It was securely locked, and there was absolutely no way she could get through it. She walked down the steps again and peered down into the depths of the staircase. To the other side of the door leading onto them, the stairs wound down into darkness.

She held up the guard's lantern and peered quizzically at it and wondered how long it might continue to remain lit. *Not for much longer,* she thought. *But what can I do?*

After a moment she began to make her way down the staircase, keeping against the outer wall where the steps were larger and more distinct.

Eventually Nia reached the bottom of the staircase. A wide passageway led off ahead, littered with stony debris. It was impossible to say how long it might stretch away for. She could only see three or four paces in front of her. Nia took a deep breath of the stale, warm air and stepped slowly forwards, keeping her left hand against the wall of the passageway as she tried to avoid the loose stones on the floor. At the limits of her vision she occasionally caught a glimpse of rats or similar creatures hastening away from this bringer of light into their jet-black world.

She walked on for a while before she suddenly stopped, thoughts of defeat growing ever larger. *There is no reason to this,* she decided. *I can't escape. All I can do is get myself lost. Either I'll be found and recaptured, or I'll roam pointlessly until I fall from exhaustion.*

Although that would be less tortuous than my fate if the guards find me.

Tiredly she rubbed at her eyes with her free hand. *Maybe I'll just curl up here and fall asleep,* she thought. *I'm sure I could do that easily enough. I'd be asleep in moments, and that would be that. I doubt I'd wake up again.*

Yet after a short while she began to walk again, one hand pressed against the wall whilst the other held the lantern. The light flickered uncertainly after only a short time, and Nia sighed to herself. She was about to be in the dark.

At the same moment as the lantern suddenly went out, she stumbled sideways into a crevice in the wall. Dropping the lantern, Nia gasped in pain as she fell through this gaping hole in the wall and landed a short while later in a pile of debris somewhere under the passageway.

Nia picked herself up and stared in bewilderment at the area outside the crevice where she had landed. A strange blue glow, which seemed to come from somewhere above, lit the dusty tunnel that she could see ahead. After a moment, she staggered to her feet and grimaced as sudden, savage pain scythed through her leg. Slowly and painfully she stepped out into the tunnel.

Nia headed to the left and limped on under the blue light for what might have been an age.

She stopped only when the screams began.

V

The sound was unearthly, a scream of utter agony, yet there was something else about it that made Nia's skin crawl. Something cold, brutal, even *mechanical. A sound from another world,* she thought, but she had no idea as to why she would think of such a thing. It coursed along and through the walls of the passageway, an ululating note of wretched despair that made her cover her ears and close her eyes, for all the good that might do.

Finally the sound died away, but another sound took its place, a dull, groan and thump that repeated over and over. To Nia it sounded like a vast, monstrous creature pounding the walls of its cell and uttering a desperate lament at the same time.

She moved along a little further and managed to dislodge some centuries-thick cobwebs. A large spider scuttled away to a small pile of debris on one side of the tunnel. Nia watched and waited until it had disappeared. She had no fear of any natural creatures, but didn't need to get in their way or worry them into attack. *Besides, I cannot know for sure that it* is *natural,* she reasoned.

The cold blue glow faltered for a moment, coinciding with an increase in the level of noise from beyond the wall, and then returned to its former level. Nia found the light oddly disturbing, not because it made the arachnid denizens of this place appear blacker than they probably were, and their thick cobwebs whiter and more ghostlike, but because it appeared to come directly from the ceiling itself rather than any light source that she could focus on. Like so much else here, it was unfathomable.

Further along the passageway, some cracks ran down the wall. In places they had caused the brickwork to crumble away slightly. Nia's heart almost missed a beat as she saw a tiny hole caused by one such disturbance, where a brick had broken and crumbled enough for her to see the tiniest glimpse of the scene in the room beyond the wall.

Blood pounded in her ears as she reached out a trembling hand and carefully brushed away brick dust and fragments before putting an eye to the aperture.

At first Nia could make no sense of the little she could see. White light flared up, dissipated into a silvery glow, which darkened to a dim yellow, and the cycle repeated itself over and over in the space of moments. She caught glimpses of movement, what appeared to be smoke, and vast machinations- cogs and wheels some distance away, and to one side, shelves upon which metal boxes had been placed. The boxes emitted lurid colours and cacophonous, high-pitched sounds.

Curiosity had now gripped her entirely, and with all caution forgotten, Nia picked away more of the crumbling brickwork around the hole, in order that she might behold more of the bizarre scene.

Now she saw what appeared to be a large glass box on the left side of the chamber, within which something stood. As the smoke cleared and the light dimmed slightly, she finally saw it in detail.

It appeared to be a human man, entirely naked, legs slightly apart and arms outstretched to his sides, each of his limbs held securely in place by coils of metal that wound around the wrists and ankles before they cut savagely and suddenly into the flesh of the shins and forearms.

This must be one of the places where the Watchers torture people for information, Nia thought, horrified. *Has Kelandra ever come down here to do just that? If they find me again, could that be me standing there, helpless and in agony with metal spikes and coils driven through me?*

The man's mouth remained open as if fixed in a scream, though he himself made no sound as far as she could tell. Perhaps the thumps and groans came from the strange wires and boxes attached to the glass box that confined him.

On the other side of the chamber, just out of Nia's view, a door opened and closed. Footsteps sounded and came nearer. Nia drew back slightly from the wall, her heart lurching. A moment later, she heard conversation, muffled at first. Then it grew clearer before it once again became indistinct after two shapes moved past the hole she had made.

"...not... they lose a certain..."

"No... strengthen the course... yes, because..."

"Fifty years ago, it was never..."

"The source... something else interfering..."

"We're missing... process fails at different stages..."

Nia pressed against the cool stone of the tunnel, trying to make sense of what she could see, for this seemed to be no ordinary torture chamber. Who were these men? What were they hoping to achieve?

Were they members of the Seven, none of whom she had ever set eyes upon?

The voices grew louder and clearer once again presently as the two men casually made their way back. In the background, the strange machinery hummed and thudded, and the prisoner sobbed pitifully. He had, she realised, only been doing that since the arrival of the two men.

And then, when the two men drew nearer once again, Nia heard a conversation that turned her entire world upside-down.

"Some difference still exists," one voice spoke up, sounding frustrated, even angry. "The High Watchers, the originals- albeit with many new faces since their coming- possess that essential vitality. That *lost* vitality. There's a secret to their constitution, and we're no closer to figuring it out after all this time."

The other voice sounded a little younger, higher of pitch. "We'll find a way eventually. To every problem a solution. You said so yourself."

"Yes, Stephan- but you know how long we have been engaged in this. The creative technique still has something missing." The man's tones became laced with fury. "It *still* will not yield up its mystery, and we don't know why. We have made perhaps two hundred Watchers in the last ten years, and no more than a dozen have been of any use."

"Luudhoq does at least provide us with an inexhaustible supply of subjects," Stephan reasoned.

"Useless subjects, mainly," the other man retorted. "Parts of the process *always* work- they never remember anything of their former lives, the new skin is never rejected once the first stage completes... but getting to the end of the first stage is almost always a problem."

Mesmerised, and thoughtless now as to everything except this numbing revelation, Nia once again placed one eye near the tiny hole in the wall, helpless as a moth drawn to flame.

She saw the two men face each other about five paces away. Neither of them had the look of a Watcher, but Nia felt, as she gazed upon them, a sense of absolute evil that even a Watcher could not project. Both men- she was now certain that they were human men, and surely two of the Seven- wore white robes over their clothes that blended uncomfortably well with the overriding white appearance of the chamber. One of them, the one who was called Stephan, looked quite young, whereas his companion was of late middle age.

"Omir, why do you think the madness takes some, or ill health?" Stephan asked as he stared thoughtfully at the prisoner.

"Another question with a less than certain answer," Omir said. "It's a matter of missing ingredients somewhere along the pathway. We choose only fit and healthy men and women, yet the process often undoes much of their vigour." He paused, and then said simply, ominously: "Twelve."

"Twelve?" Stephan queried.

"The number of originals that still remain. The *High* Watchers as the ignorant thousands call them." He shrugged. "As you'll know from your studies, it may be that we cannot simply *use* the blueprint with any high degree of success. We can be under no illusion, Stephan. In the old world it might have worked, but *this* technique was never used. That continues to be a point of frustration. Sometimes

I think this world itself conspires against us, thwarting our attempts to recreate everything we need."

"Many of the created Watchers are of good use," Stephan pointed out. "They keep the peace. They possess many of the fine qualities of the originals. They watch the filth of mortal humanity like shepherds, ensuring the flock never strays."

Omir chuckled suddenly, and the sound made Nia draw involuntarily away from her position for a moment. "Some behave more like wolves than shepherds. Have you noticed how they pick the weaklings out? They *hunt*. And in one sense we have always been successful. They retain no memory of what they once were. Easy enough to convince them they were drawn from the void, rescued by us, their benefactors." His expression became dark. "In time, even the originals will be no more, and then we must rely on this... *new breed*, if we may still call it new. And so, the secret to perfecting them must be found."

A deep rage and frustration seemed to have infected Omir. He made his way over to the glass structure where the prisoner still twitched feebly. Omir raised both hands towards the restraints, which responded in sickening fashion by burrowing even deeper into the prisoner's wrists and ankles. Although Nia could not be sure, they also appeared to change shape.

Thin silvery veins of some metallic substance began to work their way through the man's arms and legs, and the sound of the machinery rose to a pounding, screeching crescendo. It drowned out even the sound of the prisoner's agonised screams. Nia remained helplessly glued to the spot and watched this bizarre horror unfold. No doubt she would have remained transfixed, if Stephan had not slowly turned and stared directly at her.

Despite her terror, Nia did not flinch initially. *He is just looking this way,* she told herself. *He has not seen me.*

But her hope was ill-founded. As the sound of the machinery faded, the prisoner sagged in his restraints and Omir walked back shaking his head angrily, Stephan pointed in her direction and said, *"We are being watched."*

Nia remained rooted to the spot for what seemed an eternity. Memories flashed by of numerous dreams she had had, where her legs had grown so leaden that she could not walk- and all the while her enemies approached.

When she finally tore herself away from the sights and sounds beyond the wall, however, and began to half-run, half-hobble down the tunnel, she felt that she might not be able to stop until exhaustion claimed her. On she lurched, mindless as to the thick cobwebs, which she flung aside, tripping over small stones and other rubble left over from ancient times. Small, mostly unidentifiable creatures scuttled away from the panicked giant in their midst.

The tunnel stretched away for a further few hundred paces before ending abruptly at a crooked stone staircase that wound downwards in a tight spiral, into the gloom. Nia paused in her flight and gathered her wits about herself sufficiently to review her situation.

Such contemplation did not take her long. The stairs might go down into the earth itself, where she might wander lost until fatigue and madness took their toll, or they might simply come to a blocked end and force her to collapse and give in at their base or climb the steps in the faint hope of finding another way out.

But Nia knew that to go back was to face certain capture and certain death. As far as she could tell, only the one way back existed and soon enough her enemies would be waiting for her there. She stared back down the passageway. The blue glow flickered quickly, dimmed and then brightened a little. She could still hear the faint sound of the thud and pulse of the torture equipment.

Suddenly a loud crack sounded, and some type of weapon smashed against the wall in the distance. She could not know but felt certain it was exactly where she had stood and observed. A cloud of dust billowed into the air. They were so desperate to apprehend her that they were willing to break the very foundations of this place.

Her mind made up, Nia tremulously began her descent of the stone staircase. She moved as quickly as she dared without losing her footing. Only the thought of tumbling down the steps and lying broken, agonised but still conscious at some lower point, kept her from an even swifter descent.

Soon enough the sounds of rock being smashed, and of something harsh and mechanical trying to make its way into the tunnel, faded into the backcloth of musty silence as Nia navigated turn after tight turn of the stairwell. She almost lost her footing several times. On occasion she stopped for a moment to try and ease the worsening pain in her knees and thighs. She wondered blackly if her enemies might fall in their haste and tumble down the steps, smashing into her and causing them all to fall to slow and painful deaths.

No, she reminded herself. *The Seven are eternal, immortal. They don't fall down steps in the dark. Nothing can destroy them.*

Nia found that the blue glow faded entirely after a while, so that she was stepping into total darkness.

She realised bleakly that she could have no idea how far down the staircase might go. The thought even occurred to her that this downward route might itself be a sorcerous construct into which she had walked, that she might therefore spend forever descending these stairs, condemned despite her numbing fatigue to step through the blackness for all eternity.

At a later point, however, a faint glow- yellow, this time- began to suffuse the darkness, and Nia could see the steps in front of her. She increased her pace a little, and hoped that her spiralling ordeal might at last be nearing its end. A short while later, the last of the increasingly uneven steps gave way to a wide, clay-walled tunnel that led away before her. The yellow glow, though still dim, was more than adequate to see by. Nia walked as swiftly as she could, managed to avoid most of the puddles on the ground, and continued for what could have been hours.

Then a deep rumble commenced, as if from far above, and parts of the tunnel roof began to crack and give way. Large chunks of stone tumbled down. Nia broke into a run despite her exhaustion, as the rocks fell all around her.

The tunnel continued for at least another three hundred paces, and Nia almost threw herself along it. She stopped only when she could be sure that the rock fall had stopped. Behind her, dust and rubble thickly covered the ground. Before her, the tunnel began to slope gently upwards. Foul-smelling water ran in rivulets along the edges of the tunnel floor. Nia staggered onwards. She slid and lost her footing on the damp stone underfoot as the tunnel became more slippery.

At one point a little later, she fell forwards and lay on the wet ground for a while. She listened to the dripping of water and other, faintly cavernous sounds that could have come from anywhere.

Somehow, she struggled to her feet, blinked back tears of utter exhaustion and misery, and began to walk again. The tunnel continued gradually upwards. *Can this all be part of the Sanctum?* she wondered. *I've walked so far now, I could be out in the city, or even outside Luudhoq altogether.*

The thought filled Nia with renewed hope as she pressed on. Time passed, and could have amounted to days for all she knew.

Eventually the tunnel narrowed and turned upwards at a greater rate, to a point of sharp light in the distance. *Daylight,* she thought, not sure if she ought to believe it. Using her last reserves of energy she clambered up towards the tunnel exit and wondered with a curious mix of excitement and dread what she might find when she emerged.

The light was, of course, bright only by comparison with the dim yellow glow to which she had become accustomed; when she emerged through the muddy hole in the ground, Nia spent a moment in bewilderment at the landscape around her: seemingly endless marshland wrapped in thick, cold fog.

Then, as realisation dawned, so did the reality of her situation, and she sank down on her knees on the soft grass of the hillock. She sobbed and almost wished she had been captured and never allowed to get this far.

She had emerged into the great south-western marsh, the Bonemord, and as its name grotesquely suggested, no one ever escaped from this place.

For a long time- an entire night, she realised later- Nia drifted in and out of troubled, exhausted slumber. Occasionally she sat up and stared hopelessly into the gloom, noting the darkening of the mist-laden sky and sometime later the inevitable approach of what passed for dawn in the Bonemord.

All hope having now been abandoned, Nia judged that nothing could be gained from prolonging her existence, and so she ate what remained of the biscuits she had taken from the jailer. Swallowing the last few stale and soft crumbs, she gazed into the foul waters of the marsh which surrounded the island on which she sat. Here and there, ripples disturbed the surface. A few times she thought she saw something black and sinuous move slowly through the depths; a water-snake, perhaps.

If I threw myself into the swamp, Nia considered, *how long would it take for me to be devoured? Not long, surely. So many flesh-eating creatures inhabit these depths. I think I would make quite a delicacy for them.*

A moment later, she heard faint voices, and for an instant decided that madness had claimed her already. Then panic cut through dull defeat as she realised that the voices came from behind and below her- in fact, from the earthy tunnel she had scrabbled through to reach the Bonemord.

She could hear at least five different voices, and then a sound that chilled her even further- a low, rumbling growl, like that of a large dog or wolf. "A damn *traildog*," she whispered in dismay.

Traildogs looked more like large mountain wolves than dogs. Their most outstanding attribute apart from their sheer endurance, Nia recalled numbly, was their ability to follow a scent or trail far better than any other living creature. This ability somehow remained undeterred by such things as running water, or even sorcery devised to confuse or divert a scent or trail.

A simple matter for it to find me, she thought wearily.

Nia made a sudden decision. She took off her boots, tossed them into the water, and watched for a moment as they sank. Then she dived into the Bonemord and began to swim swiftly away. Many thoughts flashed through her mind, but two amongst them were paramount - firstly, that she would rather be ripped apart by the unknown monstrosities that lurked in the Bonemord than surrender to her pursuers, and secondly, that her end would come swiftly, sharply and imminently. The pain would be savage, but it would last a mere instant.

The mists had drawn a veil behind the escaped prisoner and the black waters by the time Omir, Stephan and the traildog emerged from the tunnel. Having realised that its quarry had thwarted it, the traildog uttered a low howl of frustration and pawed the soft ground, ripping out a deep clod of earth.

Omir pursed his lips in a half-smile. "A pity," he said softly. "I would like to have borne our spy back for questioning. Still, even I could not create as many shreds from a living being as the creatures here."

He gave Stephan a cold stare. "We need to see that this tunnel- this whole damned warren- is filled and sealed, made impassable throughout. No one must ever tread this way again."

They departed, and silence enveloped the Bonemord again, punctuated only by the occasional grim sounds of unseen creatures as they disturbed the waters.

XV – Dust

I

Garret stood facing the window, deep in contemplation. On the other side of the room, Daniel of the Seven waited for his comrade to speak. He had waited since midday and the sun now sank towards mid-afternoon.

"Where do you expect they will go?" he mused eventually.

Daniel knew immediately who he referred to. "They will stay north of Mornkastle. They fear ever returning to the south."

Garret's lip curled in amusement. "And yet they sought to *unify* north and south?"

"It will never happen," Daniel said dismissively.

"Of course it will not." Garret turned and glanced at him. "We should still be able to reach them, no matter the distance. Destroy them. That which makes them what they are is *ours*. No matter the distance, we should be able to reach out into the empty lands to which they've fled and turn their insides dark."

"Yes- under suitable conditions, it's possible." Daniel paused and then added, "As you know, Issele has suggested that two High Watchers be sent after them. They make useful weapons to send into that region. After all, they have no fear, no emotion, they will follow their prey until the end of time if need be..."

"That is a pointless and wasteful course of action." Garret surmised him coldly and shook his head. "How many *originals* need we sacrifice? We do not have an inexhaustible supply, Daniel. The secrets to the technology have been lost- need I really remind you? Need I remind Issele, for that matter?"

"Then what do you propose?"

364

"That we locate and destroy them ourselves, if we can penetrate the putrid veil of those territories. If not"- he shrugged laconically- "if not, they are doomed to failure in any case. The *low* Watchers can be replaced, even if the process is as frustrating and arduous as Omir likes to remind us. They are entirely expendable. I expect the madmen who preside over the chaos in the north will find a way to put an end to them and their cohorts, even if we cannot."

Daniel nodded. "Then it would be worth putting that to a motion at the meeting tomorrow." He glanced at Garret, who recognised the change in expression immediately. "So. You have more to tell me, and yet you wait until now."

"Yes." Daniel's gaze grew accusing, but at the same time Garret saw fear behind his eyes. *What does he have to fear?* he wondered.

"I heard the music," Daniel told him. "I heard the music that morning."

With an effort, Garret maintained his neutral expression. "Music," he said flatly. "What music are you talking about? In fact, which *morning* are you talking about?"

As Daniel was about to reply, the door to the chamber opened, and grim, grey-haired Anya appeared in the doorway. If anything, she looked more forbidding than ever. Without apologising for the interruption, she simply told them, "You need to see this."

The two men exchanged glances and followed her out of the room.

The three of them strode down the corridor beyond, along a side-corridor and then up two flights of spiral stairs. Garret felt something cold move and nestle in his stomach as he recognised where they were going. They were headed for the chamber where Omir and Stephan routinely questioned and tortured the child with the Gate-visions. Almost without his knowledge, an invisible shield wrapped itself around him as they approached the door leading into the chamber. *That I should wrap myself in defence like this,* he thought scornfully, yet he maintained the shield nonetheless.

Anya took a key from her robe pocket and unlocked the door.

As the door opened, Garret fancied for a moment that something within sighed regretfully- a light breeze perhaps, although the windows were always kept shut. Daniel took a sudden step back, perhaps a reaction to the same thing, whatever it might have been.

The three of them stepped through one by one into the round chamber. Afternoon sunlight poured through the thick glass windows to illuminate the musty room. Garret glanced quickly around and saw only a half-full bowl of water and a few crumbs, the remains of some stale bread that the child had been permitted.

He turned to Anya. "Where have they taken her?"

"They have not *taken* her anywhere." Was this the only time he had ever seen Anya look even remotely *troubled?* Garret thought so.

"Then where is she?"

"We don't know, Garret. No one knows."

Unable to believe what he had heard, Garret strode over to one of the windows, partly to hide the sudden, inexplicable rage that threatened to overcome him. In silence he gripped the edges of the window sill and stared down at the city.

Now would be a good time, something inside whispered to him. *Kill someone. Kill several. Kill a dozen.*

But he could not. He gazed out over Luudhoq, at the vast puzzle of streets and alleyways, at the far-away throngs of people and vehicles that streamed along the thoroughfares, at wretched mortal life dumbly *continuing.*

Then, somewhere amidst the movement, the sun and stone and glass and every complexity in between, he became aware of a dim, persistent presence, something he could describe only as a shadow without form observing balefully from across the vastness of the city.

367

If you enjoyed *Secret Roads,* the next book in the Aona series, *The Endless Shore,* is available on Amazon and from paperback publisher Completely Novel – www.completelynovel.com.

Please also take the time to review this book on Amazon and Goodreads and any other book review websites.

If you'd like to keep up to date with news from the author, subscribe to the newsletter at www.simonwilliamsauthor.com

www.ingramcontent.com/pod-product-compliance
Lightning Source LLC
Chambersburg PA
CBHW070421170726

48291CB00002B/299